RUTHLESS

A CRESCENT COVE ROMANTIC SUSPENSE, VIPER FORCE, BOOK TWO

MARLIE MAY

RUTHLESS

From *Hummingbird Press*

Cover art by *Black Bird Book Covers*
Find them on Facebook **here**

❈ Created with Vellum

For Mom.

You never had the chance to read my books,
but I know you would've been proud.

Thanks for telling me to
'write the damn book'!
Miss you.

ACKNOWLEDGMENTS

For my children who give me
endless support.

My friends & critique partners who
make my books infinitely better.

To Léonie Kelsall, a dear friend despite the
physical distance between us.

Jes Ireland for reading & listening
at all hours of the night.

And, lastly, for my own personal hero,
my retired Seabee Chief husband.

I couldn't do this without all of you.

**Only Eli, a wounded ex-Navy man
is ruthless enough to protect Mia
from someone lurking in her past
who's determined to destroy them.**

Doctor Mia Crawford moved to Crescent Cove, Maine to escape an abusive—and now jailed—ex-boyfriend and forget what happened one night on a dark beach in Mexico. She settles into the peaceful coastal community, psyched to be close to her brother, Flint, who runs Viper Force. An added incentive is Flint's new employee, Eli Bradley, a man who asked her out eight months ago when she couldn't ever imagine dating again. When someone stalks her, she turns to Eli.

Eli never forgot Flint's younger sister, Mia. Sure, she shot him down, but they now live in the same town and she says she's open to more. Things soon heat up between them, and she offers a future he never thought he'd have. When someone breaks into her house while she's sleeping and writes #1 on her bedroom mirror, he'll stop at nothing to eliminate this threat. A kidnapping attempt is followed by #2 painted on her front door, and he fears it's only a matter of time until Strike 3.

No way in hell will he let anything happen to Mia. But her past overshadows the present—and a shocking revelation puts her in the sights of a murderer. It'll take Eli's considerable military skills and the MacGyver tricks he's picked up at Viper Force to keep the woman he's falling for safe.

1

MIA

Waves crashing on the Mexican beach masked all sounds—except for the footsteps coming up fast behind me.

My skin crawled with fear. Earlier, someone had shadowed me as I shopped for souvenirs in town. I'd tried to lose the creep and only after I'd raced down an alley and jumped into the back of a cab, shouting for the driver to *go-go!,* had I escaped.

No one was ever going to hurt me again.

Inhaling sharply, I pivoted and swung out my beach bag, smacking the person's shoulder.

A man dropped to his knees on the sand, releasing a surprised curse. As quickly as he'd fallen, he burst to his feet, his feral gaze trained on me. His hand flew to his thigh. A weapon?

"Crap!" I backed away quickly. The setting sun eclipsed his face, making it impossible to make out his features. Had the man from earlier found me?

My heart thundered in my chest, and I instinctively took the stance my military-trained brother, Flint, had drilled into me. Fists raised. Feet squared. Ready to kick. My snarl collapsed when I got a better look at my opponent.

Double crap.

"Eli?" I gasped out. Horror and embarrassment surged through me like a red tide. Eight months ago, after Flint's engagement to Julia abruptly ended, I'd flown out to Port Hueneme, California to help him pack up his things. He'd needed a change and was discharging from the Navy. His friend, Eli, had been stationed there. He'd asked me out but I turned him down, telling him long-distance relationships never worked, especially with a man who was career military, getting ready to deploy overseas.

It was the only excuse I could come up with. I couldn't tell him the real reason.

"I'm sorry I hit you," I said. "I thought, well..."

Eli brushed sand off his jeans, wincing when his hand encountered his right thigh. He huffed, but from the sparkle in his chocolate brown eyes, I could tell he also found the situation funny. He swiped his hand through his thick, dark blond hair and laughed. "Flint said you'd be down here, staring at the waves. Gotta say it, Mia, you sure know how to greet a guy."

Figures. The first time I meet up with the man I'd thought about almost continuously for months, I nailed him with a sack of books. I'd never live this down.

"I'm *really* sorry," I said. "What are you doing in Mexico?"

My brother, Flint, and his employees, Jax and Cooper, were in Puerto Morelos on assignment for my brother's business, and I'd opted to join them for my last night before flying home to Maine tomorrow.

Eli was an anomaly.

"It's your birthday, and I wanted to surprise you," he said.

"Consider me surprised." I grinned, and my unease drifted away like dandelion fluff on the wind.

"Thought about sending flowers."

My eyes widened. "Here? In Mexico?"

"Well, back home." Color rose in his face. Damn, it made him even cuter. "You might not know it yet, but I'm done with the military. Moved home to Crescent Cove six months ago. Just took a job with Flint."

He lived in Crescent Cove? My heart rate doubled. "What made you decide to get out?"

His hand twitched on his thigh. "It was kind of a mutual decision." He nudged his head, indicating we should walk, and we started down the beach with waves rushing up the shore beside us. A storm at sea last night meant the surf was still high.

His gait...Did I detect a subtle limp? *Mutual decision*, he'd said. A medical discharge? Since I could tell the topic made him uncomfortable, I let it go. "You said you work for Flint now. What are *you* going to do at Viper Force?" My curiosity about what went on inside that huge warehouse my brother bought had been gnawing through my bones, but Flint had dodged my questions so far. Maybe I could tease a few details out of Eli. "Viper Force is an awfully lethal name for a company that builds and sells kiddie drones." Flint's lame explanation.

"Kiddie drones. Yeah," Eli said slowly. "That's what I'll be working on." Stopping, he bent over to pick up a pale pink shell and presented it to me.

I smiled and pocketed it, and we continued strolling. The setting sun warmed my back and other than a few birds trying to outrace the waves on spindly feet, we were alone.

"Flint said you guys will also do simple security jobs on the side, such as the one here in Mexico."

Like I believed my brother was involved in anything *simple*? The drone thing made sense. Flint had been an Explosive Ordinance Disposal Technician in the Navy. When he was twelve, he'd built a rocket and launched it into our neighbor's backyard. Mrs. Johnson's shriek made my mom jump. Mom's shriek sent Flint running. "Last I knew, Seabees didn't spend their time learning combat skills with the Marines only to provide guard duty for the local convenience store. I'm thinking that part of Viper Force sounds more like James Bond."

His gaze flicked toward the houses lining the boardwalk on our left before returning to the ocean. "That's all there is to it, I'm afraid. Convenience stores." I could almost hear the groan in his words. "But, hey, Flint said you'd just finished a month-long medical mission here?"

Decent subject change. My curiosity about Viper Force might not be satisfied today.

"I'm a doctor. When Flint moved to Crescent Cove to be near the base for his Reserve duties, I visited and fell in love with the area. And because of what..." Wincing, I pinched my lips together. When I left Massachusetts, I chose to focus on the future, not the past. "Anyway, I followed Flint and took a job at Crescent Cover General Hospital, though I won't start until after Labor Day. I'd already set up this volunteer opportunity in Mérida, and I'm presenting my findings at a conference in western Maine next week."

"What sort of findings?"

"Cardiac risk in older women. I worked with the Juniper Foundation's mission here, providing free education and testing to women who might not otherwise receive the cardiac care they need." My volunteer work meant even more to me after what happened with a woman I was unable to save back in Crescent Cove.

"That's really admirable."

"Flint set it up, actually. He's friendly with the head of the Foundation, as you may know. He mentioned the connection, and I signed on to volunteer."

"I do remember meeting Peter, the head of the Foundation. And, well, Flint's fiancée, who was somehow also associated with the Foundation."

Julia had been a nanny for one of the Foundation board members. She'd bailed on my brother and left no forwarding address.

"When Flint asked me to fly down here to provide extra cov—uh, support on this job, I mean, I was hoping we'd run into each other." The crooked smile Eli sent me made butterflies flit around in my belly. "Didn't expect to find myself dusting the beach with my knees, though."

"I'm sneaky like that," I teased. As we slowed and studied each other, I tried to ignore the warmth radiating off his skin, let alone his scent, a heady mix of fresh air and spice. This man was hot enough to make my head spin.

He tugged on the bag still dangling from my hand. "What do you keep in that thing, anyway? Cannonballs?"

I held it up, smirking. "A girl can never have too many books when she's hanging out at the beach."

"Can't be just books," he said, chuckling. "No way would a couple of paperbacks deliver that solid a punch. I'd say you've got...A twelve-pack of beer in there, too."

"Really." I tucked my hand on my hip and lifted one brow. The humor in his gaze tickled through me. "You think I'm lugging a bunch of beers around at the beach?"

He shrugged. "I would."

I rolled my eyes. "Figures." Just like a guy. "No beer."

"What are you reading, now? Last I remember, you spent some time out at Port Hueneme curled up on Flint's sofa with a romance."

"Or at the pool. We can't forget that little pool incident." When he'd come up behind me as I sat on a folding chair with my feet the water, absorbed in a particularly steamy part of my book. He'd been going wide to catch a football thrown by Flint, only to stumble against my chair and send us both flying into the water. I'd been wearing a sundress, not a bathing suit. He'd rescued me—Flint's words, not mine—but I'd been drenched through.

Eli's soft gaze drifted down my front, and his voice deepened. "Not sure I'll ever forget the pool."

Was he remembering how our clothing clung to our bodies as we stood in the shallow end, close enough I could hear him breathe? A white sundress became transparent when wet and I'd gone braless. He'd only been wearing low-hung shorts and his bare chest, broad and rippling with muscles, had gleamed in the sunlight. I'd been unable to drag my gaze away.

"I still love romances," I said in a squeaky voice, overcome by the memory of how I'd felt back then. "But mystery is on today's menu."

"You sure it's not romances?" he asked. "With sexy covers?"

"Not you, too," I grumbled. Too often, Flint teased me about my choice of reading material.

"No way. I'd be the last to pick on you for that. Besides, I read romance novels, myself."

I halted and stared up at him, my jaw dropping. "You read romance novels?"

"Love the Highlander ones the best. You read any by that

author who lives in Crescent Cove? Dag Ross. *Highlander's Fury* is the first in the series."

Who was this man, and why did I not know this about him?

"All those swords and battles." Eli wiggled his eyebrows. "And hot sex."

"Wait a minute." I scowled. "You're joking with me, right?" My voice grew hushed. "You don't really read romance novels." As I gaped up at him, I pushed my windblown hair off my face. Damn curls kept getting in my eyes. "Do you?"

He snagged a particularly unruly strand and tucked it behind my ear. "You should check out my bedside table." Whistling, he started down the beach again.

Bedside table? That took my brain in a steamier direction. I stared after him before rushing to keep up, shaking my head about his comment. "Hold on." Grabbing his arm, I pulled him to a stop. It was impossible to ignore the nice play of muscles underneath my palm. Was the rest of him still as ripped as I remembered from eight months ago?

A crazy thought occurred to me, and I frowned at the ocean. Aw, shit. Did I dare? After all, I did sort of owe him.

"Hey, Eli," I said slyly.

He turned and walked backward. Yes, he did have a limp. So subtle, it would take someone who knew about injuries to notice. "Yeah?"

"About that pool incident."

His brow narrowed as if he hoped to read my intentions in my face, but I was a better poker player than that. The word came out again, slowly, "Yeah?"

Giggling, I rushed him, my hands outstretched. But I tripped and tumbled forward, into his arms that wrapped around me.

Momentum sucked.

Eli lost his balance. As we fell, he pivoted and I landed on top of him, my dress hiked up, my legs straddling his waist.

Now, wasn't this a delicate position?

A wave flew up the shore and crashed over us before receding. Sputtering, I pushed my sodden hair off my face and wiped the salty sting from my eyes. "I'm sorry," I said. "You okay?"

"More than okay." He rose up onto his elbows, grinning at me. "Damn, girl, you *do* know how to greet a guy." His heated gaze traveled down my front.

Of course. There was nothing like a wet white sundress.

AFTER CHANGING, I met up with Eli, Flint, Cooper, and Jax outside the restaurant where we'd arranged to celebrate.

"Mia," Cooper said with a nod. "Happy Birthday."

"Thanks. Congratulations to you and Ginny on getting engaged," I said.

His smile grew wider. "Thanks."

"What's this I hear about you and Eli going in for a swim, Red?" Flint asked me with a big grin. He ruffled my hair.

Big brothers could be a major pain in the butt. "My hair is strawberry blonde, not red," I insisted for what had to be the thousandth time since I'd learned how to speak. "And you know I hate that nickname."

"Dude," Jax came up behind Eli, sporting a smirk wider than the sea. He nudged Eli's shoulder. "When you say you're gonna surprise a woman, you sure don't hold back." Chuckling, he came around to lay his arm on my shoulders and smoosh me into his side. "Happy B-Day, kiddo." He kissed my cheek. "Heard about the tote bag incident, but I must've missed the swim. Where did you learn that move, huh? Not from my boy, Flint, here, because he's too much of a softie to encourage a sweet-as-honey girl like you to dance in the ocean with a man like Eli."

Sweet-as-honey. The nickname Jax gave me after I brought a batch of cookies into Flint's office. Despite the endearment and kiss, Jax and I were only friends. Actually, I had a feeling he was *sweet* on my cousin, Haylee, who also worked for Flint. Not that he'd acted on it as far as I could tell. Whenever she was around, he went all broody and barely said a peep.

"Glad the book incident wasn't directed my way," Flint said, rubbing his shoulder. "I'd be the last one to creep up on you on your birthday."

"Yeah, sure." If Christmas hadn't stopped him from tossing water balloons off the loft while I sat on the sofa underneath, why would my twenty-ninth birthday be any different? From the slick look Flint sent Eli's way, I had a feeling I'd been pranked after all, even if Eli was unaware of the role he'd played in my brother's latest trick.

"Let's go inside, shall we?" I said, waving at the door. "How about a cease-fire from teasing on my birthday?"

Flint held the door open for me to enter first. "Don't see no white flag."

"As if. I'd never surrender."

We were soon relaxing on the restaurant's deck overlooking the ocean. Eli and I sat on one side of the wooden table, opposite Jax and Flint. Cooper took a seat on the end. We chowed through numerous plates of burritos and nachos, washing the crispy-cheesy goodness down with tall glasses of cerveza.

"What happened to your leg?" I asked Eli quietly.

His hand flew to his right thigh and he rubbed. "Just a little encounter with an IED."

"Femur?"

He nodded. "Put me out of commission for a while."

A painful injury, then. "I'm sorry."

"It's okay. Not much I can do about it now."

I could tell the topic made him uncomfortable, the last thing I wanted to do. A quick subject change was in order, stat. "So, tell me about those romance novels you love. Are the Highlander ones really your favorites?"

"Shit, bro. Romances?" Flint reeled backward with pretend horror plastered across his face. "Don't tell me you're into that stuff, too?"

Color landed squarely in Eli's chiseled cheeks. Blushing only made him look hotter because it hinted at his vulnerable side. He straightened and yanked on the neck of his t-shirt. "I've read a few."

"That's a complete betrayal of mankind." Jax's words came out serious but the sparkle in his deep blue eyes indicated he was only poking fun.

Flint sipped his beer and then cocked one eyebrow Jax's way. "Maybe if you read a few romances, you'd learn how to talk to women. Then you wouldn't find yourself blanking at inopportune times."

"Burn," Eli said with a grin. His glance between the men made it clear he was enjoying the show.

"Women like to go out with me. Talk to me," Jax said with a huff. "I..." His gaze met mine, and my mind shot again to my cousin, Haylee. "Yeah, sometimes."

Haylee's eyes followed Jax whenever he was around. Didn't he see that? Maybe I should share my favorite cookie recipes with her.

Eli turned to me. "As I was saying earlier, I really like Dag Ross's books. There's something awesome about a spunky woman who can put a beefy Highlander in his place in two seconds flat."

Repeat performance: my jaw dropped. I leaned toward him, eager to share my favorite books, but Flint abruptly pulled his phone and answered an incoming call.

He listened for a moment, then said, "Okay. Hold tight. We'll be there right away." As he put his phone away, he directed an intent gaze to me. "I'm sorry but something's come up on the job. We have to take care of this now."

"Showtime." Cooper tossed his napkin on his empty plate and stood.

So much for Flint's "cushy" security assignment here in Puerto Morelos. Fluffy security jobs never called four ex-Navy guys out on a Friday night.

I tried not to pout, because I hadn't seen my brother in over a month and I was enjoying getting to know Eli again. "I thought you were off until tomorrow."

"In my business," Flint said. "I'm never off duty."

Kiddie drones, right?

"Trouble?" Eli asked quietly, his forearms braced on the table.

Flint's gaze slid away from mine. "Someone's...gone missing." Standing, he dropped a bunch of cash onto the table. "We've gotta go."

Rising, Jax's hand darted around to his back as if he needed to make sure he was still packing.

Stop. He wasn't armed, was he?

My gut clenched. What was going on here?

Eli joined them on the other side of the table, saying so softly, I barely heard his words, "I'm in if you need me."

"Thanks."

Cooper nudged his chin toward Eli. "Talk about new employee orientation, huh? Nothing like jumping into action your first week on the job."

"Action?" I glanced back and forth between the men but their expressions might as well be carved from granite because they gave nothing away. These military guys sure held their secrets close.

"Well, no, not really action." Cooper coughed. "It's—"

"You'll go to the hotel immediately, right?" Flint said to me.

Getting up, I grabbed my clutch off the table. "Crack of dawn flight, so I guess so?" Since the celebration was over, I might as well spend the rest of my evening with a good book. After all, I had a *twelve-pack* of them waiting in my room.

Flint came around the table and hugged me. "I promise I'll be back in time to take you to the airport in the morning."

"Wait." Stepping back, I frowned. "You think you'll be gone all night?"

"'Course not," he said. "This is nothing." He rubbed my arms and stared down at me. "I'm sorry this job's ruining your birthday, though."

"It's okay." I pressed for a smile because it wasn't like he could help it. "It was still great to see you. We can catch up once you're home."

"Definitely."

Cooper nodded. "See you back in Maine."

Jax came around the table and bowled me over with a hug, saying by my ear, "Stop by the office soon, will ya? I've missed you."

I chuckled. "Chocolate chip?" Definitely needed to enlist Haylee for cookie duty.

He grinned. "Double batch, if it's not a problem."

"Deal."

We walked out front, and Jax, Cooper, and Flint strode toward my brother's rental parked in the lot and climbed inside.

Eli remained with me.

"Well," he said, his attention focused on the pavement. "It was nice meeting up with you again despite the unexpected dip in the sea." He reached into his pocket and held out a small white box. "Happy Birthday."

"Oh, wow." A thrill ran through me. He'd bought me a gift? "You didn't have to get me anything."

"Eli?" Flint called, standing inside the open driver's door. Brows lifted, he nudged his chin toward the black SUV. "Any time, bro."

Eli ignored him. "It's just a little something I thought you'd like."

My smile got bigger, because...nothing. This couldn't mean anything, could it?

"Eli," Flint said again, firmer this time.

Eli watched me, his lips teasing upward.

"As I said, I'm back in Maine for good, now." His intent gaze remained on my face. "I imagine we'll run into each other sometime?"

Excitement rushed through me at the thought of seeing him on a regular basis. Maybe...Was it possible things could be different this time? After all, I'd moved hundreds of miles away from Russell and the two men were nothing alike. "Sure, I'd like that."

He nodded and strode toward the SUV.

My pulse racing too fast from such a simple conversation, I watched him—couldn't help watching him, actually

—until he'd climbed into the vehicle and Flint squealed out of the parking lot.

Dropping onto a bench nearby, I opened the box.

My breath caught when I saw what he'd given me. The delicate silver chain winked beneath the streetlights when I dangled it. Tossing aside the box, I smiled at the pendant—a small sterling silver daisy.

Did he remember that time I'd picked a daisy and spontaneously given it to him when I'd stayed on the base to help Flint? He'd turned redder than the horizon the night before a storm.

With a soft smile, I fastened it around my neck, then rose and crossed the road to my hotel. But once I'd reached my room and sat on the bed with my book open on my lap, I sighed. It seemed a shame to spend my last night in Puerto Morelos cooped up in a stuffy hotel room. The ocean would be gorgeous now that the moon had risen, and the sultry-salty air would give me one final taste of Mexico.

As I left the hotel, I looked around to make sure no one followed. The creepy guy in town must've been an isolated incident. Someone looking for an easy tourist mark.

Arriving at the entrance to the public beach a short time later, I kicked off my sandals. I fingered my necklace as I strolled beside the water, my mind skipping with thoughts of meeting up again with Eli once we were both back in Maine.

My smile fled and my pulse kicked into overdrive when I tripped over a man lying motionless on the sand.

The metallic tang of blood hit my sinuses.

2

MIA

Heart jarring, I dropped down beside him and turned on my phone light.

Mid-fifties. Slender build. Dressed in a suit which was a weird clothing choice for a beach. He lay curled on his side as if he'd fallen.

Much like the woman I'd found down in the park back home.

Determined to give this man a different outcome, I rubbed his shoulder. "Hey. You okay?" His body slumped toward me, and my gasp cut through the air. A dark, glossy pool expanded on the ground well beyond his belly and the sharp, metallic tang of blood burned my sinuses. What was going on here?

My training kicked in, and I leaned over him, listening. Great, he was breathing. But his pulse was thready which was never a good sign. I shoved aside his suit jacket and unbuttoned his shirt. Gulping, I stared down at his belly wound that seeped blood. Crap. A slice. Not a scrape or a puncture from a fall on rocks. A deep slice, too. As if he'd been gutted by a knife.

He coughed, spewing pink foam, and I jerked back. A lacerated liver? His lungs could be injured, too.

His eyes opened, and he blinked before narrowing his gaze on my face. His flash of confusion was replaced by tight lines of urgency. "Take it." His hand rose before dropping back onto the sand. Bloody fluid trickled down the side of his face, tracing a long, white scar on his right cheek. "Take it."

"I don't understand." My words were snatched up and carried away on the wind.

He exposed a small notebook taped down snugly beneath his arm.

My breath caught. "This?" I peeled the tape back until the book came free. Flipping it over, I frowned. A normal notebook, the kind you'd pick up at a dollar store. Why...

As if he was determined to spend the last of his energy, he lifted his chest off the ground. Fear burst through in his words. "Give it to...to..." Air wheezed from his lungs. He collapsed back onto the sand and his eyes remained open, fixed and unfocused.

No pulse. Gone. Like the woman I'd been unable to save back home.

A gust of wind pelted me with sand and slashed my hair across my face. Goosebumps erupted on my arms. As I stuffed the notebook into my pocket, clouds that had engulfed the moon parted. Light stabbed down, exposing the beach. The dead man. Me, kneeling beside him.

And a bearded man. He rushed toward me, a knife in his hand.

Fear gripped my heart like a fist. I leaped up and bolted. Heavy thuds pursued me. Belly lurching into my throat, I raced along the beach, aiming for the town lights blazing ahead like a beacon of hope.

His hand slammed down on my shoulder, and I stumbled forward. My cry erupted from my throat. I twisted, trying to get away.

When he yanked me toward him, I spun. My palm connected with his nose, and the bones gave with a sickening crunch. He grunted and released me, reaching for his face. Even wounded, he shoved the knife toward me. The blade connected with the soft flesh of my arm.

My yelp broke through my clenched teeth. Fingers clamped over the wound, I fled, staggering out onto a walkway well-lit with street lights. A parking lot half-full of vehicles lay ahead, plus a cop car sitting on the road just beyond the lot. Dressed in dark blue combat fatigues, a policeman leaned against the driver's door, talking on a cell phone. Thank heaven. Mexican Federales might be known for questionable tactics regarding tourists and the random drug deal on the side but they were also known for the weapon they carried: an assault rifle.

I'd never been happier to see a gun-toting man in my life.

I rushed toward him. A quick glance behind told me the killer had melted into the shadows. Slowing my pace with relief thrumming through me, I limped over to the cop. Blood dripped down my arm, leaving a wavering trail on the pavement. My blood, and I was losing it fast. My teeth chattered as reaction set in.

"Señora?" Kudos to the cop for only blinking once at my appearance. He stuffed his phone into his pocket while another policeman leaned across the vehicle's interior, squinting up at me.

"A man," I gasped out, waving toward the beach. "Killed someone. Chased me. A knife."

The cop grunted. "Español?"

"Lo siento, no comprendo." The apology I'd mastered within moments of my arrival in Mexico. "Do you speak English?" The medical mission had supplied translators for my interactions with patients, but my Spanish was limited. I latched onto his arm. "Someone's dead." I mimicked a person stabbing someone and flapped my hands to show blood flowing from my stomach. "Muerto."

"Muerto?" The policeman peered around. A string of Spanish ensued, rapid-fire and growing louder.

"Come to the beach." I tried to tug him in that direction but he didn't move.

After opening the rear door of the car, he took my arm and steered me in that direction.

If we went to the police station, someone would understand me and they'd investigate the situation. I climbed inside the vehicle.

Hours later, I'd been quizzed by a series of Federales, repeating who I was and what had happened. Losing more of my voice with each repetition. My brain spun, making it hard to think. Skepticism grew on their faces, and if my appearance hadn't suggested I'd committed a murder, they probably would've hustled me out the front door.

They'd taken my cell phone or I would've called Flint and begged he and the guys to swoop in and save me, because I'd become useless at saving myself.

They took me to a trope interrogation room with a solitary high window covered with bars and a bare lightbulb suspended from the ceiling. A scarred table with equally scarred wooden chairs sat in the middle. And a big mirror hung on one wall, reflecting my snarled hair, my sallow face, my blood-spattered sundress.

I held back hysterical tears. Cold had sunk into my bones, and I couldn't stop trembling.

Shadows lurked behind the mirrored glass. Not a simple looking glass, then, but a way to observe me. Or wait me out, hoping I'd turn into a weak, sniveling mass who'd spill whatever information they demanded. My quaking knees told me I wasn't far from cracking.

I collapsed in a chair and tucked up my legs, wrapping my arms around them. With my chin propped on my knees, I stared forward blankly. If only this nightmare would end.

The door opened and a dark-suited man entered. He studied my face for a long moment before taking the chair opposite mine. His arms rested on the table with his hands clasped together. The relaxed expression on his face was negated by the sharp look in his eyes. He flicked his hand my way. "Please, explain what happened, Señorita."

Taking a deep breath, I repeated what I'd told the other cops. When I finished, he said nothing, just rose and left the room.

Silence kept pace with the second hand on the clock.

When he returned, he sat and studied me while I shifted in the chair. Finally, he said, "We went to the beach. There was no dead body. No blood. No imprint in the sand."

I sputtered. "A man was murdered. He'd died right in front of me. Really." I tugged my dress away from my chest, flapping the red-splotched material. "This isn't my blood. Well, some of it is, from my arm." I showed him the bandage. Three inches long, my wound probably needed stitches. They'd given me a first aid kit, and I'd applied a pressure dressing, the best I could do for now.

"Dead bodies do not rise and walk away on their own."

Hold on. I pulled the notebook from my pocket and laid it on the table between us. "He told me to give this to..." I shook my head. The details were murky. "He died before he could tell me."

Lifting it, the cop flipped through the pages before tossing it back on the table with a smack. "I believe you spent too much time in the sun today, Señorita. You found someone sleeping in the sand. Not a wounded man, let alone one who was dying." He chuckled, but his grim expression sent fear rippling through me. "As for the man chasing you with a knife, you imagined the entire incident. The cut and the blood on your dress came from a fall. This book proves nothing."

"That's not true. It's..." I snatched the notebook up and opened it. My vision swam.

The pages were blank.

Shoving back his chair, the cop stood. Taking the notebook from my limp fingers, he threw it into a trash bucket. He dropped my phone onto the table with a clatter. "Call Flint to come for you."

I blinked up at him. "How do you know my brother's name?"

"Your flight leaves early tomorrow morning," he said pleasantly. His eyes bored into mine, his stare alone ensuring I'd understand what he said next. "Tell your brother you were robbed. You came to the station to report the incident." He leaned forward with his palms braced on the scarred surface. "Forget what you saw on the beach."

"But—"

"Speak of this matter, and we will find you." He smirked. "But first, we will find Flint."

At my frantic nod, he left the room.

Half sobbing, I called my brother and stuttered out the fake story of a robbery. After, I set the phone on the table. Unable to resist, I retrieved the notebook and put it back inside my pocket. The man had wanted me to have it, and I'd take it. After, I dropped my head onto my folded arms.

Not long later, Eli stormed into the room. "Mia," he shouted. "Are you okay? Flint's with Jax and Coop. He sent me."

I stared at the cop, who watched us closely.

Eli glanced around and stiffened. "Fuck, this is..." His glare fell on the suited policeman. "What the hell did you do to her?"

My chair toppled backward as I stood. I stumbled forward, meeting Eli partway around the table. His arms wrapped around me, and I leaned into him, shaking.

"Ms. Crawford is upset," the cop said. "Which, after her unfortunate experience, is natural. I'm sure she will be fine once she returns home." His intent gaze focused on me, a lead weight around my ankle in deep water. "You and your brother live in Crescent Cove, Maine, am I correct?"

"Where she lives doesn't matter," Eli said, and to me, "Let's get you out of here. I can't believe you've been here for hours." Stepping back, he braced my arms and studied my face. "Why didn't you call us right away?"

"I..." My gaze flitted to the cop.

His intent gaze fell on Eli, and I knew the warning included him, as well.

Don't say a damn thing.

"It was just a...simple robbery." I gulped back my fear. "Can we please leave?"

"Of course." He took my hand and escorted me toward the door.

As we passed him, the cop said nothing.

3

ELI

Ten *days later*

I hadn't reached the ripe old age of thirty by ignoring the squirrelly feeling I got when someone spied on me, and I sure as hell wasn't going to start now. Yes, I was out of the Seabees and back in Crescent Cove, Maine, the small coastal town I'd left to join the Navy, but trading camo for jeans and a tee eight months ago didn't mean I was no longer a moving target.

If I'd learned nothing else when I came too close to that IED, I'd learned caution.

Sliding my body lower in the driver's seat of my Jeep Wrangler, I adjusted the mirrors and studied the vicinity through my sunglasses.

Nothing moved near the open metal gate I'd unlocked and driven through to park in front of the converted warehouse where Flint was establishing his top-secret weapons testing facility and special ops business. A covered dumpster sat to my left, and a couple of cars and a pick-up truck were parked to my right, but unless someone was hiding in one of the vehicles, I was alone.

The fence surrounding the perimeter had seen considerable work, but I could improve it over the next few weeks. I'd get to it before Flint hit me with my first assignment. I envisioned motion detection devices with cameras on the corners of the building and on the fence to provide opposing viewpoints. Spiral wire across the top. I'd get Coop to help me juice the coils with twelve-thousand volts. I knew enough about electrical installation to cause trouble, but Coop was the high-voltage expert. In the Seabees, I'd specialized in security tech. Spy equipment, essentially.

Twenty yards beyond the gate, the wind stirred the upper tree branches. The paved road stretched a quarter mile behind the gate before curving to the right. Other than a chipmunk chittering on the road, the area appeared empty. However, the prickling sensation wouldn't go away.

A flash on the roof sent me ducking behind the dashboard, the smell of overheated plastic sharp in my sinuses. I slowly lifted my head to peer over the top.

Shit. If I'd had my 9mm in hand, I would've taken out the roof AC unit where the sunlight winked.

This was not the Middle East where one guy's mistake had cost me a career. It was time to stand down.

When the feeling of being watched eased, I got out of my Jeep. I swept the area one last time but saw nothing. Could've been my imagination. As I paced toward the front door, I kept my muscles primed to dive for cover. No harm in remaining cautious.

I keyed in the code on the panel and pulled open the solid steel entry door, taking in the discrete sign above it: Viper Force R&D, a gold fouled anchor mounted below. While the locals assumed Flint's crew built remote-controlled drones for online sales, his business actually retrofitted and tested top-secret combat drones and other high-tech weapons for the military. To keep our toes in the action, Flint also took on highly-specialized tactical operations. Like his recent job in Mexico, a crapshoot that had gone south fast when his contact disappeared.

My friend's business was doing great, partly due to the government contracts our former Navy Admiral shifted Flint's way. But it would take time to build this operation into what Flint, Coop, and I had dreamed of while lying in our bunks on the Enterprise eight years ago, back when we'd shared a year of sea duty on the aircraft carrier before flipping over from regular Navy to the Seabees.

The door clicked shut behind me. I nudged my sunglasses up onto the top of my head and scanned the open room refinished with cream-painted walls, artwork, and a dark, plush carpet. Only the hint of motor oil in the air told me the front part of this building had once housed a garage.

As I approached the desk occupied by an older, smiling blonde receptionist, she stood. She smoothed her skirt along her hips, and her lips lifted further as her green eyes skimmed down my front. "Can I help you?"

Not with whatever her husky voice suggested she might be offering. She was gorgeous, and being ten, fifteen years older than me wouldn't necessarily hold me back, but I was kind of stuck on Mia.

"I'm Eli Bradley," I said.

"Oh!" Her thin eyebrows arched. "You're the newbie. Welcome." She tucked a phone between her ear and shoulder while she dialed. "I'll let Flint know you're here."

"Thanks." While waiting, I crossed the room to stare at a painting of a rolling meadow with a tree in full bloom growing in the center.

A month ago, Flint and I met up at a tea shop downtown

to discuss my signing on with Viper Force. Seeing the potential of this business, let alone how awesome it would be to get paid to blow things up, I'd given my notice at the hardware store, grateful my boss had hired more crew. I would've hated to leave him short. The day after finishing out my notice, Flint asked me to join his crew in Mexico. I hadn't even had a chance to get out here to the shop yet. Today, I'd receive the full tour.

"Eli?" someone said from behind me.

Didn't even have to turn to know who it was. *Mia.* My belly twitched.

Dressed in shorts and a snug tee, she crossed the lobby and stood in front of me, grinning. "Flint said you'd be here today."

Had she asked about me? I'd wanted to quiz him about her but Flint ribbed me enough about my crush already without throwing more wood on the fire.

"Yeah, my first official day." I rubbed her shoulder, yanking my hand back when it tingled. Tingled? That was an interesting feeling for me. Guys didn't tingle, they burned. Except, *I* tingled. Around Mia. All the damn time. "How have you been? I've been thinking about you since Mexico."

I hated seeing the light fade from her eyes, knowing I'd made it happen, but the horror of her trembling in my arms had kept me awake at night over the past ten days. I'd made sure she got to the airport the next morning, but she'd been frightened...Shit, it still churned me up that the police had held her that long, that they hadn't let her call us.

I needed to know she was okay.

Her teeth grazed her lower lip, and she rubbed a bandage on her arm and sighed. "It was a horrifying experience, but I'm putting it behind me." After darting a glance at the receptionist, she turned her gaze back to me. Her hand flicked toward an open doorway opposite the entrance, and her voice lightened. "I left some cookies in the breakroom if that's your thing."

Ginny made me cookies whenever I begged but lately, she'd been busy baking cookies for Cooper. Not that I was jealous. Too much. But I was literally wasting away. "What kind of cookies?"

"Chocolate chip." She tilted her head and her strawberry blonde curls swept across her shoulder. Her hair—plus the scattering of freckles across the bridge of her nose—socked me in the gut whenever I saw her, just like when I first met her eight months ago. I'd kept picturing burying my face in those silky strands. Stroking it. Stroking *her*.

The wrong thoughts to be having about a woman who'd shot me down.

Even now, I still wanted her. Her being in Maine and me in California was the reason she'd said no. Would she be open to something more with me this time around?

"I'll definitely try your cookies," I said in a husky voice. And anything else she might offer. No harm in getting my hopes up, even if nothing came of it. I could deal. When my dad left me when I was eight, I'd gotten a solid lesson in handling disappointment.

"What are *your* favorite kind of cookies?" she asked with a twinkle in her green eyes. "I could keep you in stock like I do for Jax."

Jax. Fuck. He'd been all over Mia's cookies in Mexico. Kissed Mia, too, even if it was only on the cheek. Was there something brewing between them? Figures we finally lived in the same town and it might already be too late for me. "I'm partial to white chocolate macadamia, but I might be a chocolate chip fan after tasting yours."

"I hope they'll be the best cookie you've ever eaten." Her gaze darted to my lips, and color rose into her pretty cheeks. Why? Our conversation was completely benign. But then, Ginny had said I was clueless around women. Something about needing keys to a castle, whatever that meant.

But wait. Was there more going on here between me and Mia than cookies?

I wanted to smack my head. Shake some sense into my brain because I needed to read this situation right.

"I have a feeling your cookies are awesome." My slight emphasis on *cookies* was a bold move on my part, but oh, well. In for a pound, as everyone said.

"Maybe, umm..." She stared down to where the toe of her pink sneaker traced along the carpet. "I could make you a special batch of cookies. Drop them off at your...Well, I'd hate to bring them here and watch Jax eat them all before you got to try one."

"How about I—"

"You could—"

"Eli," Flint called from down the hall behind the main desk, interrupting us as we spoke at the same time. He emerged from the doorway and approached. "Right on time." Looking down at my empty hands, he frowned. "Hey, weren't you supposed to bring donuts?"

I snorted. "Damn. I meant to bake muffins." A long-standing joke between us, I'd forgotten how it got started or what it even meant. "But Mia brought cookies." Definitely needed to grab one or two or ten before Jax made off with them all.

"Probably don't need the carbs anyway." Flint patted his flat belly. "Since leaving the service, I've had to work double-time to maintain my boyish figure."

Mia snorted and rolled her eyes, but her rising grin couldn't be denied.

"You never were one to slack off," I said. Coop told me Flint had installed a gym here and that strength training and ongoing martial arts instruction were a big part of the program. Not that I planned to let my hard-earned skills slide. After a tour and de-briefing, I'd hit the gym and then go for a long run, especially if I planned to eat a bunch of cookies.

My physical therapist had discharged me a month ago, saying I'd reached my new norm—which was nowhere near the endurance I'd had before my injury. The thought of hobbling around for the rest of my life about killed me. No way in hell would I accept limitations on what my body could do.

I took in Flint's slacks, button-up shirt, and patterned tie, and tugged on the hem of his tailored jacket. "You're goin' squishy now that you're no longer at the military's beck and call."

Either that or I was way underdressed in jeans and a tee.

"Is he ever." Mia nudged her elbow into her brother's side, and he whoofed. "No more cookies for you."

"Squishy?" Flint eased Mia aside and crouched in front of me, his arms splayed away from his body. "Just try me, dude."

I snorted. I could take my friend even if I was sick and my ankles were tied. "Dare ya."

"Boys!" The receptionist came around the desk, scowling. "You take that outside."

"Yes, Aunt Becca." Flint straightened. His lips curled up but he ducked his head and scuffed his polished dress shoe on the carpet.

Aunt? This woman—tall, long blonde hair, ample curves—was Flint and Mia's infamous retired-CIA aunt?

Shit. Here I'd been contemplating...Well, I truly hadn't been contemplating anything. But still.

Her arms crossed on her ample chest, and she tapped the toe of her stiletto on the carpet. "I may only be a few years older than you, Flint—"

Flint coughed.

Her frown deepened. "But I'm still prepared to take you over my knee, just like did while babysitting you all those years ago." She directed twinkling eyes my way. "You, too, if you get out of line."

My turn to cough. Taking more than a decent step backward, I took in the humor shining on Mia's face. She was enjoying the show.

It made sense Becca was here. Knowing Flint, he'd never pick just anyone off the street as his receptionist. He'd need someone capable of taking a bull down with a few strategically placed blows, let alone one with top security clearance. That would be Becca. The outer gate was wall number one, the entry door wall number two, and Becca was wall number three. Flint kept the place locked behind an impenetrable fortress.

After shaking her finger at us, Becca returned to her chair, smirking. The police scanner sitting on the desk to her left crackled but she didn't bother glancing at it, indicating nothing important was coming through.

"Well, I've got to get going," Mia said. "I've got a date with the supermarket." To me, she added, "My cupboard is bare, which means no cookies in anyone's future if I don't get some flour and sugar." As she passed me, heading for the front door, I was greeted with her light, flowery perfume. Damn sexy. "I'll make some special cookies for you, Eli."

My hand raised toward her.

Flint lifted my jaw with his finger and chuckled. He tapped my arm. "Time to get to work, Romeo."

Romeo? Flames consumed my cheeks, and Becca's snicker rang out over Mia shutting the front door behind her.

Damned if I cared. Life had just started to look a hell of a lot finer.

There was no hiding the swagger in my stride as I followed Flint across the lobby toward the hall leading to the main part of the building. But my smile soon faded as my mind dragged me back to Mexico and what happened to Mia. Despite the isolated incident involving my sister, Ginny, due to a creepy ex-boyfriend who'd tried to kill her, Mia would soon see she was safe in my sleepy town of Crescent Cove. Nothing bad ever happened here.

"The Mexican police ever get in touch with you?" I asked Flint.

We paused in the hall and stared through the window, watching Mia get into her car, back it up, and drive through the gate.

"You know how they are down there," Flint said. "Robberies happen all the time, and she was leaving the country. They've probably forgotten about it. Moved on to the next tourist incident already." Disgust grated through in his words.

"Maybe." The situation kept bugging me. That cop... The intensity in his eyes suggested there was more to this than a simple robbery. I shook my head then shoved my hair off my face. After getting out of the military, I'd defied convention and let it grow wild, but I needed a good cut or the crew here would start calling me a mountain man. Ginny already did.

Turning, Flint nudged my shoulder. "About my sister."

"She's awesome."

Flint blinked. "Shit. You've got it bad already, don't you?"

Fire rose into my face. My gaze narrowed on Flint's mocking expression, I rocked back on my heels. "Any problem with that?"

"Not at all." Whistling through his teeth, Flint pivoted and started down the hall, away from the lobby. "Not at all. She needs someone who's...well, I'll let her decide if she wants to share what happened in Massachusetts."

"Wait." I snagged his arm, turning him to face me. "Tell me."

Flint's expression mimicked his name. "Said I'd leave that to her."

I released a curt nod. While I felt like going all he-man at the suggestion someone might've hurt Mia, Flint obviously would not fill me in. What happened in Massachusetts?

However, his comment about us seeing each other outside of work could be considered permission to do more than send Mia flowers. Not that I needed her brother's approval to ask her out. It was solely up to Mia to say yes or no, and I'd fully respect her wishes even if she told me again to get lost. But it was important to have this open and above board between me and my friend. I didn't sneak around or hide.

"In fact," Flint said with a rising chuckle, continuing down the hall. "I gave her your number."

My feet froze in place. "Why?"

"'Cause she asked for it."

Wait. "Why?" I said, stuck in repeat mode.

"Why does any woman ask for a guy's number?"

"Because..." Stunned, I couldn't think.

"She's asked about you a few times since she came out west to help me move home."

"She has?" Okay, I might sound like a puppy eager for a treat, but...Had Mia thought about me the way I couldn't stop thinking about her?

"Yup," Flint said.

"Yup to what?"

"To that thought written all over your face." His laughter faded, and his face grew serious again. "But you'll have to deal with my sister another time. Right now, I've got a few interesting things to show you before our debriefing."

My brain buzzing and my chest expanding three sizes, I followed Flint toward the back of the building that must house the R&D component of the business. At the end of the hallway, he typed numbers on a keypad to open a steel door labeled *Authorized Personnel Only-No Entrance* and waved for me to enter ahead of him.

"Encrypted codes were emailed to you by Aunt Becca," he said. He paused in the doorway. "Hope you don't mind me leaving you for a sec. I've got to take care of something urgent. Go ahead and look around. Get a feel for the operation. You know the crew already."

Nodding, I advanced into the room while the door shut behind me.

"Watch out," a gruff voice shouted from my right. "Incoming!"

4

ELI

A sharp pop was followed by a whoosh, and a swarm of tiny metal objects made a beeline for my head. I ducked seconds before the mass of glittering drones impaled my face. While my heart thumped faster than I liked, the dull black bugs buzzed over me, their tiny wings skimming my hair. They circled and sped across the room like a horde of high-tech wasps.

"Hell," I said.

"Eli," Coop called out. Wearing safety glasses, he held a soldering gun and was working on a circuit board lying on a bench fitted into the far-right wall. "What a welcome, huh?"

"Yeah."

While Coop returned his attention on the board, I studied the big open, windowless warehouse. The left wall supported low benches for hands-on jobs, plus computers with office chairs parked in front. The tall metal cabinets to the right of the benches must hold tools and equipment, though I imagined Flint also had a fully-stocked supply room. The back of the warehouse had been lined with noise isolation steel, interspersed with thick rubber mats—a bit like the kind you'd find in a high school gym only tougher.

Jax strolled over, holding out his hand. "Fancy meeting you here." Even though I could tell he was joking, my gaze still squared off with his as if we faced each other on a dojo mat, ready to see who'd come up the victor.

My stiff stance was definitely related to cookies.

"Nice to see you again," I said. While I held a black belt, the steely look in Jax's dark, blue-gray eyes told me it would take considerable skill to lay this well-muscled man out flat. Given the chance on a combat mat, I'd sure as hell try. "Didn't get much chance to talk in Mexico." Our wild goose chase after the elusive contact had kept us hopping 24/7. "You were Seabees, too, right?"

"Yup. Computer Technician."

"Computer hacker, you mean?"

Jax's grin confirmed my assumption. "Eight years. Made Chief."

Usually took longer than eight years to rise to that rank, which meant Jax had impressed the board his first time through. Hackers would be in hot demand.

"Senior Chief," I said. "Eleven years." I'd also moved up quickly.

Jax gave me a random salute but we didn't need to worry about that crap any longer. In our civilian roles, we were equals. "Flint said you're our spy."

"Spy gear, anyway." I'd specialized in cameras and other surveillance equipment in the Seabees. Went to multiple C schools.

I felt a tap on my back but when I turned, nothing but a blank, beige wall stared back at me. Shaking my head, I faced Jax again.

He waved toward the swarm darting across the high-ceilinged room in precise formation. The tiny black cloud split when it approached a steel beam, reforming immediately after passing. "I see you met our autonomous friends."

I squinted at them. "Machines run by artificial intelligence."

"They talk to each other. Learn from each other, too."

"Sweet," I said. "No joystick or controller, right? You program them with a mission and send them out to do it."

Jax nodded, his gaze intent on the drones. "Someday soon, bigger versions of these babies will replace men and women in the field. They're smarter. Faster. And expendable."

Unlike people. My hand twitched against my wounded thigh as I watched the tiny group buzz Coop, who totally ignored the mini beasts. They spun around and dove toward a camo-dressed mannequin standing in front of a rubber mat at the back of the room. After circling the figure, they zipped across the open space to dive-bomb me again. Like I was under attack by a horde of rabid mosquitos, it was all I could do to resist waving my arms.

"Right now, I'm teaching 'em how to act as decoys," Jax said, humor coming through in his voice. "They've already been trained to scramble enemy air defenses. Picture this. You've got a missile headed your way and a group of our tiny friends flies into its path and distracts it, sending it in a new direction. If we program them right, they'll divert the missile back the way it came. Imagine the surprise when we take 'em out with their own weapons."

These drones could behave like viruses to medicine and become a big part of the military's future.

Jax grunted. "Eventually, we'll mount them with cameras and teach them face recognition. That's where you come in. With your expertise, we'll send these little buggers out to hunt down terrorists. The only ethical dilemma we're facing at the moment is whether we should arm 'em with weapons or not."

Warfare was changing so fast, I could barely keep up. Would future battles be fought with armies solely made up of drones? Sounded a bit too Terminator for my taste but it sure beats dodging bullets. "Cool."

Another tap on my back. Pivoting sharply, I studied the area, finding nothing again. A low growl rumbled in my throat. What the hell kept poking me?

With a nudge on my arm, Jax redirected my attention to the drones. "We call this group of prototypes Locust 3."

"What happened to Locust 1 and 2?"

Jax grimaced. "You don't want to know."

"Maybe *I* want to know," someone said from behind us.

I spun, crouching low, my arms spreading wide in defense.

A shape that had blended in with the surroundings like a chameleon peeled itself away from the wall. Fabric rustled, and a body-less face appeared. Flint, looking too damn proud of himself. "Gotcha."

"Ass." I straightened.

Chuckling, Jax strode toward the far side of the room where the drones hovered over a table. Obviously, this wasn't the first time Flint had pulled this trick on one of the crew.

"What is that, anyway?" I asked, poking at his arm while marveling at how well he blended in with the surroundings.

"Like it?" Flint grinned, looking down. "We call it a stealth cloth." More fabric rustled when it dropped to the floor. He stepped forward, fully revealed, and turned to lift the almost opaque piece of material off the concrete floor.

He held it out toward me. "Works like a mirage, bending light away from the wearer."

I fingered the stiff fabric and hefted it. "Weighs practically nothing." I could already see the possibilities in combat situations. Like crossing an open area to avoid enemy fire. Sneaking into a hostile compound.

"Works in just about any terrain but when we made it into a suit, we sweated underneath like a sinner in church." Flint swiped a hand across his forehead and grimaced. "Still trying to figure out how to cool the soldier with mini AC powered by battery packs without making the uniform too heavy. We also need to make it thinner and more flexible, so it won't hinder movement."

"Another work in progress like the drones."

"But damn fun to play around with until we're ready to send it off for further, in-depth testing, right?" He slapped my shoulder.

I was itching to see what I could do with the stealth cloth already. Maybe I could work out something with lithium batteries.

Flint strode to a table and dropped the cloth. He returned with two sets of noise-reduction headphones. "Might want to put these on."

I settled the headset over my ears and glanced around, wondering what was up now.

A woman dressed in a calf-length pink skirt and a lacy white top exited a door on our left and walked into the middle of the room with what vaguely resembled a small RPG-7 rocket launcher lying across her shoulder. In sharp contrast to her four-inch black heels, she wore safety glasses and neon green earplugs. Her long, black braid fell past her shoulders from underneath the back of the ballistic helmet she'd strapped onto her head.

Haylee. In her late-twenties, she was our former commanding officer's daughter and Flint & Mia's cousin. Flint, Coop, Haylee, and I had served in the same Seabee company for a while, but she'd left the military about four years ago. During my interview, Flint told me he'd hired her.

Weird that she'd shoot an anti-tank missile inside a warehouse. Even a toddler-sized version would take out the back wall.

Jax leaned against a workbench, facing her, his gaze more intent on her than the drones. The tiny mechanical devices lingered beside him as if they watched—and learned—along with him.

All clear, Flint hand-signaled Haylee, who nodded.

She sighted down the barrel. When the launcher engaged, her slender body jerked but she maintained her footing.

The blast jarred through my bones.

Hitting the mannequin, the missile disintegrated much of its chest and sent it flying backward. After smacking into the thick padding behind it, the fake guy crumpled onto the floor. Obviously, she'd fired a souped-up blank. Enough to knock out a target but still leave the building standing. But the angle...She hadn't been aiming directly at the mannequin.

I hauled off my headset. Curving ammunition? I'd heard rumors about—

"Hot damn!" Haylee set the RPG-7 on the floor. She yanked off her helmet and tossed it and her earplugs aside then danced in a circle, swaying her hips, her arms waving overhead. "Enemy soldier down. Enemy soldier down. Got any more dudes with attitude hanging out in the back room, Jax? 'Cause I have so got to teach them a few lessons."

His attention directed downward, Jax mumbled something that could've been yes or no or who knows what. An odd contrast to how outgoing he acted with Mia. Wait...Mia had teased Jax about being shy but I'd seen nothing to confirm that in my interactions with him.

But if he was hot for Haylee...Was that it? If he was one of those guys who could talk it up with any woman except the one he was interested in, this situation was going to be tough. Working together would be a big enough challenge, let alone asking her out.

Almost made me want to make some popcorn, put my feet up in a recliner, and watch the show.

Haylee's attention flicked in my direction, and she hooted and ran toward me. As if to confirm my assumption, Jax's eyes followed her with distinctive yearning.

Stalling in front of me, Haylee grinned. "Finally, the company's back together."

"Plus, me," Jax added forlornly, coming over to join us.

"It's okay, honey. You're part of the family, now." Haylee looped her arm around his waist.

Jax's breath hissed out. Damn. It was all I could do to hold back my grin.

He stepped away from her as if she'd burn him on contact.

Did Haylee read the situation the way I did? From the way her smile trembled, I'd say no. Her back stiffened and she presented it to Jax. That would teach him. Ha.

She pouted at me. "Can't believe you live local and didn't come to see me already. I moved to the area a few months ago."

"Don't remember you calling me to let me know. How about we get together next week?"

"Will do. I've missed you." She tapped her chin, and a

speculative gleam filled her eyes. "Since you've been blowing me off, you owe me."

I rolled my eyes. "Name your price." Haylee always had been good at getting her way. And if she was interested in Jax... Definitely needed to make that popcorn.

"I have a feeling you might have a little tequila hanging around somewhere," she said.

She'd gotten wind of the bottles I'd brought back from Mexico. "Deal." Planned on giving her one once I heard she was a part of Flint's crew.

"If you guys are finished destroying things for the moment," Flint said, slanting a glance toward the pulverized mannequin. He tilted his head toward the door. "Uncle Sid and Gabe have arrived. It's time for our meeting."

"Perfect." Haylee linked her arm through mine and tugged me along, totally ignoring Jax, who continued to watch her. "I'll show you where the conference room is while you tell me what you've been up to since we last saw each other."

We left the shop and walked down the hall.

Inside the conference room, a tall, gray-haired man stood in front of the long row of windows. As Haylee left me to round the table, the man turned, a big smile rising on his face. "Honey." He kissed his daughter. He nodded to his nephew, Flint before his gaze fell on me. "Damn, if it isn't Eli. Heard you'd joined the crew."

"Admiral Rhodes." I strode around the table and shook our former commanding officer's hand. This man had replaced the father who'd abandoned me as a kid, watching over me and guiding me throughout my career. I was a better person solely because of him.

Some guys took up golf when they retired, but Admiral Rhodes filled his free time with consulting work for the government. Only in the area for the summer—he and his wife owned a home on the coast—Flint mentioned he'd be driving out today to join us.

"None of that. It's Sid, now," the Admiral said.

I tugged on my collar and resisted the urge to salute. While we were close, being on a first-name basis with this man would take getting used to.

Sid nudged my shoulder with his knuckles. "Work on it." He took a seat.

Gabe Jameson pushed back his chair and stood, his hand extending. "Great to see you again, Eli."

I'd met Gabe during a six-month training at Camp Leje-une where we'd spent too much of our day time crawling through swampland, followed by too many late nights drinking beer and playing football under the lights. I'd run into him in the Middle East a few times, as well, and looked forward to working with him again.

Flint couldn't have picked a better team.

"Okay everyone, let's get started." Flint waved to the captain's chairs surrounding the table.

"Anyone else coming today?" Sid asked. He took a long swallow of his coffee.

"This is it for now." Flint turned to me. "I'm trying to recruit Hawk, but I'm not making much headway."

"He's still in Afghanistan, isn't he?" I asked. Hawk was another Chief with a few months left in his current tour, last I'd heard.

"I wanted to get a jump on him early. Plant the idea in his head before he reenlists."

"I'd love to work with him," Coop said from beside me. He tapped his pencil on the table, frowning. "I might have a few other guys in mind I can send your way."

"That would be awesome," Flint said. He opened a

manila folder, pulled out a sheaf of papers, and slid one across the dark, gleaming oak table, toward each of us. "Update on our Mexico project. After we ran into issues, I did more investigation. Discovered our contact had been compromised. That's why he went missing."

Double agent? If I knew Mexican drug cartels, the man was now feeding the stingrays.

"You think the cartel eliminated him before he could give us the goods." Gabe studied the paper. He tugged on his light blue patterned tie that contrasted with his darker, expertly-tailored jacket. Dude dressed up all the time, even when he hit the local bar scene.

"Hard to tell how," Jax said. "We locked him down behind a wall of security."

"If he'd remained inside the perimeter, a flea wouldn't have been able to reach him," Flint said and added for Sid's benefit, "From all appearances, he disarmed the system himself and walked out. The alarm triggered and the guy at the gate notified us. We beat it over there fast, but our contact was nowhere to be found."

"Had a tracker on him, too," Jax said.

"Removed it and dumped it in a flower bed," Coop offered dryly.

"Whoa," Haylee said. "What's going on with this job?"

Flint grunted. "Not much, now. Without him feeding us information, we're dead in the water. We're also missing the data he promised. And Maestro's true identity."

"Fancy name for an asshole," Sid said.

I had to agree. Anyone who'd bring laced drugs into the country and sell them to kids should be locked away for the rest of their life.

Our assignment was to provide intel to take down a small branch of the larger drug cartel tree by gaining evidence implicating cartel sympathizers high in the Mexican government. This would then be used to discover who the organization was affiliated with here in the U.S. One man—or woman—who controlled the entire northeast operation. The Maestro.

From what Flint told me, the guy who'd gone missing in Mexico had kept all the details in his head. With him gone, the project was stalled. Now, Flint would have to scramble to find someone else who'd be willing to risk his skin to squeal on his bosses.

Sid leaned forward, and his voice boomed. "Have you thought about sending another operative back in?" His glance cut to Jax, who was staring longingly at Haylee sitting beside him.

Haylee being Sid's daughter would make any sane man think twice. Rumor had it Sid had done everything he could to ensure she received the safest deployments, which must've irritated Haylee, a weapons specialist and gunner's mate. The way she'd taken out that sniper with one shot in the Middle East told me she was as eager as the next Seabee to jump into action.

Maybe Jax would be up for it, though. From what Flint told me, the guy thrived on danger. First to bail out of a helo while under enemy fire. Rappel down a cliff into hostile territory before the rest of the crew could even dream about popping the safety off their weapons. Heard he even crash-landed a plane in the desert once. *Before* he got his pilot's license. But if he wasn't careful, Sid would burn him alive. Haylee's father hadn't just policed her military assignments. One guy she dated suddenly found himself on an eighteen-month mission on the border between North and South Korea.

Flint nudged his chin at Jax. "See if you can hack into

their networks. I need something—someone who's desperate, someone we can tap into on the ground."

"Absolutely," Jax said. He made a note on his paper.

Flint focused his attention on Haylee and Gabe. "Even though I used him in Mexico, Eli has just started. Coop will handle his orientation because I've got to go to D.C. with Uncle Sid."

"If..." Jax gulped. "If you're thinking of sending Haylee"—his gaze cut to her again—"I can go, too."

"Actually," Flint said. "I really need you here stateside." His attention returned to Gabe. "Which leaves you two the only ones available for recon."

Sweat broke out on Sid's forehead, and his coffee cup smacked the wooden table. "But—"

"Always happy to head south for vacation." Haylee shot her father a weighted look before smiling at Gabe. "Time to pack your swimsuit, buddy. Don't forget sunscreen or that baby-fine skin of yours will blister."

As hardened as we all were from multiple tours, it was doubtful Gabe had anything baby-fine left on his body.

Jax stiffened, but I knew Haylee. Always a tease, she didn't mean anything by her comment to Gabe.

I studied Gabe and Haylee's assignment, which seemed simple enough. Fly into Cancun and settle inside a plush resort. Hang out at the swim-up bar for a day or two to give the impression they were there for some fun and relaxation.

Then disappear, going undercover.

5

MIA

"9-1-1. Please state your emergency."

"Guts and heads are strewn across my windshield." While wedging my phone between my ear and shoulder, I shifted my shopping bags to my right hand.

The dispatcher's voice might've started out serious but it ended prissy. "Is this a prank call, Miss...?" Was the repetitive sound in the background the woman tapping her shoe?

"Mia Crawford. Doctor Mia Crawford, I mean. I work... well, I'll soon work at Crescent Cove General Hospital." I'd bought a house and moved here two months ago, but I'd delayed my start at the hospital until after Labor Day. A fortuitous plan, because I not only needed a break after what happened in Mexico, I planned to attend a two-day conference where I'd highlight the Juniper Foundation's progress in reducing sudden cardiac death in the over-fifty female population in the Yucatan. "I start in September, actually."

The sweat trickling down my spine—let alone the reek rising off the entrails strewn across my windshield—made the month very clear. A carcass, or, in this case, bits of multiple carcasses, didn't fare well in this heat.

"I don't understand," the woman said. "Could you please state your emergency?"

"Oh, yes. Back to the guts." A few beheaded creatures stared up at me, their eyes milky white and accusatory in death. Skimming my gaze across the plump, slimy strands lying in loops and curls on the glass brought out my shudder. Flies flitted around, enjoying the feast.

This was why I'd turned down that surgical fellowship. I could handle blood as much as the next doctor, but innards made me squirm. We all had our weaknesses.

"Is anyone injured?" the dispatcher asked. Her voice grew louder. "Wait. Did you say heads?"

"Sorry, I should've been clearer." I winced. "Not human heads. They're fish." If the scales glinting among the gook were anything to go by.

"Fish heads? If this is an act of vandalism, you probably need police assistance."

"Yes, please." With my key fob, I unlocked my car and juggled the shopping bags onto the backseat. "Can you notify someone? I want to fill out a report." Not that I expected much to come of this. It had to be a sick joke perpetrated by a teenager. Whoever had done it was probably sitting in a car nearby—an air-conditioned car if they were wise—snickering while watching me squirm.

"I could call Sheriff Moyer. He's local to your area."

"I'd appreciate it."

"Where are you?"

"At the supermarket."

"Located in which state and town?"

"Oh, sorry. Crescent Cove, Maine. As for the supermarket, it's on East Main. The only one in town."

While some people might be put out by the lack of a mall or exciting places to dine, Crescent Cove's rural location was a big reason why I'd moved here. I'd needed an escape, and a sleepy Maine town fit perfectly. Everyone I'd met so far was kind and non-threatening. Nosy, but that meant they watched out for each other, another huge plus after my nightmare with Russell. The welcome I'd found in this community allowed me to relax my guard for the first time in months.

Until someone took sick pleasure in strewing fish parts on my car.

"What's the make of your vehicle so the sheriff can identify you when he arrives?" the dispatcher asked.

I bumped the back door closed with my butt and leaned against the overheated metal. "Older Toyota Camry. Light blue."

"You're lucky," she said, her fingers tapping away. "The message is now out, but he's in your area already. You should see him in—"

Her words were cut off by a siren growing louder. A white SUV with a police emblem on the side screamed into the parking lot, and the sheriff got out. He squinted around before zoning his attention in on me.

A uniformed woman strode around the vehicle to flank him in front of the grill.

"I take it he arrived?" The dispatcher's chuckle came through the line.

"Yes. Thank you very much."

"Anytime." She ended the call.

Approaching me, the man thrust out his hand. "Sheriff Moyer." He gestured to the woman, who rocked forward onto her toes, her hands on her hips. "Deputy Patricia Franks." She nodded. The Sheriff removed his broad-brimmed hat and scratched his thinning salt-and-pepper hair before plunking the hat back on his head. "Understand you called 9-1-1. Something about fish heads?"

"Yes." I waved at my windshield. The reek overwhelmed my sinuses even from four feet away. "I was in the supermarket for about twenty minutes. Shopping. I came out to this."

"Hmm." Sheriff Moyer frowned and leaned toward the car. "Looks like pogies to me."

"The guts or the heads?" I asked.

"Both."

Confused, I flicked my gaze between them.

"Pogie is another name for menhaden," Deputy Franks said as if that would make perfect sense to me. At my blank stare, she added, "An oily fish used as bait. Pretty common around these parts." She rocked forward again. "Imagine the perp snagged a bucket of them down at the pier. Tossed 'em your way. Well, your car's way, that is. Not sure why, though." Her brow narrowed and she swept a flinty gaze down my face. "Doctor you said?"

"Yes. I moved here from Massachusetts a few months ago." I ran away after my ex was convicted, actually, but no need to mention that. I'd left that history behind me.

"Glad to have you," she said. "We need more medical personnel in town."

The hospital had been excited when I approached recruiters. Said they rarely saw more than those recently finished with residency applying to work in a small town far from big city life, let alone someone who'd begun a cardiac fellowship. I'd been fresh off a rotation in Boston, which only made them more eager to sign me on.

The Sheriff pulled out his phone and fumbled with a stylus, grimacing. "Damn office told me I had to get with the current technology. Far as I'm concerned, there's nothing wrong with a note made with pen and paper."

Deputy Franks leaned near to me, shading her mouth from the sheriff with her palm. "They can't read his writing."

The sheriff huffed, but the Deputy's eyes sparkled, giving me the feeling these two joked around on a regular basis.

She pulled her phone and started taking pictures of my car while the sheriff laboriously typed out his note.

"You say you came out of the store and found it, just like this?" he said.

"Yes."

"Didn't touch anything?"

"Just the back door to put my groceries on the seat."

"Your vehicle was locked?"

"Of course." I'd never leave my car—or house, for that matter—vulnerable.

"All right." He watched Deputy Franks a moment before stepping forward to join her. "Let's see what we're dealing with here."

I moved back, leaving them to their investigation.

A woman pushed a shopping cart between my car and the one next to mine. She must've caught the smell, let alone the disgusting display strewn across my windshield, because she released the handles of the cart, turned green, then doubled over and heaved.

Deputy Franks, who was passing us, squeaked and hopped backward. The sheriff swallowed deeply and brought his phone close to his face as if the screen could block out everything going on around him.

Rushing to the woman's side, I shifted the cart aside and supported her under one arm while holding her long chest-nut-colored hair away from her face. As her belly settled, I patted her back. "Hey, it's going to be okay."

"Ugh," the woman said, straightening. All color had fled her face. "I'm really sorry."

"I get it." I smiled in sympathy. "I'm beyond tempted to join you. Are you dizzy? Feeling all right for the moment?" At her nod, I popped open my back door and grabbed a fistful of tissues from the box on the floor and handed them to her. "Here. You seem to have hit the pavement, but you can wipe your face with these."

The woman rubbed the tissues across her forehead and mouth. She grimaced and bunched them in her fingers. "I don't know what's wrong with me."

"It's completely understandable." I grimaced at my car. "One look sent my belly into spasms, too. You want to sit down?"

"Sure." After rolling the cart to the back of the other vehicle, she keyed it open with her fob. "This one's mine, obviously." Abandoning her groceries for the moment, she opened the driver's door and sank into the seat.

"I'm a doctor, by the way," I said. "My name's Mia."

"Lark," she said. "I actually meant this isn't the first time I've been sick." Reaching into her pocket, she pulled out a tin of mints and shook them in the air. "I'm living on these babies lately."

"If you've been sick for some time, maybe you should be seen by someone?"

Lark's lips twisted with humor. "Other than you?"

"A real visit, I meant. I'm actually a cardiologist, not a general practitioner." Well, I'd be a full cardiologist once I completed my fellowship. "You should get checked out. Make sure this is nothing serious."

"I should." Lark leaned the back of her head against her

seat and rubbed her face while sucking on a mint. On her left hand, a huge diamond and sapphire ring winked in the sunshine. "I can't keep going on like this. Dag, my fiancé, is worried out of his mind."

"It could be a virus. Plenty of those going around."

She squinted up at me. "Viruses make you hurl your guts out every morning like clockwork?"

I tapped my chin, having an ah-ha moment. "Not usually. But...a baby might."

Lark's hand shot to her belly. Her eyelids popped open, and tears glistened in her teal eyes. "Oh, my, you think so? The idea did occur to me, but with the stress of the wedding, and..." Her face colored. "Too much information, right?"

I chuckled. "Your doctor would have to run a few tests to be certain, but I assume pregnancy is a possibility?"

"Yeah." The word came out dreamy. Lark stared forward, through the windshield, a big grin blooming on her pretty face. "But I can't be pregnant right now," she said softly. "I'm getting married in two weeks."

I rubbed her shoulder. "Sounds like the perfect wedding present to give your soon-to-be hubby."

"Yeah." Said in an even more dreamy tone. "Dag's going to beat his fists on his chest and hoot, and then call his parents. His mom...She'll scream her head off." At my frown, she added, "She's dying for grandkids. But I'm getting ahead of myself." With renewed energy, she swung her legs out of the car and stood, staring toward the supermarket. "I need to go get a test." After putting her groceries in the back of the car, she started toward the store but turned back to face me. "Thanks for your help, Mia."

"You're welcome. Good luck with the wedding and..." I wanted to hug her because she seemed so happy but settled for a grin instead. "Everything else."

"Thank you!" Hand cupping her flat belly, Lark essentially skipped toward the supermarket.

I turned back to Deputy Franks, who was strolling around my car, studying and photographing it from every angle. "Nothing else seems to be out of the norm." Opposite me, she bent forward then returned to this side of the car with a black bucket in her rubber-gloved hand. "Evidence," she said pertly. She tilted the top of the bucket toward me, revealing residue of the crime: fish scales.

"I assume this is a sick joke," I said. "It's not like anyone has any reason to target me." Not any longer, now that Russell was in jail.

"Imagine so," the sheriff said, still writing. "We'll ask at the pier. See if anyone's missing some bait."

"You think a fisherman did this?"

The sheriff turned sharp eyes my way. "You having problems with fishermen?"

"Only with their fish."

Distracted from his note, the sheriff drilled me with intent gray eyes. "What do you mean by that?"

"I can't eat it."

"Why not?" Deputy Franks lowered the bucket into a garbage bag. After securing the top, she removed her medical gloves. "Fish is pretty much a staple on the menu around here."

"I'm allergic. I carry an EpiPen." The itchy rash was bad enough. The potential of being unable to breath guaranteed a quick trip to the ER. But I stayed away from fish and hadn't had a reaction in years.

"Might want to let us clean this up, then," the deputy said, slanting a glance at my windshield.

"Maybe someone down at the pier saw someone skulking in the area," Sheriff Moyer added, tucking his stylus and phone into his breast pocket. "Might gain some further evidence by asking around, but I'll say right now, it's doubtful we'll figure out who did this."

"I didn't think you would. I just wanted to report it."

"Why don't you drive your vehicle around to the back of the supermarket?" he said. "They have a dumpster out there, and I've got paper towels in my trunk. We can clean your windshield off lickety-split then hose 'er off for good measure. They've got an outside faucet, as well."

"I really appreciate it."

AN HOUR LATER, I'd put my groceries away and had started mixing a double batch of cookies.

Should I call Eli and invite him to come over for a baking session? A bold move on my part, but I'd turned him down when he asked me out in California. A decent guy who appeared to respect boundaries, I knew I'd have to make the first move this time.

Assuming I dared. After what happened with Russell, I had good reason to be leery of letting anyone close. Caution had become my norm. Hence my turning Eli down months ago when he asked me out. Everyone said time healed all wounds and, with Russell in prison, plus counseling, I'd started to put what happened behind me.

Put his abuse behind me, that is. My burgeoning trust in men sure wasn't coming easy. Yet, Eli felt different. Though I'd only known him a short time, I was certain he'd never lift a hand or raise his voice in my direction.

Which was why I'd made that comment at Viper Force. While I'd been burned, I didn't want to be alone forever.

Something about Eli called to me like no else had before, even Russell.

I hoped he understood my suggestive comment, because my interest in him hadn't waned. He was still fun. Sweet. And cute. Cuter than before, actually, with that mop of dirty blond hair hanging in his eyes. Made me want to stand on tiptoe and brush it to the side.

Now that two-thousand-miles no longer stretched between us, and Russell and his abuse was locked away in my past, I could take a baby step forward.

It was noon, though, which meant I couldn't call Eli right now. He'd still be at work.

Measuring out shortening, I scraped it into the bowl then added sugar and vanilla. Eggs. Mixing in between. Soon, I'd add white chocolate chips and macadamia nuts.

And, if I found the nerve, I'd invite Eli over for a cookie tasting session.

I WAS GOING to kill Walter.

Not really. I loved my fluffy orange kitty boy more than life itself. But he was fidgety tonight, keeping me awake along with him. Normally, he'd eat his wet food while I ate my dinner, then he'd climb onto my bed for a bath and a pre-nighttime nap. When I joined him, I'd nudge him to the side and climb under the covers. Even more of a slug-a-bed than me, he'd remain close until morning, stealing heat from my body and creating a lumpy challenge to weave my legs around whenever I rolled over.

Walter hissed, and I jumped, my heart skipping a beat.

Moonlight filtered through the lace curtains on either side of my bed, giving me just enough light to see my cat perched by my feet, his unblinking eyes focused on my closed bedroom door.

Walter plunged over the edge onto the floor when I sat up. He padded stealthily to the door and sniffed. After shooting me a narrow-eyed look over his shoulder, he pawed at the door and meowed pitifully.

Did he have to go to the bathroom? The litter box was in my laundry room, off the kitchen. Or, he might want a midnight snack. Far be it for me to deprive him of a few kibbles.

He clawed at the door.

"Okay," I grumbled, shoving aside the covers to climb out of bed.

I'd bought this house a few months ago—a single-story cottage, actually, with one bedroom, a tiny kitchen but decent-sized living room, one-and-a-half baths, and a study. A basement and a tiny, cobwebby attic, plus a nice backyard completed the property. It was perfect for a single person or maybe a couple with a baby. A quiet but mostly friendly neighborhood— excluding the peculiar older man next door, Elwin—it offered peace after the horror I'd been through with Russell.

"What do you want, buddy?" I asked Walter.

He meowed again and butted his head on the door.

"I'm coming, I'm coming." My bare feet silent on the carpet, I joined him, my fingers reaching for the handle. "Please tell me this place didn't come with mice." Or bats, the thought of which made me shiver despite the seventy-degree air drifting in through the open bedroom windows.

What else could it be, though? My cat wouldn't care about cars passing on the street, and the neighbors on both sides were elderly and went to bed each night earlier than

Walter. They wouldn't decide to play a beer-infused night-time game of corn hole in their backyards.

When I opened the door, Walter scampered out, moving so fast his claws scraped on the hardwood floor in the hall. Maybe he needed exercise. Should I follow him? Not for the exercise but to see what had drawn his interest.

Wrapping my arms around my waist, I shook my head. Not following unless I wanted to witness him stalking a mouse or leaping on a bat. Ugh. I could deal with the carcass in the morning.

Turning, I stumbled back to my bed, glaring at the clock that shouted one-ten a.m. in big red numbers. Double ugh. While I didn't have to get up and go to work in the morning, I did have to finish my presentation for my upcoming conference.

Because I'd chickened out on calling him, I also wanted to bring cookies to the shop for Eli. And beat Jax away with an imaginary stick and a stiff hint that he was not to lay one figure on them until Eli had gotten a share.

A howl from somewhere deep in my house sent goose-bumps rippling across my skin.

"Walter?" I shouted as I leaped from my bed and rushed into the hall, tripping over a box of textbooks I'd left here with the intention of putting them up in the attic soon.

Rubbing my sore shin, I flicked the light switch, but nothing happened.

Great. Lights streaming in the front living room windows told me the rest of the street had power. Maybe I'd blown a fuse? Flint had already insisted my place needed rewiring.

Another howl, coming from the study down the hall and on the left, made my heart stall before thumping faster than a horse racing in the Kentucky Derby.

Flashlight. Darting into the kitchen on my right, I rifled

through the junk drawer and found one. My fingers trembling, I clicked it on and swept the beam around. Nothing out of the ordinary stood out to me. No mice or bats peering at me, either, thank heaven.

"Walter?" I croaked out, leaving the kitchen for the hall. I tiptoed toward the study. The living room loomed on my right, a dark void that didn't invite entry. Shadows lurked everywhere. Truly, it was just the sofa, the recliner, and a bookcase, but still.

Definitely needed to install nightlights along with new wiring.

On the road out front, a car drifted by slowly. Did it hesitate at my house? I resisted the urge to press myself against the wall. My skin prickled, telling me I'd be wise to hide.

"Why would someone care about me walking around inside my house?" I asked in a low voice. "It's not like anyone knows I'm on an adventure with my cat in the middle of the night."

That's all this was, an adventure. Nothing creepy.

Keep telling yourself that.

I approached the study on light feet. Stopping beside the open doorway, I leaned forward and shot my flashlight beam inside like a bright weapon.

Nothing moved.

"Walter?" I whispered with a scratchy voice. One full of fear.

A harsh meow from somewhere in the dark room sent the tiny hairs bolting upright on the back of my neck.

"Where are you?" I asked, making myself enter the room. If Walter had gotten into trouble, I wanted to help him. The old wooden floorboards creaked and groaned beneath me, giving the situation a Stephen King feel. Not a pleasant thought while exploring alone in my dark house.

I crept forward, slashing my light back and forth.

The neat piles of paper on my desk suggested nothing had been disturbed. To the right, the open closet door revealed dark shapes—winter coats I'd stuffed inside because the front hall closet was too small to hold things from all four seasons. My grannie's rocker stood sentinel in the far-left corner of the room.

Moving slightly.

As if someone had recently pushed it.

Thump-thump-thump, the curved rocker boards ground against the hardwood floor. Had Walter nudged it while scooting by?

Another meow, this time filled with panic that was echoed inside me.

I whirled around, darting my light toward the built-in wooden cupboards spanning one wall. Eventually, I'd store board games and other infrequently used items there. For now, a pile of boxes waited in front and to the sides of the cupboard doors, which latched.

A scraping, clawing sound made me jump out of my skin before I exhaled sharply and strode forward. My unease plunged from my shoulders like a saturated blanket.

"Walter?" How had he gotten himself locked in there? I could swear the doors had been closed the last time I was inside this room.

I opened the furthest cupboard on the left, and Walter leaped out. He hissed as if I'd forced him inside the tiny area and slammed the door in his face. Scrambling across the room, he flew through the doorway and bolted right, toward my bedroom.

"Okay." Wiping my curls off my face, I shook my head. Walter must be jittery. Everyone knew it was stressful settling into a new place. He'd stayed with Flint while I was in Mexico because I had nowhere else to leave him. Two new homes in a short span of time would upset anyone, let alone my normally easy-going fluffball.

No need for me to keep my back up any longer, however. He'd taken a late-night stroll and somehow gotten himself locked inside the cabinet. Rescued, he'd probably huff when I joined him in bed and give me the cold shoulder because, naturally, it was all my fault.

Sighing, I followed him back to my bedroom.

I'd call Flint in the morning. Maybe he could recommend an electrician.

Oh, wait. Flint had left a message on my phone saying he was flying to D.C.

Who else could I call?

Per usual, Eli's name jumped into my mind. Could he offer some electrical advice outside the electrical feelings he generated inside me? If he couldn't give me a name of someone I could call, one of his friends probably could. He'd grown up in Crescent Cove, and he'd lived here for months before I moved to town.

My feet padded softly on the wooden boards as I made my way back to my bedroom.

Walter lay on the quilt, glaring as I strode inside.

"It's not my fault you got stuck in there." I stomped toward him. "I have no idea why you decided to go hunting or whatever it was you were doing in the middle of the night. You did this deed all on your own." Climbing up onto the still slightly warm spot on the bed, I pulled the covers to my waist. "Maybe save the next adventure for daylight?"

I'd dropped onto my back and was about to turn off my flashlight when Walter growled.

"What now?" I sat up and glared at him.

He stared toward my bureau that held a large mirror, where something...slithered along the glass.

My heart rate tripled and my mouth flashed dry. What...?

I directed the beam to the mirror and, at first, light shot back at me, blinding me to everything else. But then I made out something bleeding down the glass.

Something red.

My belly lurched, and my skin crawled as if a thousand spiders had dropped onto me from the ceiling.

A number one?

I grimaced as the red blood—paint?—leached down the shiny surface.

Fresh.

Horror clawed through my guts.

Someone had been inside my house. My room.

Were they still here with me now?

6

ELI

My phone beeped, snatching me from a deep sleep. For a minute, I clutched my thigh and pictured myself back in the hospital. In pain. Always in pain.

But the agony had faded. My leg no longer hurt and it did what I asked it to do. Most of the time.

Reality shoved itself back into my brain, reminding me I was back home in Maine and no longer part of the military. Not necessarily by choice, but who the hell wanted to trade deployments overseas with my buddies for a training job stateside? It hadn't been easy turning them down, telling them I wanted out. But they'd essentially bailed on me because I was no longer capable of full duty. I had to leave. Move home. Find a way to keep my injury from ruling my life.

My phone beeped again, and I lifted it off the bedside table. Mia's number. At quarter-past-one in the morning?

"Hey, Mia," I said in a gruff, sleepy voice.

"Eli!"

The stark terror in her tone sent me bolting upright. In

seconds I stood beside my bed, seeking a weapon. Which was stupid since she wasn't even here. I'd have to get to her before I could defend her.

"Mia. What's happening?" I essentially yelled into the phone.

"Someone's inside my house!"

My heart plunged all the way to the center of the Earth. "What?" Wedging my phone between my shoulder and head, I hauled on the jeans I'd tossed on a chair before going to bed. Commando, but no way would I take the time to grab boxers even though zipping my pants fast would be dangerous. "Get out of the house. Go to a neighbor's house. Lock yourself inside a secure location. I'll be there in seconds."

"I'm in my car. Don't think I could drive right now, though. I'm a wreck." Shivers came through in her words. "I've locked the doors." A cat meowed, and she shushed it in a gentle tone. "Can you...I hate to ask, but Flint's away. I'm scared."

I'd fling myself across a canyon to help her. "What's your address?"

She rattled it off and I memorized it as I stuffed my feet into my sneakers and, snatching up my keys from the small table beside the front door, raced from my house to my Jeep. I drove like a maniac to her place, roaring into her driveway. Leaping from my vehicle, I rushed over to the blue car parked ahead of mine.

Mia's tear-stained face stared out from the driver's side window. She pressed the button, unlocking the doors, and I wrenched it open.

Lowering a big, fluffy orange tiger cat onto the passenger seat, she jumped from the car and shut the door behind her. And tumbled into my open arms.

"Hey, it's okay," I said in the most soothing voice I could muster. My hands shook. My voice croaked. I'd been a wreck driving over here, worried someone was hurting her. That I wouldn't make it time.

Pulling herself from my arms, she leaned against her car and wiped her face. "Sorry. I was...messed up there for a minute. Things lately...in my life, that is...well, I've been jumpy for good reason." Her voice rose. "But there was someone in my house!"

"Still in there now?"

She shrugged. "I don't think so." Face tight, she peered in that direction. "I didn't see whoever it was, but I know they were there."

After shoving my hair off my face, I took my phone from my pocket. "I'm calling the sheriff."

"He's going to think I'm a pain in the butt."

"Why?"

She scrunched her face and street light glinted off the tears trickling across her freckles. "Fish heads."

Blinking, I paused with my finger hovering over the number nine. "Fish heads?"

Her breath whooshed out. "It's a long story." She pulled her phone from her pocket and waved it at me. "Let me do the dirty work. I've got him on speed dial." 9-1-1 must've picked up immediately, because she said, "Hey, this is Mia Crawford." She gave her address. "Yes, I called earlier."

Earlier? What the hell was going on here?

Mia paused to listen. "No, this isn't about fish heads or guts." Lines of stress appeared on her face. "Someone was inside my house." After a moment, her expression cleared. "Thank you." She tucked her phone back inside her pocket. "They're notifying Deputy Franks. She's on call tonight."

"Great." Turning, I leaned against her car beside her,

shifting my backside when my 9mm dug into the small of my spine.

Mia's shoulders lifted and fell. "I appreciate you coming over tonight."

"Call me anytime."

"You probably know Flint's away. I would've called my parents, but they live in western Massachusetts. I don't know many people in town, yet. My neighbors would be happy to help, but they're old. I can't endanger them."

Because her voice had risen and her body still trembled, I laid my arm across her shoulders and tugged her closer to my side. "I'm glad you called me. I got here as fast as I could."

Her chuckle came out high-pitched, unsettled. "Didn't even take time to put on a shirt."

"You noticed."

Her breath sliding across my skin tickled but I'd die a happy man if I could keep her in the shelter of my arms. "I'd have to be blind not to notice."

The cool night air had started sinking into my bones, but her comment warmed me up nicely. Naturally, I'd noticed the nightie Mia was wearing. Have to be blind not to. Shit, it revealed her creamy thighs and hinted at her soft shape beneath. How could something so simple turn me on?

"I thought of calling you earlier." She peered up at me. "I made you some cookies."

"I do love cookies." Knew I'd love Mia's cookies the most, not that I'd tell Ginny. She'd smack my arm and give me a scowl that wouldn't quite hide her pleased grin. "I'm glad you weren't alone before I got here."

She peered around. "What do you mean?"

When I waved, she glanced toward the windshield

where the cat stood with its back legs on the seat, front paws on the dash, winking through the glass at us with its whiskers twitching.

"Oh, yes, Walter," she said. "He...he heard something. I let him out of my bedroom to investigate and whoever it was must've locked him inside a cupboard. Poor boy. I thought he'd done it to himself. Chastised him for it, even. He's an indoor kitty and has never been outside other than on my screened-in porch. I imagine he's having the adventure of his life."

The hum of an engine told me the police were approaching. An SUV pulled into the drive, parking beside my Jeep, and a woman I assumed must be Deputy Franks got out. A tall, skinny officer joined her and they strode over to us, their intent gazes scanning the vicinity.

She chipped a nod. "Deputy Franks, and this is Deputy Cousins."

He nodded while fingering a button on the front of his dark shirt.

"Heard you had an intruder in your house, Ms. Crawford?" she asked Mia.

"Yes." Mia glanced toward her house, her teeth compressing her lower lip. "The person was in my bedroom while I was in my study. They wrote something on my mirror."

"Wrote something?" Deputy Cousins asked, frowning.

"In red. It looked like a number one. I found it after Walter woke me up, hissing at the door, and I let him out. I followed him, and when we returned to my bedroom, I saw the number."

"Hissing?" Deputy Franks blinked, and her gaze fell on me. "You, um, Walter?"

"That would be the cat," I said, tilting my head toward the car.

Deputy Cousins frowned. "Cat?"

Mia waved to where Walter pressed his face against the driver's side window. His plaintive meow reached us. "He's Walter."

"Then who are you?" Deputy Franks asked me.

I extended my hand for a shake. "Eli Bradley. Mia called me after locking herself inside her car with Walter."

"Bradley...Any relation to Ginny?"

"My sister."

"Ah, yes." Deputy Franks rocked forward onto her toes. "What a cluster that was, eh? But her fiancé took care of things neatly, now didn't he?"

"Cooper, and yes."

Mia watched us. "What happened?"

"Ginny was stalked by a former boyfriend."

A shudder rippled through Mia, and she crossed her arms and worried her elbows. Her gaze pierced the area but nothing moved outside of treetops swaying in the wind. "Stalked? How horrible."

"She's okay, now," I said. Thanks to Coop. My buddy had not only saved the day, but he'd also saved my sister's life. I'd owe him forever.

"Guy's in the pokey, awaiting trial," Deputy Franks said. "Couldn't make bail." She darted her attention toward the house. "But you didn't call me out here at two a.m. for an update on that case. Let's see what we're dealing with here, shall we? You got a back door, Ma'am?"

"Yes," Mia said. "You can enter from the deck." Pulling a flashlight from her pocket, she offered it to them. "The power's out inside the house."

"That's strange," Deputy Cousins said.

Mia shrugged. "The house is old. My brother said I should have it rewired but I haven't been around long enough to see it done."

"We've got our own lights." Deputy Franks gestured toward Deputy Cousins. "You take the back, and I'll take the front. We'll meet up inside."

They pulled their guns and flashlights, and Deputy Cousins trotted down the path leading toward the back of the house while Deputy Franks approached the porch cautiously. She opened the screen door and stepped inside.

"I think whoever it was is gone," Mia said, rubbing her bare arms where goosebumps rippled. "I hope so, anyway."

"They'd be stupid to wait for the police to arrive, but I'm glad they're checking things out."

"Me, too. It's totally creepy. Walter..." She cut her gaze to her cat. "He hissed and clawed at the door. He never wants to leave my bedroom at night. He's a deeper sleeper than me. I let him out and he howled. Scared me to death." Her voice quivered and I wrapped my arms around her again, offering her what little comfort I could. "I thought he was hurt, so I looked for him. He was locked inside a cabinet in my study." Leaning back, she frowned up at me. "Some-one...Whoever was inside my house must've done it." Her voice rose. "While I was there."

The deputies soon crossed the lawn and joined us in the drive.

"And?" I asked as they stared at each other for a long moment.

"Nothing," Deputy Franks said. "Looked around from top to bottom. I also checked out your power situation. Changed a fuse in the basement. Should fix it for now, but your brother's right. That panel outdates my parents."

"I'll call an electrician when I return from my upcoming conference," Mia said.

"Your back door was unlocked," Deputy Cousins said, his gaze focused intently on Mia.

She gasped. "I locked it. I lived in a city before moving here and ..." She shook her head as if dispelling a bad memory. "I'll never leave myself exposed."

The word "again" hung in the air between us. Flint had mentioned something bad happening to Mia in Massachusetts. We'd only known each other a short time but I ached to protect her, tell her she'd come to no harm, ensure her face never pinched with fear again.

"Take a look around tomorrow, make sure nothing's missing," Deputy Franks said. "But I'd say you must've scared them away before they could either vandalize the place or steal something."

"I'll look."

"Let us know if you find further evidence of the break-in, and we'll come out right away. Look into it."

"What about my mirror?"

Deputy Franks tilted her head, studying Mia's every movement. "Mirror was clean."

"That's impossible. Someone wrote on it in red...Well, I know it wasn't blood. Maybe paint? It was a number one."

"You sure?" Deputy Cousins asked. "Maybe your eyes were playing tricks with you?"

No way. I opened my mouth to defend Mia, but she beat me to it.

"Don't feed me that 'maybe you imagined this, little lady' crap. I'm one-hundred-percent certain someone was inside my house, that they wrote the number on my mirror." She pulled her phone and scrolled into it before thrusting it forward. "See?"

Deputy Franks leaned forward. "I don't..."

Mia growled and huffed at me. "I wouldn't make something like this up."

"Didn't think it for even a second," I said, my arms linking on my chest. The glare I fed Deputy Cousins made his fidgets still. "We'll look around once we're inside. I'm sure we'll find evidence." I'd for damn sure look around. I trusted the local law, but only until my own eyes had investigated the scene would I feel Mia was actually safe.

"You're not leaving me alone," she said softly.

I loved the complete relief in her voice, knowing I was the cause.

"Not a chance in hell."

"I think this is it, then," Deputy Franks said. "Call us if you find anything suspicious, and...Don't forget to lock your doors."

"They *were* locked," Mia ground out.

Deputy Franks lifted her hands, shifting a glance at the other officer. "I believe you."

But did she?

We watched as they got into the vehicle and drove away.

"I'll get Walter," Mia said. She paused with her hand on the door. "You...I understand if you want to get back to your place. Get back to bed. It's the middle of the night. And..."

The tremor in her voice was my undoing. I stroked the curls off her face and squeezed her shoulder. "I'll stay until morning if that's okay with you. You got a couch?"

"I do. And thank you." Relief pouring through in her voice, she opened the door and lifted her cat into her arms and nuzzled his neck. "Come here you big brute. How's momma's little kitty boy?" She kissed his face.

Was it possible to be jealous of a cat?

Inside the entryway of her house, Mia dropped Walter

on the gleaming hardwood floor and locked the front door. The cat blinked up at me. Her. Me again.

"I'll get the back door, too," Mia said.

"Let me." I nudged my chin down the hall. "In that direction, I assume?"

"Yes. My bedroom's on the back right, the kitchen's opposite." She tilted her head toward the left. "Living room's here. And I've got a study on the right—that's where Walter was locked inside a cupboard." Hugging her waist, she shuddered. "I'm so grateful they didn't hurt him."

After giving her a quick hug, I stepped back. "Wait here?"

"I'll be on the sofa."

I did a quick scan of the living room and study because no way in hell would I leave her here while someone might lurk, ready to jump the second my back was turned. Then I searched the house from top to bottom more thoroughly, not leaving an inch uninspected. As the police indicated, there was no evidence of theft. No hint that anyone had searched her belongings or done more than lock the cat inside the cupboard. Mia would have to look around before we could be certain nothing had been stolen, however.

The study cupboard had scratches on the inside where the cat had tried to free himself after being trapped. Whoever violated Mia's house had snagged the animal and locked him away. Animals were good at alerting their owners, and whoever had been inside must've wanted to remain hidden.

Or they'd wanted to draw Mia from her bedroom. The certainty of it ground through my bones, making me hyperalert, ready to take the person down to keep them from scaring Mia again.

I returned to where she waited.

"Anything?" she asked softly. She'd drawn a handmade quilt over her lap and Walter nestled against her side, his eyes mere slits, purring as she stroked his neck.

Definitely jealous of the cat.

"Nope. But we'll look around again tomorrow."

"What about my mirror?"

I shrugged. "Looks like a normal mirror to me."

She flung aside the quilt, making Walter glare. Mai darted from the room and down the hall, returning seconds later. "You're right. I don't understand." Defeat colored her voice as she slumped back on the sofa, her hand returning to Walter's side. "Hold on." She pulled her phone and scrolled into the device before turning it my way. "I don't know why Deputy Franks thought this was nothing. What do you make of it?"

Settling on the sofa beside her, I took her phone.

"I took a picture before I left the house." She leaned into my side, her sweet scent filling my senses. "See the red slash?"

This wasn't a slash; it was distinctly a number, as she'd stated outside.

One.

"First strike," I hissed out.

Mia shuddered and reeled away, staring at me. "What does that mean?" Utter panic filled her voice.

This was bad. I refused to meet her eye. "Absolutely nothing."

She bumped my arm. "Evasiveness is not a good look on you, Eli."

"Okay." I sighed and turned to her, cupping her face because I couldn't help it. I was eternally grateful she didn't pull back or tell me she didn't welcome my touch. "I think this is your first warning."

"A warning about what?" She shivered and held up her hand. "No. I know. This is a warning to *me*. What a horrifying thought. First? As in, there will be more." She pressed her fist against her mouth, her green eyes wide above her hand. "And after three strikes, I'm...out?"

Growling, I gathered her into my arms. "Not a chance with me around."

7

MIA

"I'll take the sofa," Eli said. He lifted the quilt, pausing to stroke Walter, who purred as if he hoped Eli would do it forever. Strange, because my shy cat rarely came out when someone new was around, let alone let them touch him.

However, I could well understand him enjoying Eli's lure. His comfort and his warm arms wrapped around me had meant the world to me tonight.

"You sure you're okay with me staying here?" he asked when I remained silent.

"No objection from me." I hated the shake in my voice even though, with Eli here, I had no reason to be afraid. Terror about what could've happened tonight kept plunging through me, making me quake. A creepy person had entered my house while I slept, trapped my kitty boy in a cupboard, then crept into my bedroom and written a threat on my mirror. While I was here in the house with them! My heart flipped and sweat broke out on my forehead all over again. Shuddering, I paused with my hand on the doorframe between the living room and the hall. "I'll get you a pillow. More blankets." How was I going to walk down the hall, enter my bedroom alone, and actually fall asleep? Forget sleeping. I'd lie awake and stare at the ceiling, jumping at every creak and groan released by my old house.

"Thanks." Eli dropped down onto the sofa. Like Flint, he was tall. Well over six feet. Short, my sofa wouldn't be comfortable but what else could I offer him? "You take my bed. It's a king. I'll sleep on the sofa." I didn't have a spare bedroom, though I planned to put a sofa bed in the study eventually.

He patted the cushion beside him, and Walter playfully batted his hand. "No way. This is fine."

Sure, then why did he grimace?

I linked my arms across my chest. "I insist."

He chuckled. "Insist all you want, honey, but I'm taking the sofa."

"Okay," I said in defeat. Short of dragging him down to the hall then leaping onto my furniture before he retook possession, what choice did I have?

Walter stared at me from where he snuggled up to Eli, much like I wanted to do.

For safety.

If I knew more about him...Well, I'd be crazy to offer him a place in my bed, even though it wouldn't be for sex. I wouldn't consider anything like that until I knew him a lot better. Assuming I got to know him better.

Lots of ifs in this equation, and he hadn't even asked me out again. Which he might not do after I'd turned him down. For all I knew, he was seeing someone else.

My growl slipped from me as I leaned against the door-frame. Turning him down was coming back to haunt me.

I liked Eli. Liked being with him. I had when I'd been in California helping Flint, and nothing had changed since.

Did I dare let another man into my life? If he still wanted in.

"I'm a light sleeper," he said softly, breaking through my whirling thoughts.

My smile leaped onto my face. "I'll try not to snore, then."

He snorted. "Me, too."

I glanced back at him. "*Do* you snore?" Why was I quizzing him about something like this? It was intimate business, and we were just friends.

He chuckled. "Guess you'd have to sleep with me to find out."

I studied his face, which gave away nothing. "Suggestive."

One side of his mouth quirked up. "I'm a suggestive kind of guy."

My heart flipped. I could take this conversation as interest on his part, right? Should I ask if that was what he meant?

Earlier, I'd been willing to invite him over for cookie tasting. Which was suggestive on my part.

"I'll keep that in mind," I said.

Fear kept me grounded. Eli couldn't know the uncertainty swirling inside me. The irrational worry that told me I could never trust any man enough to let him into my life.

How could I put this into my past where it belonged, and move forward?

My stinging eyes told me I was too tired to contemplate this tonight. Tomorrow would be soon enough to figure out what I wanted and discover what he might be offering.

With a brief wave, I left him, walking down the hall and climbing into my bed, pulling up the covers.

The door, I left open.

As expected, sleep wouldn't come. While I was scared someone might creep up on me the moment I closed my eyes, I also couldn't stop thinking about Eli.

Russell and everything he'd done to me shoved itself back into my mind.

I hadn't been a part of the dating scene in years, having been too busy during medical school and then establishing my career to consider going out with someone. Then I met Russell at a coffee shop. We'd gone out for months before he said he wanted to move in with me.

Then the controlling behavior began.

Where were you? he'd ask. Work was always my reply. Where else would I be? A new doctor worked twenty-six hours a day. Whenever I had a speck of free time, I wanted to sleep.

Who were you with? Co-workers. Other doctors. Nurses. Patients.

Male? Naturally. It was a hospital, not a nunnery. Female patients, too, I'd said, hoping this answer would help him feel better.

Feel better. As if it was my job to placate him, assure him he had no reason to doubt me.

I'd been a fool. I should've told him to move out immediately, but he'd been kind at other times—especially when friends, family, and coworkers were around. Everyone liked him and a few expressed envy. Russell could be featured on GQ and he came across thoughtful by showing up at my work with flowers, small gifts, or just to say hi. On the surface, he'd seemed like a perfect man. Only when I'd scratched deeper had his true identity burst through. I'd convinced myself time would allow his confidence in me to grow, that he'd relax and stop quizzing me each time I walked through the door.

Things had escalated...

"I have to work with men," I'd said. How could he expect me to avoid every man in my life?

I don't like it. Words that at first came across as vulnerable on his part. As if it hurt him to think I might flirt, let alone cheat while living with him.

Some might consider jealousy flattering. Except it could wrap itself around your neck like a noose, tightening each time he pressed for answers. I hoped he'd come to realize he had no reason to doubt me. Yet my faithfulness was never acknowledged because it wasn't about me. It had never been about me. It all rested on him and his inability to acknowledge his controlling behavior.

In the last six months of our relationship, the demands had become physical. Yanking me near as if he thought I wouldn't otherwise hear him yelling. Slamming around our apartment. Breaking furniture in his rage.

And lifting his hand, though it didn't—yet—connect.

Everything culminated the night I stayed late to help with a five-car pile-up. The ER had been swamped.

Where were you? A smack on my arm. *You were supposed to be here by nine.*

Flinching, I'd lifted my chin and explained.

Like I believe that? You were with someone else, weren't you? You fuckin' whore. His shout was sharper than a broken bottle, and his fist had stabbed out, impacting like a sledgehammer with my ribs. Unable to catch my breath, I'd gasped in pain and horror and stared up at him with tears in my eyes.

He'd pulled a gun. Waved it around before pointing it at my head. *You belong to me.*

My flesh had shriveled, and I'd cowered against the wall. Would he shoot me?

I'd run from our apartment, leaving everything behind.

Then I'd become the injured person showing up in the ER. While I'd wanted to hide, pretend it hadn't happened, breathing was torture. I'd needed help. A way out.

Photos had been followed by interviews with the cops. Me, the victim instead of the one calling the police to come in to speak with a patient. We saw it all the time. How had I not connected what so many women went through with myself?

During the trial, it came out I wasn't the first he'd done this to. Not even the second. I'd been one in a long string of abused women.

A two years sentence hadn't seemed enough punishment for him hurting me. Breaking me. Making me doubt myself when I never should. Sadly, that was all a repeat offender earned. If he hadn't threatened me with a weapon, he would've gotten three months or off completely.

Russell would leave me alone when he got out. He wouldn't follow through on the threats he'd made as they hauled him away...

Or Flint would kill him.

Embarrassed by the whole thing, even though I was not at fault, I hadn't told my brother about the real Russell until after I showed up at the ER.

While Flint still wanted to hover over me, protect me, I was determined to stand on my own two feet. But if a guy ever threatened me again, I'd be the one wielding a fist—courtesy of the training Flint gave me after the trial. I refused to stand mutely while a man abused me again.

Finally, I closed my eyes and let sleep claim me.

In my dreams, Russell chased me through the park, which was weird, since he hated nature and always joked that the pavement was the only lawn he'd ever mow. I ran along a narrow path. Up a hill, stumbling down the other side. Sobbing. Fleeing.

So much for standing up for myself.

He grabbed me from behind and wrenched me around to face him. His fist lifted.

My heart burst through my chest. I screamed and tried to pull away, but he wouldn't let go.

My eyes popped open.

A man loomed over me!

Russell. He was here. And this time he'd kill me.

"Mia," someone said, breaking through my terror.

Wait.

"Eli?" His name burst from me in a plea. My pulse decelerated in one beat because Eli was here and Russell was not.

"Mia," he said again gently.

"Yeah?"

"You okay?" He sat on the side of my bed, and his palms lightly held my shoulders. "You screamed."

I sat partway up, the blankets pooling at my waist. "I'm sorry."

"No problem. You're scared by what happened. It's only natural to have nightmares."

Yes, but this was about more than what happened tonight. My past had intruded into my life once again.

Dark in my room, I could barely read the concerned expression on his face. I couldn't make myself meet his penetrating gaze.

"It's...not just about someone being inside my house. Locking up Walter. The number drawn on my mirror."

I told him everything. Because I needed to be honest. There could be no more lies between us if I hoped to move forward.

"Fuck, Mia," Eli said when I'd finished, his hands bunching up my blanket. "I'm sorry."

"Yeah. Me, too. But it's over."

For the first time in a long time, the solid mass of fear no longer coiled in my belly. Maybe I was putting it behind me. Finally.

Now that my nightmare had retreated to the shadowy corners of my mind, I couldn't help noticing Eli's bare chest, the rippled expanse of skin above his low-slung jeans. His warm thumbs stroking my bare arms. I'd have to be dead not to feel the heat of his presence beside me. I couldn't drag my gaze away from his pecs, his washboard abs.

"You work out a lot," blurted from my lips.

Great. Way to embarrass myself.

His lips briefly flicked up, and his voice grew husky. "I like to stay in shape."

My fingers took charge, touching his skin. Gliding along his shoulders to his pecs. Warm. Smooth. He had a chest a woman could rest her head on while his strong arms held her close.

I wanted this. Wanted him. But I was scared. My breath caught, and I jerked my hands back. "Sorry. Boundaries seem to be eluding me tonight."

"Not bothering me a bit. You can touch me anytime you'd like."

His comments *were* suggestive. And though I ached to take him up on his offer, my hands still shook. I stuffed them underneath the covers before they discovered more uncharted territory. Bad enough I wanted to touch him everywhere.

Taste him.

As heat rose inside me, shoving aside the lingering

dream spell that sought to haunt me, I gulped. "I'm sorry. I..."

"It's okay." He stood and backed toward the door, taking his comfort, his alluring body, and presence away from me. "I get it. You already made it clear you're not interested in—"

"I didn't, well, what I said back then wasn't exactly true."

His head tilted, and he studied my face as if it was vital he read my mind from my expression. "Then what is the truth?"

"I wasn't honest with you in California and now you know why."

He stalked back to me and knelt on the edge of my bed. When he lifted a section of my hair, the curls entwined around his fingers as if they intended to hold him close and never let him go. "I have no problem taking this slow, Mia, but I want you. Everything you're willing to give me."

I gaped up at him. "What are you saying?" I ached for him to make his intentions perfectly clear.

"That I'm here for you. As a friend, if that's all you need. Or..." He braced his arms on either side of me, pinning my pillow to my headboard behind me. His face...His lips. If I inched closer, we'd connect. And fire would flare between us like it hadn't with any other man before. I knew it. "I'm a patient man, honey, but if you're never going to want me, you should tell me right now."

I did want him. No denying the fact. But I...

Eli is not Russell.

Everything inside me demanded I grab onto him. Cling. But I needed to feel strong about myself, about who I could offer the next man I let into my life.

Right guy. Questionable time.

But I'd be a fool to let him go.

"Can we take it slowly?" I asked. "More than once over

the past eight months, I've wished I'd taken you up on your offer."

"Cool." His lips curved up on one side. "So, you're saying this is almost a yes?"

I swallowed. "It's a full yes."

He leaned in and, when he kissed my cheek, he bestowed a promise. "Then you tell me what you're ready for and when you're ready for it. I'll be waiting." His warm brown gaze drifted down and he traced his fingertip on the pendant I wore. Always wore.

The one he'd given me.

"I like seeing you wearing this," he said in a voice scratchy with emotion.

"I...Eight months ago—"

"Your ex."

"I should've told you what happened." But the trial had only ended four months prior, and I'd been an emotional wreck.

"Why would you want to share anything like that? Don't blame you for keeping it inside."

"I'm not ashamed." Not all the time, anyway. "But it hadn't been long. I wasn't ready."

"It's been..."

"A year now since he was incarcerated. He won't be out for another year yet."

He growled. "You think it's okay if I tell you—since you're a doctor and all—that I'd be happy to kill him if he comes near you again?"

I shouldn't be thrilled by his gravelly voice speaking about committing violence on my behalf, but I couldn't hold back the bolt of excitement running through me. Was it wrong of me to want revenge?

He stroked the hair off my face, and his rough palm

trailed down to my shoulder.

Mesmerized by his nearness, I couldn't speak, but I nodded as if to say, sure, go ahead and kill Russell.

His fingers teased along my jawline. "I'm sorry about the circumstances that brought me here tonight, but I'm an honest enough man to admit I'm glad we've had a chance to talk."

"Me, too."

"And, on that note, I'll return to guard duty on the sofa, because you need to get some sleep and I..." Backing away, he left the thought unfinished and turned toward the door, saying over his shoulder fiercely, "You need me, even if it's just to hold your hand? Call and I'm here."

"Thank you," I said as he strode through the doorway.

"Anytime."

I waited until I heard my sofa creak as he settled his tall form. The rustle of the quilt I'd made as he tugged up over his body.

Until I could swear his breathing slow, indicating he drifted to sleep.

Only then did I snuggle back underneath my covers and close my eyes. And dream of a future that was no longer scary.

I WOKE to hints of coffee and bacon drifting in the air. And the sound of chirpy voices singing.

What an odd combination.

After brushing my teeth and taking a quick shower and dressing, I walked into my kitchen.

"Have a seat, and I'll bring you a cup of steaming heaven," Eli said without even turning. Working at the stove, he flicked a spatula through the air in time with the music. His broad, muscular back and jean-clad hips swayed in time with the tune coming from his cell phone sitting on the counter. "Cream or sugar?"

"How did you know it was me coming into the kitchen?" I said with a smile. "And neither."

Turning, he grinned as if that was the only answer I needed. He poured a cup of coffee from the French press I kept for special occasions and sashayed it over to the table to place it in front of me, all while whistling along with a girl singing about how she wanted something more than a provincial life. "Knew you weren't Walter, and I just...know when you're near," he said as he twirled back toward the stove.

Really, he twirled. Surprisingly graceful despite his limp.

"I could've been...I don't know, someone creeping up on you."

"Honey, you're welcome to creep up on me any old time." Lifting the spatula, he stirred something cooking in my big old cast iron skillet. The one I normally used to roast vegetables in the oven.

In addition to dance, he must've studied voice, because now he was singing in a deep, satisfying baritone about how the girl didn't shudder at someone's paw.

Wait. Paw?

"What are you listening to?" I asked with a shake of my head.

Stepping around Walter, who sat on the floor beside the stove staring up at Eli as if his life would be complete as long as Eli dropped a pound of bacon on the floor, he turned down the volume on his phone.

"Beauty and the Beast," Eli said in the lull that followed. "You like it." Said as if it was a widely-accepted fact.

"What is it?"

He gasped in mock horror, holding the spatula to his chest—right over his heart. "Please tell me you've seen Beauty and the Beast."

"Haven't." I frowned. "I've heard of the kid's movie, but...music?"

"Beauty and the Beast is one of the best musicals of all time. It ranks right up there with the Lion King."

"The Lion King," I repeated as if that would help me better understand. I took a quick sip of my coffee, savoring the rich flavors gliding down my throat. My stomach rumbled, telling me it was eager for whatever lovely smelling thing Eli was cooking.

"I can't believe you've missed out on everything Disney," he said in complete dismay. His mop of dirty blond hair shifted along his neck when he shook his head.

"The parks in Florida and California?"

"Ah, then you've been there, at least."

"Nope." Drinking more coffee, I sighed at how fantastic it tasted. "My parents couldn't afford anything like that when I was growing up. And even if they could've taken me when I got older, I was too busy with AP classes in high school then graduating with my degree in biochemistry early. After that, medical school."

He huffed, though I could tell by the way his eyes gleamed it wasn't in irritation. "It's clear your real education is sorely lacking."

I chuckled, because, really, how could he say that? "I guess?"

"I assume, then, that you haven't even been to the local Disney equivalent, either, which is just the saddest thing I've ever heard."

I cocked my head, squinting at him. No contacts made

him blurry. And even cuter, if that was possible. I slid on my glasses I'd left on the table yesterday so I wouldn't miss a single expression on his face. "Disney opened an amusement park in Crescent Cove?"

"Nah." After dishing up from the skillet, he placed a heaping platter of scrambled eggs, hash browns, and bacon on the table between us. Enough food to satisfy seventeen hungry lumberjacks.

"You don't expect me to eat much of that, do you?"

"'Course not," he said, scooping about half the contents onto his plate. He glanced up, his eyes deep, dark chocolate. "You share...don't you?"

Simple question, but the look in his eyes—okay, the *suggestive* look in his eyes—said our conversation meant two different things, the simple bit on the surface and something deeper I'd yet to discover. I'd need to be on my toes to keep up with this guy. "Yes," I said slowly.

"Eggs are good for you." He shoveled in a big bite. After swallowing, he added, "And everyone knows bacon's a food group all by itself."

"Bacon increases your risk of heart disease."

He smacked his palm on his chest. "No need to worry. My heart's already secure."

Was there a double meaning here? And, if so, who held his heart? "Something you need to tell me?"

He grinned and stuffed two slices of bacon into his mouth. Chewing, he closed his eyes and hummed before focusing his now smoldering attention on me. "All in good time, honey."

I shouldn't be turned on by a silly endearment, but I was.

"Why keep a pound of bacon in your fridge if you're worried about heart disease?" he asked.

"It's for emergencies."

"Bacon emergencies?"

"So, I've got a weakness. That a problem?" I grumbled good-naturedly. It was impossible to be irritated with Eli when he flirted. Or any other time, for that matter.

His gaze honed in on my lips where I licked off the smoky, salty flavors. "Any other weaknesses?"

Him. Definitely him. But I would not admit it. Yet.

He ate another forkful.

"Since it's clear you work out more than me," I said. "You can handle a little bacon." Was it wrong of me to want to touch his shoulders, test those muscles that flexed as he ate?

"Sorry I'm not wearing a shirt."

"Not bothering me." At all.

We skated around something wonderful. Like ice dancers swirling in an opposite circle before moving closer. Almost touching before gliding apart again.

I ached to fling back my chair, leap across the table, and climb all over him. Maybe lick the U.S. Navy tattoo emblazoned on his right pectoralis major. Never wanted to run my tongue along anyone's pec before.

"Eat up, honey," he said, his eyes shining as if he knew exactly what I was thinking and welcomed the idea. "We've got a busy day ahead of us."

"I know what's on my agenda, but what's on yours?"

He nudged his head toward his phone. "Already been in touch with Flint and, other than some brief work in the shop, I'm now completely yours."

I lifted my eyebrows and my words tumbled out, "In what way?"

His chuckle rang between us. "Any way you want but let's start with security. My exclusive bodyguard service, that is." He gave me a neat bow.

Knowing someone would have to find their way past Eli to get to me dropped my fear-level a thousand degrees.

He waved his empty fork around. "After going to the shop for supplies, we'll return here to install a security system that'll make you feel safer than the King Tut Exhibit."

"We?"

"Not leaving you alone for a second."

"I have work to do today." I needed to finish putting together my presentation for my conference.

"You do your work, and I'll do mine. Jax will help with the install."

I should've considered a security system the moment I bought my house. "Okay."

"Can you get your work done this morning and leave your late afternoon and into the evening free for me?"

"Why?"

"We need to continue your education."

I blinked while heat flashed from my skin to my core.

"Mia?" he murmured, his lips curling up as if he knew my every secret thought.

"Yeah?" Okay, so I sounded dopey, but jeez. When a hot guy teased and flirted and essentially said he was yours for the taking, what else could a girl do? I wasn't sure my heart could stand it, but I'd sure as hell try to keep up.

"Finish your breakfast, and we'll get going. Later on, I'd like to spend some time together. Assuming that's okay with you."

"I'd really like that." Unable to help myself, I licked my lips as my gaze drifted down his chest to the beginning of his washboard abs showing above the table.

He was right. I did need a little education.

8

ELI

I'd laid awake a long time after returning to the sofa. Not just because it was uncomfortable—a six-four man did not sleep well on any living room furniture.

It wasn't because I had to keep my jeans on—though I didn't want to shock Mia.

Or because she wore my pendant, which about made me want to leap through the roof.

Her essentially saying she'd been thinking about me as often as I'd been thinking about her had also thrilled me to my core.

I'd remained awake because I kept thinking about her ex, what he'd done to her. What I wanted to do to him in retaliation. If the guy wasn't already in jail, I'd have no hesitation committing violence.

I wanted to hold her. Tell her I'd make sure no one ever harmed her again.

But she wasn't mine. She'd never be mine even if we ended up together. She'd always belong to herself. To feel whole again, to welcome me if that was what she desired, she'd have to rediscover the strength she kept hidden inside, not take it from my offering arms.

I rose by five and got in touch with Flint. He'd roared through the phone when I told him what happened last night. He told me to forget about the shop once I'd finished tweaking a small project. Mia would be my sole priority. I was to install a security system worthy of the leader of a first world country. Stay by her side until the cops figured this out.

Which fit in with the plans I'd already formulated in my mind. No way would I leave her to face this alone.

While Mia went to her study to get started on her work, I cleaned up after breakfast, washing, drying, and putting everything away. All while singing along with the Little Mermaid. Man, I loved this music. If I ever had a kid, they'd know every single word to these songs. We'd sing them in the car when we went for ice cream or on a trip. In the shower or bath. And I'd save up. Take him or her to Disney, where we would jump on every ride and get every character to sign our autograph books. We'd even dress up in costumes.

I favored a pirate for myself but if a daughter wanted me in princess gear...

"Getting ahead of yourself," I said softly as I tucked the cast iron skillet into the drawer where I'd found it. "No girlfriend, let alone a wife. No kids in your foreseeable future. Take this one step at a time."

"Come with me to the shop?" I asked in the doorway of Mia's study after leaving the kitchen. "I know you have work to do but maybe you can bring it with you?" I couldn't leave her here by herself until I knew she was locked behind a fortress.

"I can finish these notes and hang out with Aunt Becca."

She stood and stretched. Yeah, I watched. Couldn't help it. I'd be a saint not to admit that I lusted after each and every one of her lush curves. And her freckles...I'd die a happy man if I could trace my fingertips across them. Lick them. "Perhaps I can help you pick out tools and materials out back. I'd love to know what goes on in Flint's shop," she said with a soft smile as I opened the front door.

A reminder never to underestimate this woman's curiosity.

Outside, I scanned the vicinity to ensure everything appeared as it should then gestured for her to step onto the porch ahead of me while clicking on my fob to unlock my Jeep doors. "While I appreciate your offer, I'll gather the tools and materials after I finish my own small project."

Her brow furrowed, and she locked her front door and pocketed the key. "Darn. One of these days, I'm going to find out what you guys are doing for real. Kiddie drones, my ass."

Chuckling, I waved to my vehicle while studying the road, the neighbor's houses. The trees. Nothing. No movement. I wouldn't let down my guard. Opening the passenger door, I waved to the seat. "Hop in."

We stopped by my place, where I showered and changed, then drove out to the shop. While a few cars appeared to follow us, one even for over a mile, they all peeled off in different directions before a sweat broke out on my forehead.

Mia sat in the front office with her notebook open on her lap, her Aunt Becca watching her like she was the only person who could save the world. My need to stay hyper-alert relaxed for the moment.

I strolled out back, finding the main R&D warehouse empty—since Gabe, Haylee, and Flint were out of town and Cooper had taken the day off to work on wedding plans with Ginny. I picked up where I'd left off with Locust 3 yesterday.

Face recognition software was going mainstream, from cops to banks to the military. My current assignment was to program and test the drones and ensure they performed as accurately as possible. Once I was confident the beasties could be expected to perform as asked, I projected a wide array of photos onto the back wall and stood "among" the faces.

With a flick of my finger on my phone app, I released the swarm.

While I turned my head away, the mechanical insects rose off the bench and buzzed toward my section of the room. In seconds, they hovered in front of me. Stared at me. Tracked my every movement when I tried to hide.

A successful hunt.

Nothing made me happier than watching them on my app while they relentlessly watched me.

After another hour tweaking, ensuring the program functioned seamlessly, and taking notes indicating what needed to be worked on next, I left the back room and met up with Jax, who must've recently arrived at the shop.

"Eli, buddy," he said when I entered the supply room. "Flint filled me in on what went down last night. Damn strange and horrifying, all at the same time. Mia's...pretty shaken up."

I growled. "Man, I wish I could..."

"You and me both," Jax said grimly. He gestured to three boxes on the floor near the door. "I've put a few things together already. Nothing's too good for Mia." He dropped a couple of glass breaks into a plastic bin beside his feet.

Snagging an empty tote from a pile near the door, I stuffed a few more breaks inside, then some passive infrared detectors. I'd install them on walls and the ceiling and point one at each window and door. The devices put out a pattern of beams. If someone disturbed them, the device would set off the detector and trigger an alarm on both Mia's, Flint's, and my phone. I'd have to make a few programming adjustments to accommodate Walter, because his movements couldn't be predicted.

"She need a new security panel?" Jax nudged his chin to a stack of them on the shelf.

"An entire rewiring, actually, but I'll get to that over the next week." I'd enlist Coop's help since he was basically an electrician. Another local friend could do the final inspection and sign off the necessary paperwork after we finished. I lifted a panel and added it to my collection, also tossing in a spool of wire. While I planned to add a generator and battery back-up to Mia's system in case of power outages, I'd wire everything into her main panel. Lifting the two bags I'd filled, I took them out to my Jeep, nodding to Mia, who chatted with Becca, as I passed. I returned to the supply room for more materials.

Pausing while taking a box of zone modules off the shelf, Jax glanced over at me before flicking his gaze toward the door. "I was wonderin'. You think Mia's seeing anyone?"

Why did Jax's mouth quirk up fast before thinning?

Unwelcome hackles rose along my spine. Hell. Was Jax interested in Mia? Sure had seemed that way back in Mexico. All that talk about cookies.

I told myself to back down. No way would I act like the possessive jerk who'd hurt her. She could see whoever she pleased.

I just hoped she'd be pleased to see me.

Besides, he was hot for Haylee, right?

Unable to hold back a low grumble, I chucked a keypad

into another tote. It clanged against another spool of wire
I'd already set inside. "Wouldn't you already know if Mia
was seeing someone?"

"Maybe." Jax's expression came across a little too slick
for my taste. "And maybe not."

"You sound uncertain." I had to goad him because, while
Mia and I weren't a thing, I had high hopes we one day
would be.

"Aren't you curious to know if she's seein' someone?" he
asked.

Pausing with my hand on another spool of wire, I
sighed. "Why are you asking me all this?"

"Because I like Mia. She's got spunk. And she's hot."

Sure didn't like Jax mentioning hot and Mia in the same
sentence, but I shoved off the uptight feeling generated by
the comment. Jax must be fooling with me, trying to get on
my nerves. I had no intention of hiding my interest. "The
fact that your boss is her brother might put her off," I said
gruffly.

Jax shrugged and returned to the shelves. He sorted
among the supplies and lowered a few more items into his
plastic bin. "If that's the only thing keeping her at arm's
length, I'd just do a little persuadin'."

The idea of Jax persuading Mia to do anything with him
burned through me like lava. But I checked myself. Again. I
had no right to feel irked by Jax's interest. Assuming that's
what this was.

"She *is* seeing someone," I said, my spine rivaling a steel
rod. "Sort of. At least for one maybe date."

"Sort of seeing someone for a maybe date?" Jax let his
full grin shine through, making it clear this was all teasing.

Seeing was stretching things a bit, but Jax didn't need to
know that.

"Ah," he said. "Beat me to it, did you?"

"Mia and I..." There wasn't a Mia and me at all. Just plans for the afternoon. Who knew what could happen after that?

With a smirk, Jax lifted his voice, sounding more like a high school cheerleader than a full-grown man. Ass might as well prance around the room while he was at it. "Do you think it bothers Mia?" He threw my own words back at me. "You *do* work for her brother."

"Hard to say." My smirk rivaled his. "But I'm also willing to do a little persuadin'."

Jax followed us out to Mia's home in his truck and, while Mia returned to her study, we hauled everything into her front entryway.

"We can get this installed in no time," Jax said, scanning what he could see of Mia's small house as if he'd never been there.

I shouldn't be pleased he hadn't stopped by to visit, let alone to sample her cookies.

"I'll handle the outside," he said, hefting one of the tool pouches.

"Perfect. I'll work on the inside, then." I returned to my Jeep for the rest of my tools, lugging the bags and a ladder into the house.

The study was my first priority.

"What does that do? I already have smoke detectors," Mia asked me a few minutes later, as I stood on a ladder installing a device on her study ceiling.

"Not a smoke detector. This is a glass break. It's got a microphone that listens for the specific acoustical frequency generated by breaking glass."

She tapped her chin. "Sounds complicated."

Glasses. I'd noticed her putting on glasses at breakfast. She must wear contacts the rest of the time. The glasses gave her a super-hot librarian appearance. I wanted to lift them off her face, tug her up from her office chair, and lay her back on her desk. Follow.

Shit. Needed to stay with the program, not give into the erotic daydreams charging through my mind. We were going on a sort of date today. I wouldn't read anything more into this than the moment.

"Will it..." She blinked, her lashes super-long behind those hot-librarian glasses. "Eli? You with me here?" Chuckling, she looked ready to wave a hand in the air between us. "Will these *glass breaks* alarm like a smoke detector?"

"Yep. Most of the time, the person breaking the glass will take off, because they'll figure you've been alerted."

She peered around her study and focused on the cabinet used to lock Walter inside. "What if I'm not here?"

"We'll program the devices to send an alarm to your phone."

Her expression loosened. "I'm likin' these glass thingys already."

And I liked that she was feeling more secure, that I could give this to her. I stepped down off the ladder and started to mount a DS150I beside the door.

"And what's that?" Mia rose from her chair. She tossed her pen aside, leaned her hip against the gleaming wooden desk surface, and watched me. It wasn't the norm for someone to hang out while I worked, but that shouldn't make me fumble with my tools. Why did it?

"A passive infrared detector," I said hoarsely. Tightening my fingers on the device, I swallowed the lump in my throat that must be making me fidget. Nothing else.

A quick turn showed her gaze gliding down my backside. Hell, was she checking out my butt?

She chuckled again, her gaze rising to meet mine. Her eyes had softened to mossy green. Fuck, I hoped she'd been checking out my butt. "It's a what, again?"

Focus, Eli. If my tongue fumbled as much as my fingers, Mia would think I had major issues. Which I did, all revolving around her. Being in her presence only made me want a lot more. "It detects a change in infrared radiation emitted by or reflecting off an object. In other words, it sends out beams that'll sense if someone comes in through your windows or doors." I planned to install a bunch of these with battery back-ups in the woods surrounding Flint's business. Mia had been inside the building yesterday when I swore someone was watching.

Was all this connected? I couldn't see how, but I never discounted my instincts and they were electrified at the moment.

"A beam. You mean like a laser? It would be nice if it would zap someone."

I liked the eagerness in her voice, that she was ruthless. "So says the doctor."

She laughed. "Gruesome of me, isn't it?" Her smile fell and her arms slid across her waist. "I'm having a hard time drumming up any sympathy for whoever broke into my house last night."

"I don't blame you." The same feeling ground through me. "Unfortunately, no lasers. This device—" I tapped it. "Watches the air. It'll know when there's a change in temp, such as a warm body passing through the pulses. If disturbed, the device will notify you via your security panel. Which I'll also mount. Your phone app will tell you something's up."

"And you and Flint will be notified, as well?"

"Of course."

"Cool. What if I want to open the window?" She waved in that direction. "Will that set it off?"

"You can bypass the zone via the app on your phone. These babies will be armed mostly at night when you go to bed. Otherwise, you'll trip it yourself just moving around your house."

"What will I do during the day, when I'm here alone?"

"You can selectively arm zones. Say you're sitting in your living room watching TV. You'll arm your kitchen, your bedroom, whatever room you don't plan to enter."

"Okay, but how do I arm the room I'm in? As you're aware, Flint has taught me a few moves, but I'm no black belt."

She used one of her *moves* on me in Mexico. I was never going to forget my view of Mia in a wet sundress. "We're upgrading your door locks. Remember, none of this does more than notify you if someone's trying to enter your house."

"Have to admit. I'm sad about the lack of lasers." Her smirk fell fast. "You're saying I'll essentially have an early warning but nothing else."

"With early warning, you can act. If the barriers are breached, you get out of the house. Lock yourself in your car again. Call the police. Me. Flint. Jax. Your Aunt Becca. Someone you trust. Knowledge of what could be coming is the key." I paused after dropping a screwdriver back into my tool pouch. "Do you own a handgun?"

"No. Not sure I want to, either."

"Unless you're willing to train and practice, a gun could do you more harm than good." Owning a weapon wouldn't necessarily make her safer. Too easy for someone more experienced to take the gun away and increase the stakes by using it against her.

She cocked her head and studied the detector I held in my hand. "Is all of this part of the standard security system you'd install for Flint's business? Say, one you'd install locally?"

In some ways, yes, but not locally. Our business catered to embassies, small government official offices, and the officials' private residences. Nothing commercial and no houses outside of Mia's. "Not quite."

"Would you call this one top of the line, then?"

"Top of the line is for civilians."

Her frown created creases on her face. "Then this system would be used for..."

"VIPs." A simple explanation and the most I'd give.

Would I always need to keep the specifics of my job hidden, or would I someday be able to share part of it with a person I loved?

"Awesome." The grin Mia fed me smacked into me like a bolt of lightning.

I loved that I could give her some sort of reassurance.

Stepping down off the ladder, I carried it into the living room, leaving Mia alone to complete her work. She strolled in a while later as I was finishing up and getting ready to start on her kitchen, and scanned the room. Her ready smile fled, and a quiver went through her frame. "I thought of something else. What about the windows? Someone could still get inside, even if the system's alarming. For now, I can shut them and run the AC, but the windows are where I'm most vulnerable."

"You've got locks." I'd been pleased to see all new windows in her house, but even a lock could be forced. Reaching into one of the boxes I'd hauled inside, I pulled a handful of pre-cut pieces of wood from my bag.

She slid her finger along one. "If I'm going to stake a vampire, this needs to be sharper on one end."

"Sometimes, the simplest things provide the best security." This was why Flint hired all Seabees at the shop. We could create something out of nothing. A Seabee could fight with a gun or his fists and feet, all while MacGyver-ing his or her way through the situation with the innovative construction skills drilled into us by the military.

Mia's eyebrows lifted. "What will I do with a stick? Hit the person with it? I guess that would sort of fit with my Hippocratic Oath. Do no harm. Well, not too much harm unless I sharpen it and gouge them."

"Not a bad idea, but how about using it for this instead?" Walking over to a window, I stood the piece of wood upright in the channel where the frame would slide. "With this here, no one can lift it, even if you forget the lock."

"Hmm. I like it." Returning to my bag, she pulled out the rest of the wood. "I'll install this security device myself." She went to each window in the living room, carefully placing the sticks in the channel. "Thanks," she said as she headed across the hall to her study.

Sometimes, the best security was one you could control yourself, be it an app on a phone or even a small piece of wood. And there was nothing that made a person feel better than the sense they were secure.

Jax poked his head into the kitchen, where I'd moved my equipment to continue my installation. "All finished up outside. We've got motion detector lights, cameras that record and store on a hard drive in the basement, and I put in the security panel. Crappy old wiring everywhere like you said. I'm glad you're making that a top priority."

"Mia deserves the best."

"You know?" Jax slapped my shoulder as I passed him on my way to mount a break. "I like how you think. I like *you*. Mia could do a hell of a lot worse."

"We're nowhere close to anything like that."

"Oh, I think you're closer than you think." Jax paused in the doorway. "Do you want me to work in her bedroom next?"

"I'll do whatever's needed in her bedroom."

He snickered.

Hadn't meant it like that. "You know what I'm saying."

Jax turned partly away but I still caught his grin. "I'll leave whatever needs doin' inside the bedroom to you, then." Laughing, he strolled into the hallway, meeting up with Mia. "Hey, sweet-as-sugar. I'm about to head back to the shop. Anything I can do for you before I leave?"

"Let me give you some cookies." She rushed into the kitchen, took a bag from a box in the cupboard, and dropped a few cookies inside before sealing it and handing it to Jax.

He kissed her cheek. "You're too good to me."

"I'm beginning to think I should open a bakery." Her gaze darted to me. "Though I might make cookies for only a few select customers."

Was there more to this conversation than just cookies?

The front door clicked behind Jax, and I heard him engage the lock.

Mia glanced up at me. "I deployed the window sticks and finished my presentation." Her pinkening cheeks high-lighted her smile. "Which means it's almost time for my education. I'm completely yours for the rest of the day."

Descending the ladder, I strode toward her, pleased by her comment. I swept my arm around her waist, a bold move on my part, but if I didn't test this, I'd never know where this could go. "Seems I'm not the only one who can play the suggestion game." Hell, if only I could gather her close enough to show her how awesome she made me feel.

Her green eyes gleamed like rich jewels, and her voice went husky. "You might find I'm good at a lot of games."

She was going to kill me if she was not interested in taking things further than our sort-of date.

"Your room's the last." Backing away, I waved to her bedroom in general. "Then, I'm done."

"Perfect." She glanced down. "What should I wear?"

"Something comfortable. Casual." Climbing the ladder, I finished installing a sensor. "We're going to have fun."

Her head tilted. "Where are we going for this education, anyway? A library?"

She'd taken off her glasses. While I loved seeing her beautiful eyes shining in her face without lenses between us, I missed the hot-librarian of my dreams. Maybe, some-day, I could talk her into wearing them.

And nothing else.

Definitely getting ahead of myself.

Finishing up, I returned my tools to my leather bag and dropped it beside the front door. I'd lug everything out after we got back. "Do you mind stopping by my place so I can shower and change again?"

She ran her fingertip along my bristly jawline. "I guess you probably want to shave, too."

I hadn't taken time this morning. "Which do you prefer? Beard or no beard?"

Tapping her lips, she studied my face. "Have to admit I do enjoy a close shave most of the time, but the look you're sporting right now—a little scruffy because you've spent almost twenty-fours making sure I'm safe? It's sexy on you."

Maybe I wouldn't shave again ever.

After locking up Mia's house, we went to my place. Mia puttered around in my living room while I got ready. When I emerged from the hall, I found her studying the photos on display across my mantel.

"This must be Ginny," she said, pointing to a picture of my sister. "She's pretty. She looks like the woman standing beside her who I assume must be your mom because your eyes are the same."

Just seeing my sis and mother brought a smile to my face. The picture had been taken a few years ago when Ginny was home in between trips overseas. Formerly a traveling photographer, she'd returned to Maine after someone kidnapped her. She'd had a tough time of it, but was beyond happy now with Cooper, planning a wedding and a future together.

"No pictures of your dad?" Her gaze spanned the frames again.

"Don't have any."

Her fingers trembled over her lips. "I'm sorry. Is he dead?"

Turning, I strode into the middle of my living room. "Might as well be."

She studied my agitated movements while nibbling on her lower lip. "I'm sorry."

"He bailed on us when I was eight." And I'd thrown away every photo I had of him when I was ten, because he hadn't called, hadn't visited, hadn't done a damn thing to show he cared. That familiar sense of abandonment rose inside me again, but I squashed it like a pesky fly and shrugged. "It's okay. I barely remember him."

Not true, but now was not the time to share. Who wanted to drag down a fun moment with talk about lost promises?

"Oh." Mia waved toward my kitchen. "You got a delivery while you were in the shower."

My heart stopped. "You went to the door?"

"Sure. It rang." Pausing, she frowned. "Shouldn't I have answered it? You're here."

"I wasn't beside you."

"I'm a big girl. I can take care of myself."

"I agree, but I'm squirrelly after what happened." I strode toward the kitchen. "What was delivered?"

"A treat from your grandfather. One of those cupcakes with a note."

My steps stalled, and my skin flashed with fire. "My grandfather's in a nursing home and no longer remembers who I am."

9

MIA

Eli bolted into his kitchen.

His harsh swear pulled me into the room behind him. I hit the doorway in time to see him stuffing the white box holding the cupcake into the trash.

"Did you touch it?" he asked, spinning around to face me.

"No. I just peeked inside the box."

His breath rushed out. "Good. No way to know what's in it, if anything." He shook his head. "My grandfather has Alzheimer's. Gran died of cancer a few years ago and Dad grew up in foster care. I don't even know if his foster parents are still alive."

After shoving the note that had come with the box into his pocket, he strode over to me and lifted and squeezed my hands. The anguish on his face—no, the horror in his eyes—made my breath catch.

"What did the note say?" I asked.

"Nothing." But he wouldn't meet my eye.

I sighed. "People don't deliver cupcakes with notes containing nothing."

Releasing my hands, he dialed his phone and spoke when someone answered, "I need to find out who sent a cupcake that was recently delivered to me." A pause. "Yes, a cupcake. Chocolate? I didn't look closely. There was a note. Delivered to me, Eli Bradley." He rattled off his address. "I see." After hanging up, he tucked away his phone. His sigh slipped from his chest. "Someone came in and ordered it, paying cash. A man, average build, but the owner doesn't remember any other details."

"What did the note say?"

He tucked his chin, and his hair flopped forward, onto his face.

"Please. Eli. We're..." I lifted my chin. "We're in this together, right?"

The lines of worry on his face smoothed, and he took my hands again. He tugged me into his arms and held me against his chest where his heart beat too fast. "You..." His chin rested on the top of my head. "I just want to keep you safe."

"Tell me."

Stepping back, he tugged the note from his pocket and handed it to me.

She'll never be yours.

While the world crashed around me, the piece of paper slipped from my limp fingers and fell to the floor. "What does this mean?" My skin flashed cold. "Russell. It has to be him. How..."

"He's in jail, right?"

Pleading came through in my voice as I tried to make some sense of this. "My lawyer would tell me if he got out early." The sense of calm I'd rebuilt since finding the number on my mirror snapped in two. I staggered, but Eli caught and held me up. "She promised. But he has friends.

Some blamed me for him going to jail." It was nearly impossible to speak through my tight throat. "One of them would've been happy to send this."

"Maybe."

"I'll call my lawyer right now." Because, if Russell was out...He'd come after me and it wouldn't just be with cute cupcakes and notes. Those might be a warning but only the start of something more. Something terrible. My hands shook as I yanked my phone from my pocket, but I found the strength to speak with a controlled voice.

Unfortunately, I only reached her answering machine. *Out of the office. Please leave a message,* which I did.

"She'll get back to me," I said in a rough voice. "She'll tell me Russell is still locked behind bars. She'll tell me what to do about...this." The last word grated out of me. I lifted the note from the floor, though I didn't need to read it again. The words were embedded in my mind. "She'll never be yours," I grated out. Typewritten, which meant the handwriting couldn't be traced. I crumpled it, stormed to the trash, and threw it away. "I'd say that's my decision, wouldn't you?"

He linked his arms on his chest and leaned his hip against the fridge, which hummed softly. "Always will be."

"I'm sorry you're mixed up in this." Wilted, I propped myself against the counter. Would I always feel insecure, vulnerable? Alone?

"I'm not sorry," he said with complete certainty. "I want to be here for you in any way you need me. I said it already, and I'll keep on saying it until I'm sure you truly believe my words."

The walls around my heart—flimsy already—crumpled. How could I keep a barrier in place between us?

I swallowed, overcome with the realization that this *was* the right time.

The right man.

"I'll notify the sheriff," Eli said.

"You think this is related to someone entering my house last night?" How far would Russell go to find revenge?

Eli shrugged as he dialed his phone. "Feels as if things are heating up, though this was mostly directed at me."

The sheriff asked him to bring the note and cupcake to the station, which Eli said he'd do.

"The fish," I said after he'd finished relating the sheriff's request.

He frowned. "Fish?"

"Someone dumped a bucket of bait on my car windshield yesterday. I thought it was just a sick joke, which it could be. Last night could've been a simple robbery attempt, right?" I wanted so much for all this to be random events, but did I dare consider it an option? Probably not. "Someone might've entered my house solely to steal from me. When I got up, they fled. Maybe I'm mistaken and the mark on my mirror wasn't a one."

"It was a one. We're going to be extra careful with you from now on."

"You can't stay with me around the clock."

He raked his fingers through his hair, mussing it. "As far as Flint's concerned, you're my sole project. But you're not an assignment. To me, keeping you safe is more important to me than myself."

"You're..." I shook my head. "Thank you." There was no way to express the relief I felt that I wouldn't face whatever this was alone. "As you said, the cupcake threat was directed at you."

"Us."

"True." I curled my lips upward as my anxiety fled like a storm on a summer's day. Because... "You know what I think we should do?"

He shook his head but studied my face as if trying to read my intent.

"I think we need to go on our date."

His smile rose to join with mine and he strode right up to me, placing his palms on either side of my waist, bracing them on the counter. Not pinning me in place as much as protecting me like a treasure in his arms. "*Date,* huh?"

I bit my lip. "That's okay to say, isn't it?"

"Hell, yeah." His head dropped close to my ear where he breathed. Tingles spread through me and heat centered below my belly. Barely touching me, he could set me aflame with a few simple words. His arms wrapped around the back of my waist. "Mia, Mia, Mia. What am I going to do with you?" He pressed a soft kiss where my neck and shoulder met and I shivered with desire.

"Educate me?" I said with plenty of sass in my tone.

He chuckled. "One of these days, you are so going to get it."

There wasn't anything I wanted more.

My senses were filled with his scent: warm and clean with a hint of spice. Unshaven, I ached to feel his roughness on my skin.

Now that I'd realized I wanted more, how did I tell him?

He dropped his chin onto my head, the position we were settling into as if it was ours.

"Eli?"

"Yeah, honey?"

"I know I said I wanted to take things slowly."

"You set the pace. Always."

"I'm ready for more. Not sure how much yet, but I don't want to hold myself away from you any longer."

Easing back in our embrace, he stared down at me with what looked like the world in his eyes. "Then let's get started." Leaning close again, he whispered by my ear, "Time to be educated." Stepping back, he took my hand and tugged me out to his Jeep where he held the door while I climbed inside.

He put the top down. In no time, he'd backed down the drive and headed out onto the road. We traveled to the western side of town, an area I'd yet to explore fully.

"Woo!" I flung my arms up into the air, fingering the warm breeze. Because it was hot, I'd worn a lime green t-shirt and pale blue jeans shorts. My hair streamed behind me.

I couldn't remember when I'd felt this happy. This relaxed. Despite someone being inside my house the night before, I wanted to laugh until tears streamed down my face.

With a quick smile my way, Eli caught a band of my hair and ran it between his fingers. "Silky flames shot full of sunshine."

I leaned into his palm when he caressed my cheek. "What a poet you are."

He wiggled his eyebrows. "Wait until you get to know me better, then you'll be introduced to all my charms. There's a lot more to me than an excellent singing voice and slick dance moves." Teasing came through in his voice.

I couldn't wait to get to know him better.

We pulled into a large parking lot and cruised around until he luckily found a spot only a few rows back from the main entrance, where he shut off the engine.

I took a final sip from my water bottle and tucked the

drink underneath the seat where it would stay cooler than in full sunlight and caught my first view of our destination.

Mounds of fake snow glistened in the sun, mountains that looked real enough a kid could climb to the top and slide down the sparkle-encrusted surface. Wire had been strung through the trees and poles, spanning the entrance and extending on both sides, and they'd hung a multitude of fake snowflakes that twisted and spun in the breeze. Evergreen trees festooned with lights and colorful bulbs added to the ambiance.

And music. *Let is Snow* drifted from the speakers.

Kids danced beside their parents as they streamed toward the entrance.

"Christmastown?" I said in awe.

"Yeah." His voice came out as a sigh.

Turning in my seat to face him, I smirked. "It's August." I tapped his arm. "And you've been holding out on me. This isn't Disney."

"It's actually better than Disney." He unbuckled. "Let's go!" Like a little kid, he tumbled out of the vehicle and came around to open my door. "Come on. You're wasting precious time."

Holding hands, we strolled up to the ticket booth, where Eli paid a guy with a bushy white hair and beard. His tag said, Franklin, Owner.

"You folks have fun, now," the man said as he secured paper bracelets around our wrists. Round and as jolly as Santa himself in a red tee, black jeans, and a red hat with a white pompom, the man's pale blue eyes twinkled, and his *ho-ho-ho* was filled with laughter. I couldn't imagine how much fun he must have working at a place that brought so many kids joy and fun. He tilted his head toward a box on the counter. "Don't forget your necklaces."

"Necklaces," I said. They looked more like extra-long shoelaces to me, the kind with plastic-coated tips.

"Since I'm a red necklace guy, you okay with green?" Eli asked, lifting two out from the colorful pile.

"Sure. I'll help you complete the Christmas theme." What was I getting into here?

Eli secured it loosely around my neck.

"Not the most exciting jewelry I've ever received." I fingered my silver daisy to show him again how much I loved the gift he'd given me for my birthday.

"You just wait," he said with a grin, taking my hand and pulling me toward the entrance to the park. "The elves are going to give my daisy hot competition."

"Nothing will give your necklace hot competition," I said. "And elves?"

"Not tellin'."

I rolled my eyes.

We exited out into the holiday-themed amusement park. A fake winter wonderland with huge grinning snowmen, icicles hanging everywhere, buildings leaden with fake, glistening snow, and staff dressed in elf suits complete with curled up shoes with dangling bells. From the speakers, *Let it Snow* had moved on to *Walking in a Winter Wonderland*. Eli grinned and, spanning one arm around the back of my waist and linking our fingers together with the other, he danced me around in a slow circle while I giggled.

It was surreal to hear holiday tunes while waltzing in eighty-five-degree weather.

Releasing me as the music changed over to *Rudolph the Red-Nosed Reindeer*, Eli squeezed my hands. "First up on the list is Frisky."

I snickered. "You're saying you're feeling frisky?"

Tugging me close again, he encircled my waist and leaned close to my ear. "Around you, I'm always frisky."

Just like that, I was on fire once more, eager for his kiss. His touch. Melting faster than a snow cone for reasons other than the late-day heat. I had no idea what *frisky* thing he planned for me but had to admit, I was beyond eager to find out.

Excited kids and grinning parents streamed around us and squeals filled the air, telling me this was not the place for a make-out session.

Talk about deep regret.

We smiled sheepishly at each other and backed out of our embrace, but we didn't release each other's hands.

It wouldn't be dark for some time yet since Maine was on daylight savings time, but white, red, and green twinkle lights strung around overhead added to the festive atmosphere. The scent of cinnamon sugar cookies—piped in or for real?—drifted through the air, making my belly perk up and rumble.

If I didn't know better, it could be December 24.

"How is this like Disney?" I asked Eli.

"Rides, characters, you name it." His eyes gleamed as he looked around.

"Rides? I am a rollercoaster girl."

"Then you'll be able to check the Kringle Kaper off your rollercoaster bucket list."

"Can't wait."

A little girl about six-years-old barreled into me, almost knocking me over, and I steadied her with a laugh. Who could be irritated while *Silent Night* drifted around you?

"Sorry," she chirped, looking up at me with pink cheeks, scattered blonde hair, and joy shining from her eyes.

"I'm terribly sorry," someone said from behind me, and I

turned, recognizing his voice. "She's just excited about Frisky."

"Mr. Taylor!" I said. "How are you?"

"Now, I told you to call me Jim." His deeply lined face gleamed with soft humor that fell far too soon. He scratched his thick, salt and pepper hair. "As good as can be expected, I guess. Staying busy, especially with special people like this." With a soft smile, he stroked the little girl's head.

She smiled up at him, revealing a gap on the bottom where she'd lost two baby teeth. "Come on, Grampie. I gotta get to Frisky before they're all gone." She fingered her shoelace necklace.

"You know there are plenty for everyone, Macy," Jim said. His pale blue eyes twinkled when he glanced at me. "She loves this place. It just lightens my heart to bring her here. My Stephanie loved it, too."

Macy tugged on his hand, stretching out his arm. "Please!"

He chuckled. "Okay, okay." And to me, "Nice seeing you again." His nod took in Eli. "And your young man."

Eli's hand tightened around mine as Jim walked away with his granddaughter. "Friend?"

"Sadly, yes."

"Why sadly?"

"His wife, Stephanie. She's one of the reasons my job is so vital." I shivered at the memory because it also reminded me of the man dying on the beach in Mexico. "She died in my arms in the park. I'd been taking a walk and I found her slumped on the grass. I did CPR but it was too late. She was already gone. The autopsy showed late-stage congestive heart failure. She must've been unaware of how ill she was because it was untreated."

"You leave tomorrow for your conference, right?" He

gestured for us to join the back of the line waiting for Frisky, whoever that was.

"Yes. It's an overnight event being held in Ashford, which is three hours north and west of here, in the mountains." I laughed. "The hotel is nestled in the base of a ski area and it should beautiful this time of year. The Juniper Foundation is desperate for funds. My presentation—plus the talks to be given by others in my field, will encourage our attending donors to open their purses and wallets."

We inched forward toward Frisky. Who was short. And moving. All I caught was a mechanical arm in a green suit with white trim, waving. Was this worth waiting in line for?

"Do you have another mission in Mexico planned?" Eli asked.

Remembering the man with the knife chasing me, cutting me, the policeman and his threat, sent chills through me as if I stood in a real winter landscape. My happiness dimmed, but I kept my lips in a smile to give nothing away.

Fearing for Flint and Eli, I'd said nothing about what happened.

"I've switched to stateside projects for now," I said as lightly as possible. Nightmares of that night still haunted me. "Next fall, I'll be in Puerto Rico for a month." Stress from the hurricane combined with poor living conditions put older women on the island at higher cardiac risk.

He tugged on a strand of my hair. "You're special to do this."

"It's important I give back even a little of what I've received throughout my life. I've had it easy compared to so many others in the world." The little boy in front of us jumped in the air and squealed, reminding me we were here to have fun, not talk about heavy topics. "But enough of that. I'm feeling frisky, and my need has yet to be satisfied."

Eli's eyes smoldered.

Teasing him brought out all the joy I kept trapped inside. I hadn't known him long, though we'd spent a lot of time together—with Flint—eight months ago in California. How long did I need to be with someone before I knew I could trust him? Warning signs had been there from the start with Russell. Was I missing something with Eli?

My gut suggested I'd read him right.

"Let me see if I can satisfy your need," he said in a husky voice.

We moved forward. When the curtain of children parted, Eli dragged me toward a tall, mechanical elf that swayed back and forth, a huge smile on his face. He held a bucket, offering it to whoever passed by.

"Frisky is one of the twelve elves of Christmas," Eli said solemnly.

"Thought that was twelve *days* of Christmas."

"Here, it's elves." He picked a few things from the basket and held out a tiny sphere with a hole in it.

"A bead?"

"F is for Frisky." He pointed to the letter etched on the side. After tugging me out of the way so others could reach Frisky, he undid my shoelace necklace, strung the bead, and returned it to my neck. "One down, eleven to go."

"We're making an elf Christmas necklace? How fun."

"One bead for each new memory."

"No memories, yet."

"You just wait." He took my hand and tugged me toward another line of kids winding their way through a fenced-in path. "It's time to meet Santa and Mrs. Claus."

A short time later, it was our turn to ride a cherry-red sleigh that took a track winding through the woods and up a gradual incline. Emerging from the forest, our sleigh stopped at the top of the hill, in front of a huge gingerbread house. Fake cookies siding and frosting crusted-roof, but the candy cane lampposts and gumdrop chairs out front looked so real I could almost taste them.

Eli held me back when I started toward the front door, following a set of twins dressed in identical red frilly dresses.

"Confession time," he said. His chest rose and fell and I wondered what huge secret he was about to confess. That he was scared of Santa? "I need to fill you in on your competition." When I blinked, he grinned. "When I was twelve, I had a huge crush on Mrs. Claus."

I reeled back, pressing my clasped hands to my chest in mock horror. "No!"

"Did."

"But...but..." I shook my head and laughter burst out of me. "Okay, since we're here, you should introduce me to the competition. Will I need a weapon to defend myself from the wrath of unrequited love?"

"Nah. I'm over her now."

"I guess I'm relieved?"

Leaning close, he murmured, "I've moved on to someone better."

Heat filled my cheeks. I took his hand and squeezed. We were going to need to talk soon, because he'd knocked down the walls surrounding my heart and was forging his way inside.

We stepped through the front doorway and were greeted by Mrs. Claus, a petite older lady who reminded me a bit of a gray-haired Julia Roberts. Beaming our way, she wore the requisite pointy glasses and long gown with an apron across the front, wrapped around her slender curves.

"Eli," she called out. "Long time, no see, sweetheart."

Sweetheart?

His face flushed while I tried not to laugh, because I could tell she was just teasing.

Tapping her heel on the white chocolate tiled floor, Mrs. Claus pointed to her cheek, and Eli leaned forward and gave her a quick kiss.

Her sparkling eyes turned my way, only growing wider as her gaze took in our held hands. "Ah, Eli. Alas, I see you've replaced me with someone else."

"Nice seeing you, Mrs. C., but we're actually here for Santa," Eli said, tugging me further into the room while I shook my head at his embarrassment. Mrs. Claus was the cutest person and I would've liked to chat about the boy Eli had been back then. Maybe I'd have to make my own trip to Christmastown again soon for a visit.

"Always Santa." She sighed. "As if the big guy in red is the only one who can dole out treats." She lifted a tray my way. "Cookie?"

"Oh, no thanks," I said with a laugh as Eli led me toward the line weaving its way across the room.

"You plan to sit on his lap?" I asked slyly, leaning into his shoulder.

"While I am wishing for something special this year, I won't need Santa for that," he said in all seriousness.

"Tell me. Are you on the nice or naughty list?"

He chuckled. "Definitely naughty."

I just shook my head.

After seeing Santa, we followed others toward a rear door.

"Don't forget Curly," Mrs. Claus called out. She pointed to the far-left corner of the room and the stout mechanical elf who had, of course, curly hair, and we collected our beads and strung them on our necklaces outside.

As the afternoon waned, we made our way through the amusement park, patting real reindeer and riding the Kringle Kaper, which barely provided barely enough thrills for a toddler.

After eating a homemade cinnamon sugar cookie that we decorated with frosting and colored sprinkles, we strolled through the snowflake forest, aptly named for the crystal flakes dangling around us. While a little girl chirped *Up on the Housetop* through the speakers, we kept to the crushed stone path winding through the light woods. At the end of the forest, we walked through an arched tunnel with real, manmade snowflakes drifting down from above. A sharp contrast to the hot evening we'd been sharing, a light dusting soon coated Eli's shoulders, his hair, and his incredibly long eyelashes. It reminded me of confectionary sugar and made him look completely lickable.

At the end of the tunnel, I stopped to savor the last bit of chilly air and we laughed while we brushed each other off. The flakes melted, drizzling down my face.

"Oh, oh," Eli said with mischief lightening his voice.

I glanced up at him and smirked. "Shouldn't that be ho-ho-ho instead?"

"No, it's a definite oh-oh, mistletoe." He pointed up. "I'll have you know that Mrs. Claus broke my poor old twelve-year-old heart when she told me Santa brought her here for a kiss at the end of each day."

"You know they're probably not a couple in real life."

"Somehow, I found a way to keep going after she shared that news." His voice deepened. "Before you crush me further, I believe it's time for a little education, don't you?"

Heat swirled in my belly. "Mistletoe education?"

"There's a legend about the plant."

I'd just heard about the kissing, which I was eager to

explore. His lips were so close. I just needed to stand on tiptoe while he lowered his head and—

"Remember Balder and the Goddess Frigga?"

Blinking, I dropped back onto my heels. "Can't say I do."

"Frigga, the Goddess of Love, was worried about her son, Balder, the God of the Summer Sun."

"Okay," I said slowly. "What does that have to do with mistletoe?"

"Hang in there, I'm getting to the good part." He swallowed, and his gaze seemed to focus on my lips, which tingled. "Frigga knew that if something happened to her son, the Earth would end, so she went around asking every being and plant to promise not to hurt him. They all agreed. Except she missed one plant—"

"The mistletoe, of course."

"Yup. And Loki, the God of Evil knew it. He made an arrow and placed a sprig of mistletoe on the tip, then tricked Balder's brother, the God of Winter, into shooting Balder with it. The world instantly became cold. For three days, everyone tried to bring Balder back to life and only Frigga was able to do it with her tears, which turned into white berries on the plant. Since then, the plant is considered blessed and legend says that anyone who stands under the mistletoe will never be harmed and is entitled to a kiss."

"Who told you this?"

He smirked. "Mrs. Claus."

"Ah." I snickered. "Are you suggesting, now that you've renewed your acquaintance with the love of your life, you want to wait here just in case she shows up and she and Mr. C. are not truly a couple?"

"Absolutely not." He wrapped his arms around my waist. "I told you. I've moved on."

The tingles in my lips spread down my neck to my chest, where my heart thrummed faster.

"No pressure, Mia," he said gruffly. "Tell me what you want from me."

"Let's see if we can replace your fantasy of kissing Mrs. Claus with something a hell of a lot better." I stroked his shoulders and, with my fingers teasing the back of his neck, urged his face near to mine. "What are your thoughts?"

He stole them all with his kiss. His lips warm on mine, he tugged me closer, pressing my body against his own while his fingers tickled along my spine.

A soft moan rose from deep inside me as he deepened our kiss, his tongue stroking along my lips until I parted them to let him inside. Our tongues teased as snowflakes fell around us, sparks of chilly moisture on my bare arms and legs.

Inside, flames licked along my bones, and, when he lifted his head, I gasped out a protest.

I wanted more.

"I think the legend is true," he said softly. "Because I sure feel blessed."

I hadn't thought I could feel warmer, but I did. Standing on tiptoe, I kissed him again quickly. As if I needed to solidify this fragile bond we were forming between us. "I'm feeling blessed too." There was something about the magic of Christmas, even if it was only August, that made my heart thrill.

Holding hands, we emerged from the snow tunnel and out into the fading sunshine. Golden beams slanted through the woods behind us, sparkling on the fake snow and making the entire world gleam.

"So, not to mess up this Disney-inspired fantasy of yours," I said. "But I've got to go to the bathroom."

"There are some near the entrance." He led me to the building. "I'll run into the men's room and meet you back here? Then we can find the rest of the elves and complete your necklace."

A piece of jewelry I was going to treasure forever because it would remind me of this day.

I essentially skipped into the women's room, hyped up from Eli's kiss and the feeling that he and I were starting something new and wonderful. I didn't take long, but after finishing, my thirst called to me. Since the women's room exited in two locations—to the park or the gift shop—I opted to stroll through the items for sale to the entrance. While I could buy a bottle of water, I'd left mine in the Jeep. No reason I couldn't zip out there and grab it then return to Eli.

Franklin nodded as I passed him.

"Be right back," I said. "Do I need my hands stamped or something? I'm running to our vehicle."

"Just keep your wristband and you're all set," he said with a smile.

As *Feliz Navidad* floated around me, I hummed along and danced to the tune.

Sing and dance. I chuckled. When was the last time I'd had this much fun?

Too long.

I had a feeling my future was going to be filled with more times like today at Christmastown and that Eli would be a big part of my happiness.

Approaching the Jeep, I scooted around the back since a car in the spot ahead of Eli's had backed in so close my legs wouldn't fit.

Since I'd left my water bottle under the seat, I opened

the door and rested my knee on the floor mat while leaning forward to see where I stuck my hand.

I was straightening, water bottle in hand, when someone came up behind me. Must be Eli, who'd figured out my plan. I reached over the stick shift to grab his water, planning to hand it to him.

Turning with a smile, I gasped when I took in the man standing in front of me. He wore a ski mask that completely covered all but his eyes, nose, and mouth, making it impossible to identify him.

"What are you—" Before I could finish the thought, let alone flee, he grabbed me and slapped his sweaty hand over my mouth.

Struggling to escape his grip, I released a mangled scream.

He spun me around, pressed me against the hot metal vehicle, and wrapped a cloth around my eyes. I couldn't see! While I flailed and fought, kicking and punching and screeching, he wound another cloth around my mouth. A third bound my hands behind my back, leaving only my feet free. But I couldn't see and could barely maintain my balance. Kicking became a challenge, but I was determined not to go down without a fight.

My breathing ragged, I gagged against the dirty cloth and shrieked around the material.

Did he really expect to get away with this? We were in a public place. People were everywhere around us.

Please, someone. Help!

Yet most were having fun inside Christmastown, not wandering in the parking lot like me. Stupid. I'd been stupid to come here alone.

He yanked me away from everyone, making me stumble past cars parked in the lot. Heading away from the entrance.

My sandals tripped me up, snagging on what felt like a curb surrounding a grassy area. I fell against a tree, and he fisted the back of my shirt, holding me upright.

"Go." His voice, gruff and scratchy, did not reveal his identity.

While he was masked, nothing about his build or voice suggested I knew him.

"Where are you taking me?" I mumbled around the cloth, unable to hold back the panic rising inside me. "Why are you doing this?"

He jabbed my backside, making my breath wheeze out fast. "Shut up."

Whimpering, I kept moving forward.

Eli would be waiting, worried about why I was taking so long. If I was lucky, he'd figure out where I was and come running.

Not much chance of that.

I needed to find a way out of this all on my own.

The crunch of gravel underneath my sandals told me we were moving through the dirt area of the lot we'd driven through to reach the paved section when we arrived. The lot was huge. If he took me too far, no one would hear my cries. Rushing forward, I made a break for it. With my head tipped back, I could sort of see. A black car loomed ahead of me, and I slammed into it, knocking the wind from my lungs. I crumpled across the back.

Groaning, I flailed on the overheated vehicle, hot metal burning my skin. My belly ached, and my lungs had forgotten how to suck in air.

The car cheeped as it was unlocked, and a click sounded beneath me.

Shit.

While horror rippled across my skin, the man grabbed

the back of my shirt and hauled me onto my feet. Something creaked, like a door opening. "Get in."

"What? I can't see where I am, what's going on." What was he doing to me? Sobs filled my throat, but I choked them back with a deep swallow.

With a grunt, he lifted me off my feet and tossed me inside a hot compartment. I cried out when my arms and legs abraded on a rubber surface.

The trunk.

Before I could scramble toward the opening, the cover slammed closed, leaving me alone in dark, humid silence.

"Hey," I mumble-yelled around the cloth. "Don't do this! Please!"

I had to get out before he drove away. Flint had drilled into me that once someone took a kidnapped woman from the original area, her odds of escaping diminished considerably. But my hands were tied behind my back and I wore a blindfold. Only my feet were free.

How was I going to escape?

I scrambled with the knot pinning my wrists together, tugging and straining.

It wasn't loosening. The sound of my heartbeat thrashed in my ears.

Footsteps crunched on the gravel, traveling away.

I carefully picked at the binding around my wrists, but he'd tied it too tight. Sweat pooled on my forehead and trickled down my face. My fingers grew slick.

He opened a car door and the vehicle shifted when he settled inside. The door banged closed.

Wracked with full-body trembles, tears saturated the cloth wrapped around my face. The vehicle started and the man slammed the transmission into gear. While I whimpered, the car surged forward, chucking me off balance.

Bumping through the lot, we gained speed. How far until we reached the road? Did I have fifteen seconds? Or less?

Renewing my efforts, I pulled harder on the knot, breaking a nail. I pinched the material. Wrestled with it. It scraped my skin raw as I struggled, the fibers digging deep. Warm blood made the rope slick and my fingers tacky.

Yes, the knot was loosening. I could get free.

Please, let it happen soon. Once he hit the pavement and picked up speed, my odds would go down.

The car veered right, and I slammed my shoulder into the side of the trunk. Grunting, my arm spasming with pain, I ignored the panic flaring inside me and kept working on the knot, slowly sliding the sticky bits of fabric apart.

My wrist tie burst, coming undone, and my hands flopped at my sides, spasms making them shake. Not wasting time, I wrenched the blindfold off my face.

The vehicle drove faster, bumping along the uneven surface.

I had to get out of here.

Outside, someone shouted my name.

Eli. He must've come after me. Had he seen the man stuff me in the trunk?

"Eli," I shrieked. "Help me!"

I scrambled across the carpeted mat and located the trunk latch. Closed, of course. But wait. Something glowed.

An inside release.

I yanked on it and the trunk flipped open. Fresh air rushed in, cooling my face. Drying my tears trickling down my cheeks.

The car picked up speed, sending gravel and dirt pinging behind the tires. We hit a pothole and, jarred, I fell back into the tight space.

I crawled back onto my knees as the vehicle squealed out onto the main road leading toward town. Clutching the edge of the trunk, I sucked in a deep breath.

Eli raced down the road, heading my way. No matter how fast he pushed himself, the vehicle was leaving him behind.

Determination filled his face, and he pumped his legs faster, his limp barely discernible. But he'd never catch a car that could speed for miles.

Wobbling onto my knees again, I clung to the edge so I wouldn't be dislodged and hitched one leg over the side.

It was now or never.

Collapsing on the mat and whimpering while hoping Eli would somehow catch up and save me was not an option.

My teeth slamming together, I bailed from the trunk.

When someone screamed, my heart stopped completely. Could've been someone having fun on a ride. Kids squealing with excitement. But I knew it was Mia. Just knew it deep in my bones. Something was terribly wrong.

My skin flashed fire, and terror sent me bolting into the ladies' room.

"Jeez, dude, get out," a woman shouted, but I ignored her.

"Mia!"

No response.

A second exit. Shoving the door open, I flew into the gift shop, looking around feverishly, hoping to find her there. Kids begged parents to buy them stuffed animals or *anything, please!* while I raced toward the entrance.

"Franklin," I yelled, panting even though I'd only run a few steps. "Did you see the woman I arrived with anywhere?"

"Sure did." With an easy smile, he squinted out the big picture window, pointing toward the parking lot. "She said something about grabbing her water from her vehicle. That she'd be right back. Silly, but she worried that—"

"Thanks." Snarling, I slammed through the main entrance door and hit the parking lot at a dead run. "Mia!"

She wasn't at my Jeep.

Fuck.

A dusty white Chevy sedan drew my eye as it bounced through the gravel-strewn part of the lot going too fast for an area with families around.

I took off after it, convinced the driver of that vehicle was somehow connected to Mia's disappearance. Not sure how I knew, but the certainty was turning the blood in my veins to cement.

"Stop!" I scrambled around cars, racing toward the vehicle. My heart pumped. My muscles strained. My leg where I'd injured it spasmed, irritated by the demands I made. Go faster. I had to catch that car.

As bone-searing pain stabbed through the femur, my body shuddered in response. But I kept going, pushing for more speed.

Dust stirred by the vehicle's tires choked my lungs, and rocks ricocheted around me, but I didn't slow. I strove to catch up, to achieve the impossible.

The car was pulling away from me.

I had to catch it. Mia. Please, no.

The trunk popped open, and Mia rose up onto her knees, where she wavered. Catching me running, she strained forward. "Eli!" She grabbed onto the trunk edge, but the car veered to the right, and she dropped back inside.

I drove my body harder, demanding more speed. *Do not fail me now.*

Mia appeared in the opening again. She flung her leg over the edge of the trunk.

While my stomach roiled, her body dropped from the vehicle, slamming on the road. Like a broken rag doll, she tumbled before coming to a full stop.

My mouth flashed dry. She wasn't moving.

The Chevy slowed, brake lights flashing hot. Red, like blood. Like death.

A rock lay on the road in front of me. I snatched it up as I raced toward Mia. With a mighty heave, I threw it at the car. It flew past where Mia lay motionless and, with a loud bang, hit the car's taillight, breaking the thick plastic. White and red fragments rained down onto the road.

Unlike Goliath, I was unable to take down the beast with one blow. The car swerved but kept going. Dirt and rocks flew around me, and a cloud of dust choked the air, making it impossible to breathe.

The vehicle took a bend in the road with tires screeching and disappeared, the roar of the engine fading.

I reached Mia and slammed onto my knees beside her. Ignoring my aching leg, I reached out, wishing I could snatch my hands back, because I'd rather live in a world where Mia was still with me than roll her over and have my worst nightmare become fact.

On her stomach, her arms splayed on either side of her head, she lay too still. Her red curls lay scattered across her unmoving face.

"Mia," I murmured in a cracked voice, and my eyes stung. Please. We'd barely started getting to know each other. Life couldn't take her from me this soon.

I touched her shoulder, soft and tender. Praying that her warm skin meant she still lived.

Her eyelashes fluttered, and she moaned.

My heart flipping, I leaned over her and spoke softly by

her ear. "Hey. It's okay. It's me. Eli. Stay still, honey. Let me check you out before you move."

She moaned again and shifted her arms, dragging them closer to her body.

"Where does it hurt?" I ran my gaze down her frame, assessing for damage. While I was no medic, I'd done my share of combat-related first aid.

Road dust coated the bare skin of her arms and below her shorts. Her back. All of her, actually. Seeing her wrecked felt worse than dragging my guts through a bolt hole.

"I'm okay." She pressed her palms onto the road and started to lift herself up, but groaned and collapsed again.

"Your arms. Legs. Back. Does anything hurt? How about your head? Your neck?"

"No." She pushed again, and I helped ease her onto her side. Then onto her back, even though I knew I should tell her to stay as she was until I could get the EMTs here.

She blinked up at the sky, and her face tightened. "What the hell...?"

"White Chevy. You were in the trunk but escaped. Do you remember what happened?"

Her brow pinched. "Going to the lot for the water bottle I left in your Jeep. Someone grabbed me." Her lips fluttered upward before dropping. "You were running after me." Her palm dropped onto her belly. Did she have internal injuries? "You came for me."

"I'd leap across the Grand Canyon to help you, honey." Not that I'd done anything that heroic. All I'd done was run after a vehicle. I leaned forward, speaking quietly again. "Can I give you a quick once-over?" While my heart demanded I carry her off the road, take her to safety, my head told me I couldn't move her any more than she already had until I was sure she wasn't seriously injured.

Her gaze met mine. "Sure."

Starting at her feet, I removed her sandals. I carefully slid my fingertips over the bottom of her feet, her toes, the tops, and on to her ankles.

She twitched.

My heart rate tripled. "Where does it hurt?"

A soft smile curled her lips. "No pain. Just tickles."

The relief in my grin made my cheeks ache. "Hold still and let me check you out some more."

"You playing doctor instead of me?"

"Damn straight, I am."

Her eyelids drooped. Had she hit her head? I ran my fingers over her scalp but didn't feel any cuts or bumps. Maybe she'd just had the wind knocked out of her.

"I'd love to play doctor with you, Eli," she whispered.

My chest cracked wide open and welcomed her inside. Once I was sure she was safe, that she hadn't been harmed by her fall, we needed to talk.

Our kiss was quick, partly because I couldn't help myself, mostly because I needed the reassurance she'd be okay. Then I gave her a more thorough examination, turning up nothing but a few scrapes and reddened areas that would likely turn into bruises.

"Honey, you can play doctor with me any day of the week. I'm available 24/7."

"I'm not delirious. I didn't hit my head," she said. Though I urged her to remain still, she sat up. "I meant it." Her arms went around my shoulders, and she gave me a soft kiss. "We need to explore this. Us. Soon."

"You name the time and place and I'm there. But right now, we're calling an ambulance."

"I'm fine." But her half-smile didn't reach her eyes. "Don't need an ambulance."

"Why not? You're a doctor. After a fall like that, you know you need to be checked out."

"I can tell nothing's wrong." She glanced around. "Crap. I'm sitting in the middle of the road." Her voice rose. "I need to get up before someone runs me over."

I helped her stand, and when her knees trembled, I scooped her off her feet. Yeah, she could probably walk, but I needed to hold her. I started back down the road and I had to admit, my legs were shaky. Watching Mia fall out of that car and tumble across the road had about killed me.

Her arms linked around my neck, and she snuggled close. "Thank you, Eli. For being here. For rescuing me."

"You rescued yourself." I hadn't done a damn thing.

"I tried to fight him off, but he wouldn't let go."

"You're clever. You found a way to escape." I'd never been more grateful for anything in my life.

"He tied my hands. But I worked on the knots and found the inside trunk release."

Seeing her bloody wrists and knowing the wounds had come from her struggles stabbed through me worse than a knife. "Smart. You kept your head."

"I remembered everything Flint taught me."

"Did you see the person who took you?"

"A man," she said, her words brushing my chest. "He wore a mask. The skiing kind that covers the entire face except with holes for his nose and mouth. And he blindfolded me. But his build. His voice...There was..."

"What?"

She shook her head, and her coppery hair slid along my shoulder. "I don't know who he was or why he tried to take me."

"Your ex..." As far as I knew, she hadn't heard from her lawyer yet.

"Similar build, but I can't be certain. And, for all we know, he's still in jail."

"I really think you need to be checked out in the ER."

"I'm okay." Her voice did sound stronger.

We arrived at my Jeep, and I lowered her onto her feet. "You know a fall like that can give you a serious injury." She could be bleeding internally.

"I promise to tell you if something feels wrong or hurts."

I relented but was determined to keep all my attention on her from now on. She wasn't getting out of my sight. "I'm calling the police."

She drooped against my car. "You think they can figure out who did this and arrest them?"

I'd memorized the numbers on the plate.

While Mia slumped in the passenger seat, I pulled my phone and spoke before returning it to my pocket. "The dispatcher said the sheriff would be here soon."

"Who needs regular criminals? I keep them hopping all on my own."

The sheriff and Deputy Franks arrived not long after, bringing with them a cloud of dust from their rush down the road.

Mia got out of my Jeep and explained what happened.

"Can you identify the voice?" the sheriff asked, his phone and stylus in hand.

"I think he purposefully lowered it, made it sound gruff."

"To mask it?" Deputy Franks asked. Her intent gaze swept the area. "This suggests it's someone you know."

"Maybe?" Mia's hands snaked around her waist. She shrugged and explained about her ex while I put my arms around her. Her body trembled.

"We'll notify the Staties, see what they can come up with. It'll be easy enough to look into your ex. Make sure he's still incarcerated." The sheriff nodded to me. "We'll also run that plate. Quick thinking on your part."

"You'll be around town for a while if we have any further questions?" Deputy Franks asked Mia.

"I'm leaving for Ashford tomorrow morning. I'm speaking at a conference."

"We'll call an ambulance, Ma'am," Deputy Franks said, her concerned gaze taking in the purple shadows blossoming on Mia's arms and legs. "You look pretty beat up."

Mia was lucky she hadn't been more seriously hurt.

And I was damned grateful she was safe. I wanted to track down the man responsible and make sure he was locked behind bars for a very long time, but there was nothing I could do until we had a name.

"I just want to go home," Mia said. She sounded so lost and alone. I tightened my arms around her, wishing I could help her feel better. But all I could do was lend her my strength and the protection of my presence.

The sheriff finished up his notes and tipped his hat. "We'll keep you informed about our progress."

Deputy Franks rocked on her heels with her fists propped on her hips. There was no disputing the steel in her voice and expression. "Rest assured, we're on the case."

"How about we take a quick look around?" the sheriff suggested to Deputy Franks.

"'Course."

"We're okay to leave?" Eli asked. "I want to get Mia home." Where I could barricade her inside her house, with me and my 9mm standing between her and the door.

"We've got both your numbers," the sheriff said over his shoulder. "We'll be in touch." They strode toward the road.

Tightening my arms around Mia, I rested my chin on her head. "I'm going to do everything within my power to make sure no one harms you again. This ends here. Today."

She leaned back in my embrace and lifted a shaky smile. "Thank you."

The confidence in her eyes made my heart swell twenty times its normal size.

We arrived at her house and I helped her from the car, supporting her with my arm around her waist as we slowly moved up the walk.

Anger burned through me faster than a spark landing on a line of dynamite because we had nothing. No name. No description.

No motive.

Mia took her front steps with jerky strides and opened the porch door, where she made her way slowly across the creaking, weathered floorboards to the front door.

I hated seeing her in this much pain.

Pausing with her hand over the lock, her eyes widened as she took in the wooden panel. "Eli."

The number *two* bleeding bold red paint on her front door made my pulse flatline.

11

MIA

The sheriff arrived with a squeal of his tires in the driveway. His brow furrowed as he took pictures and samples of the number on the door. He told me he was gravely concerned about this, that it was his top priority.

I was to remain inside. They'd patrol the area on a regular basis.

He asked me to send him the photo of the number one on my mirror.

However. There was always a *however*. Unless they knew who to arrest, there wasn't much they could do. They were terribly sorry, but they had nothing.

Two strikes.

I dreaded the form the third strike would take. After that, it would be lights out. *I'd* be lights out. My throat ached. I couldn't swallow. And my body had been battered by some unknown fiend.

After the sheriff left, I stumbled down the hall to shower while Eli scrubbed the paint off the door.

My tears mixed with the water pulsing from the shower-head. I sagged into the tiles and pressed my fist against my mouth as I keened. Shivers quaked through me even though the water was hot enough to fill the glassed-in space with steam.

It had been a year since they'd hauled Russell away to lock him up. Silly me for thinking I'd repaired the emotional damage he'd delivered. How had I ever believed I was strong enough now to handle anything? The high walls I'd built crumbled as if they'd been made of clay, and I once again became the puny weakling who'd cowered from Russell. The sad, hopeless women sitting on the ER stretcher all those months ago. Dressed in a johnny, my bare legs dangling in the air, my bruises exposed for the world to see.

Me, exposed for the world to see.

Though I tried to check them, my tears kept falling. An imaginary hammer in my head pounded a relentless beat. The scrapes from where my bare skin met the pavement stung, and my bones ached. Every muscle protested the abuse my body had taken when I fell from the back of the car.

Life had won. It had beaten me.

I'd been snapped in two all over again.

"Hey," Eli said softly from the other side of the opaque glass. "You've been in there awhile. You okay?"

I'd never be okay.

Struggling to regain control of myself, I sniffed. Didn't work. Tears continued to fly unchecked down my face.

He cracked the door. "I'm…So, this isn't anything…I just want to hold you." When I sighed but didn't protest, he opened the door and stepped inside, fully clothed. "Come here." Arms wrapped around me, he tucked me close, his chin resting on the top of my head. He patted my back as I sobbed. "Let it out. It's gonna be okay."

When nothing remained inside me but shudders, he took my hand and helped me step out of the shower where he dried me like a parent with a small, wounded child, murmuring soothing sounds while he did it. Then he helped me dress in a tee and lounge pants he must've snagged from my room.

"I'm sorry," I said through quaking lips.

"You did nothing wrong." Lifting my feet one by one, he slid on my fuzzy slippers.

"You're trying to protect me, and I took off on my own. I should've told you where I was going. Asked you to come with me."

Straightening, he cupped my face. His hair flipped up at his collar, soft curls generated by the heat of the shower. "I messed up, not you. We were having fun. Hell, I was thinking more about kissing you than keeping you safe. Didn't suspect things would escalate this fast when I should've." He growled. "I wasn't careful enough."

"It's not your fault."

"And I don't think it's yours." He swept me off my feet and carried me out into the living room. I wanted to protest that I could walk, could do this under my own steam, but I chose to let him do it instead. He wanted to protect me and shelter me, and I needed to be held.

Settling on the sofa with me on his lap, he snuggled my handmade quilt around us and wrapped me up in his warmth underneath.

I couldn't stop shivering. Despite how hot it was today, my reaction to the near-kidnapping had taken hold.

Walter jumped up beside us and nestled half on/half off Eli's thigh. His purr, normal and centering after a day that had started with incredible promise yet ended with horror, dragged the pain from deep inside me and scattered it, leaving only my throbbing shell behind.

I stroked Walter's head, trailing my fingers down his neck and underneath his loose collar. While an identification microchip had been placed by the vet, I'd also bought Walter a jeweled collar with my information printed on the back.

With a sigh, I settled against Eli's chest.

"I'm wet," he said wryly.

"I kinda noticed." Dampness had sunk through my clothing but how could I complain when he'd sacrifice his own comfort to give me reassurance?

"At this rate, I'm going to need to keep a full wardrobe here."

"I think you should," I whispered into his neck.

Pressing himself back into the cushions, he stared down at me. "I was joking."

"I wasn't." I lifted my gaze to meet his, knowing my growing feelings must be blazing in my eyes. I'd been determined not to let another man close again. But Eli, with his warm arms, his gentle touch, his humor? He'd crept up on me when I wasn't looking.

Whatever I felt for him was too new, too fresh to expose to the night air.

I cleared my throat. "Would you—"

"I can—"

His phone beeped on the coffee table.

"That would be Flint," Eli said. "I texted him the details about what happened earlier."

Of course he'd notify my brother. I was glad he had.

"Fuck, Eli," Flint shouted through the line when Eli answered. "What's going on up there?"

"Mia's here with me," Eli said. "You're on speaker."

"Good. Mia." Flint breathed my name in a shaky voice, his bubble of anger bursting instantly. "You okay, sis?" Caring and frustration came through in his words.

"I am." Beaten but maybe not quite broken. Not any longer. Eli had a way of making me feel whole again.

"Things are going crazy down in..." He coughed. "Anyway, I can't get home until day after tomorrow. You stay put. I need to know you're safe."

"I'm leaving for my conference tomorrow morning."

"You can't go now," he said as if he had complete control over my actions.

"It's just for two days." Normally, my back would ramrod and I'd voice protest, but I'd lost my oomph when I bailed from the back of that Chevy. "I have to go. You know that."

"Your life could be at stake."

"Many lives *are* at stake." How would one person—me—be more important than the women who could be helped in the future by money raised during the event?

"This is only a freakin' presentation. You're not the first responder to a disaster."

"In some ways, I am," I said with a lift of my chin. He couldn't see the gesture, but it elevated my voice and added strength to my words.

"Can you wait to go until I get home, then? In other words, show up late. Sure, you'll miss some of it, but you'll reduce exposure."

"I need to be physically present for all of it."

"Maybe drive out solely for your presentation and return home immediately after."

Hide behind my VIP security system, he meant.

"As you know, it's not just the presentation," I said. I hated to remind him of something—someone, actually—he'd rather forget but he was the one to introduce me to Peter, the head of the Foundation, whom Flint had met through his former fiancée, Julia. "I need to network with the philanthropists throughout the conference, talk them into opening their pockets and giving generously to the Foundation."

Sure, my findings would spark interest, but the real meat of the event lay in the networking, the influx of money they could contribute. "If I only come and go, my impact will be substantially lower." After the presentations finished for the day, the Foundation had planned events for the evening and the next morning where I and other speakers would mingle to reinforce the information and drive home how valuable their donations could be.

"I'm afraid for you, Mia," Flint said. "You know I'd—"

"I'll go with her," Eli said, his arms tightening around me. "I don't plan to leave her for a second anyway."

A long pause followed before Flint's gruff voice bled through the line. "Appreciate it. You know how worried I am."

I leaned forward. "Eli's—"

"We're—"

We broke off and shared a smile, because it was clear we'd both been about to tell Flint our relationship was changing.

What we had might be new, but it wasn't fragile.

"I want Jax to go with you, too."

Eli's grunt revealed his satisfaction. "Was hoping he was free."

"The second I'm back," Flint said. "We need to talk,

figure out what's going on." His voice lowered. "I wish I could get there sooner."

"It's okay. I'm safe." I snuggled into Eli, inhaling his scent of man, wet cloth, and strength, which shouldn't have a smell but fit him perfectly.

Eli cleared his throat. "You said things are heating up down there?"

I watched his face but couldn't read anything in the tiny lines.

"Well," Flint said. "Gabe and Haylee are on the trail of a new contact."

"Cool."

"Where are they?" I asked. I'd only met Gabe a few times when I stopped by the office, but my curiosity was sparked by this veiled conversation. And I'd always worried about my cousin, Haylee, wanted her to be safe. What was she involved in?

Eli shook his head vehemently, even though my brother couldn't see the movement.

"On assignment," Flint said abruptly. "Out of the country."

Kiddie drones, right? My lips twisted. There was a heck of a lot more going on at Flint's business than recreational toys.

These guys...These Seabees. They might've left the Navy but the military had remained with them. I had a suspicion my brother ran a bunch of government-sponsored, covert operations. Missions under the direction of their former boss, my Uncle Sid. Why else would a Navy Admiral bother hanging out at a business that made 'toys'?

"I see," I said, even though I didn't. But pressing would only bring on more vague answers. And while curiosity drove my interest, I had enough to deal with at the moment without worrying about whatever trouble Flint might be getting into.

"Haylee and Gabe are okay?" Eli asked.

"Not a care in the world." On the surface, Flint's words came through loose and relaxed, as if Gabe and Haylee had gone to Cape Cod for the weekend. While he might believe he could hide it from me, we'd grown up close. An edge had come through in his voice. "They're relaxing, soaking up the sunshine."

Eli nodded. "Keep me in the loop, then."

There was no reason Eli needed to be updated about a fun vacation, right?

"Will do," Flint said. "Gotta go, now. Meeting. Be careful, Mia. Stay safe."

I couldn't be any safer than where I was right now, wrapped securely in Eli's arms. "Please, don't worry about me."

"Can't help worrying. You know that."

I'd feel the same if it was Flint in danger instead of me. "Love you."

"Love you, too." Flint ended the call.

I eased around in Eli's arms to fully face him with my knees braced on either side of his thighs. Walter blinked, and his purr hummed around us before he snuggled his nose deeper into the quilt and drifted back to sleep.

The dampness of Eli's clothing might bring out my shivers but his body radiated warmth. It soaked into me, sparking a different sort of heat. One I was quickly beginning to believe only he could initiate.

Our Christmastown kiss had taken our relationship in a new direction. While a week ago, no one could've convinced me I'd be eager to spend all my time with one man, things had changed.

I'd changed.

The fear that had haunted me for a year had flown for the moment, replaced with a longing for something I'd never felt before. Maybe the danger I found myself in right now heightened my emotions, but how could I hold myself back from him when he gave me everything I could ever need? And our situation was tenuous. I didn't know what tomorrow would bring, whether I'd be alive or dead within a week. I could hold myself back or grab onto something wonderful and savor it for as long as it lasted.

While staring into his sinfully chocolate brown eyes, I slid my hands up his shoulders and fingered his curls. "Do you—"

"Mia, I—"

There we went again, speaking at the same time. The comedy of the repetition brought out my laugh.

"You go first," he said.

Did I actually dare speak about this growing closeness between us? "I just..." My chest rose and fell with my sigh. "The mistletoe legend that said whoever stands underneath a sprig will never be harmed. In some ways, you're my mistletoe. When I'm with you, I feel confident, secure. Like nothing and no one can harm me."

His fingertips tickled along my waist and underneath my tee to stroke the sensitive skin on my back. "Exactly the way I want you to feel."

"But I..."

"What?"

"This isn't just about you providing security, is it?" I knew the question was stupid the moment I spoke it. He kept saying he was here for me, that he wanted me, that it was solely my decision.

My insecurity ate at me like cancer.

He reeled back against the sofa, and his hands stilled on my back. "Hell, no. It's a lot more than that for me."

"Me, too."

"When I heard you were moving to Crescent Cove, I thought it would be awkward between us when we met up again, and I'll be honest here,"—his voice deepened—"I fully respect your right to tell me you aren't interested in going further, because I would never pressure you into something that makes you uncomfortable. Especially when my role here is to keep you safe. But I—"

"Oh, I'm interested." My words came out firm, but I lowered my gaze from the intensity in his, because the emotions swirling inside me felt raw and exposed. But also, hopeful. "I've thought about you a lot since California, and knowing this was your home town only added to its draw." I swallowed back my lack of self-confidence and continued in a firm tone, "While I wasn't ready back then, I am now."

He cupped my face and lifted it until our eyes met. "Then we start over from here."

"One step at a time."

"Like I said, you set the pace."

Part of me wanted to speed things up and find out where this would go, but another part of me wanted to savor this moment. Because this was new and different and wonderful. Something to be savored.

I tilted my head. "The other part of that mistletoe legend..."

His grin sent happiness shooting through me. "You saying you might be open to another kiss?"

I pulled his face closer. "Why limit ourselves to just one?"

Our lips came together.

The rising fire inside me couldn't be denied. Moaning, I pressed into him, drinking in everything he gave.

Our tongues met, tentative at first until fully unleashed. Wild.

I raked my fingers through his hair and strained closer while he groaned and cupped my butt.

Somehow, he'd gathered up the severed pieces of me and fused them together.

Eli groaned again and his fingers eased underneath my shirt and traced along the seam of my bra. His thumb stroked my nipple through the silky fabric.

I jerked back and gasped.

"Too much?" He panted as if he'd run ten miles. Or like I'd pant if I ran ten miles. Eli seemed to have plenty of stamina.

"No." I yanked off my tee.

His gaze drifted to my breasts peeking above my lace black bra, and his breath hissed out. "Fuck, Mia. You're gonna kill me."

Reaching behind, I unhooked my bra then tossed it aside. I needed his touch more than I needed air.

He trailed the back of his fingers along the tops of my breasts then cupped each mound with his palms. His thumbs on my nipples were replaced with his mouth and his tongue stroked the tip while his fingers teased the other.

His hand continued down my belly, and I arched back to give him full access.

I couldn't hold back my wince when his hand skimmed along a bruise.

"Shit," he said. "I'm sorry. You're sore." Lifting me up, he eased me onto the sofa beside him, on the opposite side of Walter.

I'd set the rules, suggesting we take this slow, but I

wanted to wrench them back and replace them with a cry of need.

But he was right. I ached all over.

He helped me dress in my bra, his fumbling fingers telling me that while he might've undressed women in his past, he'd helped few of them put their clothing back on after.

"Tee," he said, feeding my arms through the sleeves and sliding the fabric down around my waist. He followed his ministrations up with a kiss that was a mix of sweetness and passion.

It only made me yearn for more.

"We've got plenty of time," he said while he held me with his chin nestled on top of my head.

But did we?

A knock on the door drove us apart.

"Expecting anyone?" he asked, instantly on alert. His hand darted around to the back of his waist where his handgun hid. He'd locked it in his Jeep's glove compartment when we were at Christmastown, but he'd tucked it back under his shirt while we waited for the sheriff.

Rising, he padded barefoot into my entry where he turned on the porch light and carefully edged a slice of the curtain to the side. His posture losing its hyper-attention, he disengaged the locks and opened the door.

The elderly couple who lived in the house on the left of mine stood on the porch.

Elvira peeked through the opening, and her smile widened when she spied me coming toward them. She lifted a white container my way. "The Price is Right just ended and before we headed to bed, we thought we could stop by to—"

"Tell you we've got a bone to pick with you," her husband grated out, his fists clenched at his sides. His thick, bushy white eyebrows wedged together, and his equally white combover slid across his forehead before he raked it back.

"Now, Elwin." Elvira bumped his side with her generous hip. "None of that. I told you to let it go."

Face darker than a storm at sea, he grumbled. "Coming and goings, all the damn time."

Beaming, Elvira pushed the plastic container into my hands while I gaped back and forth between them. Comings and goings?

Elvira continued, "I made my grandson brownies but my daughter-in-law says he can't have them." Her voice came out high-pitched and prissy as she mimicked. "Sugar makes him hyper."

Elwin loomed forward, engulfing the porchlight with his tall, broad-shouldered presence. "Before you moved into this neighborhood, it was quiet. Peaceful. Safe."

Whoa. Wait. I—

"Frankly," Elvira said, propping her hands on her hips after I reluctantly took the container of brownies. "I don't believe a bit of sugar hurt anyone."

"People creeping around the backyards at all hours," Elwin shot out.

Elvira's smile grew even brighter, and she winked at Eli. "Who can resist chocolate?"

"Hold on," I said, lifting my hand. Unease crept through me on cloven feet, making the hairs on the back of my neck stand on end. "Who's coming and going at all hours?"

"People parking on the street, stomping through my hedges in the middle of the night," Elwin said with menace. "I won't have it, I tell you."

"Love to bake," Elvira said cheerfully. "You like cookies?" She dipped her head toward Eli. "You're a hearty young man. Bet you love a plate of hot-from-the-oven treats."

Eli wrapped his arm around my waist. "Mia makes the best cookies in the world."

Sweet of him to say, considering he hadn't tried one yet.

"Elwin, you said you've seen people creeping around at night?" I wedged my way into the brief gap in the stacked conversation. Neither Elvira or Elwin was giving the other— let alone us—a second to breathe.

"So many people trooping around on nefarious missions under the moonlight, I'm starting to believe you're dealing drugs." Elwin chewed through the words.

"What?" I gasped out.

"But you haven't tasted my pumpkin chocolate chip cookies yet." Elvira shook her finger at Eli. "They disappear by the plateful at the church suppers."

"Saw it on 60 Minutes." Elwin yanked on his button-up shirt collar. "Doctors prescribing for each other all the time, then turning around and selling the drugs to school kids."

"I'm not selling drugs to kids!" I said in horror. "I'm training to be a cardiologist."

"Even Anna-Marie, who owns a home on the water, buys my cookies." Elvira nodded pertly. "Despite the fact that we've got a new teahouse in town and the owner's a trained baker. She even once said—"

"That's what the doctors interviewed on 60 Minutes said. They're in prison, now, and maybe you should be there with 'em. You won't be bringing that kind of shenanigans to our neighborhood. I'm telling you right now"— Elwin poked his finger forward, nearly impaling my chest before Eli tucked me behind him. "I will not stand for it. You shut down your meth lab or whatever you've got going on here that calls people out at night when they should be sleeping snug in their homes, or I'm reporting you to the police."

"The sheriff has already been out today," Eli said.

"I guess it's okay to share, considering you're a new neighbor. I have a secret ingredient I use in all my treats." Elvira clucked her tongue. "Not that I'll tell anyone what it is. Even on my deathbed."

"See? See?" Elwin's voice rose in volume. "The sheriff has been out, filing reports? Knew it. You've had one run-in with the law already and before you know it, your lawn will be overgrown, drunks will be sleeping in your bushes, and property values in the neighborhood will tumble."

"Now, you can't make me tell," Elvira said with a sly grin. "Some folks swear by a pinch of vodka, but I—"

"You put vodka in cookies?" I asked, both appalled and intrigued at the same time.

"Someone broke into Mia's home." Eli's words might come out soft but they contained a palpable edge of steel. "I assume you told the sheriff that when he interviewed you, Elwin?"

Elvira leaned close to me. "Okay, you twisted my arm. I'll share. It's coffee powder. Makes chocolate taste more chocolately and my pumpkin cookies? Gives them that extra something that plain old makes them pop."

"Haven't spoken to the sheriff yet, but I intend to." Elwin nudged his pointy chin toward Elvira. "Come on, now, mother. It's time we were back in our home." He added to me, "Be aware I keep my doors double locked at night. You and your druggie friends won't invade my home while you're stoned out of your minds."

My eyebrows rising all the way to my hairline, I was unable to do more than sputter.

"Now, Elwin, don't you think we should be getting

home?" Elvira beamed at me. "You want anything, love, you just let us know."

"Fair warning." Elwin's scowl deepened. "I don't take time to ask questions when someone skulks onto my property at night." His curt nod drove his final point into my bones. "My shotgun's always loaded."

ELI

"That was completely fucked," I said, shutting the door and engaging the locks.

Mia shook her head, and her breathing shuddered from her lungs. "I've never had such a bizarre conversation in my life. Elwin was beyond creepy and Elvira? I have a feeling that woman needs a big hug."

"People skulking around at night," I said with a laugh, though having what I already knew confirmed was not something to laugh about. After scoping out Mia's backyard earlier, it was clear whoever broke in last night wasn't the first to seek entry, though the tracks peppering the fence between her and her neighbors' properties were old. A few days at least. The hedges spanning the back of her house had been trampled, especially beneath her windows. And someone had forced their way into the side door of her detached garage. From the prints I'd found, a variety of individuals had been on the premises. *Before* Jax installed the exterior security system, which meant we had nothing we could use to identify the perp.

The big question was: why were they so eager to get

at Mia?

Mia tossed the container of brownies on a table near the door and snaked her arms around her waist. "He saw people in my backyard."

"Yep."

"And he thinks I run a meth lab and I'm dealing drugs to kids. Or both." Her worried green eyes met mine. "What's going on here? Elwin's 60 Minute-inspired drug theories aside, we know something's up. Someone broke into my house last night and fled when I investigated. And then today, this person or someone else tried to kidnap me. If it wasn't for the painted numbers, I'd think the two events weren't connected."

They were. I was convinced of it. I took her hand and led her into the living room. We dropped onto the sofa again and she bumped Walter over to sandwich between us, snuggling into my side. I buried my fingers in the floofy, multi-orange fur on his neck and rubbed. His satisfied purr rang between us.

"I don't like any of this," she said.

"Me, neither." I tucked my arm along her shoulders.

"It doesn't make sense."

The pieces of this random puzzle needed to come together soon or I was going to go rogue. My 9mm dug into my spine but no way would I set it aside. Keeping it ready to use in Mia's defense at any given moment had become my sole focus. "We're assuming your ex is somehow involved."

"Not sure who else it could be. Although..." She frowned.

"What? Any other ideas?"

"Not possible." She shook her head and a shudder ripped through her frame. "That was far from here, and I've done what they..."

"What are you talking about?"

"Nothing." Her face had gone completely blank. Pale, too. I wanted to press her but she'd dealt with enough today already. "Other than Russell, I can't think of anyone who'd want to hurt me."

"We'll know soon whether he's locked up or free." If he was loose and after Mia, he was about to get a taste of what he'd delivered. Tenfold.

"Doesn't matter. Even locked up, he could find a way. His friends weren't happy with me after the trial."

"They threatened you?"

"Twisted lips, long stares, and mutters that sounded suspiciously like, *watch your back* were enough to make me want to take a new name and move to the other side of the world."

"Give me their names, and I'll call the sheriff and ask him to find out where they are and what they're up to."

"I will." Her yawn broke through her quiver.

Ten-o-clock. We should go to bed soon. "What time do you want to leave tomorrow?"

"Ashland's a three-hour drive away, and check-in for the conference is from eleven to noon, followed by lunch and then the first presentations, so maybe we could head out by seven, seven-thirty?"

I kissed the top of her head then closed my eyes and took in the flowery scent lingering on her curls. "Tomorrow, we can stop by my place on our way north and I'll shower and pack. Suggestions for clothing?" I doubted jeans and a tee would suffice.

"How do you guys dress when you're doing bodyguard services at a function like this?"

"Depends on the function. Will this one be casual or formal?"

"Caught 'ya." She blinked up at me. "I knew there was more to Flint's business than kiddie drones."

"We do provide security on the side," I said carefully. "Casual stuff. You already knew that." The moment this situation calmed down, Flint and I were going to talk. Mia didn't need to know every facet of what I did for a living, and I would never share top security clearance information with someone not working for the business, but I was done with hiding. Being dishonest with her about my job ripped through my bones like a chainsaw.

She sighed. "While I'd love to wear yoga pants and a tee, they won't fit in well with cocktail parties and the first night's formal ball. I'll be wearing fancy dresses and heels."

I wiggled my eyebrows. "Spiky heels?" Damn, but I was picturing her wearing nothing but those spikes propped on my shoulders while I...

"Eli?" She waved her hand in front of my face and laughed. "I lose you there for a minute?"

No, she'd found me.

"You're going to make me think I'm boring."

"Not a chance." Turning to face her, I cupped her pretty cheeks and gave her a slow, deep kiss. If only I could keep on kissing her forever.

"We need to go to bed, but you don't need to sleep on the sofa," she said after we parted.

That made my breath hitch...and my body respond.

"You can sleep in my bedroom."

Double wham. She couldn't be inviting me to her bed for a hot round of sex. Could she?

Wait. Sleep in the *bedroom*. She'd been careful to enunciate the words. Not sleep in her *bed*.

"You suggesting your floor instead?" I teased.

"Since you can't have slept a wink last night on the

sofa, you can share my bed with me." She stroked Walter, who purred, but her hand soon stilled on his fur. "We don't..."

"Have to do anything," I finished for her. My body needed a strict reminder that my primary duty tonight was ensuring her safety, not making her shout out my name. "I wouldn't mind keeping a closer eye on you."

She scooted forward on the sofa and stood, staring down at me. "You don't plan to sleep?"

"Not deeply." With someone eager to tag Mia with a number three, I'd be foolish to relax my guard for even one second.

"You're going to be exhausted if the police don't figure this out soon."

Rising, I clasped her hands. "Sleep's overrated." At sea, the norm was twelve-hours on and twelve-hours off, seven days a week. Free time was spent getting ready for your next shift. Being on a boat in the middle of a rough ocean didn't provide much to do or anywhere to go during your free time. The highlight of your life became getting back to work, so we often worked over.

Who needed sleep?

"I'll scoot into the bathroom and do my teeth and every-thing else," she said.

Chuckling, I swept my hands toward my body. "I really need to get out of these damp clothes. I'll sleep in my boxers if that's okay with you."

"Sure, though I might have a few of Flint's things around you could wear, if you want. A t-shirt? Maybe shorts."

At home, I slept in nothing, but that could prove embar-rassing in Mia's bed. "I'm happy to take a look." If only for something to wear until I could get to my place in the morn-ing. With high humidity this time of year, there was no guarantee my jeans would dry overnight. "Unless I can use your dryer."

"Of course. It's in the basement," she said from the doorway leading to the hall. "I'm glad to run your things downstairs if you'd like."

"I can do it while you're in the bathroom."

"Then I'll see you in my bedroom," she said softly and disappeared down the hall.

Fuck. I'd about kill to find a way into Mia's bed, but not like this.

I followed her, making sure she was secure before I took the basement stairs two at a time to the dryer where I hauled off my jeans and tee and threw them in. While they tumbled, I returned to the first floor and leaned on the wall outside the bathroom, feeling conspicuous in my boxers. I tried to tell myself this wasn't much different than lounging on the beach in swim shorts.

Except for my partial woody.

Protection. Protection. Protection. That was my primary directive. I repeated the litany in my mind.

The door opened and Mia walked out, pausing to glide her gaze down my slouched form.

"Damn," she whispered. "How the hell do you expect me to..." Her wide eyes met mine. "Okay. Well." She blinked fast then said softly, "I am so screwed."

Nudging off the wall, I eliminated the short distance between us and stroked her hair. I was having my own hot damn moment. Did Mia have to wear such a short night-gown to bed? "Silky," I said, feathering my fingers along the side of her waist. Beyond sexy.

So much for the *partial* woody.

"It's just...umm. I don't own any flannel nightgowns."

I snorted. "That, I'd have to see. But you'd look hot in

anything." As well as nothing except those heels.

Stepping back before I could haul her into my embrace and devour her, she said, "I put a toothbrush on the sink. I keep spares for friends. You're welcome to anything else in the bathroom, naturally."

"Thanks." I eased around her and went inside, where I was tempted to take a cold shower.

Joining her in the bedroom, I found her nesting underneath the covers with Walter splayed out by her feet. He winked at me, and I told myself I found acceptance in his gaze, because I was going to do my damndest to someday be welcome in Mia's bed for reasons beyond protection.

"My bed's a king. I don't imagine we'll even know the other person's here," she said lightly.

I was going to be fully aware of her delectable body lying nearby the entire night through.

"No bundling board, then?" I said with a laugh.

"Do you need one to behave?"

"Honey," I said as I turned off the light, pulled back the covers, and climbed into the warmth beside her. "You need to know right now I never behave."

"A promise or a warning?"

"Take it whichever way you'd like." Dropping my head onto the pillow, I left the covers down around my waist. I was hot enough to burn down a building.

Mia scooted over until she lay snug against my side, and I tucked my arm underneath her waist to draw her even nearer.

It felt good to lay with her in the dark.

But sleeping beside her without touching her was going to fuckin' kill me.

∾

A LONG NIGHT PASSED, during which I sported a half-woody whenever Mia snuggled closer, sighed, or just plain existed. The old house creaked and groaned, but nothing and no one provided a decent challenge.

I roused to the soft chirp of the alarm.

Heaven lay my arms.

Do not touch.

Not too much, that is. Would kisses on her head and face be considered strikes against me? Couldn't help it. I'd never be able to resist her.

Mumbling, she rolled onto her back, and I followed, rising partway over her, propping my head on my elbow.

Even in sleep she stunned me with her soft curls a riot around her face, her smooth, freckled skin peeking above the rounded neckline of her nightgown, and her rich, honey scent.

She hummed when I nibbled her collarbone. "Eli."

I loved that my name was the first word from her lips when she woke.

"Time to rise and shine, honey." With my teeth, I slid her nightgown strap aside to give me better access and kissed her exposed shoulder. "We've got a road trip ahead of us."

"I don't want to get up."

Okay with me. I'd be happy to spend the entire day here, tasting Mia.

The stretch she released sent flames roaring through my veins and solidified a whole new dilemma my boxers would never completely mask.

"You want the shower first, or should I?" I tossed back the covers. Time to get this show on the road or I'd be crawling all over her, begging to touch her skin.

Aw, hell, her nightgown had ridden up during the night. And she wore a lacy scrap of fabric she might call underwear but I called pure seduction. I could rip it aside with my teeth as I explored.

Did oral sex count as providing bodily protection?

Flint sure as hell would never agree.

"How about you shower first while I make breakfast?" *Focus on the physical tasks, Eli, not her endless physical attributes.*

But hell. I'd much rather savor the feast I'd found here in the bedroom. My gaze could not be dragged away from the juncture of her thighs. "Mia?"

"Hmm?" Her eyes remained shut, blocking out the world.

"While I should go make breakfast, I'm beyond tempted to climb back in bed and lick every inch of your body."

Her eyes popped open and the heat I found there—just for me—made my body go fully rigid.

With a smirk I could not define, though I was eager to discern it's meaning, she scooted over to the side of the bed and slid to the floor.

Walter stared at us benignly before hopping off the bed to wind between her parted ankles.

Mia's gaze centered on the front of my boxers and fuck, her tongue peeked out and slid along her lips. "Maybe I should call dibs on licking." With a giggle, she raced from the room, shouting over her shoulder, "Too bad we're short on time!"

I growled and gave chase, shouting, "You are so going to get it, honey."

She beat me to the bathroom—though honestly, I let her —and shut the door in my face, calling out, "How about pancakes this morning? There are blueberries in the freezer."

I chuckled, more than satisfied with how she kept me in

line. I did love a woman who could give it back to me as fast as I dealt it out.

After thumping down to the basement and hauling on my jeans, I returned to the first floor and strolled into the kitchen. I opted not to wear my tee. Mia wasn't the only one who could tease.

The low simmer in my veins told me we were both going to savor the inevitable volcanic explosion.

I'd mixed up some batter and was shifting my hips while singing about painting with the colors of the wind when someone knocked on the front door.

Elwin again?

My cheery mood sunk in an instant.

After tapping my gun tucked into the back of my jeans, I stomped down the hall barefoot. If Mia's jerk of a neighbor thought he could come back here with his shotgun and make further threats, he'd learn I didn't put up with shit like that from anyone, especially directed at the woman I...

Aw, hell.

My feet stumbled, and my hands twitched. My heart...Well...

Shaking my head, I put aside the thought for now. *Front and center, Soldier.*

A quick squint through the curtain made me stand down immediately. I unlocked and swung open the door.

Ginny, my sister, strolled inside. "Settling in already?" she said with a smirk. Her playful tap on my chest was reinforced with a pleased grin. "Showing off your muscles for Mia, are you?" She started down the hall. "Where is she?"

"What are you doing here?" I called out as I trailed her toward the kitchen.

"Cool. Blueberry?" she asked as she peered into the bowl sitting next to the stove. Her glance took in the table set for two and, in the center, the daisy I'd plucked from Mia's garden and tucked in a vase. "Cozy, Eli. Maybe even romantic. I approve. Seems you've learned a thing or two about women from me, after all."

"I can handle myself around women."

Her low chuckle rang out over the soft voice coming from my phone, singing about finding everything just around the river bend. "Since you're here after what I assume is a morning after—"

"Totally not like that," I said shortly, though I wasn't sure whose honor I was defending, mine of Mia's. "I'm here solely to protect her." Sure. After my realization in the hallway, I wasn't going to come close to fooling myself about this situation, let alone my sister.

Ginny was too savvy for her own good.

"Aww." Ginny's face crinkled. "That's so sweet. Why protection, though?"

"She's..." I raked my hair off my face. "Someone was in her house night before last and yesterday, someone... stuffed her in a trunk." No way would I name it as the kidnapping it was to my sister, who'd experienced the same horror earlier this year while traveling in Istanbul. She'd made her peace with her past after the jerk was locked up, and it thrilled me that she had nothing in her future but a lifetime of happiness with my best friend, Cooper.

"My, God, Eli." Ginny's hands flopped to her sides. "Stuffed in a trunk? What's going on here?"

"Your guess is as good as mine. We suspect Mia's ex could be involved."

The tremble Ginny released told me my statement had hit home but she tightened her spine and pivoted back to face the stove. If I knew my sister well—and I did almost as well as myself—she'd take comfort in simple tasks. Because her kidnapping had also been caused by an ex.

As expected, she lit the gas underneath the frying pan and plopped a pat of butter onto the surface then watched it melt. "What are you listening to?" she said brightly. Fake cheer, but she was making an effort to redirect the conversation. "You and your Disney tunes." With a chuckle, she turned off my phone.

She dipped into the batter and formed perfect circles in the pan. "You're going to take care of this situation." Said as a statement, not a question. After sliding the perfect pancakes onto the platter on the counter, she added more batter to the pan.

"Hell, yeah, I am."

"Good." She tossed me a pert nod. "Were you planning anything other than pancakes for breakfast? Sausage? Bacon?"

"Sure, whatever."

She opened the fridge and removed the package of bacon, then laid strips in a second pan. The sizzling essence of smoky heaven soon filled the room.

"I'm going with her to the conference."

"Then she'll be completely safe." Tension eased from Ginny's frame as her gaze slid down to my bare toes. Her lips twitched upward. "Not dressed like that, though, right?" Leaning away from the stove, she flicked my hair. "Getting kinda shaggy, aren't you?"

"If Mia has scissors, will you..."

"Of course."

She'd cut my hair before. Back when she was a teenager, she wanted to be a hairdresser. Since she hadn't done too bad a job, I'd asked her to cut my hair after that, which she'd done until she started traveling for her career as a photographer.

"The conference is swanky, from what Mia told me." Her lips pursed as she studied my jeans. "Don't forget. You're representing us Bradleys and—"

"Totally on it." Contrary to what she might be suggesting, I was capable of cleaning up well. "You didn't tell me why you're here."

"Flint mentioned to Cooper that Mia was going out of town at the same time Flint would be in D.C. I'm taking care of Walter." Her quick flip of the bacon created splattering sizzles. "Mia asked me to come by this morning so she could explain his routine." A quick glance took in the window break I'd installed on the ceiling. "I assume that's not a kitty cam."

"I upped her security."

"I love how you Seabees think."

"Coop will be here with you whenever you're checking on Walter, correct?"

"Before? Maybe. Now? One-hundred-percent, yes."

I nodded.

A shudder rippled through her, and I was sad I'd reminded her of the horror she'd experienced in her past.

"What's the plan for the conference besides you hovering over her 24/7?"

She must know I was all over this already. But I held in my huff, knowing her questions were motivated by concern and a need to turn a scary conversation into something productive. "I have a few ideas in mind, and Jax is coming with us as back-up." While I couldn't rush ahead and install a security system worthy of the Queen of England in Mia's hotel room, I could rig a few things I'd collect at the shop. Discreetly, that is. The facility would have its own security system in place. A baby system, likely, but decent enough that it might pick up on one or two of my tricks if I wasn't careful. No need to offend anyone.

Ginny dropped the heaping platter on the table then took in me leaning against the doorframe. "You want me scarce while you two savor this breakfast I just slaved over?" Her smile grew as she took in the setting again. "I could...I don't know. Take a walk. A long walk, if that's even better."

I crossed the kitchen and pulled out a third plate from the cabinet. Added a cup for coffee, which had finished brewing. "Join us." Romance could be delayed long enough to enjoy a meal with my sister. I didn't see her often enough as it was, with her and Cooper together all the time.

After getting to know Mia better, however, I understood why she'd made the suggestion.

Ginny's arms slid around my waist from behind while I poured three cups of coffee, and she gave me a quick hug. "I'm happy for you, Eli," she whispered. "You deserve the best life has to offer."

"So, do you."

"I found it with Cooper." Stepping back, Ginny turned to the doorway.

My heart flipped as Mia strolled toward us with a big smile on her face.

There was no holding back my low whistle.

Damn. She wore a deep green dress that hugged her luscious curves. She'd fixed her hair in some kind of arrangement that looked complex but maybe wasn't, with a few curls highlighting her high cheekbones, the rest coiled up in a mass on her head. The dark stuff she'd outlined her green eyes with made them smolder.

And she wore heels.

Black, higher-than-Mt.-Katahdin heels.

13

MIA

I f a car wasn't trailing us, I would've sat back in the Jeep and relaxed. Chatted with Eli while savoring the scenic ride northwest to Ashford.

He'd left the top up this time to keep a red—no, make that a *strawberry blonde*—rat's nest from forming on my head. Respectful on his part since he knew how important it was for me to make a good impression.

Gnawing on my lower lip, I turned in my seat and squinted through the back window. My unease did not drop just because the car was a maroon Toyota, not a white Chevy sedan. "Who can it be? We know it's not him." *Him*, meaning Russell.

"Nope."

The sheriff had called before we left and told us my ex was still locked up securely in jail. Unless he'd escaped within the last hour, someone else had been riding our rear bumper all the way from Crescent Cove.

As for the white Chevy, they'd run the license plate number Eli gave them and discovered it had been reported stolen a few days prior. The police located the vehicle last evening, abandoned on a dirt road about three miles from Christmastown. They were running prints but couldn't say if their tests would yield any results.

Two leads gone like fog burning off in the early morning sunshine.

Actually, Eli was not convinced someone was following us. Something about no bugs or his vehicle being clean, whatever that meant.

I was convinced, though I was leaving the losing-the-tail task to him. Or Jax, whose SUV followed the Toyota.

Rubbing the wound on my arm I'd received in Mexico— it itched like a bugger—I slumped back in my seat and stared out the window at the dense forest we passed. This part of Maine was quite rural, with only a smattering of houses centered in each tiny town, surrounded by woods and craggy hillsides stretching into infinity. While a few official towns had been formed with real names and the occasional post office, much of northwestern Maine was a collection of unorganized territories who'd ditched names for numbers and no longer collected local taxes.

Now that I'd had a decent night's rest, which I'd miraculously accomplished despite Eli and his delectable body lying in the bed beside me, I was no longer a quivering wreck. Anger had shoved fear aside. Someone had a personal vendetta against me. One of Russell's friends? If so, they seemed to be making a lot of effort to exact revenge on a woman who'd done nothing wrong. One would think it would be easier to send me hate mail.

Or fling a bucketful of fish guts on my windshield.

Stress about who it could be, let alone why they were after me, kept me hyper-alert, prepared to bolt from any perceived threat. It made it nearly impossible to get the rest of my work done. With my presentation coming up in a few hours, I needed to shove aside my apprehension and skim through the notes lying on my lap one last time.

"Daily weights. Low sodium diet. Strict I&O," I mumbled, adding to Eli, "That means intake and output."

"Naturally." Eli kept his eyes on the road.

"The rural areas of Mexico have the highest incidence of death from preventable diseases. Getting proper medication and treatment to them is an ongoing challenge."

"Your work there must help a lot of people then."

"As I said, I focus on women's cardiac health, and it eats away at my own heart to see people suffer when I know there's treatment that could enhance and prolong their lives, whether it be diet changes or medication or a combination of both. The Foundation's efforts have made some headway in getting them what they need, but we still have a long way to go." Abandoning my notes, I stared out the window again.

My skin prickled with goosebumps despite thick sunbeams streaming in through the glass. "We need to figure out who this is and see them arrested before they have a chance to deliver strike three."

"Strike three's not happening," Eli said. His quick glance in the rearview mirror was followed by a growl of satisfaction. "Perfect. Knew we could count on Jax."

"What did he do?" I darted a glance over my shoulder, noting just Jax's SUV behind us, the maroon Toyota gone. "Did he drive the other car off the road?" The latter was a joke to loosen the apprehension lingering in the air.

Eli's stoic face gave away nothing. "He took out their tire."

I gaped at him. "He shot at the car?"

When Eli chuckled, I smacked his shoulder.

"The vehicle turned off onto another road," he said.

"Must've been going in the same direction we were all along. At least until now."

"They were following us."

"Maybe." Or maybe not, his dry tone suggested.

I had complete confidence in his abilities. Truly. But that didn't make it any easier to set aside my anxiety. "I know what you must be itching to say to me."

He cocked one eyebrow my way, and his eyes gleamed. "Oh, you do, do you?"

"You think I should chill out, leave all of this to you and Jax, and enjoy the conference."

"Not quite."

"Really."

"I do hope you'll trust me and Jax to keep you safe, though we need your participation as well. You need to notify us if you see something unusual or suspicious. We can't do this alone. We're a team and you're a full member."

Hmm. "Okay. I can do that."

"But that isn't all I was thinking."

I turned to face him again because his voice had gone husky, making me eager to watch him while he spoke. His sexy tone, combined with his darkening eyes, made me want to tug him back to my bedroom and stay there a good long while. Add to that how he looked with his tight haircut courtesy of Ginny and his button-up shirt topped with a casual yet perfectly tailored blazer.

I was so lost in him, I'd never be found.

"What *were* you thinking?" I asked.

His gaze traveled down my legs. "About those fuckin' heels."

I tilted my foot, posing as I smiled at one of my favorite indulgences. I might live in yoga pants and flip-flops much of my free time, but when I kicked things up, I splurged. Nothing beat four-inch red bottoms. "You like my shoes?"

"I do. I keep picturing them...You..." He cut off with a groan.

"Picturing them..." My brow cleared as I got an ah-ha moment. "I think I understand."

"You do?" The hint of a squeak in his voice suggested vulnerability.

A muscular, physical guy like Eli could intimidate whoever he pleased. Knowing that something growing between us brought out his softer side thrilled through me like a double shot of tequila. It made me drunk on him, and it created an answering need in my soul.

But I did like to tease and this presented a prime opportunity. "I assume you intend to stay in my room."

A long pause followed as he shifted the Jeep into a lower gear to take us to the top of an extra-steep hill. We coasted down the other side, winding our way into a heavily-wooded valley. "Staying in your room tonight is the best way to protect you."

"I'm all about avoiding that third strike. But when I booked my room, I requested a king-sized bed."

"I'm relegated to the sofa, then." He sounded resigned.

"I think we need to share the bed."

His fingers tightened on the steering wheel. "Like last night."

"Well..."

The GPS chimed, directing us to turn off the main road onto a smaller route. Eli drove about a mile with Jax right behind then turned the Jeep onto another paved road that climbed a small mountain in a switchback pattern.

Since his attention needed to remain on the twists and turns in the road, I held off finishing my thought. A bombshell, I wanted to deliver it while he was solely focused on me.

Our vehicle emerged from the tree-lined road to find the hotel perched on the peak ahead of us, surrounded by sloping lawns peppered with oval gardens overflowing with colorful flowers. Behind us spread the valley and beyond the hotel, taller mountains rose almost to the clouds. Ski trails —green this time of year—snaked down the mountains in grassy ribbons.

"I feel like we've stepped into a scene from a Stephen King novel," Eli said as he slowly approached the entrance of the dark, grim structure.

"Is it the rough black granite exterior or the towers that give you that impression?"

"I think the towers are supposed to make it look like a castle."

"Not doing it for me. I'm thinking of horror films, too." Some might consider the creepy setting intriguing but after what I'd been through recently, the ambiance gave me the chills. "How about we tell ourselves it's the setting for one of your Disney movies?"

"Then I should be singing about letting it go." His smile made me join in, though I didn't get the joke. "Aww, come on. Elsa? She's a queen."

Must be a favorite character. "If she's royalty, I'm in. Just call me Queen Elsa."

"Cool. I always did think Elsa was hot."

"Hot? We're talking Disney princesses here, right?"

Taking my hand, he squeezed it. "No, we're talking about you."

That made my heart flip. But, then, just about everything this man said or did made my heart flip. It was a wonder my head wasn't cartwheeling along with it.

Actually, it was.

He drove up to the broad entrance and parked his Jeep underneath an enormous stone and stained-wood awning.

A valet dressed in a red jacket with black buttons topping dark pants and shiny shoes strode up to my door and opened it. Half bowing, he flicked his hand toward the entrance. "My Lady."

Rolling my eyes, I stepped out and turned to watch Eli round the front of his Jeep and join us. His grin held secrets only I could understand.

Excitement about the creepy location.

Questions about my king bed comment.

Affection for me.

And humor about the guy calling me My Lady. Maybe this *was* a fairytale setting.

Jax pulled up behind Eli's Jeep and got out. "Some place, huh?" he said, handing his SUV keys to a second valet who hustled around the vehicle to the driver's side. "You two go inside." Jax's flinty gaze swept the span of lawn sloping away from the front of the hotel and the thick, snarled hedges looming on either side of the awning. "This is too indefensible. Too...insecure."

Did he think someone would rush at us with guns blazing while we stood out in the open?

Shivers rippled across my skin, and I fidgeted from one foot to the other. My sexy, Eli-inspired mood fled, leaving only spiraling apprehension behind.

"Our cases are in the back of the Jeep," Eli told the valet, handing over the keys with a folded bill.

"I'll get them right away, Sir, and bring them inside." He handed Eli a luggage receipt. "Give this to the front desk when you check in, and they'll get someone to bring your bags to your room."

"Thanks." Eli took my hand. "Let's get you inside, honey."

We crossed the broad, high-ceilinged foyer with chandeliers highlighting ornate, golden trim and paintings of stern old white men hanging on the walls, to the front desk. I gave the concierge my name and Eli handed her the luggage receipt.

"Ah, Doctor Crawford," the woman said. Her tag read, *Suzie. How can I help you?* She squinted at the computer screen. "I see the Juniper Foundation gave you a complimentary upgrade to a suite. It's in one of the towers. Lucky you! There are only seven rooms in each tower, one per floor. Fortunately, while the north tower is fully occupied, the south—where your suite is located—isn't, so it'll be extra quiet. It has a great view. The room's enormous. And it even has a large, in-room jacuzzi." Her suggestive look took in Eli standing beside me.

Naturally, my mind immediately shot to us sitting in the jacuzzi. Naked. Then moving to the bed... I was getting ahead of myself. We needed to talk about where this—we— were going before testing that jacuzzi, let alone the bed.

I wanted to tell her that if my life wasn't in danger, he wouldn't be here. I'd be sitting in that jacuzzi alone.

However, the predatory interest Suzie showed Eli sparked a feeling I'd never experienced before: jealousy. Which was silly because Eli wasn't mine. He may never be mine.

And maybe that was why I felt jealous.

"That's really sweet of the Foundation," I said. The moment I saw Peter, I'd have to thank him, though I suspected Brianne, his assistant and a friend, might've played a big part in this.

"You two are sharing the suite?" Suzie asked, her gaze gliding down what she could see of Eli.

I linked my arm through his and beamed up at him. "Hear that, sweetie?" I winked. "We've got to try out that jacuzzi tonight."

So, I might be laying it on thick, but I couldn't help it. My eyes *were* green.

Gaze blazing hotter than a rampant brush fire, Eli leaned in close to my ear and murmured, "Only if you promise not to wear flannel."

"Actually," I whispered. Time to drop that bomb. "King bed and...I didn't bring a nightie."

He gulped, and "fuck" hissed past his lips. I snickered while his body went rigid. "You..."

"Me?" I said coyly. This wasn't a true tease because I fully planned to deliver.

"I keep saying it," he said softly, partly turned away from the clerk to ensure only I could hear. "You are so going to get it."

"You promise? Because I can't wait."

He cleared his throat and tugged on his shirt collar before leaning his elbow on the swirling marble counter surface. "Let's get this show on the road, then, shall we? I'm eager to check out that...jacuzzi. But first, our associate," he nudged his head toward Jax, who loomed behind us like the bodyguard he truly was, "needs a room near ours. Next door if possible."

"Oh," Suzie burst out. Leaning around Eli, her smile grew even bigger as she took in Jax. "The tower rooms are on individual floors, so I won't be able to put him next to your suite unless I move you back to the main hotel."

"Anything on the floor above or below?" Eli asked.

"Let me see." Clicking on her computer, she nodded.

"The suite below yours is free." She peered at Jax. "Name, sir?"

"Jackson Ramsey," he said in a deep voice, strolling closer.

Being flanked with two hot guys made my pulse soar. In their tailored jackets and pants, they resembled James Bond on steroids. I swore I could see Suzie's heart fluttering, and the glance she shot me contained pure envy.

"Yes. Okay," she said, staring at her computer. "I *can* put Mr. Ramsey in the room below yours. Will...you be alone, Mr. Ramsey, or is someone joining you?"

"I'm by myself." He stalked right up to the desk, his face completely neutral. As if he didn't hear her innuendo let alone see the interest in her eyes. It was clear he did not understand the impact his presence had on women, let alone Suzie. "This room have a king bed? Because I like to stretch out."

"A king bed, yes." Head bobbing, her cheeks pinkened. "All by yourself? Now, isn't that a shame. And you're here for the conference, as well, I assume?"

He grunted affirmation and turned away from her. His attention passed over me to the woman standing off to my left and he nudged me close enough to Eli our sides brushed, as if he needed to ensure he could thrust himself between me and the woman if she spontaneously pulled a weapon. Considering her cane supported her substantial limp and her blue-gray hair and wrinkles told me she had to be at least eighty, it was doubtful she'd present much threat. But I appreciated that he took this job seriously.

No wonder Flint had hired Eli and Jax. These guys must be dynamite on any assignment.

"Are you a doctor like Doctor Crawford?" the woman asked Jax, pulling his attention back her way.

"No, I'm her—their"—humor filled his dark blue eyes when they slid to Eli—"bodyguard. He's arm candy."

Eli scowled but the gleam in his eyes told me he didn't mind the tease.

"Oh!" She fanned her face. "You're much cuter than the bodyguard in that movie." Her quick cough was covered with her hand. "Sorry. I didn't mean to get personal." Sure. With a stiffened spine and smoothed face, she handed us our programmed keycards, projecting a more businesslike manner. "Can I do anything else for *you*?" Her gaze remained on Jax. "Or,"—she coughed again—"Or, yes, for Doctor and Mr. Crawford?"

Eli grinned. "I believe we're all set. Thanks."

Suzie's slender shoulders thrust back. "Here's my card." She slid it across the marble surface toward Jax. "You need anything at all, and I mean anything. At any time. Call me."

Nothing like good customer service. I chuckled as red suffused Jax's chiseled cheeks, leading me to believe he'd finally picked up on her interest. Really. At this rate, Haylee could strut around in front of him naked and he'd take ten minutes to notice.

"We'd like to sign in for the conference," I said to Suzie. "Where is it being held?"

"The Foundation has booked the top floor of the main hotel. Gorgeous view of the valley and ski areas from up there." Standing, she leaned across the counter, pointing to a bank of elevators at the back of the foyer. People bustled around, some pulling rolling luggage, others striding toward the entrance. A few sat on the plush furniture reading books or scrolling on their electronic devices. "You'll find the conference on the sixth floor. There are signs pointing the way, but you can't miss it."

"Perfect," I said. "Thanks."

"I'll have the bellhop bring your luggage to your rooms."

We rode the elevator to the sixth floor and, upon exiting, walked over to the full wall of glass encasing one wall to take in the view. In winter, everything would be covered with snow and the valley must resemble a scene from the North Pole in a Christmas movie. Shades of every variation of green carpeted the landscape this time of year, interspersed with splashes of colorful flowers. Palatial houses dotted the hillsides on the opposite side of the valley, and the small mountain that housed the hotel sloped gradually downward, the lush surface broken by crushed stone walking paths, a gazebo, and fountains shooting blue-tinted water into the air.

"Look! A moose," I said, my eyes wide. Hard to believe, but one actually stood on the front lawn munching on grass, seemingly oblivious to the people pointing and snapping photos.

"Haven't seen one of those in years," Jax said.

"If you drove around looking, you wouldn't find one. But they'll stroll onto your lawn when you least expect it," Eli said.

Leaving them to the panoramic view, I approached the conference registration desk.

"Mia!" Brianne, the Foundation President's assistant, rose and zipped around the desk to give me a big hug. "How you doin'?"

I grinned. "Great. You?"

"Fine."

"Thank you for the upgrade. We haven't been to the room yet but I imagine it's going to be awesome. I feel like a princess." Disney or otherwise.

Her eyes sparkled. "Knew you'd appreciate it, and Peter said you needed a treat."

I swept my hand toward the literature lying on the smooth surface. "I see Peter roped you into working registration today."

"Yeah." Her full lips twisted, and she tugged on one of her dark braids. "The guy we hired quit. Something about suddenly needing to move to Florida." Her pretty face stilled. "But we haven't talked since you got back. Are you okay? I heard about what happened in Mexico. You must've been terrified."

"How did you find out?" I'd told no one about the incident except Flint and even then, I'd stuck with the robbery lie, not revealing anything about the man who'd died in my arms, let alone the bearded guy who'd chased me.

"How *did* I find out?" Her tweezed eyebrows furrowed. "Can't remember. Maybe from Peter?" She shrugged. "Or online? I'm not sure."

Online? I'd be stupid to post anything about the incident on social media. Drawing attention to what happened was the last thing I wanted to do.

Brianne shook her head, making her braids sway across her back. On chunky heels, with the slit in the back of her tight skirt flicking on her thighs, she returned to her seat behind the broad desk. She lifted a packet, extending it toward me. "Here's your stuff. Your lanyard's inside, as is a schedule, though I'm sure you know when you're speaking this afternoon. This isn't your first rodeo; you know the routine."

I'd spoken at two other conferences for the Foundation in the past, in different locations.

I nudged my head toward Eli and Jax. "The guys are my guests. I notified Peter this morning that they were coming."

"Of course." Brianne handed me badges they could pin to their chests. She nudged her head to her right. "Lunch is informal. You know how Peter is about appetizers being enough for a full meal. But I put my two cents in and he agreed to endless champagne." The sound of clinking glass and murmurs of conversation drifted toward us. "We've commandeered the smaller ballroom, saving the larger one for tonight's more formal event." Rising again and coming around the desk, she leaned in close to me. "Either of the guys single? Because..." She grinned and shook her hand as if it had been scorched. "Whoa."

"Umm, no." Maybe? I mean, neither of them was officially with anyone. Although, I had high hopes for Haylee and Jax. And Eli...Well, I had very high hopes for Eli and me.

"Girl!" Her elbow nudged my side. "You go."

"Oh." I blinked. "The three of us are not...well, only Eli's with me." Sort of. I spoke with a voice I strained to keep from sounding possessive. There went my green eyes again. "But Jax..." This felt disloyal to Haylee, but it wasn't as if my cousin and Jax were a couple. "Jax, the slightly shorter guy, if six-two can be considered shorter, is single."

"Lovely," she said. "Maybe you'll introduce me later?"

Magnet Jax, meet metal once again. How could a guy so hot be this oblivious to his attraction? It was one of the ten mysteries of the world.

"Sure." After attaching my lanyard around my neck, I nudged my head toward the hall where my on-stage appearance awaited me. My cheeks were going to ache from smiling within fifteen minutes. "See you in a while, then?"

Brianne winked at me, but her attention was fully on Jax. "One second after the last guest has registered."

I laughed and crossed to the window to give the guys their badges. "Ready?"

"Always," Eli said.

"Then, let's go." I linked my arms through theirs and we strode down the hall. "First up, the smaller ballroom for some mingling during lunch. It's casual, appetizers."

Jax grimaced. "Appetizers? Like, little tiny bite-sized bits of food? I'm famished."

"Just snag something whenever a server passes, and you might take the edge off your appetite by midnight."

"Where's a good steak and potatoes when you need them?"

"At dinner?" Though, if I knew Peter, the Foundation would serve something he considered more refined than the hungry man twosome.

Jax came to a full stop. "You didn't say ballroom, did you? You know I'm an informal kind of guy. I'm not good with chit-chat."

No one would ever accuse Jax of being too talkative. He epitomized tall, dark, and extra silent. With a hefty dose of brooding thrown in on the side.

"You're going to do fine." Was he suggesting he hadn't attended an event this size before? I knew he was shy because it had taken more than a few batches of cookies for him to squeak out a gruff thanks in my direction, but this was a little extreme. Hopefully, he'd feel okay once he'd gotten inside and could see what he was dealing with.

He slapped his jacket with both palms. "Despite the borrowed duds, I'm not exactly high-class."

"You look awesome."

His shaky grin slipped out. "You think so?"

See? Totally unaware of his appeal. "Totally awesome."

As we continued down the hall, his demeanor grew stiffer. "What are we dealing with here, anyway? Twenty, thirty people? Will anyone be armed?"

I blinked. "This isn't a hostile foreign country. While I'm

stressed about what might happen next, I don't think strike three will come from this group. These are wealthy donors, not assassins. Bringing two bodyguards with me feels like overkill."

"Whoever's after you knows you," Eli said. "They've studied your routine. You attending this conference isn't a secret. If they're smart, they'll find a way to infiltrate the event."

Infiltrate. As if this was a warzone.

"I know almost everyone here," I said to reassure him. "And I trust them with my life." Not that it would come to that. The philanthropy network was smaller than anyone thought and they came because of their generous spirit, not to eliminate the person seeking their donations. "We're talking two hundred, maybe three hundred people."

Jax's lips thinned. "Great. Just great."

I patted his arm, feeling sad that he appeared stressed. While I was confident he could handle this job no matter what we found inside, I hated seeing him upset. "This is the smaller ballroom. Tonight, the bigger event will be held in the large ballroom but it'll be with the same guests." Plus a few who always arrived late due for various reasons. At events like this, there were always stragglers. But he seemed concerned enough already without adding that detail.

Jax nodded, his gaze locked on the door ahead of us. "Let's do it. A few hours and we're out of here, right?" All color had blanched from his face.

Taking his arm, I hugged it. It was never easy striding into a new group, projecting a confidence you didn't feel. "We can take a short break before dinner, but eight, ten hours tops."

His hand reached underneath the back of his jacket where I knew he must keep a weapon. Color returned to his face, suggesting he found comfort in grounding himself in the job, rather than the situation. "All right, then. I'll deal."

We reached the end of the hall and a sign on an easel indicated we were in the right location. A man in a red and black outfit like the valet's opened one of the gilded, two-story doors. "Welcome," he said with a wave to the interior.

Eli and I strode inside, my heels clicking on the glossy marble tiles. Jax followed, grumbling about escaping as soon as possible. Then adding how he hated fancy schmancy events and ties and that he was going to stand out like a pink kitten in a wolf den.

Inside, men and women dressed in their daytime best chatted in various sized clusters. The *small* ballroom could probably hold five-hundred people and, to my surprise, it looked to be at near capacity. Kudos to Peter and the Foundation for drawing such a large group to this isolated location.

A bit more people than I'd expected, but, other than to Jax, this was awesome. More opportunities for me to network and solicit donations.

I snagged a flute of champagne from a passing tray suspended at chin level by a server and peered around while taking a sip of the bubbly refreshment.

Eli rested his palm on my lower back, and Jax hovered on my other side.

As a mix of both introvert and extrovert, I was happy to get out of the house and interact on a regular basis, but I equally savored playing the recluse. Today, my extrovert would need to shine.

Passing on the champagne, Jax and Eli prowled around me like starved panthers until I lifted my eyebrows and waved for them to back off. To work the room for the Foundation, I needed access to someone other than them.

With a quick nod at Eli that must be part of a secret, silent exchange I'd somehow missed, Jax rushed toward the main entrance. Bailing already?

When his lips moved without making much sound, and his finger traced a small, flesh-colored device snugly planted in his ear, I realized splitting up was part of their plan. A device in Eli's ear matched. Jax leaned against the wall beside the entrance and crossed his arms on his bulky chest, glaring at anyone who came within five feet of him.

"I'll remain with you," Eli said softly. "Jax will do ongoing reconnaissance but keep within shouting distance."

Reconnaissance. "This isn't an embassy in a hostile country."

"Just doing my duty, my lady." His eyes gleamed, and he leaned near. "Later, I'm happy to turn back into your arm candy."

That brought out my laugh. I savored the heat building between us, knowing that eventually, my job here would be over and we could be alone.

Eli stilled, staring past me.

A man dressed in a custom-made suit came over and gave me a hug and a quick kiss on the cheek.

"Mia, Mia," Peter said. "Delightful to see you. You have something to drink?"

Smiling, I lifted my glass in a toast. "Lovely event already, Peter. Congratulations."

He tapped my arm. "You know I owe it all to Brianne. She could organize this conference in her sleep."

"She's wonderful." I sipped my champagne. "Thanks for the room upgrade, by the way."

"You're welcome." He braced my forearms with his hands and beamed down at me. "You know how much I appreciate your efforts."

"Speaking of which, I'm looking forward to my presentation."

"And I'm looking forward to hearing you speak." He tossed a quick look over his shoulder, toward the enormous stone fireplace centered on one wall with two-story windows flanking the sides. "I realize you just arrived, but Janice Bennington is here. Brianne somehow worked miracles and talked her into dropping in by helicopter from Boston this morning. Since you've been so successful with her in the past, I'll leave her to you."

In other words, *could you go talk with her now?* I chuckled. "I'll do my best."

"This must be one of the friends you added last minute?" Peter asked, slanting his attention at Eli.

"Yes." I slid my hand around Eli's waist and introduced them, and they shook hands.

"I hope you enjoy the event." Peter lifted his arm and called out, "Cordelia!" He added to me, "Gotta fly. Schmoozing awaits."

"See you later," I said as he hurried away.

Time to start my own version of schmoozing. I needed to do my part to ensure the financial success of the Foundation.

After another fortifying sip of champagne, I tucked my arm through Eli's. "My first opportunity to shine is standing with her husband beside the fake, unlit fireplace. The infamous Janice Bennington."

"The older woman using the server's platter as a dinner dish?"

"Jax would approve, I imagine. Her husband, Thurston, is beside her, but she's the powerhouse in their relationship." We started in that direction and I lowered my voice. "Old money. Big money. Part of the one-percent." In my mind, I rubbed my hands together. In reality, I leaned into Eli's side, enjoying sharing this moment with him. "Just watch me in action."

Eli's palm tickled down my back to the bottom of my spine. "I don't believe I'll be able to take my eyes off you for one second."

The feeling was mutual.

"Janice," I said warmly as I approached.

"Doctor Crawford!" The slender woman turned briefly to the stout man at her side. "You remember Doctor Craw-ford—Mia—don't you, Thurston? She stopped by our home a few months ago, before she left for her mission in Mexico. It was wonderful to see her."

Thurston dipped his head. "Nice to see you again, Doctor Crawford. Enjoying the summer weather?"

"Yes. It's been humid but the AC makes it bearable," I said. "But who could be upset with a little humidity in this gorgeous location?" I swept my hand toward one of the tall windows that framed a stunning view of the ski area behind the resort.

"It's not the Hamptons," Thurston said. "But it has its own quaint charm."

"I can't wait to hear your presentation," Janice said to me. "I'm beyond thankful I've able to make a difference, even if only for a few poor souls. I'm sure you plan to high-light my contribution?"

"The mission would've been impossible without your support. We—the Foundation and I, that is—are grateful for your kind generosity. As are the women served by your ongoing donations."

Beaming, Janice turned to Thurston. "I was recently telling my husband that I'd like to double my—"

"Lemon Tahini Crostini?" A tall server thrust a tray

between us. His gaze drifted to me. "The head of the Foundation specifically asked me to make sure you sampled them before anyone else."

Janice's ring-bejeweled fingers darted out, and she snatched one up and popped it into her mouth. Closing her eyes, she wiggled and sighed as she chewed. Her throat worked with her heavy swallow.

"Ma'am?" the server said pointedly while tipping the tray toward me. His gaze drifted around the room as if he was scoping out who to tempt next. "Would you like a Crostini?"

Why not? If I didn't eat something, the champagne would go right to my head. "Thanks." I lifted the tidbit and popped it into my mouth. A burst of lemon was followed by—

"I adore smoked salmon, don't you?" Janice snatched up two more of the treats.

Salmon? Fish!

Sputtering, my free hand flailing, I spat the Crostini onto the floor then took a big gulp of my champagne. After swishing vigorously, I shot the liquid toward the fireplace. It hit the rough granite blocks on one side and splattered a woman dressed in a bright blue cocktail dress standing nearby. She squeaked and stumbled backward, her arms spiraling. Her champagne glass crashed to the floor, adding more spraying liquid to the mix.

Janice reeled away from me, disgust cratering her face. "What are you...?"

The server pivoted, nearly sending the Crostini tray spinning into the crowd like a sterling frisbee.

"Mia?" Eli's voice rose in alarm, and his arm tightened on my waist. "What's wrong?"

"Fish!" I moaned, swilling more champagne and spitting

it toward the fireplace again. "I'm allergic to fish." I lowered the empty glass onto the mantel and clenched my fists against my head. I couldn't focus on anything except my breathing. My pulse. Both galloped too fast. Was I having a reaction already?

"Fuck," Eli shouted. He ripped away from me and bolted toward the server, who was racing for the door.

Flinging himself forward, he tackled the man.

They slammed onto the polished marble tiles.

14

ELI

Wrenching the server over onto his back, I took a good look at him. Hadn't seen the jerk before in my life.

Unaware of Mia's allergy, I'd watched in growing horror as she choked and grimaced, her face turning red. Someone had deliberately fed her something they knew might kill her, and I was going to crush the person responsible.

With two fists, I hauled the guy up to chin level. His body shook and his feet—suspended above the floor —flailed.

"You a friend of Russell's?" I shouted. Around me, people dressed in fancy clothing cringed. A few took photos or made recordings I feared would be flashing across social media with the hour. Too many people thrived on scandal.

The guy's fading sputter and florid face made me realize he'd be turning blue and slumping unconscious soon. When Jax stormed up beside me, his expression grimmer than a pastor at a funeral, I shoved the guy into Jax's waiting hands. "Hold him. Find out who sent him, who's responsible. Don't release him except to the police. I've got to go to..." I raced back to Mia who sat in a chair with Janice rubbing her shoulder and cooing for her to take deep breaths. The woman from the conference registration desk knelt by Mia's other side. Her tag said, Brianne. She stood when I approached.

My heart clawing its way up my throat, I slammed onto my knees in front of the woman I...Hell, yeah, I loved her. It would be easier to hold back the Mississippi River after a hurricane than my feelings for Mia. I took her hands. "You okay, honey? What can I do? Call a doctor?"

"I'll go find Peter," Brianne said as she hurried away.

"Call a doctor? Mia *is* a doctor," Janice said sternly.

"I don't need anyone," Mia choked out. She cupped her face in her hands. "I got rid of it in time."

"EpiPen. Do you need an EpiPen?" I asked, frantically looking around, hoping multiple pens would appear before my eyes.

"I'm going to be all right," she said. "I've only ever had a rash and...and some tightening in my throat...from seafood in the past. Pen's in my purse." Which sat on her lap. "Haven't ever needed to use it." When she lifted her face, her shimmering eyes met mine. "I carry it...in case the next reaction is serious."

This was serious enough to give me a heart attack. The thought of losing her sliced through my spine like razor wire.

"Can I help?" someone asked from behind me. "I'm a doctor."

"I'm okay, Joe," Mia said, glancing up at him. "Really."

"You sure?" He patted her shoulder and stooped down beside her. "Were you choking?"

"Allergy."

"Benadryl? I've got some in my room."

"Thanks, but I don't think I'll need it."

"Okay, then. Call me if I can be of any assistance." At her nod, Joe rejoined the crowd.

No rash I could see on Mia's face, arms, or the part of her chest revealed above her dress. "How's the throat? Any tightness or difficulty breathing?"

"Normal."

"Mia, I'm incredibly sorry," Janice said, her face pinching.

Mia patted Janice's hand that rested on her shoulder. "Not your fault. Once again, though, you've...saved someone's life. My life."

"Me?" Janice's face suffused with color, and she pressed her fluttering hand to her chest.

"If you hadn't said salmon, I might've swallowed before realizing what I was eating."

"Oh." Janice's voice quivered and her fingers stroked her throat. "You're right. I did save another life." Her pale blue eyes lit up. "Where's Thurston. Thurston!" Her arm thrust up into the air and she waved her hand to catch her husband's attention. When he turned, she rushed in his direction. "We need to call our bank. It's not too late to make that transfer to the Foundation." Pausing mid-flight, she beamed back at Mia. "I'll make the donation in your honor."

"Thank you," Mia said, and to me in a low voice, "I'm willing to do just about anything to help the Foundation, but eating fish in exchange for a donation is pushing my limit."

I couldn't hold back my chuckle, but it was filled with raw emotion. Standing, I swept her off her feet. "We're going to our room."

She clutched her purse to her chest. "Hot to try that jacuzzi?"

"Hell, yeah, but not until you're fully healthy and able to participate." I loved how close we teased to the truth, that we were thinking the same thing much of the time, guiding each other toward what I hoped would be something awesome. But right now, I could only focus on making sure she was all right.

She linked her arms around my neck and snuggled into my throat. "I really can walk, you know."

"And I really need to hold you." My gut clenched again at the realization of how horrifying this situation could have been. I could've lost her when I'd only just found her.

Jax joined us, bringing me to a halt as I'd started weaving through clusters of staring people. Some still chatted and drank, but the majority watched us like spectators straining against the yellow tape at a murder scene, eager to see evidence of the crime.

"You left the guy with the police?" I asked Jax. If so, they'd arrived quickly. Hotel security must've called them after I took the guy down to the floor.

Jax's lips tightened and he snarled. "Had to let him go."

"You're kidding me."

"Security showed up when I was questioning him. The guy said he didn't know about her allergy, that Peter told him to offer the tray to the lady standing by the fireplace. He thought that meant Mia. Security said it sounded like an honest mistake and not a crime. They didn't want to involve the police." Face filled with concern, he leaned around me. "You okay, Mia?"

"Yes," she said. "I'm feeling silly being held in Eli's arms in the middle of a crowded ballroom, however."

I had no intention of putting her down. As long as I created a fortress around her with my body, she was safe.

"The guy works for the caterer," Jax told me quietly,

scowling at a couple inching near, no doubt eager to obtain gossip. At his glare, they backed away. "I questioned the owner of the catering business, too. Said the server has been with her for only a short time but the references checked out."

Maybe there wasn't anything nefarious about this, but I couldn't shake the uneasy feeling chewing its way up my backbone. I'd only be able to relax when I got Mia home and locked behind her doors.

"So, he's free after nearly killing Mia," I said, disgust coloring my words.

"Hey"—she waved her hand at us—"not dead here. Alive and very much kicking."

"The catering manager said the perp has a history of problems with law enforcement, though he's kept out of trouble for eight months," Jax added quietly.

Perp. Jax had not named the server an innocent man, and I liked how he thought. Jax and I knew that until all the facts were revealed, you didn't trust anyone other than those in the inner circle.

The server had a history of legal problems, huh? More pieces to the puzzle, though lots of people made mistakes then straightened out their lives.

"Eli?" Mia said, her voice lifting.

"I want to question him myself," I said, peering around but unable to find the man. "Track him down again and hold him. Cuff him if you have to. Detain him until I can return from taking Mia upstairs and securing the location." Before I returned here, I'd rig a few things in our room that should keep trouble away. Wasn't leaving her vulnerable.

Jax grunted and started for the main entrance. "I'm on it, bro."

As I followed him at a slower pace, weaving around

people who wouldn't get out of the way fast enough, Mia tapped my arm. "Eli."

"Yeah, honey?"

"I can't leave. I've still got work to do. And I'm fine. I'm not having a reaction."

"I want you secure," I growled out.

"I'm not a bank vault," she grumbled. "Hauling me to the room and locking me inside behind whatever you can come up with on the fly will accomplish nothing. If someone wants me, they'll find a way to get me. You'll be down here while I'll be up there facing...whatever. Meanwhile, I've got to make my presentation. If I stay here, you can keep an eye on me." The last came out placating, making me realize how bossy I was sounding. Not how I wanted to behave.

Peter strode over and stopped in front of us, essentially blocking the exit. He swiped his dark hair back and straightened his suit jacket then brushed off the shoulders as if he'd just crawled through an obstacle course.

And I was the one who'd played tackle football with the staff.

"Mia." He patted her arm. "I'm truly sorry. I had no idea about the fish allergy."

If he was sorry, why wasn't he looking her in the eye? I shoved aside my niggling suspicion because it was groundless. Peter had worked at the Foundation for years. In fact, Flint had introduced Mia to Peter, who'd arranged all her medical missions. Hell, Flint's former fiancée had worked for one of the Foundation board members as a nanny. The Foundation—and Peter—couldn't be involved in whatever was going on with Mia.

"I'm partly to blame," she said with a shake of her head. A few of her soft curls had escaped her arrangement. They slid along my shoulder. "I always ask before eating anything but I've been scattered lately. I should've verified there was no fish before stuffing one into my mouth."

She must be hungry. We hadn't had anything to eat since breakfast and my belly was gnawing a hole through my spine.

"You friendly with Mia's ex?" burst out of me, directed at Peter, who flinched as if I'd stabbed him with a sword.

"Eli, please. Stop," Mia said. Acceptance filled her eyes, telling me she understood why I was determined to question everyone. But the twitch of her lips indicated she wasn't cool with my public examination of her friend.

Stiffening, Peter raked his gaze down my frame. "I assume you're referring to Mia's former partner, Russell?" He released a curt nod. "I do know him. Of him, anyway. Mia spoke about him a few times when they were still together."

I doubted she told him the horror stories she'd shared with me.

Mia tapped my arm. "Put me down, Eli. I mean it."

People around us stared, whispered, took pictures.

I'd bare everything inside me to protect Mia, but I didn't want to cause her embarrassment. Her face looked...normal. Flushed cheeks but that could be explained away by her recent distress. Her voice came out like it always had, not scratchy or hoarse, which might've indicated a looming reaction. She said she'd gotten rid of the fish in time.

Muttering about my worry for her, I lowered her gently onto her feet. Thankfully, she remained steady, though she clung to my hand. If even her pinky finger trembled, we were out of here.

She was right, I could keep a better eye on her here. We'd stay, but Jax and I would be even more hyper-vigilant than we'd been already.

"Thank you." She kissed my cheek, whispering by my ear, "You're the best. I don't know how I could've handled this if I'd been alone."

I took her hand and squeezed it, telling my inner defender to stand down. For now. Frustration burned through me like battery acid on my skin. Not with her but with this untenable situation. I hated Mia being out in the open like this. Each person who came up to her could be the one after her, and I wouldn't see it until it was too late.

"My presentation is in fifteen minutes," Mia said. Her upper teeth pressed down on her lower lip. "I need to get set up or I won't be ready."

"I assume it's all on a thumb drive?" Peter asked.

"Yes." Mia lifted her purse.

"Brianne made sure everything was ready. This will be seamless," Peter said. "All you need to do is go up to the podium, insert your drive in the computer, and you're free to begin. Your presentation will be displayed on the screen while you speak and you can scroll through your slides with the remote.

"You've eaten nothing since breakfast," I said. "Can we get you something before you speak?"

"That might be a good idea," she said.

"I'll handle this," Peter said. He lifted his arm to signal a server who rushed over, tray in hand.

The crowd around us drifted off like dust on a tailwind now that the drama was over. Most chattered in hushed whispers or went up to the bar for drinks.

"No fish here, correct?" Peter asked the server, scrutinizing the tray of appetizers.

"These are vegetable quiches," the server said with a smile. "Try one. They're delicious."

The offering looked like half-bites of scrambled eggs

with minuscule multicolored pepper chunks to me. I took one and popped into my mouth, chewing thoroughly, examining every feature before swallowing. "Tastes okay to me. No fish."

"You're...Okay." She chuckled. "Since I'm a queen, it appears I've now got a taster."

I'd take a bullet in the chest if it saved her. Stealing the tray from the server, I tilted it her way, waiting while she took one.

"I appreciate you looking out for me," she said with what looked like her heart in her eyes.

Did I dare hope she felt about me the way I felt about her? I wouldn't rush her. We'd been thrown together. Tension was mounting as the situation escalated. I knew my own heart and mind, but I'd give her the chance to either fall for me or...

Abandon me like everyone else had in my life.

The burning in my gut told me I needed to get over my father taking off when I was eight before it influenced my actions any further as an adult.

If Mia wasn't interested in me, it wouldn't be abandonment. It would be her exercising her right to her own future.

I'd show her how good we could be together and let her decide. Although, I never went into a battle I wasn't prepared to win. I was more than open to using all the persuasion I could muster.

She seemed to enjoy my kisses, my touch. I'd start there.

∼

WHILE MIA GAVE her PowerPoint presentation—spoken from a podium at the end of the ballroom and overseen by my bribed hotel security guard, I located Jax—and the server. But I wasn't able to get any more information out of him than my friend had. The guy honestly thought Peter meant Janice, he didn't even know Mia, let alone Russell, and he just wanted to get back to his job. Newly married, he needed the income.

I returned to the ballroom feeling more aggravated than relieved. Not with the guy who'd made an honest mistake as far as I could tell, but because Mia had again been thrust into a situation that could've caused her harm and I'd been unable to prevent it.

Something was going on here but I couldn't figure it out.

Mia finished to roaring applause, the crowd eating her talk up faster than the appetizers. While she smiled and took the last questions, a number of people rushed over to Peter, clamoring to make donations.

As much as I wanted to wrap her up in cotton to ensure no one could ever hurt her, it was clear her work was vital. This was about more than me or her or us.

Lives were at stake.

I was glad I'd curbed my jerk-like tendency to hide her away. She deserved this chance to make a difference.

Joe, the doctor who'd offered Mia help after she accidentally tasted the fish walked up to the podium and gave a presentation about his advances in alleviating pediatric malnutrition in Central America. Mia and I mingled with no further suspicious activity directed her way.

After the applause died down, Peter took his turn at the mike. "I've been told dinner is ready. If you're feeling as famished as me…" He chuckled and rubbed his belly.

Jax snorted in disgust. "Those little egg things were no more satisfying than eating a handful of popcorn."

Peter waited for the polite laughter to die down before finishing, "The caterers are excited to serve our meal."

Red-coated servers swept open sets of doors on the wall opposite the towering fireplace. The succulent scents drifting from the dining room made my belly perk up and rumble.

"I've been told our entire meal was crafted from organic, locally grown products," Peter said.

"Woods," Jax grumbled. "We're surrounded by nothing but freakin' woods. What? We eating toothpicks for dinner? I'm going to lose twenty pounds before morning."

Mia tapped his arm, doing nothing to hide her smile. "Behave and I'll send you home with cookies when we get back to Crescent Cove tomorrow."

Hopefully not my cookies.

"You can have all the cookies in my house except the white chocolate macadamia ones I made for Eli," Mia added as if she'd read my mind.

I smirked at my friend.

"I'll try to be good," Jax said dryly, hanging his head. But his lips curved up.

We followed everyone else through the doors into the dining room, taking a table with three people Mia had spoken to earlier—from whom she'd obtained a generous donation.

While Mia expounded further about her recent mission in Mexico and the patients she'd worked with there, the first course was placed in front of us, a tiny plate with an even tinier serving of lacy, multi-colored greens flanked by three minuscule tomatoes.

Jax, sitting on Mia's other side from me, groaned.

I tucked into my salad, sharing his sentiment but knowing I was wiser not to speak up. I really didn't want to sleep on that sofa.

Some sort of lamb dish with more vegetables and a few

slender potatoes was brought out next, fortunately, accompanied by baskets of piping-hot rolls Jax and I slathered with butter and consumed until nothing but crumbs remained.

Somewhat sated, I'd settled back while they cleared the plates, my arm lying across Mia's shoulders, when Jax's voice came through in my ear. "Ten-o-clock. By the door."

The server who'd offered Mia fish stood alone, intently studying the guests.

Not suspicious all on its own. After all, he worked for the caterer and the crew appeared busy. On duty tonight, he could be awaiting direction.

A bearded man joined him and they partly turned away from us to speak, their positions making it impossible to read their lips. Was the other guy also one of the catering crew? The jeans and tee he wore said otherwise. He couldn't be part of the conference crowd or he'd be dressed to the hilt, like us.

The bearded man glanced our way, and I swore his gaze narrowed in on Mia.

I sat forward, poised for whatever might come next.

My belly twisted when Peter joined them.

15

MIA

"Something's up," Eli said softly beside me.

Was he speaking to Jax via that earbud thing or to me?

"What?" I asked, waving away the chocolate torte a server offered. Finished with food for the evening, I dropped my cloth napkin on the table.

"Want me to check it out?" Jax's attention remained focused on the entrance to the ballroom, not on the enticing dessert the server placed in front of him. Totally not in character. My skin prickled with unease, and I squinted in the same direction but saw nothing unusual.

Back to us, a guy in a tee and jeans hurried out into the main hall. Peter stood speaking with a few guests at a table near the exit, his face alight, his hands braced on their shoulders.

The server who'd accidentally given me fish ducked through a doorway that must lead to the kitchens.

"Let's…" Frowning, Eli trailed off.

Peter strode up to the podium mounted on a small stage at the end of the room.

"On it." Jax stood. He wove around tables at a near run, aiming for the exit to the hall.

Peter tapped the mike, redrawing my attention. "I hope you all had enough to eat. I've been told there's more food available. No need to go to bed starving."

A few people chuckled.

"Before we take a short break to get ready for the final event of the evening, the grand ball, I wanted to thank all of you for coming, for giving so generously of your time and"—he faked a cough—"for opening your wallets." His smile greeted the laughter. "Special thanks to Doctors Mia Crawford and Joseph Splain for their stunning presentations. But while our volunteer medical staff have worked hard to provide quality healthcare to people in third world countries who would otherwise go without, their success is only possible because of your generosity. I, and everyone else working at the Foundation, thank you from the bottom of our hearts."

Nods from people around me acknowledged his words.

Peter left the podium and moved through the room, stopping to speak to the guests.

Eli stood abruptly, his dessert untouched, his attention directed toward where Jax had rushed from the room.

"What's up?" I asked.

"Nothing."

"Eli," I growled. "We've been over this before. Don't keep things from me."

His weighted look took in the others at our table who watched our exchange raptly. "How about we go to our room?"

My heart flipped even though I knew he only meant we could get ready for the ball, not strip and jump into the jacuzzi, let alone the bed. Still, my pulse flamed already at the possibilities the end of this evening could bring. I ached to see where our relationship could be heading. I needed to know if there could be more to us than a few kisses.

Bold of me to offer myself to him so soon, but I couldn't help it. I was falling hard and fast for this man.

"Okay, let's go." Smiling to the others at our table, I said, "Will we see you later at the ball?"

"Yes, I look forward to it," one woman said and the others nodded while eating their dessert.

Rising, I took Eli's hand, and he hustled me toward the hall. When we left the dining room, my smile dropped, and I shook my head. "While I'd like to think your sole interest in rushing me from the dining room is to get me alone, I have a feeling there's more to this than that jacuzzi." Like, something involving Jax and his own flight from the dining room.

Backing me against the wall, Eli took both my hands in his and leaned in close. His breath heated my ear. "I *am* curious about that jacuzzi."

Everything inside me tingled. But he was avoiding giving me an answer again. "Eli. Tell me what's going on."

He kissed my jawline, my neck, and my collarbone. "Jax is just checking out a few things."

Jax? Who was that? I could barely think, let alone remember what we were talking about.

"Let's go to our room, okay?" he said. Before I could reply, he took my hand and ushered me down the hall to the elevators.

We stepped inside, facing each other. We'd need to ride down to the ground floor and then take the private, south elevator to reach our room at the top of the tower. "Since we'll be dancing, maybe I should take my heels off and wear flats to the ball?"

"Don't let my eagerness to see you wearing nothing but heels keep you from going with what's comfortable."

Flames licked through my veins as I pictured myself dropping back on the bed. Eli spreading my legs and stepping between them, lifting my heels up onto his shoulders.

My heavy gasp revealed my need. Damn, I was wet already and he hadn't even touched me.

All I could picture was his exquisite seduction.

"I...I..." Crap. I'd lost my train of thought again.

Nudging me backward until my butt met the wall, he dropped his mouth onto mine, capturing my breath, my lips, and my heart all over again.

I wrapped my arms around his neck and strained forward, pressing myself against his rigid, muscular frame.

The elevator came to a stop and the doors swept open, revealing the lobby. We burst apart like kids caught making out behind the bleachers in the high school gym, even though it didn't appear anyone was watching.

Eli's eyes—darker than sin—met mine, and I read a promise for tonight.

"This ball. How long before it's over?" Eli asked as we took the south elevator and then walked the short distance to our room.

"Too long."

He chuckled and squeezed my hand. "While I'm tempted to steal you from the Foundation for the rest of the night, I know how important this is to you. This is your chance to shine. I want you to celebrate your accomplishment. I won't hold you back."

"We could leave after a few dances. Sure, I could network until midnight if I wanted to, but I don't."

"Take the time you need. I can wait."

I wasn't sure *I* could wait. "I want to be alone with you," I confessed.

Eli sighed out my name.

Jax caught up with us, emerging from the stairwell located at the back corner of the short hall, breathing as if he'd taken the stairs all the way from the ground floor in ten seconds flat. He nodded at Eli. "My room's beneath yours. Five rooms below that, then the level with the lobby. We're dealing with a single elevator, two stairwells for egress—one on each end of the hall."

Eli opened our door and quickly scanned the room as I stepped inside. A huge king-sized bed dominated the center with acres of plush, pale blue carpet surrounding it like an ocean around a gorgeous, tropical island. Floor-to-ceiling glass panes spanned one wall and, in the valley below, lights twinkled like fireflies. The moon hung full above the mountain peaks, barely eclipsed by soft night clouds. On our right were two closed doors. The closet between them stood open and the gown I'd brought hung beside a zippered bag that must contain Eli's evening clothing. Our overnight bags had been placed at the foot of the bed, on the floor.

The jacuzzi, oval and empty, had been submerged partway into the floor in the center of the glass wall, inviting me to fill the tub with piping hot water then slip inside and enjoy the view.

Jax lounged behind me, against the open doorframe.

After checking out the rooms on my right—two bathrooms—and ensuring they were secure, Eli came over and squeezed my hand. "I'll only be a minute. Why don't you start getting ready while I speak with Jax?"

"Now would be a good time to tell me what you think is happening. Does it involve the server? I saw him speaking with another man, though I didn't see his face." I glanced back and forth between them but I might as well be trying to make Walter sing the national anthem than get an answer.

Without answering, Eli ducked into the hall, swinging the door shut behind him.

I tiptoed over and cracked it open enough to spy on their conversation.

"Nothing," Jax said. "The bearded guy works in maintenance. Said he's friends with the server. The caterer works here all the time and the two men often hang out together at the end of the day."

"Why did Peter speak with them, then?" Eli asked quietly.

Peter? My eyebrows flew up and I pressed my ear against the door crack, eager to hear more.

Jax grunted. "Said Peter asked him to leave. He didn't fit in with the guests."

"You believe them?"

Why wouldn't he? This sounded like nothing to be concerned about.

"No reason yet not to, but..."

Eli sighed. "Yeah."

Yeah, what? This conversation was taking me nowhere.

"Ball, huh?" Jax groaned out. "This is gonna be worse than standing on an aircraft carrier in dress whites, manning the rails while we pull into Subic Bay, Philippines. Too damn hot. Too damn muggy. And too many people. I'm sweatin' already."

"I appreciate the back-up."

"Mia okay?"

"Fine."

"We were fuckin' lucky."

"Yep," Eli growled. "I'm not letting her out of my sight until we've caught whoever's responsible for all this."

"No damn strike three."

"Not a chance."

"I'll change and be back fast," Jax said. "Let's get this over with. We can leave at the crack of dawn tomorrow, get her home where it's safe. Flint will be back soon and we can strategize about what we need to do next."

I couldn't leave early. Peter expected me to put in an appearance at breakfast and talk a few more sponsors into making bank transfers.

Feet shifted in the hall.

Leaping away from the door, I kicked off my heels and dashed over to my overnight bag. I had just enough time to lift it, toss it on the bed, and unzip it.

Eli shut the door as I turned and pushed a tangle of hair off my face. My smile wavered while embarrassment swept through me.

He leaned his back against the wall, arms crossed, a smirk on his handsome face. "Any questions or did you get all your answers a second ago from Jax?"

While I had plenty of questions, there were none he would answer. And I would not apologize for snooping. "Navy men. I rest my case."

Grinning, he sauntered across the room, not stopping until I was pinned between the mattress and him.

"We leave after one dance, right?" he murmured, kissing my neck. When he sucked my sensitive skin just above my collarbone, I moaned.

My spine tingling, I shivered with pent-up craving.

"Three dances?" I whispered.

His arms scooped around my back and he held me up as if he knew my legs could not support me. Which was completely true. His lips feathered along to that spot where my neck met my shoulder. "How about one dance?"

"What?" I blinked. "Oh, dances? I could probably sneak out after two."

His tongue trailed to the tops of my breasts straining against the scooped bodice of my dress, and he kissed one of the mounds. "One dance?"

"Half a dance," I squeaked out. "That's my final offer." If he released me, I could fall back on the bed and yank him down on top of me.

Chuckling, he tugged me away from the mattress and then stepped backward.

"Wait," I said frantically, my hands twitching. "We, um... have time for a quickie." One stoke of his fingers between my legs, and I'd scream.

Reaching around me, he lifted and chucked his case onto the bed before I could stretch out and claim the surface. Claim him. "No quickie. Once I start, honey, I'm not stopping for a very long time."

"But, but..." I really couldn't complain about that, now could I?

He crossed the room to the closet and unhooked my dress from the rod and dropped it over my arm. From my bag, he pulled my bathroom tote. "Anything else you need to get ready? There are two bathrooms which means we can dress at the same time."

"Um." I was totally flustered, unable to think of anything but tasting his skin. "I guess I need my make-up bag, too. Panties."

One eyebrow cocked up. "As much as I'd enjoy peeling it off you, how about skipping that lacy scrap of material you call underwear?"

"Go...without anything underneath my dress?" Wait. Peeling? I quivered.

But the idea of no underwear...so forbidden and tantalizing, had never appealed more. *We'd* know, but no one else would.

He nudged me toward the bathroom where he dropped my make-up bag and shower tote on the sink after removing them from my unresisting hands. My dress, he hung on the hook on the back of the door.

"I'll leave the underwear decision up to you," he said. He backed from the room and shut the door.

I essentially collapsed against the vanity and fanned my face. Hot damn. I didn't know whether to scream out my frustration or tell Eli that even half a dance was not necessary.

"Meet you out here in ten minutes," Eli said.

"Ten minutes? I'll need at least twenty."

"If you can do it in ten, you can model for me before Jax arrives. I'll be waiting on the bed."

16

ELI

My body rigid, I strode into the other bathroom, stripped, and stepped into the shower.

Double fuck. Even a blast of cold water wasn't enough to cool me down.

After toweling off, I dressed in my suit and combed my hair, grateful Ginny had cut it earlier.

I didn't know if I'd be able to keep this seduction going much longer without exploding but I sure as hell planned to try. When she'd offered a quickie, I'd had to clench my hands into fists and grit my teeth to keep from nudging her back on the bed, shoving her dress up, and driving myself all the way to the hilt.

Our first time needed to be perfect. Taking her like that, even if I made sure she came before me, would be a complete waste of something special.

If I hoped to win her heart, I had to give her everything tonight, not just a hasty tumble on the bed.

But, yeah, it was going to kill me.

Ducking out of the bathroom, I was grateful I'd beaten her into the room. Because I did want to keep the heat going between us. I needed to get her so hot and panting she couldn't think of anything but me.

I dropped onto the bed, lounging on a cluster of fluffed pillows, and kicked up my feet, hoping she'd come out before Jax showed up.

The bathroom door swung open.

No Mia.

Then her bare stretch of leg strutted into the air— showing off an awesome spiked heel.

Wearing a black silky dress, she swung partway into the room, hugging the doorframe with her hands, stroking them up the white painted trim. Her hips gyrated. My body...Fuck.

Humming a vampy tune, she pumped her hips, pursed her lips, and tipped her head back so her gorgeous, fiery hair dangled down her back.

What a freakin' tease.

The goal here had been to keep her heated up, not me.

While my jaw hung open, I watched with complete absorption.

Circling out into the room, Mia sauntered across the carpet and stopped at the foot of the bed, her hair a wild mess of curls around her face, her arms over her head, her eyes closed while she swayed.

Slits opened up each side of her floor-length dress, exposing enough skin some might consider the garment indecent.

A total turn-on for me.

Still humming, she swiveled her hips and slid her tongue across her lips.

"So, tell me," she said in a sultry voice while I sputtered and tried to maintain some sort of inner control. She sashayed around to the side of the bed and flicked her hand to her body. "Will this do?"

"You're gorgeous." Sliding off the bed, I circled her in what felt like a mating dance older than time.

Color rose in her cheeks, and her posture relaxed back into the Mia I knew best. I might beg for the vamp again before morning, however. "Thanks."

So much creamy skin available to touch. I ached to kiss my way from the arch of her foot strapped in the higher-than-sin heels, to the tops of her thighs. She spun and posed with her back to me, tossing a come-hither look over her shoulder. Dipping low, the silky black fabric hung in loose folds, exposing her spine to just above the crests of her awesome ass.

Her hair. Her glorious hair. Wearing it swept up earlier had added to her sophistication. Now, tickling across the bare skin of her back, it shouted pure siren. If only I could sink my face into the silky strands before tasting every speck of her hot body.

"Not bad, Eli," she said after giving me a full perusal. She flicked the collar of my white button-up shirt.

Not bad?

"Honey," I said, my voice scratchy and gruff. She'd stolen my heart, my wind, and my will to resist her.

But hell, *not bad*? I patted the front of my jacket and stared down. What was missing that would take me from 'not bad' to 'hot date' material for the evening?

"Aw, poor baby," she said with a pout. "Don't tell me you can dole out the tease but can't take it?"

"You are so going to get it," I growled, reaching for her.

She giggled and evaded my grip, backing toward the door. "Don't forget. You said no quickies." Her voice went high pitched as she mimicked. "Can't start something we can't finish, my dear." She propped a hand on her generous hip. "Besides, Jax might stroll in any minute. Don't want to give him the shock of his life."

I had a feeling Jax would understand.

Damn minx was going to drive me insane. She was wild. Insatiable.

I advanced toward her, ready to toss her onto the bed anyway, then follow, but Jax banged on the door.

"Guys," he said. "About ready?"

"I was just kidding, you know." Mia strolled closer to me, not stopping until our bodies brushed together. "You look incredible. Too damn sexy for my own good."

"I like that you think I'm too damn sexy because the feeling's mutual."

Her lips quirked up on one side. "What we're starting is special, isn't it?" Her voice came out bold yet hesitant, all at the same time.

I swept my arm around her waist and gave her a quick kiss. "*You're* special. Infinitely precious to me."

Jax banged. "Guys?"

She gulped and stared up at me with shimmering eyes. "Aww, I feel the same." Backing out of my embrace, she waved at the door, her voice croaky. "Better let Jax in before he breaks it down." Releasing a laugh, she wiped the corners of her eyes. "And before you ruin my make-up. I'm going to look like a raccoon if you keep up the sweet talk."

After stroking her cheek with my knuckles, I unlocked and swung open the door for Jax.

"Good, good. Was getting worried there for a minute." His gaze fell on Mia. "Whoa. Someone turned up the heat." He slapped my back. "I feel for you, dude. Tough night ahead."

I was up for it.

"Jax," Mia said, giving him a quick kiss on the cheek. "You look great."

"More than not bad?" I said with a smirk.

"I'm going to have to beat both the ladies and guys off tonight." She lifted her clutch. "Unfortunately, instead of a stick, I've only got this."

Dressed in an equally dark suit, my friend looked ready to walk down the red carpet at the Emmys with a model on each of his arms.

"We ready to head to the ballroom, then?" She winked at me. "I'm eager to get this started. The sooner I make the rounds and solidify a few more donations, then dance for half a song, the quicker my real evening can begin."

The jacuzzi. The king-sized bed. Me and Mia. All. Night. Long.

"Half a dance?" Jax tossed me a puzzled look. "We gettin' a reprieve?"

My body warmed at the thought of returning to our room where I'd slowly strip every bit of material off her body. Then I'd drape her across the bed and start at the bottom and work my way to the top. Or vice versa. I wasn't picky.

I roped myself in before I got so into the idea, I could think of nothing else. To protect her from all threats, I needed to remain alert and on guard.

"Early night, Jax," I said.

His tense expression eased. "Cool."

Looping her hand through my arm, Mia tugged me toward the door. "Come on!"

We returned to the floor the Foundation had booked and strolled to the ballroom, which was situated on the opposite side of the hall from the registration desk, and went inside.

While packing my suit, I'd worried I'd be overdressed. So not true. Jax wasn't the only one looking ready for the Emmys.

The ballroom for the evening event had to be twice the size of the other, and more people had arrived for what must be the biggest event this part of the state had ever seen. Clusters of people dressed in black, with a few splashes of red and silver, stood chatting, cocktails in hand.

We grabbed drinks, a dirty martini for Mia and soda water for me and Jax.

"I'll go lurk in the shadows," Jax said with what could be considered a smirk but probably represented relief. Dude obviously hated crowds. Our covert surveillance earpieces had been tuned to our own, private frequency and encrypted to ensure whatever we said couldn't be overheard by others. Anyone savvy enough to consider spying on us would only hear gibberish. It was vital that whoever was after Mia not know our next move until it had already happened.

"Before you do that, can I get you to stay a moment with Mia while I..."

Jax snorted. "Go to the bathroom?"

"Something like that." I gave Mia a quick nod and strode from the room. Out in the hallway, I made a phone call and then returned to the ballroom.

"All set," I told Jax, who retreated to his spot in the shadows, near the entrance.

My hand low on Mia's back, we made our way around the room. It was a pure joy watching her in action, using her friendly, slightly folksy manner with some potential donors, but switching it up to pure sophistication with others. She could read someone in seconds and knew just how to draw them out, make them feel as if they were the only ones who mattered.

Rivaling a goddess, she glistened more brightly than an emerald on a white satin surface.

I couldn't believe that she'd soon be mine even if it was only for one night.

"Three's a charm," Mia said eventually, holding my arm and leaning into my shoulder. "Only one thing left before we can blow this joint."

"The—"

"How about a dance?" Peter said, coming up behind us. His grin took us both in.

"Oh, sorry," she said, mischief filling her eyes. "But my dance card's full."

Peter's grin fled, replaced with a scowl, even though it was clear from Mia's light tone she'd been joking. "I thought we could...talk."

"How about next week?" She must've picked up on odd nuance in the air because a frown brewed on her forehead. "Call me anytime. I don't start my new job until after Labor Day."

"I wanted to discuss a few...things. Including your next medical mission."

Her fingers fluttered against the sides of her martini glass, and her gaze darted to the exit.

Tension spiked through me immediately. Why did his comment make her nervous?

"I can't go back to Mexico," she burst out.

"That, I don't understand." Peter pressed for a smile but it didn't come through in his tone or posture. "Let's dance and you can tell me all—"

"I'm happy to go anywhere else for my next mission, though we agreed I wouldn't be sent again until next year,

Mexico is not an option." Said with such finality, even I wouldn't argue.

Was this solely because of the robbery? She'd been terrified when I picked her up at the station, but she must know robberies could happen anywhere, even in sleepy Crescent Cove.

Peter's scowl only deepened, taking us both in, which made no sense. He had no reason to act this way with Mia, let alone me. It got my back up. Made me want to bluster between them, push him aside, then take her somewhere else.

"As Mia suggested, why don't you call her?" I said softly, barely restraining my ire. This conversation scraped like a fingernail along my nerve endings. The undercurrent of... something suspicious couldn't be denied. "How about that dance, now?" I said to Mia.

"I thought you'd never ask." Her smile came out shaky. Definitely something bigger going on here.

With a nod to Peter, I took her hand and led her over to the wooden dance floor where couples swayed to the 90s music played by a live, four-piece orchestra. Nothing beat a cello-violin version of a Backstreet Boys hit.

"That was a weird conversation," I said, sliding my arm around her waist. Feeling grateful Ginny had shown me the rudimentary elements of the waltz, I spun Mia across the parquet flooring as the cellos and violins spun, *I Want it That Way* seamlessly into *Quit Playing Games*.

Mia shrugged and lifted a fake smile to the couple swaying near us. "I'm not sure why it matters to Peter where I go next. I can help people anywhere."

"Why *are* you so opposed to Mexico?"

Stumbling, she righted herself with a hand on my shoulder. "It was a scary situation for me."

I hated pressing, but to defend her, I needed to know the full picture. She was hiding something. "The robbery?"

She gnawed on her lower lip then smiled brightly up at me. "Yes. The robbery." Her fingertips tickled across my neck, and she swayed closer. "Can we let it go? I want to focus on you."

So did I, but... "What aren't you telling me? What else happened in Mexico?"

Her breath sucked in. "Nothing. What gives you the idea I haven't been completely honest?"

The fact that she was staring past me, not making eye contact, for one.

"You'd tell me if someone hurt you, threatened you, whatever, right?"

A fake laugh burst from her. "Of course. But nothing did. It was a simple robbery. Well, other than the cut on my arm, but that come from...concrete. When I fell."

Simple robberies and falls on concrete don't keep people from returning to an entire country. What wasn't she telling me?

"Our half dance is done," she said with satisfaction. Her lips curled up in a real smile, and her voice deepened. "Can we go back to our room, now?"

I didn't want to let this go. If I could persuade her to tell me what was bothering her, I could fix it. But pushing this when she obviously didn't want to discuss it would only upset her further, the last thing I wanted to do.

My protective instincts dueled with my heart. I did want to take her to the room.

To shelter her. Show her how great we could be together. To love her.

Despite my unease with our conversation about Mexico,

the slow dance with her had built my anticipation for what might come next, once we'd returned to our suite.

Maybe, just this once, I could relax and leave Jax to handle the job. Then I could focus on the gorgeous woman in my arms. Short of a bomb exploding in the building, nothing could harm her while we were together.

"By the way, I...opted to go with something a little more intriguing," she said slyly.

I missed a step but recovered quickly, dipping her backward—because I could. And because her laughter trilled out, telling me it pleased her. "I have a feeling *intriguing* is going to just about kill me."

Lying in my arms, she grinned up at me. "I know you suggested no panties, but I opted for a thong."

We left Jax at his door and took the tower elevator ride up one floor to our suite, holding hands.

I should be nervous about this.

Someone wanted to do me harm, and Eli had stepped in to keep it from happening. Would we be together, let alone contemplating hooking up otherwise?

Unlike other bodyguard situations, we'd grown close fast and taken our relationship in a different direction.

Yet, we'd been friends first. Our attraction had heated up eight months ago, when we first met.

If I hadn't been burned by Russell and I'd told Eli yes instead of no back then, where would we be now?

Russell. The name sent anxiety racing through me, and I tensed. After what happened with him, was I foolish to let someone into my life again?

"You okay?" Eli asked when we stopped outside the room. "You're quiet." He teased one of my curls between his fingers. "You seem...hesitant. If you're not sure about—"

"I want this," I whispered. "I want you."

His knuckles stroked my cheek, and his voice deepened. "Then I'm yours. For as long as you want me."

What if I wanted him forever? For him, this could be a short-term thing, something to be savored before he moved on. While I...I was greedy. I wanted it all.

I gulped. "I'm scared."

"Russell."

"Maybe?" I glanced up at him, but his face gave nothing away. "He made me feel worthless. As if it was his right to do what he did, and I was wrong to feel he shouldn't. Too often, I took it because I believed I deserved it."

"Jeez, Mia, you're ripping my heart out."

"I only want it if it's freely given."

He pulled me into his arms. "Honey. You don't need to feel afraid. I'll never hurt you. I want you, for sure. But so much more."

Could he ever love me as I was starting to love him? Or would he hurt me? Not like Russel but in a different way. It wouldn't be on purpose, like with Russell's abuse, but it might sting just as bad.

Looking back, I had a hard time believing I'd truly loved Russell. My initial caring got tangled up with my need to please him at all costs to myself.

Eli pulled something new and exciting from deep inside me. If I handed him my heart and he eventually tossed it aside, it would devastate me. It would leave permanent scars.

"Loving someone doesn't have to make you vulnerable," he said.

But it did. It opened you up to hurt. Pain.

"I'm sorry I've turned this into something so solemn." Regret made my words come out jerky. "That was never my intent."

"It's okay. We're working through this together. I'm here for you. You tell me how you want me." He stepped back, releasing me. "We can take this as slow as you need."

"Eli," I said, then repeated his name until he looked at me, because he'd been staring over my head. The stark yet hopeful look in his eyes reached into my chest and severed something vital deep inside me. "I'm yours. However *you* want me."

Gathering me into his arms again, he held me a moment before leaning back to look down at me. "Let's go inside, huh?"

I nodded and took his hand.

He swiped the card over the lock and swung the door open. Following me inside, he shut the door but when I reached for the light switch, he stilled my hand. "Leave it? I set something up for you. Well, I hope you like it." His footsteps padded across the carpet, heading toward the wall of glass. A scraping was followed by flickering light that touched down one by one, slowly creating an oasis.

Candles encircled the tub, which had been filled with steaming water and...I crept closer. Flower petals floated on the surface.

My fingers were drawn to the pendant he'd given me. "They're..."

Returning to me, he stood close, breathing softly. "I know people would say I should've used fancy flowers like rose petals but somehow, daisies felt better." When I said nothing, he cleared his throat. "Is it too much? I don't want to push this." No mistaking the hesitancy in his voice. Was he worried I'd pull back from this, reject him?

If I shoved him away, I'd be denying myself.

"I love it. You did it for me." No denying my smile. This

man...Just when I thought I knew him, he did something that twisted my heart in a knot.

"If you want, you can get in. Sit back. Relax. There's wine. Enjoy it. I can...Sit on the bed."

I chuckled because... "Really. Sit on the bed? While I lounge in the jacuzzi and drink wine?"

I could feel his grin even if I couldn't see it. "I wouldn't mind if you shared the wine."

"What if I want to share the jacuzzi, too?"

"I'd say yes."

While scooped low in the back, my dress rose high in the front. It was simple to slip it off and step out of the soft, silky folds.

I not only wore the heels he'd seemed absorbed with, I'd also planned another surprise. Would he see it in the dimly lit room?

"Fuck," he breathed, and I could feel his gaze gliding down my body.

Nothing showed a woman off better than a black bra and matching thong and garter. I stepped briefly out of my shoes and unclipped my stockings, slowly inching them down my legs.

"Double fuck," Eli said. "You're..."

"Teasing?" I said. Turning, I purposefully bent forward and slipped my heels back on my feet.

He had said he was interested in seeing me wearing not much other than heels.

Groaning, his fingertips slipped down my bare butt cheek. "You're going to drive me out of my mind."

Feeling empowered, I sashayed around him, lifting his chin as I passed. "I think you're overdressed, Eli."

"You're right." He groaned again. The heat of his gaze

caressed my back as I walked toward the tub. "Fuck, Mia. You're burning me alive."

Everything inside me tingled. A heady thrill of anticipation told me this was going to be good. *We* were going to be good.

Tossing aside my heels, I stepped down into the tub. "What's taking you so long?" While I loved to tease, I was so going to get it. The thought of him being with me shot sparks all the way to the ends of my nerves.

He shrugged out of his jacket and slowly unbuttoned his shirt. From the quick of his lips, I got the feeling he'd regained his composure. While a vulnerable Eli made me ache to hold him, a confident Eli made me eager to yank him near and cover him with kisses.

While I settled onto a bench in the water and rested my arms along the sides, he stood beside the tub, staring down at me. "I don't want to scare you."

"Are you trying to tell me you're either porn star huge or lacking?"

"Honey, I'm anything but lacking."

"Show me," I breathed.

His white shirt then pants hit the floor, followed by his boxers. Straightening, he stood motionless, letting me glide my eyes from his broad, muscular shoulders to his narrow, rippled abs to where he jutted out toward me.

"Not lacking," I said with a half-smile. Anything but.

Leaning forward, he poured two glasses of wine. After, he climbed into the tub and settled beside me. He handed me one of the glasses, then draped his arm across my shoulders.

We sipped our wine and stared through the windows. The moon might be hiding but stars filled the sky, winking through wispy clouds. Below, in the valley, lights gleamed. Up here, above it all, we ruled.

"How are the bra and thong doing in the water?" he asked before sipping his wine again.

"They're wet and clingy." I wrinkled my nose. "And scratchy."

"Don't forget sexy."

"I like being sexy."

He turned to face me. "Take it off if you want."

I did want. Everything.

Unclipping my bra, I pulled it away from my body and tossed it onto the floor. Daisy petals floated around me, tickling my bare skin.

Eli swept them aside and gently cupped my breasts. His thumbs, thick and calloused, stroked across my nipples.

Tipping my head back, I closed my eyes. A moan slipped past my lips.

His mouth descended, stopping to drink from my lips before kissing downward from my jawline to my neck to the tops of my breasts.

He shifted lower in the water, kneeling in front of me.

The hot liquid, swirling around me, heightened this moment. My heart soared, fluttering in my chest.

He took my nipple into his mouth, sucking gently at first but then with more urgency.

My sharp gasp cut through the air, and he lifted his head. "You like?"

"Yes. Don't stop!"

Chuckling, he stroked his tongue across my nipple again while his hand pinched the other.

Heat swirled inside me, centering in my core. I thrust my hips forward, seeking...everything.

His fingers tickled across my belly, and he cupped me

between the legs. His thumb deftly slid my thong to the side, and he rubbed.

My gasp cut through the air, and I pushed against his hand. "Yes. That."

Lifting his head, he said, "Love the thong, honey, but this thing has to go. Do I rip it off with my teeth or..."

Rip it with his teeth. The aggressive, animal-like image blooming in my mind made fire flash through me.

Moving a few candles aside, I dropped a towel on the tub surround, rose out of the water, and lowered myself onto my back on the soft surface.

Eli rose above me, grinning. "Teeth it is, huh? I do like to bite."

"Let's see what you can do with panties." And everything underneath.

"I'm all about removing them, actually."

My smile must blaze on my face. "You keep making threats but I've yet to see action."

Bracing himself over me, he nipped at my neck. "Just watch me."

He feathered kisses down my neck to my breasts, where he stopped to play. Pinching and sucking, and rubbing.

While I writhed beneath him and begged for everything.

His fingers trailed across my belly and he stroked his thumb down the strip of fabric between my legs.

Gasping, I arched up.

"I've been dreaming of this forever," he said.

"Me and a jacuzzi?"

"You wearing nothing, spread out before me. A feast I can savor until dawn."

"What are you going to do with me now that you have me?" I said while spreading my legs wider. Yes. Touch me there...and there...

He knelt between my thighs and stroked my slit again with his fingers. "Show you what you've been missing."

I snorted. "Cocky, aren't you?"

"I don't do anything halfway." He tugged my thong to the side and exhaled, his breath making me shiver with arousal.

But his tongue...His mouth...His teeth.

Nibbling and sucking and biting and stroking. In seconds, my thong was gone and his mouth...Hell, his mouth was everywhere.

I whimpered and thrashed my head.

He looked up with satisfaction burning on his face. "Yes?"

"Yes. Now!"

"Not too fast. I'm eager to explore." He slid his fingers inside me while he bit and sucked. While I urged him on, he moved in and out. Over and over. I writhed and moaned and couldn't get enough.

"Fuck. So wet, Mia. I'm going to explode."

"No," I keened. Sobering, I shook my finger at him. "Better not."

While he licked and stroked and rubbed, he hummed, and pressure built inside me, a fire only he could put out.

I tipped my head back and lifted my hips, meeting his fingers.

"I've got to..." he growled out, leaving me only long enough to lean over the tub and pull a condom from his jacket. A quick rip with his teeth, and he rolled it on.

"I'm on the pill," I said. "And I tested after..."

"Haven't been with anyone in over a year. Tested after, too. But I'm keeping you safe." He rose above me, bracing his arms with his palms beside my shoulders. "How do you want me, honey? Like this or do you want to flip over?"

Bracing my heels on the side of the tub, I lifted my hips toward him, seeking... "Just get inside!"

He chuckled. "Like this?" He pushed just inside my entrance before pulling back out. His arms trembled and his breath came ragged. "Or do you prefer it like this?" He shoved inside me, hard and deep, penetrating me to the hilt.

Shrieking, I writhed and begged him for more but he remained motionless as if awaiting my command.

"Screw me, damn you."

He growled by my ear. "Love it when you talk dirty."

"Eli."

"Yeah, honey?" Hip shifting, he kept up a slow and deep seduction.

"Now."

"Like this?" Picking up speed, he drove into me, over and over while I panted and urged him on.

"Yes," I cried out, my body humming, riding a wave toward the peak. I no longer knew if I was answering or just calling for more.

Both. Because my muscles were tensing. I was rushing toward the sky.

While he rubbed between my legs and kept plunging deep inside.

"Take it, honey," he said hoarsely. "It's yours."

Harder. Faster. Skin slapping together, our bodies fusing. The pressure built inside me. Heat and flames licked along my nerve endings. I gasped and clutched his shoulders and then shuddered, screaming his name.

Head back and muscles more rigid than steel, he crashed with me, groaning and shaking, following me in the wake. Collapsing on top of me, he whispered my name. He sheltered me in his warm arms.

While I slowly slid back down to Earth, he stroked my face and side. Kissed my face, my neck, and my chest.

We dried each other off, our laughter soon turning into something steamy.

We tumbled onto the bed together in a tangle of limbs, our mouths coming together.

THOUGH I DIDN'T INTEND to fall asleep, my eyes eventually closed, and I drifted into a dream where Eli held me close, keeping me from harm.

If only that shrill screaming would stop, then I could hold onto the dream...

Shrill screaming?

My eyes popped open and I jolted upright.

The fire alarm.

I smelled smoke.

18

ELI

I leaped from the bed, staring around feverishly, but didn't see any flames. The candles we'd left alight flickered, but they hadn't tipped over or started a fire.

But something—or someone—had.

"We need to get out of here," I yelled over the harsh squeal of the alarm.

Gasping, Mia slid from the bed and rushed to her overnight bag to dress. I followed, yanking up my jeans and hauling a tee over my head. I stuffed my bare feet into my sneakers and quickly tied them.

"Maybe it's...I don't know. Someone left something in a microwave too long?" she shouted over the noise.

"Not on this floor. We're alone." At the top of a tower. A long series of stairwells awaited us, and fuck. I didn't like this. I felt like we were being driven to a certain action. "Too many coincidences." I grabbed my Jeep keys and slung our overnight bags crisscrossed over my shoulders. Once we left this room, we weren't coming back. We'd jump in my Jeep and beat it the hell out of here.

I didn't like how vulnerable we were here. Yes, I'd rigged

up a few things to give warning, to trip someone up if they tried to take me down inside the suite, but we had to leave the sanctuary I'd created. And none of this beat the system I'd installed at Mia's house.

I might take the heat from Mia come morning for leaving if this was just a false alarm, but at least I'd know she was safe. She could make it up to the Foundation after this was all over.

Once I'd taken out whoever was after her.

She snatched up her purse from where she'd left it on a table near the door and, as I stepped into the hall, she looked back into the room wistfully.

Tonight had been special. The start of something new and wonderful for us. I hated seeing it end early, too.

Out in the hall, we coughed, our lungs sucking in smoke that billowed from down the hall to our left. One stairwell available then, because we couldn't go in that direction. No visible flames but they wouldn't take long to catch up. Constructed of wood and stone, this place would be engulfed in minutes.

"Jax," she said hoarsely. "We've got to help him." Holding her hand over her mouth, she tried to filter the air.

I helped her tug up her tee, as well as my own over my face. "Breathe through this."

We took a flight of stairs down one floor and emerged in the hall housing Jax's suite. I ran to his room but when I banged on his door, it creaked open.

Why was it unlocked? I felt like this scene was moving too fast; I couldn't keep up. The doomed feeling of inevitability washed over me.

Shoving the door wide, I rushed into the room, my gun drawn. My heart raced, hyped up on adrenaline. I halted when I was hit by a wall of smoke.

Though dark in the room, the smoke hung thickly as if the fire waited here, smoldering, until it gained enough energy to consume everything around it.

I ducked down low where the air was slightly clearer, and inched forward. "Jax!" He wouldn't have left without us, which meant he was here somewhere.

"Jax!" Mia echoed from the doorway.

Someone groaned from deeper inside the room, yanking me in that direction. Fear licked up my spine, telling me to run, to get out of here, now. But I would not abandon him.

Jax lay on the floor, unmoving. Unconscious from inhalation?

As I approached, a pool of red revealed itself, surrounding his head.

Fuck. "Jax." I dropped down beside him and shook him. "Wake up."

He groaned again and shifted before going motionless again.

Mia dropped down beside me. "Let me see him." She ran her hands along his spine and limbs quickly then across his head. When she gasped and yanked her hand back, it came away bloody. The face she turned to me echoed the grim emotions inside me. This was bad. "He took a blow to the head. He could have internal bleeding. We've got to get him out of here."

The three of us had to get out of here. As soon as possible.

"I'll get him." Drag him out if I had to. "You go."

"What?" She reeled away from me, then coughed as the smoke filled her lungs. A few more seconds of this, and we'd both succumb. "You can't do this alone. You need help."

"I need you to get help for me. Take the stairs because you can't risk getting stuck in the elevator. Get to the ground floor and find someone. Security or the fire department if they've arrived. Send them up the stairwell. I'll meet them and we'll get Jax out together."

I could tell she wanted to resist, insist she could help haul him out, but her shoulders slumped before her spine tightened. "I'll do it." She leaped to her feet and, clutching her purse like a lifeline, raced from the room.

On heels. I shouldn't chuckle. Our situation was beyond dire. But those heels...

"Jax, buddy." I shook his shoulder again, and he groaned. "I'm going to get you out of here but you've got to help me."

"Eli," he mumbled. "Someone..." He slumped unconscious again.

No missing his ominous tone.

Coughing, I covered my face again with my shirt. Dizzy, I could barely stand. I hefted Jax onto his belly then lifted him up to his knees with my arms underneath his. Once slumped against me and more or less on his feet, I pivoted him around to face me. Choking on fumes, I gasped and fought to drag in clean air, but I was fighting a losing battle. I dropped down, my shoulder meeting his belly, and maneuvered him into a fireman's lift. We'd trained to do this in the military until it was seamless—no soldier was ever left behind.

I stumbled from the room.

"Fuck, dude. You're freakin' heavy." Pure muscle weighed a lot and while Jax was a few inches shorter than me, he was broader.

The physical therapist told me not to hold back on my training. Thankfully, I'd listened. But my spasming leg told me that, if I made it out of here alive, I needed to increase my training.

I moved out into the hall where the smoke hung thicker than a black curtain. I couldn't see. My eyes burned like I'd doused them in bleach. The heat and chemicals seared my lungs.

Left, or right? The smoke made me punchy, confused, unable to remember which way to go.

And sleepy.

Don't go there. In a fire, sleeping equaled death.

The stairs. To the right. Twelve fuckin' flights to the bottom.

I could do it. I *would* do it.

I dragged my feet in that direction, hauling an unconscious Jax with me. If he went down, I'd go down with him. Then pick him up and haul him further.

Reaching the door to the stairs after what felt like one-thousand years, I propped Jax against the wall, bracing him up with my knee, and hauled open the steel door.

Farther down below, Mia yelled, "Eli?" Panic ruled in her voice.

"I'm—"

Footsteps rushed up from farther down the hall. No other rooms. Couldn't be another guest.

Before I could pivot to confront what I knew had to be an incoming threat, someone hit me from behind, the blow landing solidly on my head.

The world blurred. Jax, released from my hold, slumped to the floor. A burst of clean air shot up the stairwell and I could only pray there wasn't fire below or I'd turn the stairwell into a chimney.

As I nosedived toward the floor, the bearded man I'd seen talking to the server—and to Peter—rushed past me. He clattered down the stairs.

After Mia.

19

MIA

When I scrambled from the bed, I'd dressed in yoga pants and a tee but my flip flops had gone missing and were nowhere to be found.

No time to look. I'd slipped my feet into my heels. Running down the stairs in these babies was going to be torture.

I'd only hobbled down a few flights to the fourth floor and was contemplating ditching the shoes and going barefoot when the door opened above me.

"Eli?" I called out. He was faster than I'd expected. While no one answered, it had to be he and Jax. With only one suite per floor, there was no one at the top of the tower but us.

I'd hated leaving him to rescue Jax alone, but he was right. Dragging Jax down multiple flights of stairs would be beyond my capabilities. I'd slow us down solely because I wasn't strong enough to be a full member of the team. He needed help and, as much as I wanted that person to be me, someone stronger could make the difference between living and dying.

Go faster!

The thuds of shoes coming down fast told me this couldn't be Eli. He'd never leave Jax. Who could it be? If it was someone who worked at the hotel, I could wait for them and send them up to help Eli. But a rising terror inside me told me this wasn't someone who worked at the hotel.

Should I hide on the fourth floor?

Eli had suggested the fire had been set. If so, this could be the beginning of strike three, and I'd be in considerable danger.

I wouldn't go down without a fight. I had too much to live for to give up now. My career, Flint. Eli.

I rounded the next flight of stairs. The third-floor landing waited ahead. My heels banged on the metal treads despite my effort to move quickly yet silently.

I reached the third and kept going. Should I exit the stairwell and see if anyone there could help Eli? Although, Suzie at the front desk had said we were alone in the south tower, that most of the guests were in the main hotel and the north tower. And the fire could be stronger on any of the floors. If I left the stairs and something happened, Eli would never find me. Deviating from our plan could make the difference he needed.

Second floor. The clatter of my heels echoed around me.

Harsh breathing roared up behind me, making me jump.

I spun, lifting my fists. I tried to tell myself it was another guest, but I knew...

I just knew.

"You!"

The bearded man from Mexico rushed down the stairs toward me.

He'd tracked me. *Found me.*

He grabbed my arm and hauled me in close, pressing a gun against my temple.

I gasped and struggled, but couldn't break free of his hold.

He shook me until my teeth rattled. "Where's the notebook? It's not in your house."

While I should be trembling and pleading for him to let me go, rage roared through me. "You scared Walter. And me!"

He hauled me close enough his hot, foul breath coated my face. "The notebook. Where is it?"

"All this time...it was you. First strike, second strike, and now the third." My time *was* up unless Eli arrived. The odds of that were slim. He was helping Jax. For all I knew, he was still getting Jax out of the room.

The man frowned. "I don't...Just give me the notebook."

"I..." Terrified out of my mind, I couldn't think.

"Where is it?" he roared.

Where had I put it? When I'd returned from Mexico, the dress had been inside my suitcase, wrapped in a plastic bag.

Should've thrown it out. Why hadn't I?

The notebook was still in the pocket. And the dress...

"Your friends upstairs didn't have it, either. Thought I'd get it from them."

"What did you do to Eli and Jax?" I tipped my head back, peering up the open section in the center of the stairwell. "Eli!"

Not hearing his reply sent fear bolting up my spine like jagged lightning.

I tried to haul my arm out of the man's tight grip. If Eli was okay, he would've replied. He couldn't still be on the sixth floor. He'd be in the stairs with Jax by now.

The man reinforced his hold and shoved the gun hard

against my head, the blow making me wince. Sweat drizzled down my spine, but my body flashed cold.

Was this it? Would I die here in the stairwell?

Fear roared through me. He'd kill me like he had the man on the beach in Mexico. "Where is Eli? What did you do to him?" I yelled, unsure why I wasn't cowering. The gun would end my life in one second yet I still found a core of resistance inside me.

"You mean the guy upstairs?" He grinned. "Think he's asleep. Not a very good bodyguard, now is he?"

"You hurt him!" My anger escalated, flailing through me, giving me the strength of Wonder Woman. I pushed the man hard. Adrenaline charged through my veins like molten lava.

I had to get away and find Eli. He could be burning!

The man grabbed my clutch and tried to wrench it from me. "It in here?"

Strapped around my wrist, he only hauled me forward.

I scrambled back, freeing myself from his hold and spinning, yanking my clutch from his grasp. This was over. I was done with running. Shrieking, I charged at him, pushing, shoving, screaming nonsense.

His foot dropped down one step. Arms spiraling, he tumbled backward, falling down, down. Tumbling over and over until he smacked on the next lower landing. The gun discharged, and he shuddered.

"Mia!" Eli approached from above, Jax braced on his shoulders, somehow remaining upright. He reached this landing and carefully lowered the semi-conscious Jax to the floor. "You okay? I heard you scream."

"Yes." My gaze fell on the man lying unmoving below us and reaction took over. My arms and legs shook, my throat tightened, and tears welled behind my eyelids.

Eli followed my gaze. "What the...? The guy from the ballroom? Jax said he's the maintenance man."

"He had a gun," I blubbered out. I pressed my knuckles against my lips hard enough I flinched. "He tried to kill me in Mexico, and he followed me here."

"What?" Eli shouted. He glared toward the motionless man. "I don't understand. Why would someone who tried to rob you follow you all the way to Maine?"

"He wanted something else..." Shaking my head, I started down the stairs but turned. "When he fell, the gun went off." Had it hit him? "He's...I don't think he's worked here long. Assuming he works here at all."

Eli had suggested the person after me would know I was attending the conference, that they'd follow.

"This was it," I said. "Strike three. I stopped him."

"This is..." Around us, the alarm continued to blare, and lights flashed. "We can talk soon, but we've got to get out of here first."

"I'll help with Jax." Having a purpose would allow me to push the rest of my horror aside. "We only have a few flights left before we reach the ground floor."

Together, we got Jax to his feet. Stumbling like he'd chugged a six-pack, he slurred his words and was more hindrance than assistance, but we got him down the next flight of stairs to the landing where the bearded man lay with blood expanding in a brilliant circle around him.

The gunshot *had* hit him.

Dead?

No, not dead, but soon. When I stooped down to roll him over, he stared up at us, his dark eyes watering.

"I..." I lifted my chin. "I'll get you help." He had a chest wound, and I worried he wouldn't last long. Like with the woman in the park, there wasn't anything I could do. We needed to get Jax out, then I could send someone up the stairwell to help him.

His breathing slowed, telling me there wasn't time even for that.

"Mia," Eli said, supporting Jax. "The firemen will come for him."

"It'll be too late." If nothing else, I'd kneel beside him while he left this world for the next. Because it was clear by his rough breathing and the glazed look in his eyes, he wouldn't be with us for long. Everyone deserved to die with someone holding their hand, even a murderer.

Eli lowered Jax to the tile floor, leaning him against the wall with his legs splayed forward, his head lolling against the cinderblock wall.

The weirdest thing about all this was that we had yet to see a fireman. A quick look at my phone told me it hadn't been long since the alarm woke us. The impression of many lifetimes passing had only been minutes.

"Why did you do it?" I asked the bearded man. "Tell me." He'd killed another man, chased me on the beach.

What was so important about a blank notebook?

Unless it wasn't truly blank.

"Give the...notebook," the man gasped out. His hands rose to his chest where dark blood squirted out. He'd hit an artery deep inside and would bleed out in seconds. His hand fluttered before dropping back to his side. "Give it...to my sister. Tell her to..." Gulps consumed him, and he coughed, spurting more blood. "Tell her to destroy it. Don't let...the maestro...get it."

"Maestro?" I asked.

Eli took in a sharp breath of air.

"Traitor," the dying man said.

From the way he gurgled, we didn't have much time.

Even if EMTs arrived this minute, they'd be unable to save him. He'd lost too much. In trying to harm me, he'd instead dealt himself a lethal blow.

Curiosity overwhelmed me, and I leaned closer. Why did I linger? I should be escaping the burning building. "Who's your sister?"

A soft smile lifted his lips. "You know. Julia," he hissed out.

I reeled away from him, "What?"

His head tilted sideways, and his chest stopped rising.

"He's gone." Chills wracked my frame. My eyes met Eli's and it was clear we shared the same conclusion.

Julia, the man had said.

Flint's ex-fiancée?

20

ELI

"Why did you lie to the police?" I asked Mia as I popped my Jeep into a lower gear and drove up a steep incline.

"You caught that, did you?" She stared out the window.

"You said you didn't know the guy."

"Actually, I don't. Know his name, that is."

"But you've seen him before."

"Yes."

"He's Julia's brother?"

"I think so."

What was going on here? I trusted Mia completely, but she needed to spill.

"Flint will be home today. I need to tell him...no, show him something. Both of you."

"If you're still in danger, I can't protect you unless I know all the facts." I was a jerk to press her after the trauma we'd been through, but the thought of someone still eager to hurt her tore through me like a jagged blade.

"The guy who just tried to hurt me is dead. You know

Russell is in jail. Seems like I'm relatively safe for the moment."

I growled, because the hospital was straight ahead and it was clear I wouldn't be getting any answers before we arrived. "I'm not letting go of this."

"And I'll tell you all you want to know," she said in a scratchy voice. We'd all experienced various degrees of smoke exposure. "Let's go see Jax first."

"All right." I parked my Jeep in a visitor spot. The EMTs hadn't been able to revive the guy in the stairwell and he had been pronounced at the scene. Jax, fortunately, was okay. He'd been checked out and told he needed more tests. They'd taken him by ambulance to the hospital. They'd also suggested I see a doctor, though my head must be tougher than Jax's because I hadn't bled and I'd only been stunned, not knocked out. My brain pounded like I'd drank an entire bottle of tequila last night, but I'd live.

"You need to let them examine you, too," Mia said as she unbuckled and opened her door.

"I'm okay." We got out.

Meeting me at the front of the Jeep, her breath caught. "I'm grateful you weren't more seriously injured." Lines of worry had etched her face. "But it's not just the blow to your head. Smoke inhalation isn't anything to play around with."

"I'm more worried about Jax," I said, taking her hand.

"He's going to be okay." There was no denying the anxiety in her voice.

We hurried up the walkway to the main entrance.

"After we're sure he's okay, we'll talk about the guy back at the hotel," she said softly. "We can patch into Flint and I'll fill him in at the same time or we can wait for him to arrive home."

I'd never been good with waiting. I needed to know why

the guy tried to kill her in the stairwell and how the server and Peter were involved.

What did she need to tell me? This was about more than a robbery in Mexico. The guy naming the maestro proved it. It was tied in with our job.

We went inside and they directed us to the ER. The clerk sitting behind the desk rose and took us back into an area with a long row of bays. She pointed to where we could find Jax. Pushing aside the curtain, we stood motionless, staring at him. He lay on a stretcher covered with a white sheet with his eyes closed.

As we approached, he woke.

"Hey," he said in a scratchy voice.

"How you doin'?" I asked, rubbing his shoulder.

He shrugged. "I've seen better but I'll live."

"Jax." Mia took his hand and squeezed it. "I'm sorry."

"Not your fault."

"What happened?" I asked. "Your door was open. I found you lying on the floor."

"In a pool of blood." She shuddered.

He frowned. "I sat up awhile, watching TV. Then I...went to the bathroom. I think. Got ready for bed. I came out and the room was dark." He winced. "Someone was waiting."

"Don't strain yourself," Mia said. "I imagine you have a concussion."

"I'm pissed, actually. Someone jumped me and I didn't hear them, didn't even know they were there."

"Have you been to CT yet?" Mia asked.

"Yes. All clear."

She slumped against the stretcher. "Phew. I was really worried."

"I'm going to be okay." He patted her hand as if she was the one needing reassurance. "He came up behind me and it was lights out. Never had anything like that happen before. I was complacent. Thought the only threat was only to...Mia."

"He's dead," she said with a lift of her chin.

"Who the hell was it?" He turned to me. "Did he come after you, too?"

"Me," Mia said. "He *was* after me."

And I was determined to find out who the guy was as soon as possible.

The curtain parted and the doctor came in. "Well, you're going to be okay, Jackson. No bleeding on the CT. Vitals check out fine. But we want to keep you overnight and repeat the CT in the morning. You had quite a blow to the head. Took ten stitches to close it up. Sometimes we don't see bleeds right away but will on the repeat. Neuro will see you, too, though I'm confident we're only dealing with a concussion here."

"But—" Jax started to rise but Mia gently pressed him back down on the mattress.

"This needs to be taken seriously," the doctor said. "If we're not careful, you could have lasting damage. Head injuries have been in the news a lot lately for good reason."

"You need me," Jax said to me. "I've got to get out of here."

"The guy..." Mia said. "I think he was the one we were... concerned about."

In the stairwell, she'd said this man followed her from Mexico, but I wasn't buying that as the only explanation. Something bigger was going on here.

"At least you don't have to worry about that any longer," Jax said. His shoulders eased onto the stretcher. "I'll be out of here tomorrow, then."

"I can send Becca for you," I said. "Your SUV, too."

A nurse came in as the doctor was leaving. "We're going

to take him upstairs to a room, now. If you'd like to follow, we can get him settled and you can visit with him some more after that."

"Why don't you two go home," Jax said, waving toward the door. "I'll hang out here. I'm sure you have a few things to talk about."

We couldn't talk here, not in front of the medical staff. This didn't just involve a man who'd accidentally shot himself in the stairwell, only to die from the wound. With the maestro names, this tied into what went on down in Mexico.

I caught Mia's eye, and she nodded.

We started to leave when Jax called out, "I want the deets when I get home."

"Yup," I said. I'd fill him in as soon as I could.

A short time later, we were back in my Jeep and driving down the main route home.

"How do you know this guy?" I asked. "Because you did. Or, he knew you."

She pulled her phone and started typing. "I'll call Flint and tell you both at the same time."

"Mia?" Flint said through speakerphone a second later.

"Hey. How are things? I've got you on speaker, by the way. I'm with Eli and we're driving home."

"I'm doing fine, but you didn't call me so you and Eli could chat. What's up?"

Mia explained about the fire in the hotel, that Jax was in the hospital but would be okay, and about us leaving early.

"A fire? Eli..."

"Yeah." No need to ask what he'd meant. Flint wanted to know if Mia was safe. "It's over. The guy who was responsible is dead."

Flint's breath whooshed through the line, and his voice

rose with worry. "You're sure you're all right, Mia? I wish I could be there with you, sis."

"I'm okay." Reaching over, she took my hand. "Eli was with me."

Not when I needed to be, which burned through me like a raging wildfire. I'd known I'd take a risk sending Mia off alone, but what else could I do? If she'd stayed, she could've died. Sure, she could've helped, but there was no guarantee we wouldn't be overwhelmed by the smoke. I hadn't really sent her for help. Though I would've welcomed it, I could get Jax by myself. But I needed her out of the hotel fast.

I'd played right into the guy's hands.

"You don't know how much I appreciate this, Eli," Flint said. "You being there for Mia. I owe you."

"I'd do it again in a heartbeat. Keeping Mia safe is the most important thing to me."

"I can take over once I get home. You must be worn out."

I was tired. Stress, lack of sleep, worry about Jax and Mia, plus getting knocked over the head would do that to a guy. And we'd gone to bed late...

"Mia and I—"

"We're..." she said at the same time. The soft smile she gave me was filled with heat and promise. "Eli and I..." She broke off, but at my nod, added. "We're together, now."

It felt good to hear the words spoken. Right. I wanted to kiss her, show her what she meant to me, but I had to focus on driving and the conversation. I could show her later, though.

"I...see," Flint said. "Damn well better not hurt her," he growled, but a hint of humor came through in his voice, telling me he was happy for us, that he welcomed this.

Had he known all along that we'd fit together so well?

"I wanted to talk to you both at the same time, which is

why I called rather than wait until you got home," Mia said. She turned sparkling eyes my way. "And Eli wants to hear what I have to say immediately."

"Okay." A strong hint of reservation came through in Flint's voice.

"The guy that fell had a gun. I pushed him and when he landed, the gun discharged, and he was shot in the chest. It was clear he'd hit a main artery and there wasn't anything I could do for him. He died while I knelt beside him."

"Mia! You're all right?"

"I wasn't hurt at all."

Flint's breath chugged out. "I'm grateful this is over, that he didn't hurt you or Eli. Why was he after you?"

Pulling up to a stop sign, I turned out onto another road.

"He wanted something a man gave me in Mexico, but I don't know why. It doesn't make sense because it looks like nothing."

"Wait," I said, darting a look at her before returning it to the road. "Back up a second. Is this somehow related to your medical mission?" The robbery took place in a different location, but Peter...Was he involved? I hadn't mentioned my suspicions to Mia but I sure would to Flint once we had a chance to talk alone. Besides, the guy had mentioned the maestro.

"This happened after my birthday dinner. You guys had left."

"You said you were robbed." Still wanted to rip a bunch of cops apart for how they'd treated her.

She pulled her gaze from mine, down to her lap where she'd set her phone. "There never was a robbery."

"Mia," Flint growled out. "Tell us what's going on."

"I decided to take a walk on the beach after you guys left."

"Thought you went to your room?" I tapped the wheel with my fingers, wishing I could pull over and hold her because she looked ready to fall apart. But we needed to get home. While the guy in the stairwell was dead, my earlier hunch was proving true. I had a feeling this situation was just starting to heat up, not cool down.

"I did go back to my room, but I was bored. It was a gorgeous night." Her laugh came out bitter. "Well, it was gorgeous when you guys were around. But it was my last night in Mexico and I decided to take a walk on the beach. I tripped over a man lying in the sand."

I had a sick feeling where this was going. It couldn't be... could it? "How does this tie into the guy in the stairwell?"

"Before the man lying in the sand died, he gave me a small notebook. It was hidden on his body." Her face pinched. "He was dying. I think a lacerated liver from the knife wound, and—"

"Knife wound?" Flint shot out. His voice deepened. "Mia, I—"

She held up her hand and, as if he could see, he said nothing further. "He was desperate for me to take the notebook."

"Where is it?" I asked. The one good thing about getting an early start was that the roads were nearly empty of other cars. We were making great progress and would be home in about an hour. With things still uncertain, we needed to get to a secure location.

"That's a great question," she said.

"The notebook," Flint said. "Eli. You thinking what I'm thinking?"

Too much of a coincidence. "The notebook," I said to prompt Mia.

"The man in the stairwell told me to give it to Julia."

Flint's breath wheezed out. "Julia? It can't be…"

"He said to give it to her, that she'd destroy it. When I questioned him about the name, he said I knew who he meant. It *is* her."

"Fuck," Flint ground out. "This is all…yeah."

Tied together, he wanted to say but wouldn't in front of Mia.

"Did Julia have a brother?" I asked. I'd only met her a few times. Pretty, petite. Haunted eyes.

"She told me she was alone but I guess that was a lie like everything else." No denying the disgust in Flint's voice.

He'd mourned that woman for months. Went frantic trying to find her, but she must've ditched her phone or blocked him because he'd had no success tracking her down. She'd disappeared as if she'd never existed, leaving Flint behind with a shattered heart.

"What are the odds?" I said.

"We need that notebook, Mia," Flint shot out. "Where is it."

"At my place." She gnawed on a fingernail. "Tell me why it's important because, to me, it looks blank. You don't know how close I was to throwing it out. Actually, I kind of did."

Flint groaned and I was tempted to groan along with him. "Please tell me you didn't get rid of it."

She half smiled. "Well, it's in the trash but it hasn't made it to the landfill yet." Her smile fled. "But I mean it. I'm not saying anything else until you tell me how all this ties together." Her gaze lifted to me. "Please?"

"I'm sorry, Mia," Flint said. "I can't say much more."

"It's…part of a job," I said carefully.

She smacked her fist on her thigh. "I knew it. Everything that's happened is connected to Flint's business, isn't it? It has never been all about me. That guy…" Her voice broke.

"He's been after me for the notebook. It's part of some top-secret job you guys are doing for the government, and I somehow stumbled into the middle of it."

Silence reigned between Flint and me.

Turning in her seat, she gave me a look that should've pinned me in place or at least made me squirm. If she was good at reading me, only the tightening of my jaw would tell her she'd squarely hit her mark.

"Why not admit it?" she said. "Oh, wait, if you tell me there's a connection, you'll have to kill me."

Flint huffed. "It's not like that."

"Then tell me."

I yanked on my t-shirt collar. "You know I'll never hurt you."

"Come on." She tapped her temple. "You're not the only one who can connect clues. I knew right from the start that you guys are secret operatives. Kinda like James Bond. Only without the sexy accent."

I shot her a sharp look. "You think James Bond is sexy?" Which one? The old guy from Scotland or the new guy... who was hot.

She rolled her eyes. "Doesn't everyone think James Bond is sexy?"

I raked my fingers through my hair.

"Strange that I can find humor in this tense situation, but what else can I do? Cry? I'm done playing the wimpy heroine like this is some action movie." She grumbled. "You think I haven't connected the fact that my sweet Aunt Becca —who happens to be retired from the CIA—randomly took a job with Flint because she wanted to keep her mind active? Last I knew, the best way to do that is by playing Sudoku. I've joked with Flint about how he's kind of a James Bond with MacGyver thrown in for fun. You know, the—" She made air quotes. "Special Ops stuff combined with all that construction experience. And he hasn't denied it."

Flint grunted, giving nothing away.

Her lips twisted. "You guys don't fool me. Not any longer. I just can't—" Her voice cut out, and she swallowed deeply. "I thought I was dealing with all this. Someone breaking into my house. Throwing me in a trunk. The seafood which you and I both know seemed unrelated but is now highly suspicious. And now a guy who chased me on the beach in Mexico after killing a man tries to...well, I don't know what he planned for me. But I'm part of all this, whether you like it or not. I have to know what's going on here. Be honest with me. Please."

"I think there *is* a connection between the man you found dying on the beach, the man with the gun in the stairwell, and a job we were doing in Mexico," I said, because she was right. We needed to tell her. Maybe not everything because much of what we did would need high clearance to share, but she was involved whether we wanted her to be or not. She had the right to know why her life had been threatened.

And I was past done with lying.

"No shit," she said with relief in her voice.

"We'll tell you what we can," Flint said. "Eli?"

I turned onto another secondary road. Cooler air drifted through the open windows from the woods on either side of us and swirled through the car. "Our knife-wielding friend obviously wanted the notebook. Nothing new for you there. And since I'm surmising the dead guy in Mexico was our contact on a job that I will not share further details about—on a threat of impalement by you Uncle Sid—I'm leaving it at that for now."

"I don't need to know everything about your secret project," she said.

"In Mexico, we were tasked with providing protection for a government contact, but the guy left the safe location where we'd hidden him."

"Taken?" she asked. Astute.

"Maybe."

"You'd hidden him near the hotel where we were staying," she said with certainty.

Flint grunted. Yeah, he shouldn't underestimate his sister. "Half a mile or so down the road."

"Why was he walking on the beach in a suit?" she asked. "It was hot. Too hot for clothing like that."

"Things are adding up," Flint said. "Not that the suit alone proves anything."

"Mid-fifties. Slender build," Mia said, frowning. "Older scar running down his right cheek."

"Crap," I hissed out. "She *did* find our guy." Somehow, I'd hoped all this would turn out to be unrelated. I hated that Mia's life had been endangered in Mexico, that she was thrust in the path of harm here where she should be safest.

Hard to believe this all tied together, but this was too close, too coincidental. How the hell had it happened?

"Where exactly is that notebook, Mia?" Flint's raised voice made me picture him leaning forward, the phone clutched tightly in his hand. "We need it."

"In my house."

"Hidden," I said. A statement. Because, if it had been lying around, the guy would've found it.

"It's blank." Her brow furrowed. "Why would I need to hide something like that?"

As I turned onto her road, I was grateful we'd be home soon.

Home. Funny how Mia's place felt like home already. If we stayed together...Best not to go there. Whatever we had was new. Untested. But I ached to find a place with her permanently.

Did I dare trust her not to bail on me like everyone else had?

I shook my head, hoping I could shove off the thought, but it lingered, a sour taint in my mouth. Trust should be given freely, not demanded.

"When I got home, I unpacked in my basement," Mia said. "I put my clothes into the washer. The dress was stained with blood." She glanced at me. "You remember."

I'd never forget. The fear on her face...Why hadn't I realized there was more to the situation than a simple robbery?

"I didn't see any point in washing the dress. The blood had set; I'd never get it out. So, I tossed it into the trash beside my dryer. It's only chance that I haven't emptied the bucket yet."

"And the notebook?" Flint asked.

"It's in one of the dress pockets. Funny..."

"What?"

She turned a frown my way. "The cop in Mexico threw it into the trash. I retrieved it. If the guy on the beach wanted me to have it, I was determined to keep it. Now, I wonder if that cop was involved."

"I'M glad you still have it," Flint said. "Get it, Eli, and bring it to the shop. I should be home in, oh, four hours, assuming my flight's on time."

"We can run some tests," I said eagerly as I turned into Mia's driveway and turned off my Jeep. "If this came from our guy and I'm pretty sure it did, this is a major breakthrough. He...Flint, the guy in the stairwell? He said not to let the maestro get it."

"Fuck," Flint sighed out. "This is it. I'll let Haylee and Gabe know. We can pull them out. Oh, hey," he added. "They're calling my flight."

"We'll see you soon," Mia said.

"You will. Bye."

She tucked her phone into her purse and turned to me. "It's over, then. Finally. No more hiding?"

"You don't need my bodyguard duties any longer."

Her face tightened but she reached out and took my hand. My heart along with it. "That might be true, but I still need you."

21

MIA

When we arrived home, Ginny was waiting, sitting on the sofa with purring Walter on her lap. "You're home early!" she said.

"We ran into some problems at the conference," I said as Eli closed the door behind us. A lot of problems.

"Walter was the bestest boy," Ginny said in a cutesy voice. "So snuggly. I need to get a cat. Cooper keeps talking about a couple of dogs. A big, vicious one and a tiny, cuddly one. Or is it the other way around? But Walter here made me realize how nice kitties can be."

I picked Walter up and gave him kisses. "Did my boy miss his mama? Bet you did." When I put him down, he strolled over to weave around Eli's legs until Eli scratched him behind his ears. Walter's rumbling purr rang out again. "Thank you for taking care of him."

"Any time. He's the sweetest thing."

Walter strolled back to the sofa and blinked up at Ginny, who stroked his back. When he jumped onto the sofa and curled up on a quilt, Ginny rose.

"That's quite the neighbor you have there," she said.

I sighed. What now? "You mean Elwin, I assume."

"That's his name?" Ginny's lips twisted. "He didn't introduce himself. Not officially, anyway. He's handy with his gun, however."

Groaning, I rubbed my aching head. I needed to take some aspirin. Or have a shot of tequila. "What did he do?"

"Sat on his porch with a rifle pointed this way. Even shouted that it was loaded when I went out to my car to get something. I believe he thought I was you. Hello. Red hair?"

"It's strawberry blonde," I said.

"Sure. Anyway, I called Cooper and asked him to make an official appearance. He showed up in one of his uniforms and had a sit-down with Elwin. Told him that if he didn't put away his rifle, Cooper was going to take it from him and put it away for him and Elwin wouldn't like where Cooper put it."

"Cool." My chuckle slipped out. "Maybe he'll leave me alone from now on."

"Hard to say." She tilted her head. "But I don't think he wants another interaction with Cooper."

"I owe him cookies." Lots of cookies.

Ginny chuckled. "Don't fatten him up too much. I want him to fit into his uniform for our wedding. Which is only a few months away!" A thrill of excitement came through in her voice. Rising, she lifted her purse off the coffee table. "Let me know if you need me to come hang out with Walter again. Despite your neighbor, it was a lot of fun." She winked at Eli. "Maybe you'll want a getaway weekend or something."

"I will." I hoped Eli would want a getaway weekend, too. Soon.

Ginny left and I locked the door behind her and engaged the alarms.

"Let me get that notebook for you," I said.

We went down to the basement and over to the washer and dryer. The trash bucket was wedged into the gap between the wall and the dryer and I had to yank hard to get it out. Lint clumps in the bucket masked anything underneath, which could be why the man from the stairwell hadn't searched further.

For some reason, I'd avoided emptying this trash bucket. Who knew why I hadn't chucked it out completely. Maybe I saw the dress as a symbol of what happened in Mexico. My memories were more than enough to keep my heart jolting into action, but the dress was a tangible object. Real. It proved the incident had happened, that it wasn't all in my mind. That it hadn't been a simple robbery.

And maybe I'd kept the dress as a challenge to myself. When I felt it was finally over, I could burn it in my backyard firepit. Set the memories aflame and watch them disappear into the sky.

I upended the trash bucket. A shudder rippled through me when my fingers touched the crusty, dark burgundy stains on the fabric. The man's blood, mixed with mine. I was grateful I'd survived but a wave of sadness flowed over me, because he hadn't.

"I can't believe you..." Eli stared at the dress.

"Most of it's his blood. He died right in front of me." The words choked out of me. "But you want the notebook, not my sob story about what happened."

He wrapped his arms around me and rested his chin on my head. "It was a traumatic experience for you. Whenever you want to talk about it, I'm here to listen."

"Thank you." I released a long breath. "I never gave the notebook another thought because it was blank."

"To the normal eye, maybe. We'll figure it out."

"Another one of your James Bond tricks?"

"For this, I'll tap into my inner-MacGyver."

I rested my head on his chest. "MacGyver always took down the bad guy and saved the heroine." Like Eli.

He leaned back in our embrace. "You're incredible, Mia. You took down the bad guy on your own. Saved yourself. Again."

"You're right." Someone had tried to hurt me and I'd fought back. Made a difference.

Stepping out of his arms, I lifted the dress off the floor and shook it to unfold it. "Pocket." I reached inside and pulled the notebook out, extending it toward Eli. "How could something so simple mean so much to this many people?"

Eli skimmed through it and grunted.

"What do you see? Because I still see blank pages."

He shrugged.

"Eli." An edge of warning came through in my voice.

"Hmm?" He looked up from the notebook. "We're hoping to find names. Our contact in Mexico promised names."

"He died trying to give them to you. Names can't be worth a life."

"Nothing is worth a life, but these names could save many lives once the people we're after are arrested."

"So, this is it." Tension flowed off me like a soft blanket onto the floor. "I'll still keep my security system armed because I like feeling safe, but we've solved this mystery."

"We'll need to analyze this." He tucked the notebook into his pocket and we returned upstairs and went to my study, where I dropped off some of my paperwork on my desk. "But this is the end of you feeling scared. Though..." He coughed. "I'm still more than willing to provide bodyguard—and arm candy—services upon demand."

Stepping forward, I hugged him. "In case you didn't figure it out, I'm a needy woman. I do have demands."

His arms went around my waist as his mouth came down to meet mine. "And I plan to meet your every need."

"Do you have to leave for the shop yet?"

"In fifteen minutes or so." He leaned back in my arms. "What do you have in mind?"

I just smiled.

What was it with me lately? Whenever Eli was around, I wanted to drag him off to bed. Or seduce him. Would I ever get enough of him?

Fourteen minutes left before he had to leave. Thirteen, if I was realistic.

I couldn't. I shouldn't. Like I had a choice?

I peeked up at him over the top of my glasses. "Do you, um..." Was that my voice coming out deep and husky? "Do you want to go to my room before you leave?"

One of his eyebrows quirked up. "What's wrong with here?"

"Here?" I peered around my office. The old rocker wouldn't work. The floor was hard. And there was nothing else here other than boxes I'd yet to unpack and...

"How about lying back on your desk, honey?" he said, tugging on the hem of my tee. "Take everything off and lie back. Enjoy."

Oh...

"With those glasses, you look like the sexiest librarian imaginable."

I'd always thought they made me look owlish. Maybe I should wear them more often.

We had thirteen—no, twelve—minutes to drown in this moment. For me to drown in Eli.

His breath coming fast, he pushed my things off my desk and they clattered on the floor.

Once we'd stripped, I reached for my glasses.

"Leave 'em. They're a freakin' turn on." Nuzzling my neck, he sucked the soft flesh where my shoulder met my nape. My breath hissed from my lungs, and I moaned.

"Love that sound. I'll never get enough of you shattering in my arms."

The elastic flew from my hair, and the silky strands dropped around my shoulders in a soft wave. At his urging, I lay back on the flat surface.

"There's nothing more erotic than you spreading yourself in an invitation for my touch." Standing between my splayed thighs, his body surged. "I want you." His groan filled the silence, echoing in the empty room. Leaning over me, he braced one hand on the wooden surface and slid his fingers between my legs. While creating intricate circles, he kissed me, plunging his tongue inside, mimicking the movement he'd soon deliver.

My chest heaved, and I gasped.

"I can barely hold myself back." He trailed his lips down my neck, sucking, grazing his teeth along my skin until I quaked.

Soft mews came from my throat, and my breathing hitched. I arched into his touch.

When he slid his finger inside me, I knew I was ready.

"I've gotta be here," he groaned out. "Now."

I panted, and my head thrashed on the table. "Eli."

He fumbled with a condom, almost losing it while flinging aside the package.

"Lift your legs and scoot closer to the edge," he grated out.

Complying, my ankles locked behind his back.

"Higher."

My eyes opened, but I felt dreamy and languid. "What?"

"If your legs are higher, I can go deeper."

My heels found his shoulders.

As he placed himself just inside my soft folds, I reminded myself we still had a few minutes. He could go slow. Take his time.

We still had ten—no, make that nine—minutes before he had to leave.

Rubbing me harder, he held himself back.

"Ahh." I strained upward, my legs flailing. "Eli. I can't wait. I want you."

"The only invitation I'll ever need." Falling into me, he shifted his hips, making sure he delved everywhere, rocking against my core.

I moaned and rose up to meet him.

Planting his palms on the table, he pulled out and drove back inside. He alternated his pace until my cries grew in volume. Then he moved faster, and I could feel him getting harder, longer.

"Oh, yes," I cried.

Lowering himself onto me, he buried his face in my neck as he buried himself in my body.

I shuddered beneath him and my spine coiled tight. His name crested my lips.

As I shook around him, he groaned and shot toward me.

Rapture took us over the edge.

Our breathing slowed along with our hearts, but he remained collapsed on top of me as if he couldn't find the strength to move.

I laughed, my belly twitching. "Hey. You're heavy."

"I'm just going to stay here for a while. You think they'd mind at the shop? I can tell them I'll bring the notebook in tomorrow."

"I have a feeling they'd like you to bring it in today. In one minute, actually."

"You timing me?"

It was clearer than a spring-fed lake that this man was different from any other. I loved him, and I'd tell him soon.

Eventually, we rose. I scooted into the bathroom to wash and dress, and then he did the same. We met up in the foyer.

"I'll take the notebook into the shop. See if there's anything we can do to analyze it. Coop and Flint are there already."

"Will you be able to tell me whatever you find?"

He shrugged. "That's up to Flint. Sorry." He took a deep breath. "I may never be able to share everything I do with you. I don't like it, but there it is."

"I get it. You're doing something bigger than us. Something important. Sometimes, things like that have to be kept quiet." Not much different than my job. I also couldn't bring work home with me. Patients deserved confidentiality. "I'm just glad this is all over."

"It may be over, but *we're* just beginning."

My heart thrilled at his words. "Want to come to dinner?"

"Love to."

"I happen to have some white chocolate macadamia cookies we can have for dessert."

He gave me a quick kiss. "I can't wait."

I followed him outside, onto the porch.

"What time can I expect you?" A quick glance at my watch showed it was only eleven in the morning. It felt like a lifetime had gone by already but it had only been a few hours since we woke to the hotel on fire and I then had the run-in with the man in the stairwell.

"Five-ish?"

We kissed again.

"I'll stay tonight?" Vulnerability stole into his voice.

Didn't he know what he meant to me? But I hadn't told him. "Eli. I love you. I want you here all the time."

His sharp inhale made me worry I'd spoken too soon. Said too much.

"Ah, Mia," he growled out, pulling me into his arms. "I love you, too."

"Then hurry home soon."

"Home." He grinned. "I like that." He left me and strode to his Jeep. After he backed it down the drive, he pulled out onto the road, tooting his horn as he drove away.

I waved and turned to go back inside. Something drew my eye...

Elwin sat on his front porch, glaring my way.

A shotgun lay on his lap—pointed in my direction.

22

ELI

Our former C.O. and Flint and Mia's Uncle Sid, and Flint found me and Coop in the back shop testing the notebook.

"What have you tried?" Sid asked, patting me on the shoulder as he leaned over the bench. "Great job obtaining this, by the way."

"Mia's the one who takes the credit." I chuckled. "I was just arm candy."

Sid frowned.

Flint laughed. "Bet there's a story there."

"And then some." I nodded to the notebook lying on a workbench. "I've tried the standard cheap invisible ink tricks. A flame and lightbulb didn't reveal anything, so no diluted lemon juice."

"That would be too easy," Coop said. "Also tried grape juice concentrate and nada, so it's not baking soda ink."

"I've heard you can write with milk and then use an iron to reveal writing?" Sid said.

"Yes, and no," I said. "Didn't work." I nudged aside one of the more persistent drones. I'd programmed them for face recognition and they loved honing in on me. Should've used Coop's face instead.

"How about simple old white crayon that can be revealed with dark, watercolor paint?" Flint asked. He traced his finger down the open page. "Don't feel anything, though."

"I read you can sometimes use a well-diluted highlighter then expose the writing with a blacklight, but nada to that one, too," Coop said.

"Why don't I take it D.C. and share it with the boys?" Sid reached for the notebook.

"I'd like to keep it here a little longer, Uncle Sid," Flint said easily. "This job has screwed me over for weeks. I'm determined to figure this component out myself."

"Well, okay." An easy smile filled Sid's face. "I'll be real curious to hear what you discover. The sooner we get those names, the sooner we can arrest maestro and stop the flow of drugs into the U.S."

"I can't wait for that day," Flint said.

Sid's gaze drifted to the notebook again. "Well, I don't have a problem giving you boys a few days to work on this, but if you run into problems, we might want to involve Washington."

A subtle reminder that, while Flint ran Viper Force, this job had come directly from his uncle. Flint was the boss, but he answered to people higher than himself in the government.

"I think we're going to crack this within a few days," Flint said in a steely voice.

And there was his subtle reminder that, while Sid might feel he ran the show, Flint was the one in charge at Viper Force. The final decision to send this notebook to D.C. or not was up to Flint.

"What if we—" Flint's phone rang. He pulled it from his pocket. "Lo." The bit of humor lingering on his face dropped away. "Fuck. Yup. Sure. Thanks for filling me in. Of course. I'll be there as soon as I can." He slammed his phone down on the workbench and rubbed his face with both palms.

"What's up?" Coop asked, pulling his gaze from the notebook.

"It's..." His attention fell on Sid. "Maybe you want to sit down."

Sid stiffened. "I don't like the sound of this."

"Me either." Flint pulled up an office chair and pressed the older man's shoulders until he dropped onto the seat. "That was our new contact in Mexico." His eyes glistened when they fell on me. "Gabe and Haylee have been in an accident. It's bad. They're...They're arranging to life flight them stateside."

"Haylee?" Sid said with horror in his voice. His hands clamped on his thighs. "My daughter. Is she okay?'

"They don't know," Flint said, anguish for his cousin leaking into his voice. "They'd...Well, she and Gabe left a message on my phone saying they'd discovered something astonishing about the case. Something that would blow it wide open."

Sid blinked. "Did they say what it was?"

"Nope. Just a message for me to call. But before I could reach them, someone plowed into their vehicle head-on. Other driver's dead and Haylee and Gabe are both bad off. Gabe's worse than Haylee but she's...Well, they really don't know." He rubbed his reddened face with both of his hands.

Sid stood. When his body swayed, Coop jumped up and grabbed his arm to steady him.

"Take a seat, buddy," Coop said. "Let's talk about what the next step needs to be."

"I have to go to her. Be with her." His pale blue eyes watered and he suddenly looked old. "My poor little girl."

Flint lifted his phone. "I'll get the three of us to Cancun as soon as possible. We'll make damn sure they both get the best medical care possible."

The strain in his voice told me how hard he was taking this. He'd sent Gabe and Haylee to Mexico and now they were near death. Any boss would feel responsible. Sure, we'd been military buddies, covering each other's backs in the line of duty. I knew Flint would feel ultimately responsible, because he hadn't been able to cover theirs. Especially with Haylee being his cousin.

"Eli can hold things down here," Coop said. He nodded at me. "We'll get Gabe and Haylee out of there. They're going to be okay."

Flint nodded. "I'll run home and pack, Uncle Sid. Then meet you at the airport with Cooper. There's a connecting flight leaving at three and I'll make sure we're on it."

"Thank you." Sid stood, steadier this time than the last. "I have a bag in the trunk. Always keep a change of clothes with me. Old habit from my military days I haven't broken since retirement."

It would serve him well, now.

Flint went out to the front office to fill in his Aunt Becca, who'd have to oversee the shop while he was gone. He returned in a few minutes.

"Just heard from Jax. News spreads fast."

Becca called Jax, then. I'd had the same thought.

Flint's gaze pinned me in place. "He wants to go AMA despite the doctors saying he needs to stay longer for observation and another head CT."

Of course, he did. If I knew Jax, the second he'd heard

about Haylee, he'd sprung from the bed and thrown on his jeans.

"He wants you to come pick him up," Flint said to me. "Said the world's still spinning. Doesn't think he can drive."

AFTER CALLING Mia and a little over two hours later, I'd reached the hospital where Jax waited impatiently. He leaped from the bed the moment I walked into the room but grabbed his head and staggered backward until his ass hit the mattress. He sunk down and laid flat, groaning.

"Took you a damn time to get here but I appreciate you coming," he finally said.

"I get it. If it was Mia, I'd be on the plane already."

He cricked his head and stared up at me. "Am I that obvious?"

"Only to a few of us." All of us, actually, but I'd leave him his pride. I guessed the big question was, did Haylee see what we all did?

Far be it for me to speculate. Making sure I didn't do something stupid and mess things up with Mia was enough challenge for me.

But she said she loved me, and I needed to trust in her words.

"Flint, Coop, and Sid are on their way, though. They'll have Gabe and Haylee home safely in no time."

"I'm going to her." Jax sat up on the bed and hugged his head with his arms.

"You're in no shape to go anywhere. You need to lay back in that bed again and do what the doctors tell you to do."

"Don't you get it? She needs me."

Maybe, and maybe she couldn't care less if Jax showed

up and hovered by her side. She might have no clue of Jax's feelings let alone return them. "She'll be home soon. You'll see her then."

"Going to her." Jax stood and staggered toward the door. "You either take me to the airport or I'm walking."

"It's over a hundred miles to Portland."

"I'll get there no later than tomorrow. Damn head should be feeling a little better by then."

I sighed. "I'll take you."

Jax turned at the door and a half-grin rose on his face. "Knew you'd see it my way."

I rolled my eyes but grabbed his arm when he swayed. "I'll get you to the airport as soon as I can. You got a flight arranged yet?"

Jax pulled his phone but cursed soon after scrolling into the screen. "Crappy thing." He rubbed his eyes. "Can't see straight."

I held in my second sigh. "You sure you're up for this?"

"No choice. Don't you understand?"

I did. "Let me do it for you." Scrolling to a travel site on my phone, I soon located a flight leaving a little over an hour after we'd reach the airport. "We'll be cutting it close. You might have to pick up a few things at the airport."

"I'll figure that out after I get there."

The nurse brought paperwork for Jax to sign and with a lot of tongue-clucking, arranged for someone to take him out in a wheelchair while I brought my Jeep around to the front door.

We were soon on our way south, me pushing the pedal to the floorboard as hard as I dared. Seven miles over the limit was okay with the cops, right? While I was tempted to push it to fifteen or twenty, stopping for a ticket would eat away our precious time. I was determined to get Jax on that flight.

We still had an hour left to travel when my phone rang. Mia.

"Eli!" Her words choked through the line, bringing my heart to a standstill.

I gripped the steering wheel until my knuckles blanched white. Leaning forward, I slammed my foot on the gas pedal as if that would bring me to her in seconds. "You okay?"

"It's Russell."

Crap. Her ex. "What's going on, honey?"

Jax watched me intently. At least his eyes no longer spun in his head. Hopefully, he'd feel almost normal by the time he reached Cancun.

"My lawyer called." Mia's words stuttered from her. "Russell escaped during a pre-release detail. Cleaning up garbage along the side of the highway. He escaped!"

"When?"

"A week ago. Eli..."

Her thoughts must mimic mine. Had all of this been caused by the guy in the stairwell or had Russell been involved instead?

"My lawyer apologized for not letting me know. She's been on maternity leave. She left a message with her office to call me but they messed up." She whimpered. "What am I going to do?"

"Honey. It's okay. I'll be there as fast as I can. What else did your lawyer say?"

"Russell borrowed a friend's car a week ago. The police are looking for him but they haven't located him yet."

A week? It was taking them too long to find him.

"My lawyer said Russell was seen at a convenience store

in South Portland five days ago. Oh, God! The woman at the store just called the police. She'd seen his face somewhere but couldn't remember where. It wasn't until she saw a report online that she connected it to Russell. Five days ago, Eli. Five. Days! He was heading north. He's been after me all this time. Playing a game with me. Slinking through my house." Her voice quivered and I wanted to be there to hold her. Comfort her. Protect her. "He was right outside my bedroom! Toying with me. But he's escalating. I think it was him."

"Him doing what?" Jax asked.

"Strike one. Strike two. In three strikes, I'm out." Her horror charged through the line. "He'll get me this time."

"Not happening," I growled out.

"My lawyer said I should find a safe place to stay there until they catch him. It shouldn't take long. But...five days!"

"It's going to be okay." Damn, I needed to get to her. Now.

"Someplace safe?" she said again. "There is no safe place. Wherever I go, he'll follow. If I went to Ginny's, I'd only drag her into this. She could get hurt. Same with Mom and Dad. I won't endanger them. Just being near me endangers you."

"Mia. Listen to me." I tried to sound soothing but rage was roaring through me and it leaked into my voice. I couldn't hold it back. "I'll get there as soon as I can. You'll be safe. I promise."

"My lawyer said one last thing." Death ruled in her voice. She was shutting down, creeping inside herself to hide. I knew it. Silence stretched through the line for too long. "Russell...Well, his friend not only loaned him the car, but he also gave Russell a gun." Her sob broke through, crushing my heart. "She said—" Sniff. "They'll find him. Arrest him. And the judge will make sure he never comes near me again. But that'll never happen. He's smart. He won't be taken easily."

"I'm on the road right now. Only an hour away." I slammed my fist on the steering wheel and pushed the gas pedal to the floor.

"He said he'd kill me after I told the police what he'd done. He broke my ribs...broke me a year ago. This time, he'll end it permanently. Strike three. It's been him all along. The guy in the stairwell was independent in all this. He frowned when I mentioned the strikes. Now, I know why."

If only I could give her my strength. "You never told me what Russell did for a living. We dealing with a lawyer or a banker here?"

"Russell is...Well, he was a DEA agent."

Not an average opponent. It would take considerable finesse to eliminate this threat. But I'd make for damn sure he didn't get within a mile of Mia.

"It's going to be all right." Who was I fooling? She was alone. I'd left her defenseless. I glanced at the dash clock. "I'll come straightaway to you." I glanced at Jax, who stared at my phone in horror. "You can get a ride from there, right?"

He nodded.

Damn. Please keep her safe until I could get there. "Make sure your security system's fully armed."

"Has been since you left."

"Stay inside. Don't go near your windows. And lay low. I'll get there as quickly as I can."

"I will." Her voice tightened, telling me panic ruled. "I'm scared, Eli."

"He's not getting to you, honey. I promise."

"I hope you're right!"

I hated hearing the terror in her voice. When would this end?

I was done playing around. It was time to end this, but not in the way Russell intended. He wasn't only facing a defenseless woman. He'd have to get through me to reach Mia. And I wasn't backing down. I'd fight to the death to protect her.

"Hold on," she said. "I've got...Someone sent a text."

A short pause was followed by her gasp.

"Mia," I shouted. "What's going on?"

"A text message," she shot out.

"Who from?" I asked, already knowing.

"Unknown sender."

"What does it say, Mia?" I wanted to fling myself through the lines and hold her this instant but all I could do was drive like a fiend to reach her place.

"It says..." Her gulping sob rang out. "Tick tock. Ready for strike three?"

23

MIA

"Stay inside," Eli had said through the phone.

As if I dared go anywhere, now. To think earlier I'd been out in my front garden, ignoring Elwin while I weeded the beds that were so overgrown, I was afraid the neighborhood homeowner's association would sick the board president on me to demand a gardening intervention.

Now, I didn't dare look out my windows.

Walter jumped up onto the sofa beside me. I'd collapsed here after ending my call with Eli. I'd wanted to keep him on the line, clinging to him every second it took for him to reach me, but he had to drive. I wouldn't endanger him to help me feel safe.

I'd never feel safe with Russell loose.

Would the cops find him before he reached me?

I lifted my feet up onto the sofa, wrapped my arms around my legs, and clung. My whimper rang out in the room. Shivers wracked my body like a category five hurricane. Walter, as if sensing my need, snuggled closer. No purr. But having him near lent me strength. I stroked his face and neck. His bejeweled collar winked in the late-day sunlight filtering in through the windows.

My skin crawled with fear. Was Russell watching me right now?

As if he stood in front of me fuming, his hand swung out. I shrunk, trying to make myself small enough he wouldn't see me. Hit me.

Yelping, I leaped from the sofa and ran down the hall to my room. I dropped to the floor and crawled underneath my bed. Walter joined me, maybe wondering what the hell was going on but okay with hanging out here if that was my whim.

I clung to my kitty and sobbed as flashbacks poured through me like acid, burning wherever they touched.

Don't say anything. He'll find you.

I hated that I'd reverted back to the cowering, clingy thing I'd been a year ago.

I'd thought myself stronger than this.

But Russell was loose. He was coming after me. He'd find me. And this time, he'd do what he promised. He'd kill me.

"Mia," someone called out from the front hall.

I cringed, clinging to the floor and Walter, who struggled until I let him go free. He scampered out from under the bed and took off toward the front of the house. If only he was the size of a lion. Then he could defend me from this new threat.

"Mia!" the voice barely penetrated my panic. I fisted the carpet and pressed my face against it, wishing I could sink through it and hide.

Keep quiet. Don't move. Don't draw attention.

"Mia?" Whoever it was spoke softer, in a voice so full of love it broke through the shell I'd built around me.

A whimper was all I could release. Because it was clear. This wasn't Russell.

Eli dropped down onto his belly beside the bed. "Aw, honey." He held out his hand, and I grasped it like a lifeline. "It's okay. I'm here. You're safe."

"He's going to hurt me."

"I won't let him."

"He'll track me down and kill me."

"Has to go through me first. I'm not leaving you alone, Mia. I'm here for you always." He crawled underneath the bed and wrapped his arms around me, banging his elbow on the frame above while finding his spot. "It's going to be okay. I promise."

Releasing my fear, I clung to him and sighed.

I *was* safe. Nothing and no one could harm me now.

WE SAT on the sofa with Walter snuggled between us.

"What are we going to do?" I said. "I can't hide behind my security system forever."

"We're not hiding, but no reason we can't stay here until they locate Russell. The cops, despite messing up about him being locked behind bars, have got a manhunt going. They'll find him. I won't let him hurt you. Never again."

"I hate being terrified of him almost as much as I hate him."

"He hurt you. Natural to feel that way. He tapped your vulnerabilities and used them against you."

Eli wouldn't do that.

I scooted forward on the sofa. "I need to feed Walter." While he'd been comforting me, the sun had slunk toward the horizon. It would be dark soon.

Darkness could hide anything. *Anyone.*

Walter blinked up at me when I stood. As if he knew what time it was and had been watching for this moment, he rose and stretched.

His collar caught the sunlight winking through the curtains.

Wait.

Frowning, I stooped down in front of Walter and unlinked the collar.

Horror expanded inside me to the point I thought I'd explode.

"Someone, no something's different here."

Eli sat forward, his face filled with concern. He took the collar from my limp hands.

"Fuck," he said. Then again, louder. "You won't get to her." He lifted the collar and shook it. "Damn fuckin' camera." His eyes met mine. "He's been watching us all this time. From your cat's collar."

24

ELI

I held up the cat collar, making sure whoever was watching could see my face. "You want her, you'll have to come get her." And I for damn sure wasn't going to make it easy.

Time to get out of town. Take this to *my* territory. I was done hiding behind locks and doors. It was time to end this.

I knew exactly where I could take her. Where I could finally make sure she was safe by eliminating this threat.

"What's going on?" Mia asked, fear a living thing in her voice.

After dropping the collar on the hardwood floor, I crushed it underneath my heel, taking endless satisfaction in eliminating Russell's ability to spy.

"Do you have any decent pictures of Russell?" I asked.

She winced and shrugged, then pulled her phone. "I think I deleted them all but I might be able to find a few on Facebook." Her face pinched as she scrolled through the social media app and, when it tightened, I knew she'd located some. "I assume you want me to send them to you?"

"Yep." My phone chimed as they came through.

"You have a plan." She said it with such certainty, I gave her a hug.

"Definitely." Always. Instead of playing reactionary any longer, I was going to drive this to a showdown. One on *my* terms, not Russell's. "I'm going to take you somewhere." I didn't mention the location. If the creep had planted one camera, there was a good chance he not only had more scattered throughout the house but he had listening devices as well. "Can you pack a bag for about a week's time? Plan on going rustic."

"What do you mean by—"

I placed my fingertip over her lips. "Let's take a quick walk, okay?"

"Sure?" Her frightened glance shot to the windows. "Outside? What if..." Her face cleared, and I knew she got it. "Okay."

Holding hands, we left the house and took a left at the end of the drive rather than pass Elwin's house. He'd vacated the porch but there was no need to stir him up further.

Elwin was another issue I'd deal with soon, but he was more a pest than a problem. A quick call to the cops should set Mia's neighbor straight.

"You do have a plan," she said in a low voice.

"Sure do."

One of Mia's other neighbors, working in her front garden, straightened. While rubbing her back, she waved. "Beautiful evening, isn't it?"

"Perfect," Mia said with a fake smile. "The mosquitoes have been atrocious but they're not bad tonight."

"Citronella," the elderly woman said as she brushed strands of gray hair off her face. "Works like a charm."

"I'll have to get some," Mia said.

We continued walking.

"After you pack your bag, we'll go out to the shop. Before we leave town, I need to pick up a few things there."

"Weapons?"

"That, too."

"Why Russell's pictures?"

"I've got a few friends who will be eager to see what he looks like." Locust 3 would help me take Russell down permanently. Not kill him unless he escalated this to the next level, but I'd make sure he was captured and locked behind bars for a good long time.

"Okay." The smile she released told me she trusted me completely to keep her safe. "Friends are always good."

"Especially these friends."

"I'll pack then."

"We're going camping, so like I said, plan for rustic. No showers there, though you can wash at the sink. And it can get cold at night. Plan to dress warmly." Turning, we walked back toward her house. "We can't say anything else about this once we're inside. I'm worried about bugs."

"What will I do about Walter?"

"Flint's out of town again, but what about Ginny? Could we take him to her place?"

Mia pulled her phone. "I'll text her and ask. Fortunately, he already knows her. The strange, new setting will be enough to upset him without introducing people he's never met before."

"What can I do to help you get ready?" I asked quietly as we strode up her front walkway.

"Walter's pet carrier is in the basement. I'll pack while you get that and talk him into climbing inside. Then grab his dry food, which is also in the basement, plus enough cans of wet food for however long you think we'll be away."

"Plan at least a few days. And I'll be quick."

A short time later, we drove to Ginny's place with Walter howling in his cat carrier in the back. Mia's tight spine told me that while she was nervous about what I planned, she was prepared to stand by my side while I saw it through.

Couldn't ask for anyone better in my life. I just hoped I could end this situation so we could move on to an awesome future together.

After dropping Walter off with Ginny—he promptly scooted down the hall to her bedroom the moment we let him out of his crate—we drove to the shop.

Becca met us inside.

"Mia, sweetheart, you okay?" She enveloped her niece in a huge hug before pulling back in their embrace to study her face. "Flint called. I was a wreck when I heard what happened at the conference, let alone to Haylee." She strode around Mia and right up to me, glaring. "You're slacking off. You know what happens to people when they slack off."

"You grind their faces into the mat?" I said, not even the least bit concerned. In fact, I half-smiled. "Don't cash me out yet. I've got a few tricks in mind for this creep."

The sharp look in Becca's eyes made it easy for me to see why Mia's aunt had been a successful operative. Her gaze could cut a suspect in two.

"Then tell me." Becca propped a manicured hand on her slender hip. "How do you plan to redeem yourself, because I'm prepared to listen." *Prepared* was a light statement, as evidenced by the rapid tap of her heeled foot.

"I'll need a few supplies to put things in place."

"You'll tell me all about it first, naturally." Pinching my t-shirt, she hauled me into the hall, calling out to Mia over her shoulder, "Sweetheart, why don't you wait in the break room while I help Eli?" She then ground out to me, "I anticipate you'll want my input."

"I wouldn't have it any other way."

She nodded pertly. "Not sure I like you yet, Eli. I'll come with you, wherever you're taking her."

"That would be great." The back-up would be fantastic. "But it's tricky. Where we're going, there won't be room for one more."

Pausing in the hall, she tapped her lip. "Now, you've roused my curiosity."

I held open the door to the supply closet and waved for her to enter before me. "Let me explain and you can help me troubleshoot. I want to make sure I'm not missing anything."

"Perfect. We're going to make sure Mia's never threatened again."

"Definitely."

It didn't take long to show Becca what I intended.

"Clever," Becca said with an approving nod. "And you're right. I'd be in the way."

Mia emerged from the break room in time to catch me hauling a large box filled with supplies out to my Jeep.

"What are we planning?" she asked as her aunt opened the front door for me. "Armageddon?"

I paused. "Sorta." After carrying the box outside, I returned to the front office. "All set?" My eyes were drawn to the window, and I rubbed my palms together. "It'll be dark soon."

"Sure." Mia didn't sound certain. "While I'm eager to finish this, a big part of me would rather crawl underneath my covers and hide."

Couldn't blame her for being concerned about the

upcoming confrontation. I sure was. While I'd put every-thing in place then double and triple check it, there were too many unknown variables. I didn't like endangering Mia.

Becca drew Mia into her arms for a big hug. "You watch out for yourself, okay? While this big brute's prepared to take down a T-Rex single-handed, don't forget that it's we Crawford women who come through in the end." She dropped her hands down to squeezed Mia's. "Don't you forget that for a minute."

"I'll keep her safe," I said. "Promise."

We left and drove to my house. My security phone app showed my place was still armed, which was reassuring. I disengaged the system, and we went inside.

Mia followed me into my kitchen where I opened drawers and cupboards and selected items, tossing them into a supermarket bag. I stuffed my potato masher in with everything else, generating a clang.

"I didn't think we'd be cooking tonight," she said, gaping at me.

"Just making sure I don't forget anything."

"But, a potato masher?"

"You never know when one will come in handy." Glancing around, I frowned. "Nutmeg, nutmeg."

"We're making eggnog?" Crossing the kitchen, she opened the cabinets and pawed through a row of spices Ginny had left here the last time I'd hosted Thanksgiving. Mia drew out the bag of whole nuts and handed it to me. From Hawaii, Ginny had said; she'd bought them online. Grating created a little more work, but there was no reason not to cook with the best ingredients available. So, Ginny said.

"You want a grater, too?" Mia asked.

"I do." I tossed both in with the other items I'd collected. "Nutmeg's a natural hallucinogen."

Her words came out slowly. "Okay. Not going to ask."

I winked. "You'll see."

"Hallucinations? Hopefully not."

"How about getting me couple nylon knee-highs?" I said. "I keep them in the box on the top of my closet."

"Something you need to tell me, Eli?" She grinned, and I was grateful I could make her smile. My own smile only half-lifted and fell too soon.

"When you're stationed in the south, you need to worry about chiggers."

"Chiggers?"

"You know—"

"Also known as berry bugs. Part of the Trombiculidae family of mites."

I scratched my head. "All I know is they're a pain in the ass. They crawl up your pant legs and dig their way in."

"And the nylon knee-highs?"

"The nylon's just thick enough to keep the chiggers from burrowing into your skin."

Her squeamish expression said it all. "I'm grateful I live in Maine now, where we don't have to worry about anything but mosquitoes."

"And black flies, come spring."

She lifted her eyebrows.

"You just wait. They get into everything. And bite. Itches like hell."

"Back to your nylons." She started down the hall. "On the top of your closet, you said?"

"Yeah. I've got some left from when I was active."

She returned a moment later with a few knee highs and

a grin that stretched from ear to ear. "When this...is all through, you're modeling these for me. While I'd always taken you for a guy who enjoyed black undies, I notice these are nude."

Speaking of nude. We both need to wear nude again soon. Had it only been this morning when we last made love? It felt like a lifetime ago.

She giggled when I advanced on her with a pretend scowl on my face. "Not much chance of me modeling them, honey."

"Aw. I bet you'd look cute."

"Nope. No way. No how."

"Okay," she said with a heavy sigh, tossing the nylons into the bag. "What else do we need?"

I hefted the bags. "This is it."

After setting the house alarm, we went out to my Jeep. I strolled around to the back and loaded the bags, and she followed.

Stooping down after shutting the hatch, I stared at the underside of the bumper. Bingo.

"What are you doing?" she asked, dropping down to her knees beside me.

I tipped my head toward a round piece of metal sitting on the gravel drive beside me. Something I'd picked up at the shop after inspecting my vehicle. "I brought an Earth magnet."

She cocked her head. "As opposed to a moon magnet."

I chuckled and dropped down onto the ground fully. After rolling onto my back, I dragged myself underneath the vehicle, my clothing scraping on the pavement.

"Checking out the exhaust?" she asked.

"I'm seeing how clever Russell is."

"Too clever?" Her voice shook.

"Not for me." I crawled back out. Standing, I brushed off my jeans and the back of my tee, then tossed the devices I'd found—except one—into the bushes. Mia then dusted off my neck and head.

"So, what are we doing next?" she said. "*We* being a bold word choice on my part since I was doing nothing here. I don't even know what an Earth magnet is."

"We're setting up the first of my booby traps." Lifting the magnet, I tilted my head and stared underneath the bumper. The magnet clanged when it met metal.

"Booby traps. You think we'll be followed and your Earth magnet will pop off and somehow impale him? I do like that plan, but it sounds risky. The magnet might miss."

I straightened. "This baby will make sure we're not followed. Not yet, anyway."

A quick glance around showed we were alone as far as I could tell. But Russell could be spying from any location. For example, the trees along one side of my house. Or from inside my garage.

Despite the heat still lingering in the waning day, she shivered. "Not yet, you said. There's a time when we'll want to be followed?'

"Yep."

We went around our respective sides of the vehicle and climbed in. Buckled.

"Earth magnet. I assume it's not an explosive. You're not going to blow up your pretty Jeep, are you?" she asked. As if it was the best dog in the world, she patted the dash.

I turned the key and the engine growled. "Nope. I like it too much."

"And if you didn't?"

I laughed.

She tried to keep a straight face, but her humor shone through.

Damn, I loved her.

I'd do everything within my power to ensure she'd be a part of my life forever.

25

MIA

S ince he'd disabled the tracking device on his Wrangler, Eli was confident we were not being followed. Not any longer, that is. But that didn't keep him from training his eyes in the side and rearview mirrors as he drove out of town. He got onto the highway and headed north. We'd remain on I95 until we hit Lincoln, then follow Route 2 all the way to Mattawamkeag.

I tapped my flower-embroidered sneakers on the floor. "I like hitting the road with you even if it's not under the best circumstances."

If only this trip was for fun.

"My grandparents own a piece of land out in the middle of nowhere. It's got a small cabin on it, a gas fridge and stove, and a simple shower."

"You said no shower," I reminded him.

"It's a simple, rigged-up thing with a hand pull to release water that's collected when it rains. Unheated."

Not quite a shower, then, but I'd deal if we were there more than a day or so. I shivered, realizing there was only one way out of this. Russell would win, or me and Eli.

It wasn't going to be Russell.

"We'll hide in the cabin?" I said. "Is it bullet-proof?"

"Nope. It's made of rough-hewn logs—my grandfather built it himself right after he and Gran got married—but we won't be staying there. The cabin's a decoy."

"We're not going to the cabin, then?"

"Initially, but then, no."

"I'll admit I'm scared about how this will end, but one thing is certain. I trust you."

Taking my hand, he linked our fingers. "I'll die before I let anyone hurt you."

I'd do the same.

He didn't let go of my hand until we arrived in Mattawamkeag. After driving through the mill town, he turned off Route 2 onto a smaller, paved road. Three miles up, he took a right, onto the rough dirt road that led to his grandparent's property. Putting the vehicle into neutral, he engaged the brake and got out. After unlocking the padlock, he creaked open the long metal gate that he said had been here since he was a kid. He drove through and locked it behind us.

As he climbed back inside the vehicle, I asked, "Do we expect this to heat up tonight?"

"Maybe." His glance took in the dash. "It's ten. We'll get set up but I don't believe we'll see action until dawn. I'm planning on it turning out that way."

My pulse jumped, and I knew we'd have to hustle if we wanted to get things ready. "What can I do?"

"The drive is a few miles long, so we'll stop at regular intervals to mount cameras."

"Miles long?" I peered into the dark woods surrounding us. "I assume there are deer out here. Raccoons." Who knew what else?

"Bear and moose, too."

Bear. Lovely. "Will we see a bear?" I was less worried about moose, who were mostly timid creatures except during fall rutting season. We had a few months yet before we had to worry about that.

"Probably not. We won't leave food out, which would draw them in and no one's allowed to bait them out here." Shifting into gear, he drove forward, the tires bumping across potholes and ruts. "Like every other time I've come here since I was a kid, it's going to be a slow ride."

"You know he'll just walk around the gate." Staring out the window, I gnawed on my nail.

"Maybe. The gate's solid steel. I doubt he'll bring anything to blast his way through. And it's a long walk to where we're going."

To our left, the Mattawamkeag River gleamed ebony blue in the moonlight, with rushing, white-capped waves.

"You said you came here a lot when you were little?"

"Yeah." His sigh leaked out. "My dad...Well, he took off when I was eight. Bailed on me, Mom, and Ginny. I don't know what kind of kid I would've turned into if my grandparents hadn't stepped in and tried to fill the gap."

"What did you do up here? No TV or Internet I assume."

"Spent all my time outside. Ran wild." He chuckled and I could picture him as a small boy. I could tell by the way he said it that he'd been hurt from the loss of his dad, someone who should've loved him unconditionally but had abandoned him instead. "Gran let me pretty much do whatever I wanted from sun-up 'til sundown. Went fishing a lot. Swam in the river."

"The current looks strong."

"It is here and there but it's shallow in places. It was damn cold in the spring."

"Frozen run-off from the surrounding hills."

"Yep."

An few minutes passed, and we kept bumping along. The speedometer barely crept past thirty, but I imagined he didn't want to go faster. Keeping this vehicle functioning could mean the difference between life and death.

"Do your grandparents own all of this?" I swept my hand toward the endless forest.

"They own about a couple thousand acres out here."

A couple thousand acres? I couldn't fathom that amount. Growing up in the more-congested Massachusetts had made me appreciate how exciting it could be to own more than a postage stamp lawn. My small house came with almost a full acre, which I'd felt equated with an estate, though it was the norm for most of the houses in the downtown area of Crescent Cove.

"If we're not staying in the cabin, will we sleep in your Jeep?"

"We'll need some of the night to get ready but come dawn, we'll be hidden away."

"I like that you have a plan." Would Russell follow? My biggest fear was that he'd wait us out. We'd have to return home eventually. If he was patient—something he never had been—he could strike once I'd let down my guard.

I rubbed my arms to shed my goosebumps. "What if this doesn't work?"

"Then we'll try something else. I'm not giving up. He'll never get to you."

Taking his hand again, I squeezed it. "Thank you. For being here for me. And for making me feel safe."

Lifting my hand, he kissed my knuckles, my fingers. I wished he could kiss me, that all we had to think about was where we'd go on our first 'real' date. We'd done this backward. The big question was: would we get that chance? "At least we're facing this together."

"Always."

We bumped along for a few more minutes.

"We're half a mile away from my grandparents' property." He stopped the Wrangler, put it into neutral, and engaged the emergency brake. "Time to get things started."

I got out with him.

He opened up the back of his Jeep and slid a cardboard box forward. Opening the top, he reached inside and grabbed a tiny rectangular device. "Upgraded version of a game camera."

Camo pattern to blend in with the surroundings? "Is this the kind you mount on a trail to take pictures of whatever walks by?"

"Yep, only a bit more sophisticated. Something Coop's been working on back at the shop." He hauled out a small ladder and carried it over to an evergreen tree standing a few feet off the road.

I followed, watching as he leaned the ladder against the tree and returned for his bag of tools.

Opening his hand, he showed me the tiny thing lying on his palm again. "This one'll do more than take a grainy picture of something passing by. It'll detect motion but filter out anything we don't need to see, like bobcats or skunks. It's smart."

Bobcats? Great. I doubted they were as friendly as Walter.

The device was barely larger than his thumb.

"That won't stop him," I said, not unless it sprayed the area with bullets. Damn, but I was getting bloodthirsty about this.

"Don't intend to stop him with this. It's just here to let

me know he's coming. I'll mount a bunch of these babies at regular intervals along the road."

"Cute," I said, touching the box as if it might bite.

"If someone passes, it'll send video to my phone app. Attached to a battery pack, it'll be working long after we need it."

"Phone app? I thought you said there was no TV or Internet out here? I assume from that you meant no cell service, too."

"Companies are installing new towers all the time. But I brought a booster that'll amplify and rebroadcast the signal to my phone. Yours, too."

"With these cameras in place, we'll see him coming."

"Indeed." He rubbed my shoulder. "But they're not our only defense. I'll rig a few tricks in the woods once we reach the cabin. Enough to take down ten DEA agents."

I snorted. "Wouldn't want to do that. They'd send a SWAT team after us." My mood sobered instantly. "We're forgetting one thing. He's not dumb. He'll expect something like this. He'll leave the road." Swatting away a few pesky mosquitoes, I peered into the woods. "He'll go around the cameras." Filled with downed trees and dense brush, it wouldn't be an easy hike, but a determined person could do it. Russell was definitely determined.

The river roared at our back. Only someone with a death wish would try to swim upstream in this section. But he'd said there were shallower areas. Russell could walk through those.

Eli shook his head. "Why bother trooping through brush or the river when the road's handy?"

"Russell isn't rational. He must know the police are after him. He'll be locked up a very long time for escaping, let alone coming after me. And he's got the same training as you, I imagine."

"Not quite. I learned a lot overseas and from the military."

"Enough to take down a DEA agent?"

His half-smile curled up. "Enough for ten of them." Too soon, his smile fell. "We've all got a bit of the dark inside us, but your ex will think things through. He won't endanger himself in the woods because that would make it harder to get to you. He'll stick to the road."

"If he doesn't?"

"He'll deal with a hell of a lot more than cameras."

"Don't suppose they shoot laser beams?"

"Something even better."

"What's that?"

"I also brought a swarm of locusts."

"What's an army of bugs going to do?"

"Smart bugs. With some fancy programming courtesy of me. I can't reveal much about them because they're a...prototype—"

"Top secret, then."

"Ah, yeah. Anyway. Just trust me. They're on our side and they're lethal."

"Good. We need lethal. Never thought I'd say this, me being a doctor and all, but he's bringing this to me, not the other way around. I have the right to defend myself even if it means the police have no one living left to haul back into court."

Eli chipped out a nod. "My thoughts exactly. I'm not going vigilante, but I won't hesitate to remove him from your life permanently if he comes ready to fight to the death."

"So, your locust friends are part of the team. I like that we have a back-up plan."

"I hate seeing you stressed, but I won't lie to you. This was going to be a tight situation. But short of dropping in via chopper, I'll be ready for him."

"His friend gave him a car. Doubt they own a chopper." I couldn't help glancing up at the inky sky. Pitch dark, speckled with a billion stars. The moon hung high and heavy, nearly full. Only a few clouds broke up the sky. The moonlight would be to our benefit—and work against us. Russell would see us as easily as we'd see him.

Eli finished mounting the camera and stepped back to make sure it was well-hidden.

"I can't see it," I said, hands on my hips. "And I doubt he'll examine every tree along the way. That would take him days."

"My thought exactly. I'll build a mesh network that'll tie them together. They'll work as a second team, coordinating with the locusts."

"Your locusts don't fire laser beams, either, I assume, but do they come armed?"

"Unfortunately, not yet." He pulled a handgun from the back of his waist. "I've got this plus a few shotguns. We'll be prepared for him if he makes it past the fortress I intend to surround you with."

I liked that. Staring down the road, I hoped I wouldn't see lights from a vehicle coming our way. Eli said it would take time to get ready, and I wanted us securely hidden before Russell arrived.

I only hoped we'd make it out of this alive.

26

ELI

We got back into the Jeep and continued, stopping periodically for me to mount more cameras. Eventually, we reached the end of the road and I turned onto an overgrown track. Five hundred yards in, I parked and shut off the engine. "We're here."

"Custer's last stand?"

"We're savvier than Custer."

"Sure hope so." Mia squinted through the window. Wildly wooded land surrounded us, filled with old tree growth. This area hadn't seen a chainsaw since before I was born.

We were miles in from the main road. Nice and isolated. Exactly the way I liked it.

It was time for a showdown and this time, it would be on my terms. My territory.

"Where to next?" Mia unbuckled and opened her door. "I assume we walk from here."

"Yep." I joined her at the back of my Jeep, where I handed her my small bag to carry. I hefted the larger box I'd packed back at the shop. I'd come back for everything else after I got Mia settled in the cabin. I nudged my head toward a barely discernible trail leading into the woods. "Follow me." I trooped through a thin strip of deep grass growing along the road and took the trail weaving through tall tree growth, following faint steps created by deer or maybe even a bear.

"No one has been here for some time," Mia said.

"Nope. Not with gran dead and my grandfather in the nursing home. Other than the kid I hire to bring out a mower, no one's been here for years."

"I assume we'll have to de-tick ourselves when we arrive."

"Yep."

She shivered. "Never did like bugs."

We arrived at a small, open field. Over the years, I'd paid the kid to drive down here and mow the grass each summer. I hadn't wanted it overgrowing with scruff. The forest would take the land back within a few years if I didn't keep it groomed. Mom had spent her summers here, too, and she loved the place. Hoped to come up here a lot more once she'd retired.

The two-room cabin sat on the far side of the field ringed with long overgrown flower beds Gran had kept filled with hollyhocks and day lily's when I was a kid. It pleased me to see a few straggling flowers blooming even after she was no longer around to tend them.

Hard to believe such an idyllic location might soon become my own personal battle zone.

A DEA agent, huh? He'd be a formidable opponent.

The rustic cabin, built from hand-hewn logs by my grandfather, held the last of my good memories. I'd practically grown up here. My grandparents would sleep in the tiny bedroom on the back while I'd take the couch in the main room. I hadn't cared where I'd slept. Camp meant getting away from life. Fun.

Grandpa would get up early and make pancakes, saying we could let Gran sleep in as long as she pleased. But she never did. She'd emerge as soon as the sweet, maple smell hit the air. Standing in the doorway dressed in her long cotton nightie, her bare feet planted on the hardwood floor, she'd smile. "My boys," she'd always say before joining us at the small kitchen table and digging in with gusto. "You sure know how to please an old woman's heart."

Maybe, when all this was settled, I'd bring Mia back here for a long weekend. I'd let her sleep in. And in the morning, I'd make her pancakes.

We crossed the field, our feet crunching on the dry, stubbly grass.

A few feet away, Mia stopped and stared at the cabin. "You said we're not going to barricade ourselves inside."

"Remember? Decoy."

"Where will we hide?"

"Where he'll never find us. We're going wild." I unlocked and held the front door open for her.

"You mean we're going to run through the woods with sticks? Live off the land?"

Not a bad idea as long as I was with Mia, but... "Something even better than all that."

She turned in the small living room, standing on the oval braided rug Gran had made, facing me. "Any hints?"

"I'll show you soon enough. I'm going to set up a few surprises for Russell, first." I lowered the box onto the kitchen table and started pulling things out.

"Booby traps," she said with a gusty sigh. "I like this."

When her eyes gleamed, my heart did, too.

Sliding off the empty pack I'd carried on my back, I started filling it.

Mia ticked off the items as I dropped them inside. "Hatchet. Check. And...is that fishing line?"

I held up the small spool. "It's clear."

"Of course, it is. The fish would see it if it was pink." She chuckled nervously.

"As you wisely pointed out, clear's nearly impossible to see."

She frowned. "Okay." Poking inside the box, she held up a machete. "Can I keep this here with me?"

I took it from her and slid it into the sheath hanging from my belt. "Once I'm done with it, it's yours." I added a set of sheathed steak knives to my pack.

"So much for the barbeque."

"Definitely in our future."

She paused and blinked fast. "We *do* have a future."

"Never doubt it." I'd make sure it happened.

Mia pulled three long blue strips of rubber from the box. "Exercise bands. I know you love working out, but isn't this taking it a little far?"

Taking them from her, I flexed my arms, stretching the bands until they thinned. Showing off a little, but hell, I did love the gleam that came to her eyes whenever she looked at me. "These will come in handy."

She rolled her eyes and dug back inside the box, while I coiled up the bands and tucked them into my bag.

"A nail file," she said, handing it over without question. "Everyone needs one of those." Reaching into her pocket, she pulled out a pen. "I feel as if I should contribute. How about this?"

I took it from her and dropped it into the bag. "Great idea."

"I was just kidding."

"I'm not."

After zipping up the bag, I hefted it onto my back. "I'm going to step outside for a bit. Slide the bar down over the door after I leave."

Arms crossing on her chest, she nodded. "I'll, um..." She glanced around. "Take care of the cobwebs." Shuddering, she grabbed the broom from where it leaned beside the door. "And de-tick myself." Another shudder.

I stepped outside and waited until the bar thudded into place behind me.

It was time to create a few surprises.

A few hours later, when dawn was cresting the horizon, I finished. I tossed the empty backpack inside the Jeep and went around to the back bumper.

"Okay, creep," I growled. "It's time for you to come get what you've been seeking."

It sure as hell wasn't Mia.

Reaching down underneath my bumper, I removed the magnet.

27

MIA

Hours passed, and I knew I ought to be worried. Anyone would be if they had a relentless, vengeance-seeking ex-boyfriend hunting them down.

But, for the first time in a long time, I felt in control. While I'd been scared to come this far from home to a place where I knew we'd force a stand-off, as I'd waited for Eli, I'd changed. Yes, the isolated location was scary, but inside me, I had the strength to deal with it. While I hadn't realized it was there, it had grown inside me over the past few months.

I'd found myself again.

Maybe it helped that I didn't face this alone. I had someone I loved to stand beside me when I faced my demons. And, while Eli had picked the location and timing, when we faced Russell, I'd have my back to Eli's. Nothing and no one would do us harm. We were a team.

Eli's quick knock, followed by him calling out, told me he'd returned. I slid the deadbolt and opened the door. When he stepped inside, he brought with him a burst of fresh air and early-morning sunshine. Happy smells for a frightening time, but I drank them in and smiled.

"All set," he said.

"Almost." I extended my hand, and with a grin, he handed me the machete and the sheath I could wrap around my waist. After dropping them on the table, I strode back up to him and rose onto my toes. Pressed myself against him. I stroked his hair, his neck, his back. I kissed him. I'd never be able to kiss him enough. I wasn't afraid to admit that I clung to his shoulders. He was warmth and kindness and everything I needed.

Leaning back, he stared down at me, his eyes rich deep brown. He slid his knuckles along my face and fingered my hair. His grin heated me straight through. "You ready to check out my treehouse?"

My heart glowed. "Is that like taking me back to your place to view your etchings?"

"Even better."

I took his hand and linked our fingers. "You lead. I'll follow."

"We'll lead together."

My eyes stung, but I brushed away my tears.

"Grab your things." He hefted his bag onto his shoulder. "We're not returning to the cabin."

We went outside and he locked the door.

I checked my phone. Five a.m.

"He'll be here soon," Eli said. "I expect him within the hour."

Stilling, I squinted into the woods that surrounded us but saw no movement. How would he come for us? Would he rush across the field with bullets blazing? Or would he be stealthy, creeping low to the ground, a knife in his hand?

I fingered the hilt of my machete. No matter how he attacked, I was prepared.

Sometimes, the prey won, too. It was past time to take down the hunter.

We crossed the field, the dried grass crunching beneath my sneakers. Eli opened the back hatch of his Jeep. He pulled out a long, black rifle.

"I wish we'd brought a cannon," I said.

Eli paused, and his lips curled up on one side. "Thought the same thing but it wouldn't fit in my Jeep."

Bags in hand, we crossed the field again, passing the cabin on our left. After a few steps more, Eli stopped and gazed at the ground.

"We lost?" I asked.

He scowled, but it held no kick. "Not in the slightest." While listening each time he placed his feet, he stomped in widening arcs.

"We're making crop circles, then." I didn't know where my stand-up comedy routine had come from, but I welcomed it. A little humor made the tense situation bearable.

"Trying to find the opening to my treehouse."

I flicked my hand toward the woods. "Maybe we should start with a tree."

"Platforms in trees are for sissies."

Sissies, huh? I twisted my lips. "Flint had one."

He smirked and stomped his feet again. "My point exactly."

Like an old-fashioned school teacher, I shook a finger at him. "I'm going to tell Flint you called him a sissy."

Eli's fingers darted for my waist, but I giggled and stepped back, evading his touch.

"Tell your brother," he said. "And I'll give you a tickling you'll never forget."

"Throw in playing doctor, and I'll keep my mouth shut."

"Not if I'm a good doctor."

While I sputtered and tried to regain the use of my tongue—and ignore the heat spiking through me because this was so not the time—Eli smacked his feet on the ground some more.

"Ah-ha." Stooping down onto his heels, he brushed at the grass. He grunted and lifted something solid, and bits of long grass ripped as it tore.

A hatch. To a hole in the ground. A *black* hole in the ground.

"That's no treehouse," I said, my heart thudding dully. My humor had fled, replaced by rising fear. Moments ago, I'd felt in control. One challenge, and it slipped through my fingers like ground pepper.

"I told you I was a wild kid," he said. "After I built a bomb in my parent's basement, Mom kicked me out. Not completely. She said that if I was going to do things like that on a regular basis, I needed to take my activities out of the house."

"You built a bomb in your mom's basement."

"Exploded it, too. Made a mess."

I could only imagine. "The house is still standing."

"It was a small bomb." Lowering the hatch onto its back, he stared down into the hole. "I spent a bunch of summers digging a pit here, turning it into my version of a treehouse. Fixed it up slick. Spent more time out there than inside. Hence, my grandmother calling me wild."

Who was this man? Wild, for sure. Despite my dread, his enthusiasm called to a wildness inside me. If I could just find the courage to grab onto it and make it my own.

Creeping forward, I joined him, staring down. Echoes of the interrogation room in Mexico crowded into my mind, shoving aside my baby burst of self-confidence.

Eli bowed and swept his hand toward the opening. "Your accommodations await you, my lady."

Shivers racked my frame. I crossed my arms and pinched my elbows. "I can't go down there."

He tilted his head, his brow narrowing. "Oh. You worried about spiders? Let me check first." Stomping down the rickety wooden stairs, he disappeared inside. "Looks okay to me," he called up. "Not much water damage, which is surprising, considering how much time has passed." He poked his head into the early sunlight slanting through the trees. A cobweb draped across his hair, and, with a laugh, he brushed it aside. "Come on. You're going to love this."

I wished his excitement could damp down my nervousness, but my quakes grew stronger. "It's a big hole in the ground." We'd be trapped inside there. Russell would trap me and I wouldn't be able to run escape.

"It's cool. I reinforced it with pressure-treated beams. Put in a subfloor. Gran said all I needed was a cook stove and a sleeping bag and I'd be set for life. Have to admit, I slept out here a lot."

Didn't he understand? "I can't. I...I'm sorry." I hung my head, knowing I was disappointing him. Disappointing myself.

He climbed back up to ground level. Unlinking my arms, he slid his hands down to take mine, linking us together. He squeezed gently. "Mia? Tell me what's wrong."

"The hole. It's...What if he finds us? We'll have no way to run." My words stuttered out, and my ribs ached as if they'd been punched all over again. "He'll kill me this time."

"I won't make you do anything you're not comfortable

with." Releasing my hands, he gathered me into his arms and rested his chin on the top of my head. The vibration of his words hummed through me. Like always, he gave everything he had inside himself to me. "We'll hide somewhere else."

This was wrong, and I hated that I'd driven us to it. He'd set into motion a foolproof plan and, if it failed now, I'd be the reason. How could I let him down?

No, how could I let myself down?

Pulling out of his arms, I tipped my head back. Eyes closing, I let the warmth of the rising sun sink into me, bathing me from my head to my toes. I listened to the wind in the trees. It lifted my hair as it passed, and I released my fear along with the wind. Because, really, I'd never truly lost control of the situation with Russell. I just had to retake the reins.

"Everything okay?" Eli asked. He studied my face then nodded as if he saw something I'd only just realized.

I took his hand and though my smile wavered, it grew stronger until it blazed on my face. "Why don't you show me your treehouse?"

28

ELI

I led Mia down into my underground treehouse.

"Oh, my. That's a lot of stairs," she said, her voice tight.

"Twelve."

"You wanted it deep."

I snorted. Shouldn't be thinking about sex at a time like this. I strove for a normal tone. "Wanted to get below the frost line. Makes it cooler in the summer. Nature's air conditioning."

"Lovely." Her voice suggested anything but.

I snapped two glow sticks and laid them in the back corners. "These'll keep us from stumbling into each other but won't be visible from above." A long silence followed. I wished I could see her face, read her mood. "You're okay with this?"

If it was too much for her, we'd climb back out and go with an alternate plan. This wasn't the only way to eliminate a potential killer.

"I am."

I studied her face and was pleased to see the glow of

confidence that must be growing inside her. Giving someone their strength—as I'd do freely whenever she asked—was like a bandage. It covered the wound, but the true healing needed to take place inside.

I was glad Mia was finding herself. After we eliminated Russell, she could put this behind her.

Yes, we'd be hiding in the ground, but there was no reason I couldn't make this as comfy as possible. I removed a thin blanket from my bag and spread it out on the subfloor I'd installed with pressure-treated lumber years ago. Now, I wished I'd added chairs. A table. Hell, a bullet-proof room. "Want to sit?"

"Sure. Thanks." She dropped her bag and sat cross-legged. Her hands trembled, but she gave me a shaky smile. "It's going to be okay. Really. I'm not scared about being underground. It's kind of cool." Her smile grew. "Maybe we can come back someday and have a picnic here. Actually, to be honest, I'm more worried about what'll happen next."

"I understand."

"I know you'll protect me." Certainty rang in her voice. "But who's going to protect you?"

"We're in this together. We'll protect each other."

She nodded.

I finished setting things up, which meant closing the hatch until only a sliver of light could eke through. It would be stuffy inside, but no one would find us unless they pretty much stepped on the hatch. I supported the opening with a few small stones.

I also loaded my rifle and made sure my handgun was ready.

Kneeling on the steps, I was able to see a good part of the field—thanks to the kid who'd been out recently to mow. Sure, there was dead grass strewn around, but I could see well enough through the night vision scope mounted on my 308. I nestled the tip of the rifle in the tiny opening.

Had I considered every possibility? No one would ever suggest a DEA agent was dumb. I'd need to be on hyper-alert to eliminate this threat.

And elimination was probably what this would come to. I had no hope of us coming out of this alive unless Russell was either dead or severely incapacitated. I wouldn't shoot to kill but I sure as hell had no problem taking him down for a good long time.

Mia crept up and perched on the stairs beside me. She rested her head on my shoulder.

I wrapped an arm around her and squeezed. Kissed her forehead. "The last few days...Well, as tough as they've been, they've also been special."

"For me, too."

"When we're done with all this, I'd love to take you on a normal date."

Her muted chuckle rang out. "One without a kidnapping?"

"And no fish."

Her teeth gleamed in the low light when she grinned. "We have a lot left to explore with each other."

"We'll get the chance."

Her chin lifted. "We will."

"You up for movies?"

"What kind?"

"Only the best."

"Do they involve princesses?"

"And villains and heroes." My favorite kind.

"It's a date."

I gave her a quick kiss, longing to deepen it but knowing

I couldn't take the chance. If my assumptions were correct, we didn't have long.

I'd do whatever I could to avoid involving Mia in a fire-fight, but I was determined to end this and ensure she was safe forever. I wouldn't back down. I'd give this my all.

"Not long now," she said softly, mirroring my thoughts. Not a hint of fear in her voice. She'd lived through some-thing I couldn't save her from and while it ate through my gut like an ulcer, I'd be there for her from now on.

I checked the time. We'd been inside forty-five minutes. Per my calculation, Russell should arrive soon.

A pall of dread fell around my shoulders. Not because I worried about myself. I'd been in hairy enough situations before to know that, at any given moment, my time could be up. I'd come close with that IED.

I worried about Mia. Things could step beyond my control.

The scant vibration of her phone kicked my heart into overdrive.

At my nod, she answered. "Hello?" Her face cleared and she whispered to me. "It's my lawyer."

I watched her face as she listened and the utter relief spreading through her body had me loosening my grip on my rifle.

"Okay, thank you." She hung up. A mix of feelings I couldn't define filled her face. "Russell's..." She gulped. "He's dead. Deputy Franks caught him in my backyard, trying to break into my house through the back door. My alarm system tipped her off." Her breath shuddered. "He ran behind my shed and it turned into a shootout. When Russell ran, my neighbor, Elwin, shot him. Said he was finally cleaning up the neighborhood." She shuddered, and her phone dropped from her hand, clattering down the stairs and onto the ground. "I can't believe it. After all this time, it's finally over."

I'd never wish anyone dead, but there was no denying the utter relief filling me. While I'd been prepared for a showdown, knowing I wouldn't have to battle it out with Mia at my back made my gut unclench. She was safe. We both were.

We could begin our lives together from this moment forward.

My phone vibrated and I pulled it from my pocket, expecting a text from Flint or Jax or even Coop.

No text.

I held back my shout when I scrolled into the screen.

Someone had triggered the first camera half a mile back down the road. My heart rate plummeted.

A man I couldn't identify crept past the camera, dressed in camo, carrying a rifle. I zoomed in on the device in his ear: the bud component of a tracking device that allowed him to hear the signal coming from the component in his hand. It no doubt tracked the bug I'd found—and disabled for a short time—on my Jeep. He also held his phone and I spied on the spy, seeing the blinking light indicating what he hunted: from its location, my vehicle.

"What's going on?" Mia hissed out.

I feverishly clicked through the screens on my phone. "Someone just passed zone one."

"But, but...Russell's dead."

"Russell came to Maine to find you, but I don't think he's responsible for the strikes." Dread uncurled inside me, spreading poison through my limbs.

"Who, then?"

My swear ground from my throat. "I programmed the

locusts for Russell. Face recognition." I wanted to smack my head. "I've been so stupid. Why didn't I see this happening?"

I stared down at the screen, horror roaring through me like a hurricane.

As if the guy suspected I'd set up a bunch of tricks, he kept his head tucked forward, hiding his face from view.

One thing was clear.

This wasn't Russell.

Some unknown man was determined to kill her.

29

MIA

My upbeat mood fled, and my lips trembled. "I...I don't understand."

"Someone else is coming down the road and we know it's not the guy from Mexico or Russell."

"Are you sure this person's after me—us? It could be a...I don't know. A hunter?"

"Not this time of year. People hunt coyotes maybe, but only at night and with more than one hunter."

"Someone out for a walk?"

"This is private property. It's well marked. No local would trespass."

"You think they're after me." I gulped. "Who could it be?"

"Other than Peter, I'm fresh out of ideas."

"Peter?" This made no sense. He was a friend. "Why would Peter want to hurt me?"

"Good question."

"What aren't you telling me?"

"I saw Peter talking with the guy from the stairwell. When questioned, Peter explained it away, but..."

My sigh slid out and my shoulders drooped. We'd been so close to feeling safe I could almost taste it. That wonderful feeling had been stomped into the ground. "We can't trust anyone."

"Never."

I leaned forward, staring down at his phone. "You said the cameras would send you clear shots. You must be able to identify the person."

"He's wearing a ski mask."

"All right. Well." I tightened my spine. "We're ready for him. Your traps are in place."

"Damn right. We came here to take down a threat and that plan's still in place. We're ending this. Permanently." He sounded grim, and I loved that about him. Alone, I'd be terrified. With Eli beside me, a strength I couldn't define surged through me. I didn't know how this would come out, but we'd face it together. "He triggered the first motion detector. What do we do now?"

"I can't reprogram the locusts without a face. They're a prototype. Eventually, they'll be programmed to change targets. They're smart. They'll learn from mistakes like this and will be able to switch prey, but the programming for that is still up here." He tapped his temple. "Not loaded into them."

"You're sure it wasn't—" I waved my hand. "—a deer or something like that?"

"It's a man." He turned his phone so I could see what he described. "Camo. Tracking devices. A signal I can see on his phone—my Jeep. Let alone the fact that he's come loaded for bear."

A rifle. Any other weapons?

Another hum erupted from his phone.

"Zone two?" I whispered.

He nodded.

Then three and four. Each strike ratcheting another anxious notch up my spine.

Eli kept his face blank, his posture loose but ready to jump if need be. On guard but casual, to give me the impression this didn't faze him a bit.

"I'm scared," I admitted.

"Me, too. I'd be a fool if I wasn't." He rubbed my shoulder and stared into my eyes, his filled with confidence and reassurance. "We're coming out of this alive. I'll save us both."

"Since he's hitting the zones, he's staying on the road," I said softly, awe coming through in my voice. "Like you said he would."

Eli was no ordinary guy. In my mind, he was a hero, forced into a situation where he had to defend himself and me.

"This is no job, Mia." He stroked my face. "There's no place I'd rather be than right here and right now. With you."

I gulped back my tears because I felt the same. And I was terrified it would end too soon. That we'd never be given a chance to have more.

I didn't deserve him. But here I was, nestled against his side, knowing he'd give his life to keep me from harm. I wouldn't let him down. He'd fight for me, and I'd do the same for him.

Ten minutes passed. I fidgeted. Eli held himself still, staring through his scope, watching for movement outside.

"How many zones are there?" I whispered. "We spaced them out evenly, right?"

He nodded.

"This last stretch has been longer than between the

other zones." Although, I wasn't exactly watching the time. "Do you think he left the road?"

"Maybe."

"That's bad."

"Don't give up on us yet." He squeezed my hand.

"If he left the road, he'd—"

Eli's phone vibrated.

"Good," I said. "Zone five."

Eli stared down at the picture, keeping the screen tipped away so I couldn't see it. "He...found camera number five."

I leaned forward. "Let me see."

His hand dropped over the screen. "Not much to see."

"Eli." Why did he think he could keep anything from me?

"This guy has had training."

"You saw his face? You recognize him?"

"He used a hand signal for the camera's benefit. I'd say cop or military. And, no face."

"What did he say?"

Eli looked up, and his face was grimmer than I'd ever seen it. "Nothing we don't already know."

"Please. Tell me."

"He signaled, *I'm coming for you.*"

My heart stalled. Eli was right. We already knew this. Confirmation that this wasn't a hunter or a local out for a walk shouldn't shake me to my core.

"What will happen—" A scream cut my words off. "What the hell..."

The satisfaction on Eli's face drove away my unease.

"I believe he discovered the danger of playing with knives. Or your pen."

"My pen?"

"Let's hope it hit something vital."

I narrowed my gaze on Eli's face. "What did you do?" My voice was half filled with curiosity, half filled with amazement.

"Set up a few surprises to slow him down."

"Booby traps," I whispered. "You're better than any old MacGyver. Does this mean it's over?"

"Maybe. Or maybe not." He held up a finger and listened. "If he keeps on coming, we'll hear..."

A whoosh was followed by a couple of smacks.

Yes. "Looks like he found your nutmeg."

He grinned. "I think he's missing the eggnog, though."

"Just got egg on his face. Or, in this case, nutmeg on his face. Carefully dumped inside your nylon knee-highs, I assume. The one's you've yet to model for me. Let me guess, spring-loaded with the exercise bands?"

He turned briefly away from staring down his 308's scope. "They're not just for building muscle."

"But if he keeps coming..."

"The nutmeg wasn't our last hold-out." He sighted down his scope

There must still be more traps awaiting the man. Unless he somehow evaded them.

Wait. My heart rate spiked. What was that sound? And that smell?

Eli held up his hand before I could whisper a word.

Crackling.

Eli reared back, his nostrils flaring.

"What's happening?"

"A rabbit ran by the hatch."

I didn't like this. My sixth sense was scraping along my back, and it couldn't be denied.

Eli inhaled sharply, but his breath stalled before he eased it out. "Smoke."

"A campfire nearby?"

"Nobody else out here but us, and…"

My shoulders slumped. "And him." A clever fiend who'd run the foxes to ground and now planned to smoke them out.

Eli grabbed his rifle. "You prepared to move fast, Mia?"

"We're changing plans."

"Have to. He set the field on fire and it's roaring this way."

Crawling around to face forward, I squinted through the narrow opening and gasped. Flames skipped along the ground, setting the world outside alight, turning it into an inferno. "Where will we go?"

"Where you can disappear. I'll find you a safe place to hide while I hunt him down and finish this."

I wanted to insist I'd go with him, stand at his back to defend him. But I was a doctor, not a Seabee. He'd be safer if I wasn't around.

"On three. One." He took my hand and placed it on his back, encouraging me to grip his shirt. "Hold on tight and don't let go."

"Okay." My voice shook. "I'm ready."

"Two." He paused. "And, three."

Shoving up the hatch, I bolted up the stairs. When I hit the surface, I crouched low.

Smoke filled the air, making it almost impossible to see.

The hatch slammed closed behind me.

Mia! No hand on my back. Where was she?

No time to look, because someone jumped me, slamming into my side, driving me to the ground face-first. I bit dirt and arched up, shaking to dislodge the man from my back.

While the guy tumbled and flipped onto his feet, smoke billowed around us. Scorching my lungs, making me cough.

I spread my arms wide. Shit, I'd dropped my rifle. And where was my handgun?

The man dove toward me from out of the smoke, a knife extended in his fist. He slashed it forward, aiming for my gut.

I flung myself sideways and kicked out, hitting the other man in the knee cap. He grunted, but the knife grazed my previously injured leg. It sliced through my jeans and bit deep. Adrenaline blazed through me, and I blocked out the growing pain, hunkering low to avoid the smoke hanging in the air. To my left, flames leaped, dancing from tree to tree, but they appeared to be skirting this area.

Wobbling on his feet, the man blinked and said, "I promised her I'd make this right. Mia doesn't deserve love. She stole my love from me."

"Jim? Jim Taylor?" I asked, stunned. The older man from Christmastown. The guy having fun with his granddaughter, seemingly accepting his wife's death. Mia had found his wife in the park, dying of a heart attack. She'd been unable to help the woman.

He blamed Mia.

Jim wiped his face with his palm and staggered sideways.

The nutmeg was working.

"Give up," I said. "It's over."

"I took down worse than you when I was a cop in Boston." His wavering voice rose. "Don't you see? I don't have my wife, so Mia can't have you. One of you has to die, and it might as well be you." He slashed toward me with the knife again.

A shadow darted to my right, but the smoke was too thick to see who it was or where they were going. Was Jim alone or did he bring a friend? My cameras hadn't picked up anyone else but that meant nothing.

"Stephanie," the man shouted. He gouged the knife out again, and it sliced through the air. But when his gaze fell on me, his eyes cleared and he ran forward.

I struck out with my foot, hitting his arm but not dislodging the knife. He deflected my quick series of hits. While he might not be as strong as me, he'd had considerable training. Without the hallucinogen on board and the fifteen or so years on me, it was anyone's guess who'd come up the victor.

Jim whimpered and peered toward my left as if seeing ghosts. Blood trickled down his leg from a wound in his thigh—caused by a kitchen knife or pen.

I rushed him and we grappled for the knife. He crouched and, with one quick move, I lay on my back on the ground, gasping. I rolled to put distance between us and leaped to my feet, hands wide, ready to challenge him again.

But Jim was on me already, anticipating my next move. He jerked the knife forward, and his harsh breathing hit my ear. We grappled, the knife slashing between us. Smoke filled my lungs, and I coughed. The heat was getting to us both, stealing our air.

I redoubled my efforts, striking out with my fist as Jim lunged forward.

Something hit my gut at the same moment a machete stabbed into Jim's shoulder.

Jim staggered backward, his hands reaching around for the weapon. Blood seeped around his fingers. He pivoted and stumbled forward.

Smoke clouded around us, making it difficult to see.

Jim gasped. His arms spiraled wildly, and he tumbled down inside the hole I'd dug in the ground.

I stumbled forward, falling to my knees. Why didn't my legs work? They'd gone limp. Just like the rest of me. My body ached. My lungs couldn't drag in even one speck of air.

My stomach burned.

Mia rushed over to me. "No. Oh, Eli, no." She dropped to her knees beside me.

When had I fallen to the ground?

"Help me up," I gasped out, grabbing her arms, trying to rise. "Have to make sure he can't come after you."

She pulled up my shirt and wailed. Sobs caught in her throat. "No. Please, no."

A knife in the gut never did a guy any good.

Mia collapsed against my chest.

I wrapped my arms around her, holding tight. Maybe for the last time.

But I couldn't comfort her until I was sure she was safe. "Mia. Help me up."

"Lay still. I...I've got to do something. We brought a first aid kit, didn't we?" She looked around frantically. "Where is it? The cabin? Inside your Jeep?" Her voice shrieked out. "Where's the damn first aid kit?"

"Go," I said. Every breath shot agony through my belly. Damn, but it hurt. Pain was good. It meant I still lived.

Blood seeped from my belly wound. It cooled as it trickled down my side. My back squished wetly on the grass. A pool must be forming underneath me.

When had I laid down in the grass? I had to get Mia out of here, away from the flames. And Jim...I had to do something about Jim. End this. Keep her safe.

I wouldn't get out of this one alive, but I'd make sure Mia did.

Jim would be on her in seconds. I wouldn't be able to defend her. She had to hide.

I didn't want to be alone when I died, but I'd sure as hell prefer to face this alone than watch the grief shadow her eyes when death took me.

"Do something," I said. "For me."

Her hands fidgeted on my belly. She must know she couldn't pull out the knife without ending this fast, but she must feel she had to do something.

My time for doing anything had passed.

"Go." Shoving the pain from my mind, I pushed the

words out. "Take my Jeep. Keys...my pocket. Run. Hide. Call the cops, tell them it's Jim. They'll...keep you safe."

She reared back, her nostrils flaring. "You think I'm going to leave you here?"

I was used to people leaving me. Funny how this time, I was the one pushing someone I loved away. "Want you...safe."

Her hands fisted on her thighs. "Here's the thing you might not have learned about me yet. I'm stubborn. I don't give up. Not on myself. And not on you."

"Go."

"I'm getting you out of here. You'll just have to deal." She rose to her feet and grabbed my gun from where it must've landed when I fell. "I'll be right back."

I lifted my hand to hold her with me, but it dropped limply at my side.

Mia strode down into the ground. She returned moments later. "He's dead. Broken neck. Good thing." Sobs broke through her voice. "I would've killed him if he hadn't done it for me." Lowering herself down beside me, she stroked my forehead. "Hang in there, baby. I'm going to help you."

I stared into her eyes, reading overwhelming determination. Awe struck me all over again. This woman would never abandon me. Not like Dad. Or anyone else in life.

If only I didn't have to leave her.

31

MIA

Twenty grueling minutes later, I ground the Jeep to a halt at the gate. I leaped from the vehicle and ran over to enter the code. After shoving the gate wide, I jumped back inside the Wrangler and blazed through the opening. Not stopping to close the gate behind me, I left the dirt road and squealed out onto Route 2.

After I'd made sure Jim was dead, I'd roused Eli enough to get him to his Jeep. I'd kept half an eye on him during the bumpy ride down the dirt road. His breathing continued, but his pulse was thready. Blood dripped steadily down his belly and onto the floor. Its metallic essence filled the air, and I could barely hold back my screams.

I chocked on sobs and held my overwhelming fear inside.

I would not lose him.

Pushing the Jeep for speed, I raced into town and followed signs to the hospital in Lincoln.

Squealing up to the Emergency Room entrance, I popped the vehicle into neutral, yanked on the brake, and bolted inside.

"Help," I yelled. "A man's been stabbed. He's in my vehicle out front."

The eyes of a woman sitting behind a reception desk widened, and she lifted her phone.

"A knife," I gasped out. "His belly. It hit his liver. Please, hurry!" I raced back outside and yanked open the passenger door.

For a moment, I thought he was already gone. That he'd passed on without me beside him, holding his hand. But his breath drew in and sputtered out. His heart continued to pulse when I pressed my finger to his throat. He didn't turn his head or open his eyes, but he still lived.

How long could he keep going?

Behind me, a stretcher banged as nurses and a doctor pushed it off the sidewalk and over to the Jeep.

The doctor took one look at Eli and shouted, "Call a code. And get him the hell out of this vehicle." He unbuckled Eli while feeling for a pulse. "He's still with us."

They eased him onto the stretcher and covered him with a sheet that jutted into the air from the hilt of the knife. Redness soon spread in a circle around it.

Eli's face. Paler than the sheet, he looked as if death had already called him. I couldn't bear it. Arms fluttering helplessly at my sides, I clung to the foot of the stretcher and followed them inside.

While *Trauma Code, Stat, ER*, burst from the speakers overhead, they rushed his stretcher down a hall and wheeled him into an exam room.

I tried to go in with him, because I had to hold his hand. If he didn't know I was there, pulling for him, he might give up. I had to beg him to keep trying.

"I'm a doctor," I said as a nurse pulled the curtain closed in front of my face, blocking me out.

She poked her head around the curtain. "You family?"

"No. I'm...his friend."

Someone who loves him more than anyone else in the world.

Her face softened before she darted a glance over her shoulder. "I'll let you inside as soon as I can. Since you're a doctor, you know the routine. We've got to stabilize him first." She pointed. "Wait over there."

I stumbled over to a chair and dropped down. Straining, I clung to every beep of his heart as it accelerated on the monitor. Too fast. About one-forty. A body's response to heavy blood loss.

They were losing him.

Someone shouted, "Tube him, stat. And you—" A bang rang out. "I want at least three fourteen-gauge IVs with LR, wide open. Get the lab. Portable film, too. I need to know what we're dealing with here."

Propping my elbows on my knees, I dropped my face into my hands. My body crumbled. All I could focus on was the rapid beat of his heart.

Sometime later, the nurse approached. She stooped down and pulled my hands away from my face. I jerked upright, pressing my back against the hard, plastic chair. "What? He's..."

"Hey," the nurse said. Compassion filled her dark eyes. "You okay?"

I rubbed my forehead. "How's Eli?" I didn't need to ask.

The monitor had gone silent.

Tears dripped down my face while my heart fragmented into a thousand pieces. My breath wouldn't come.

I'd never breathe again.

"He's in the OR," the nurse said with more cheer than she should. "We've got a great trauma surgeon in-house and she was around, but..."

"You can be honest." I gulped back grateful tears.

"You know where he was hit."

Liver.

The nurse gushed on, squeezing my hand tight. "Doctor Lee's fantastic. The best in the state. If anyone can pull him through, she can." She rose to her feet and tugged on the hem of her scrub top, smoothing it over her hips. "Let's take you to the critical care waiting room. He won't come back here after they're finished."

No matter what the outcome.

We rode the elevator and the nurse waited while I used the bathroom to wash Eli's blood off my hands and splash cold water on my face. She led me inside a small room and gestured to the sofa. "Have a sit. This will take time, but we'll update you about his progress." She left and returned with a cup of coffee. "Drink. The caffeine will do you good. You look worn out. You're not injured, too, are you?"

"No." The word could barely escape my tight throat. I swallowed what felt like a year's worth of dust and shook my head. "I'm fine."

Unless Eli lived, I'd never be fine.

The coffee grew cold before I took my first sip. It slid down, and while the caffeine shocked my bones, a dull ache consumed my head. It matched the ache expanding against my chest wall.

While I wanted to curl into a ball and sob, I would stay strong. If...no, *when* Eli pulled through, I'd be here for him, standing by his side.

I called Flint and explained what happened.

"Ah, Mia. I'm sorry. And Eli..." His voice grew tight.

I could almost picture him straightening up from whatever wall he'd slumped against, tightening his spine. He'd mourn after he hung up but for now, he'd be strong for his sister.

"I'll call Uncle Sid," he said.

Perfect. We needed him.

"He'll deal with the cops. Don't worry about a thing. They'll, um, take care of the body. Clean up the scene."

"Make it look like an accident?" In some ways, it was. While the machete might've caused him pain and the nutmeg made him loopy, Jim had fallen on his own. He'd died while trying to kill Eli and me.

A long silence followed before Flint said, "Don't worry about all that. Just be there for Eli. I'm in Mexico right now. They flew Gabe to a trauma center in Florida but Haylee's not stable enough to travel."

"Haylee? What happened to Haylee?" Why was she in Mexico? As if I had to ask.

"It was an...accident."

"What? What? Haylee?" My body went limp as it took another emotional blow. Haylee worked for Flint which meant whatever happened was anything but a simple accident.

"I'll get home as soon as I can," my brother said.

"Thank you." My words came out dull because my worry for Eli was now compounded by overwhelming fear for Haylee.

My heart was frozen. Broken. What would I do if they didn't make it?

After we ended the call, I scooted back on the sofa. I drew up my legs to my chest and wrapped my arms around them. I couldn't stop shivering, even though the room was warm.

All I could do was stare at the wall. And pray.

Then I called Ginny. She sobbed in the phone and said she'd call their mom and come wait with me.

The coffee grew colder. As did I. People passed in the hall, but no one came inside the waiting room other than the nurse, who poked her head through the opening only long enough to say, "They're still working on him."

It wasn't enough. I had to be with him, touch him, help him hold on. Give him my strength, because I owed him tenfold.

Ginny and she and Eli's mom arrived a few hours later, while I was still waiting. We hugged and cried, and it's surprising how quickly you can form a bond with someone you've never met before when you're brought together to pray for the survival of someone you love.

Eli had his mom's eyes.

We held hands for a while then drifted to our own chairs, me on the sofa.

Hours went by. More time after that. Each moment leaching away more of my hope.

About eight hours after Eli went to the OR, Ginny's mom stood and stretched. "I'm going to go to the cafeteria for some coffee."

"Awesome idea," Ginny said, also standing. The half-smile she directed my way was as welcome as a hug. "Come with us?"

I couldn't leave. Not even for caffeine. And I couldn't imagine ever eating or drinking anything again. Not until I knew Eli would live through this.

"Thanks, but I'll stay here. Just in case they come out and look for us."

"You've got my cell," Ginny said. Crossing the room, she rubbed my shoulder. "Hang in there. Eli's tough." A sob broke through her words, echoed inside me. "I'll bring you coffee."

"Okay. Thanks."

After they left, I stared at swirling patterns on the thin carpet.

"Excuse me." A woman wearing blue scrubs and a thin cap on her head stood in the doorway. She advanced inside the room, her booted feet padding softly. "Are you Mia?"

If I denied the name, would the woman leave? Then she could tell someone else that Eli was dead. I couldn't bear to hear those words. Hands pressed to my chest, I rose from the sofa and took a step forward. My legs buckled, but I remained on my feet while my body spasmed. I'd held the crunched-up position for too long. Through the window, a pink and yellow sunset filled the sky. Would tonight be Eli's last and the end of everything for me?

Be tough. If not myself, for Eli. "Yes. I'm Mia."

The woman drew closer. And smiled. "I'm Doctor Lee. I've been working on your friend." She brushed a strand of straight black hair off her forehead, tucking it back underneath her cap. Her dark eyes, red-rimmed, met mine. "He's going to be okay." Taking my hand, she led me back to the sofa and patted the flowered cushion. "You look like you need to sit again."

"Yeah." Had the woman truly said Eli was going to be okay? Or had I imagined it? A spark of hope filled me, flickering in the dim light. "Eli's mom and sister are here. Well, they went to the cafeteria."

"Wonderful. I'm sure he'll be glad to see family." The woman's grin widened as she dropped to the chair beside the sofa. She sighed and rubbed her face. "It was a tough case, but we got him through. His liver...well, after he recovers, he's going to be all right."

Tears welled in my eyes. "Thank you." With a sudden burst of energy, I jumped to my feet. "Can I see him?"

"Sure. Follow me." Doctor Lee led me out into the hall where she paused to tell a nurse to wait for Eli's mom and Ginny and to send them into Eli's room once they returned.

I followed Doctor Lee through a set of double doors and into the critical care unit. "He's sleeping," she said over her shoulder as she walked into a room with wide glass doors. The curtain had been pulled, but she brushed it aside. "His vitals are stable. I think it's going to take something tougher than a liver laceration to knock this man down."

"Eli's strong. He's...the best there is."

The doctor patted my arm and then drew me closer to the bed. "Sit with him. He won't wake for a while due to the sedation and pain killers, but he'll know you're here. Even unconscious, patients can tell."

While the doctor left, I dragged a chair closer to the bed. I reached slowly through the rail and took his hand. I squeezed it carefully, not wanting to hurt him further. His fingers remained limp in my hand.

A nurse entered the room. She crossed over to the monitor and stared at it. Stared at Eli. The monitor again. "Lookin' good. He's recovering nicely. Do you have any questions for me?"

I shook my head. The hows and whys and what might come next could wait. Right now, I just wanted to drink in the knowledge that he would be okay.

And be here for him when he woke.

"Can I get you something, then?" the nurse asked. "Water?"

"Sure."

She left and returned with a covered cup with a straw peeking from the top. "Here you go. Something to eat, too?

We don't have much, but I can offer crackers." She smiled. "Or crackers. There's a machine in the lounge, and I'm happy to get you something from the kitchen."

"I'm okay," I said. "Thanks, though." I took a sip of water and savored the coldness gliding down my throat. Funny how such a simple thing could bring a spark of pleasure.

"I'll be out at the desk but push the call bell if you need anything." At my nod, the nurse left.

I stared at Eli's pale face, starkly white against his dark blond hair. With my knuckles, I carefully stroked his bristly cheek, but he still didn't respond. His lungs rose and fell, even, sure. And the monitor beeped steadily. Heart rate eighty. Decent BP. Oxygen levels were good, too. They were numbers he could live with.

Unable to bear it any longer, I stood and dropped the side rail. Not caring what anyone thought, I lifted the covers. They'd cut off his clothing and he wore only a cotton gown. I couldn't bear to think he might be cold.

Holding back my sob, I crawled up onto the bed and lowered myself slowly down beside him. After carefully snuggling into his side, with one arm crossing his chest and my other beneath his neck, I imagined myself feeding him strength. He could take all I had to give.

I sighed. He smelled like smoke and medicine but a faint hint of Eli still lingered. I closed my eyes and pulled it in.

Tears trickled down my face, but they weren't from fear. They were from relief.

Eli shifted. His arm edged underneath me and pulled me close.

His chest rumbled when he spoke. "You didn't leave me."

"You're not getting rid of me that easy. I'll never leave you. I love you."

"Ah, Mia." I swore his eyes watered. His voice, though

slurred and slow from the medications, deepened. "I love you, too."

My grin rising on my face, I kissed him.

From now on, I wouldn't just tell him he was mine and I was his, I'd show him.

We'd pull through this.

Together.

32

MIA

ne week later.

I SHIFTED my hips to the music streaming from my phone, belting out how I wanted to be part of his world. Eli's playlist.

While Eli said I was his favorite Disney princess, I kind of wanted to be a mermaid instead.

I backed up, dropped the oven door, and pulled out a freshly-baked batch of white chocolate, macadamia nut cookies.

Once Eli was stable, they'd transferred him to the hospital here in town so he'd be closer to home. I'd begged for a bit more leave before starting my new job to remain by his side.

He was getting better. Cranky but that assured me he was healing. Man pain was the worst, but he had been horribly hurt. In fact, my colleagues at the hospital had told me they'd let him come home soon.

Home. To me.

I was more than ready. Frankly, I was getting tired of the nurses whispering in the halls that Eli was *so hot.*

He was hot, but he was *my* hot.

I slid the last cookie off the pan and onto the rack, then reloaded the tray and popped it into the oven.

Two sharp knocks hit my door.

I stilled, listening but hearing nothing further. Except...

A deep voice singing about how he wasn't shy, he was gonna kiss the girl.

My heart flipped, and I scurried from the kitchen.

How was this possible?

After yanking off my apron and ditching the pot holders from my hands, I raced down the hall, headed for the front door. I paused to smooth my hair, my—white—sundress, and my heart rate, which was never going to slow as long as I had Eli in my life.

I couldn't keep the grin off my face. My happiness demanded it had to shine through.

I unlocked and swung open the door.

A gorgeous man stood in front of me, dressed in a soft tee and faded jeans, a Santa hat on his head with the pompom brushing his shoulder.

My laughter snorted out. "I, um. Hmm. I'm afraid Mrs. Clause isn't here. I believe she's hanging out at Christmastown with the real St. Nick."

"What if I have this?" A grin on his face, he held up a sprig of mistletoe.

"I think you'd better come inside, sir."

He limped through the doorway looking so hot that I needed to fan my face.

"Where did you get that—"

His arm swept around my waist. "Remember that legend I told you at Christmastown?"

"I do."

He dangled the mistletoe over his head. "Everyone who stands underneath it is entitled to a kiss."

I wrapped my arms around his waist, being careful not to put pressure on his sore belly. "Then we better get to it, Eli, because I've been waiting a lifetime."

LOOK FOR JAX & Haylee's story next, *Reckless*. I can't wait to share more of the Viper Force world.

~*MARLIE*

If you've enjoyed *Ruthless*, I'd love to hear your thoughts.
Would you please leave a review?
Goodreads
Amazon

I know everyone at Viper Force would say thanks.

MARLIE WRITE BOOKS WITH HEART, humor, and a guaranteed happily-ever-after. When she's not writing romance, you can find her in Maine, where she works as a nurse. She lives with her own personal hero, her retired Navy Chief husband. They have three children, too many cats, and a cute Yorkie pup.

You can find me via my website,
Twitter, and on Facebook.

OTHER BOOKS BY MARLIE MAY

Crescent Cove Contemporary Romances

SOME LIKE IT SCOT

SIMPLY IRRESISTIBLE

Independent Titles

TWIST OF FATE, May, 2019

(A time travel romance set in ancient Pompeii)

Crescent Cove Romantic Suspense

FEARLESS

RUTHLESS

RECKLESS, coming soon

Young Adult

DEAD GIRLS DON'T LIE

A young adult suspense

If you enjoy my adult romantic suspense novels, you'll also love my twisty young adult suspense that opens with a bang and keeps you on the edge of your seat until the shocking ending.

Here's the first chapter of *Dead Girls Don't Lie*. You can find it on Amazon.

DEAD GIRLS DON'T LIE

~OR DO THEY?

Seventeen-year-old Janie Davis was found wandering a
Maine beach with second-degree burns and no memory of
what happened. An accident on a yacht caused it to sink,
taking her parents and best friend down with it. Recovering,
Janie returns home under the watchful gaze of her new
guardian—an aunt who had been ostracized by Janie's
family.

Snooping uncovers the accident report. She's horrified to
learn the deaths could be murder and is determined to solve
the crime. Selective breaking and entering leads her to two
suspects: her father's shady business partner who profited
from Dad's death and her aunt, a woman with a sketchy past
she's eager to hide. Unsure where to turn next, Janie enlists
the help of Emanuel Sancini, a fellow high school senior
who thinks doing community service in the library means
he can call himself a librarian.

Their investigation leads them to crash a party where they
uncover more evidence in the homeowner's office. Discov-

ered in the act, they're forced to conceal their crime by pretending—sort of—that they snuck into the room to make out. Then Janie's brake lines are cut and only a quick plunge to the tile floor keeps an overhead lamp from impaling her in the school library. This, and the warning, *You're Next,* proves Janie's getting closer. With Janie targeted, she and Emanuel must race to expose the murderer. Or Janie could wind up dead.

CHAPTER ONE

Aunt Kristy insisted I was strong enough to go to school today, but my heart, a tiny bird trapped in my chest, disagreed. I climbed from her SUV and pushed the door shut, steeling my expression as pain shot up my arms.

My aunt came around the hood and thrust out her hand. "Give me your backpack, Janine. I'll take it inside for you."

"It's Janie," I said.

"What?"

"I told you before. Everyone calls me Janie." I tightened my hand on the strap looped over my shoulder. "And I can carry my own bag, thanks."

"Well. Okay. If you're sure. Janie." She worried her necklace, releasing a sigh, then pivoted on her heel and hurried up the walkway. I imagined she was dying to get to the teacher's lounge to put away her things. Gulp down a cup of coffee before she had to convince a bunch of teenagers that chemistry was fun. Or maybe she just wanted to get away from me.

Two months ago, Aunt Kristy moved into my home

and applied for a job at my high school. She'd done her best to be a parent since. Few people would take on raising a niece they barely knew. Considering she and Dad hadn't been close since before I was born, that said something.

"Hey, there you are," someone said from behind me.

Turning, I hugged Sean, my remaining best friend from before.

"Whoa, aren't you a rebel? I like it," he said, taking in my dark green skirt and white tee. At Finley Cove High School, we were expected to wear white collared shirts and khakis, and 'keep our appearances tidy'. Sean could be a poster child for the school dress code.

"That's me, living dangerously." I'd tucked my shirt into a skirt that landed above rather than below the knee. While my outfit would challenge the school board rules, it still felt awesome wearing something other than ratty shorts and a tee. "I, well, you know, lost weight. Nothing else fits. Think I can get away with it until I hit the mall?"

"I won't tell." His gaze fell away from mine. "You ready to hit the gauntlet?" At my tight nod, he shoved his backpack strap higher on his shoulder and held out his arm. A few months ago, he would've held out both arms. One for me and one for his girlfriend. Brianna.

The doctors said I should be grateful because I'd only received second-degree burns. Third-degree would've been worse because the nerves would be shot and I'd never regain sensation. Those doctors didn't know a damn thing. Pain could be swatted away like a pesky fly. Losing the people I loved had gutted me.

We caught up with a bunch of girls who stalled and grew silent when they saw me. I'd known most of them since elementary school, hanging out together more times than I could count to talk about hot guys, TV shows, and make-up. Frivolous stuff, but I'd been frivolous back then.

Marley's lips twitched as she took in the red patches on my pale skin and the puckers from my grafts. Another girl pretended to gag, not realizing that while my arms and hands might've been burned, my eyes worked just fine, thank you very much. Back home, I'd convinced myself my scars were battle wounds proving I'd survived when everyone else hadn't. Seen through the eyes of these girls, I was repulsive, a thing that should be hidden. I yanked my sleeves down around my wrists, wishing I could pull the material over my fingertips, as well.

"So, Janie. You still have—" Marley made air quotes. "—amnesia?"

"I don't remember much about what happened that night if that's what you're asking." The doctors said my memory might never return.

"But, but..." Marley's mouth dropped open. "What if *you* caused the accident?"

The other girls released muted giggles, savoring the drama.

"I didn't." My heartbeat pulsed in my throat.

Like my personal Pitbull straining against his leash, Sean bared his teeth and snarled.

"Kinda hard to say if you're to blame or not, now isn't it?" Marley smirked. "Considering you don't *actually* remember."

Anger slammed through me like a semi hitting a paper-thin wall. "I wouldn't hurt my parents or Brianna."

Sean elbowed himself between us. "Get lost, Marley, would you?"

With a huff, she spun and continued toward school with the other girls clustering around her feverishly whispering.

"Thank you," I said, grateful all over again I still had Sean in my life.

"Any time." We continued toward school. "Umm, about swimming. I thought about it a lot over the past few weeks." His footsteps paused before picking up speed. "Decided I'm going."

Sean, Brianna and I had been on the swim team together and had made a game out of competing for the best times. While Sean could literally swim laps around us due to his male body structure, Brianna also beat me at every meet. A foster kid, she'd worked twice as hard as me to get ahead. If only I'd appreciated that fact sooner.

"Swimming?" A shiver went through me. "How could you—I just can't."

"Going to the pool will be one of the hardest things I'll ever do but it's what she would've wanted. Yeah, I mourn her." His eyes squeezed shut. When he opened them, they glistened. "I'm going to miss her forever. But she would've wanted us to keep going."

My aunt had been after me to jump back into 'activities you used to do before the accident,' but I didn't see how I could. Going to classes without Brianna would be tough but it would ruin me to do anything else we used to share.

"I'll feel closer to her when I swim. Like she's still with me," he said.

Whenever I thought about getting into the water, my brain flashed to memories of me struggling in the sea...my head going under...our boat lighting up the night as it was consumed by flames.

"Hey." Sean peered down at me. "You look pale. You still up for this? 'Cause, we can bail, if you want."

Like that would do me any good? My grades were

skating too close to the edge already. I pushed for a smile. "I'm okay. Let's go."

Crossing the lobby, we walked down the hall to the wing lined with lockers where I ditched my backpack and pulled out a notebook.

Sean slouched against the wall. "*Are* you starting to remember what happened that night?" The hope in his voice tugged my insides sideways. If only I could give him one more memory of Brianna, a tiny speck he could hold on to.

"Some." I fiddled with a pen before stuffing it inside my pocket. "It's sporadic. Which is frustrating." Fear came through in my words. "Do you think I'm blocking it out because..."

"Janie. You weren't responsible. Forget what Marley said."

A worm of doubt kept wiggling through me, spreading its poison.

"Fireworks caused the fire. That's what the police said." He pulled out his phone and glanced at it. "Damn. I've gotta get to AP Chem." Not that Sean needed to worry about angering my aunt by being late to her class. With our school's highest GPA, he was the top candidate for the Upstanding Citizen Award, which came with a full college scholarship. If I knew Sean, he'd finish with the best grade in the class.

Unlike me. I'd be thrilled if I got a C in basic chem.

I went in the other direction, toward calc. Inside, I took my usual seat—front right and next to the window so I could look outside if I got bored.

The teacher clapped her hands. "Okay, everyone. Let's get settled."

Since I couldn't start school with everyone else in

September, Sean had brought me my assignments, but I was barely squeaking by in some of my classes. It was time to get to work. I opened my notebook and clicked my pen.

When I looked down, my heart stopped. I stared at the top corner of the white laminate desk surface where someone had drawn a tiny hummingbird in dark blue ink.

My hand flew to my right hip, and I traced the identical pattern. Brianna and I had used fake IDs to get matching tattoos earlier this summer. The fact that this one looked exactly like mine was just a coincidence. It couldn't mean anything.

An intense longing for my friend rushed through me, and tears swam in my eyes all over again. Jeez, I was hopeless.

The teacher's sympathetic gaze sliding my way only made things worse. She nudged her head toward the hall and lifted her eyebrows.

Running from the classroom, I went to my locker and dumped my stuff. I pressed my forehead against the cold metal until my ragged breathing eased.

This...wasn't going to work. Not today, anyway.

Slamming my locker closed, I ran.

I shouldn't be afraid to go downstairs. This was my house now that my parents had died.

The creak of my bedroom door sent a quiver down my spine. Old houses have rusty hinges, plumbing that sputters, and wooden floorboards that protest whenever you walk across them. History, my dad used to say. No, it felt creepy.

Out on the landing, I peered down. My aunt had left a light on in the dining room, and a yellow beam bled across the carpet covering the entryway and glinted on the table where my parents had always dropped their car keys. Where Aunt Kristy dropped her car keys, now.

Somewhere deeper in the house, a man spoke, but I couldn't make out his words.

Barefoot, I tiptoed down the staircase to the first floor. While I could poke my head into the study—where I'd determined the voices came from—and tell my aunt what I was doing, why bother? I could dart into the kitchen, drink fast, and scoot back to my room without her knowing I'd been near.

"...haven't told her?" the man said.

Abandoning my thirst, I slipped through the living room and hovered against the wall beside the almost-closed study door.

"... need to know..." my aunt said. "I...best if she *never* knows. Janie's...fragile."

Great. She was talking about me with some man.

Nothing good ever came from eavesdropping, especially when you were the subject of the conversation. Part of me wanted to run back upstairs and jump under my blankets. Hide.

Curiosity only killed cats, not teenage girls.

I leaned forward, tilting my head to place my ear closer to the opening.

The hardwood floor groaned as the man shifted. "I think you—"

"This is a closed subject," Aunt Kristy said crisply. "Are we clear?"

A long moment passed. "You *are* her guardian." She'd applied for that honor a day after the police called her.

"Legally," the man added, "It's up to you to tell her or withhold the information."

"Exactly," Aunt Kristy grated out. "Is there anything else we need to discuss before you leave?" A chair screeched across the floor as if she'd shoved it back to stand.

"No," the man said. "Just doing my duty, delivering the report as requested, now that—"

"Thank you. I appreciate your efforts on our behalf."

"Anytime, Ma'am."

"Let me walk you out." Footsteps approached, and my heart leaped against my ribcage. Pivoting, I raced into the living room and stared around frantically before diving behind the sofa. I landed on the carpet, jarring my hip against the wall. Breathing fast, I lay still, listening. As my aunt and the man crossed the living room, my hands grew clammy with sweat.

"Thank you for coming," Aunt Kristy said. "I know you're busy at the station."

Station? I crept forward to peer around the end of the sofa.

Aunt Kristy unlocked and pulled open the front door.

A cop stood with her in the entryway. After dropping his hat onto his head, he grunted. "Let me know if there's anything else we can do."

"Thanks." My aunt's hands twitched as he stepped out onto the porch. His footsteps retreated, and a car door slammed. The engine fired.

Aunt Kristy shut the front door and slumped against it. She swiped her dark hair off her face with trembling hands. "Just what I needed," she growled. The click of her heels echoed as she strode into the study.

Because I didn't want to get caught snooping, I waited until she went upstairs, shutting the lights off behind her.

Rising, I crept to my father's study and clicked on my phone light. Dad's oak desk sat sentry on the opposite side of the room with two windows overlooking the inky backyard behind. My heart pinching, I crossed to the back of his desk where I pulled out his chair and sat.

This chair had hosted my pretend rocket launches to Mars. My buggy rides down shady lanes. And Dad used to spin me around in it until I laughed and got dizzy.

When I closed my eyes, I could almost feel him.

Nothing lay on the scarred wooden surface except a green blotter and a few pens. I pulled open a drawer and pawed through pencils, a stapler, a billion paper clips, and a small framed picture of me taken when I was ten. Bank statements, a few thumb drives, and a folder with copies of letters Dad had sent to various businesses and the government. Nothing worth bringing a cop to the house at night.

The bottom drawer wouldn't budge, but I wasn't stopping now. When I wiggled a letter opener in the lock, it clicked open.

"Bingo." Inside the drawer, I found a green folder containing a letter from Dad's lawyer dated July 18, a week before the accident. Two pages of tiny print ended with Dad's printed name—he hadn't signed it yet.

My breath caught. He'd never sign it, now.

Mr. Somerfield's name jumped out at me. If I read this correctly, Dad had been planning to dissolve their business partnership, which was odd, because we'd gone boating to celebrate the upcoming release of an app Dad had designed for the company. But they had argued a lot.

Had Mr. Somerfield known about this?

Stuffed in the back of the drawer, I found a yellow envelope with *Davis Accident Report* scrolled across the front.

Ah. This was what my aunt was talking about.

I stared down at it for a long time. Did I dare look? Going through the details would make my grief fresh all over again, but looking might also drag my memories closer to the surface. I wanted to remember what happened that night, didn't I?

Raking my teeth across my lower lip, I separated the top of the envelope and reeled back when I found pictures.

They're not people you love.

The whimpering part of me insisted they were nothing different than photos I'd see on TV, but I couldn't stop the tears from filling my eyes.

When I upended the envelope, the images slid out onto the desk. Black and white and with the bodies carefully posed, the photos looked like graphic art. A gruesome nightmare played out before my eyes because they *were* the people I loved. No use pretending otherwise.

I traced my fingertip along the burned arm of the person in one photo. Long limbs. Gutted belly. Face a blackened skeleton. Horror rushed through me, making me weak.

Leaning closer, I squinted at the writing along the bottom. *Male, approximate age early-twenties. Burned beyond recognition.* One of the crewmen of the rented yacht?

Another photo: *Male, approximate age mid-forties. Burned beyond recognition.*

Dad.

My keen echoed in the room. This charred carcass with bits of flesh clinging to its bones wasn't my dad. This...this thing wasn't the man who'd rocked me to sleep when I was little and read me stories when I was sick.

If I was wise, I'd go upstairs, take a sleeping pill, and sink into a medication-induced coma. In the morning, I'd convince myself this had all been a dream.

Next picture. *Female, approximate age forty. Burned.*

Mom.

A whiff of Chanel No 5 drifted through the room. If I closed my eyes, could I pretend she was still with me or would I see flames?

Clumping the pictures together, I shoved them back into the folder then pulled out and skimmed through the accident report.

Approximate time of death of the passengers: 23:00. Four hours after we left Finley Cove, where Dad had rented the boat.

If only I hadn't talked my best friend, Brianna, into coming with us. But it had been her birthday. I'd wanted to celebrate it someplace special. I couldn't have known she'd die.

Cupping my face, I peeked through my fingers at the report.

Location of the wreck: ten miles offshore, due east of Big Berry Island. They'd found me wandering the beach after I escaped the boat and swam to shore.

A witness, Andrew Smythe, reported seeing a bright light at sea he dismissed as boaters setting off fireworks. He eventually became concerned about ongoing flashes and called 9-1-1.

The Coast Guard rushed to the scene but found nothing. It took divers and a thorough search to drag up the final evidence.

Highly combustible fuel source suspected. The heat of the flames killed the victims almost immediately. And, *the yacht burned through to the outer hull before sinking underwater, taking everyone down with it.*

I wiped my eyes, but they kept tearing. Bringing my phone closer, I stared at the last bit of information in the file.

My harsh cry rose from deep in my belly and burst into the room.

Possible homicide. Investigation is ongoing.

No, no. This couldn't be true.

Homicide?

Mom, Dad, and Brianna had been murdered.

Made in the USA
Lexington, KY
27 July 2019